ROMA
ETERNA

ALSO BY ROBERT SILVERBERG

THE MAJIPOOR CYCLE
LORD VALENTINE'S CASTLE
VALENTINE PONTIFEX
MAJIPOOR CHRONICLES
THE MOUNTAINS OF MAJIPOOR
SORCERERS OF MAJIPOOR
LORD PRESTIMION
THE KING OF DREAMS

OTHER TITLES
STARBORNE
HOT SKY AT MIDNIGHT
KINGDOMS OF THE WALL
THE FACE OF THE WATERS
THEBES OF THE HUNDRED GATES
THE ALIEN YEARS
THE LONGEST WAY HOME

ROMA ETERNA

ROBERT SILVERBERG

An Imprint of HarperCollins*Publishers*

ROMA ETERNA. Copyright © 2003 by Agberg, Ltd. All rights reserved. Printed
in the United States of America. No part of this book may be used or reproduced
in any manner whatsoever without written permission except in the case of brief
quotations embodied in critical articles and reviews. For information address
HarperCollins Publishers Inc., 10 East 53rd Street, New York, NY 10022.

HarperCollins books may be purchased for educational, business, or sales
promotional use. For information please write: Special Markets Department,
HarperCollins Publishers Inc., 10 East 53rd Street, New York, NY 10022.

FIRST EDITION

Designed by Renato Stanisic

Printed on acid-free paper

Library of Congress Cataloging-in-Publication Data
Silverberg, Robert.
    Roma eterna/Robert Silverberg.—1st ed.
      p.   cm.
    ISBN 0-380-97859-8
    1. Rome—Fiction.   2. Imperialism—Fiction.   I. Title.
PS3569.I472 R6 2003
813'.54—dc21   2002035416

03   04   05   06   07   WBC/BVG   10   9   8   7   6   5   4   3   2   1

For Frank and Renee Kovacs—
for whom much of this is a twice-told tale

And with special thanks to
Gardner Dozois for his encouragement of this
project across many years

To Romans I set no boundary in space or time. I have granted them dominion, and it has no end.
—VIRGIL, *The Aeneid*

A NOTE ON DATES

The traditional date assigned by Roman historians to the founding of the city of Rome was 753 B.C., and the Romans reckoned time from that date, designating the year as such-and-such *ab urbe condita,* or A.U.C.—"from the founding of the city." Thus A.D. 1 was A.U.C. 754, A.D. 1000 was A.U.C. 1753, A.D. 1492 was A.U.C. 2245, and so forth. All dates used within the text of this book are A.U.C. and should not be confused with dates of the system used in the Christian world.

CONTENTS

ROMA
ETERNA

A.U.C. 1203: PROLOGUE

The historian Lentulus Aufidius, whose goal it was to write the definitive biography of the great Emperor Titus Gallius, was now in his third year of research in the Imperial archives at the Palatine Library. Every morning, six days a week, Aufidius would trudge up the hill from his lodgings near the Forum, present his identification card to the Keeper of the Archives, and set about his daily exploration of the great cabinets in which the scrolls pertaining to the reign of Titus Gallius were stored.

It was a formidable task. Titus Gallius, who had come to the throne upon the death of the madman Caracalla, had ruled over Roma from 970 to 994 and in that time had completely reorganized the government that his predecessor had left in such disheveled condition. Provinces had been merged, others had been broken up, the system of taxation had undergone reform, the army had been ripped apart and reconstructed from top to bottom to meet the growing menace of the northern barbarians, and so on and so on. Lentulus Aufidius suspected that he had two or three more years of study ahead of him before he could at last begin writing his text.

Today would be devoted, as each previous day of the past two weeks had been, to an inspection of Cabinet 42, which contained the documents concerning Titus Gallius's religious policies. Titus Gallius had been much troubled by the way mystical Oriental cults—the worship of Mithras the bull-slayer, of the mother-goddess Cybele, of Osiris of Aegyptus, and many others—were spreading through the Empire. The Emperor feared that these alien religions, if allowed to become deeply established, would weaken the fabric of the state; and so he had done what he could to suppress them without at the same time losing the loyalty of the common folk who adhered to them. That was a delicate task, and it had been only partly accomplished in Titus Gallius's time. It remained for Titus Gallius's nephew and successor, the Emperor Gaius Martius, to finish the work by founding the cult of Jupiter Imperator, which was intended to replace all the foreign religions.

Someone else was already at work at Cabinet 42 when Aufidius reached it. After a moment he recognized the man as an old friend and colleague, Hermogenes Celer, a native of Tripolis in Phoenicia who was, perhaps, the Empire's leading scholar of Eastern religions. Aufidius, though he had corresponded occasionally with Celer, had not seen him in many years, nor had he known that Celer was planning a visit to the capital. The two men embraced warmly and—to the annoyance of the librarians—began at once to discuss their current projects.

"Titus Gallius?" Celer said. "Ah, yes, a fascinating story."

"And you?"

"The Hebrews of Aegyptus," said Celer. "A remarkable group of people. Descendants of a nomadic desert tribe, they are."

"I know next to nothing about them," Aufidius said.

"Ah, you should, you should!" said Celer. "If things had gone differently for them, who can say what path our history would have taken?"

"*Please, gentlemen, please,*" one of the librarians said. "Scholars are at work in here. If you must have a conversation, there is a hall available outside."

"We must talk later," Aufidius said. And they agreed to meet for lunch.

Celer, as it turned out, was overflowing with tales of his Hebrews, and spoke of little else while they ate. In particular he told of their passionate belief in a single lofty god, remote and stern, who had decreed for them an intricate set of laws that controlled everything from how they should speak of him (it was forbidden to utter his name) to what foods they could eat on which days of the week.

Because they were such a stubborn and difficult tribe, he said, they were often in trouble with their neighbors. Having conquered a large portion of Syria Palaestina, these Hebrews—who also called themselves Israelites—founded a kingdom there, but eventually were subjugated by the Aegyptians and forced into slavery in the land of the Pharaohs. This period lasted hundreds of years. But Celer declared that he had identified a critical moment in Hebrew history, some seventeen centuries in the past, when a charismatic chieftain named Mosaeus—*Moshe,* in their language—had attempted to lead his people on a great exodus out of Aegyptus and back to their former homeland in Palaestina, which they believed had been promised to them as an eternal homeland by their god.

"And then what happened?" said Aufidius politely, although he found none of this very interesting.

"Well," said Celer, "this grand exodus of theirs was a terrible failure. Mosaeus and most of the other leaders were killed and the surviving Hebrews wound up back in slavery in Aegyptus."

"I fail to see—"

"Ah, but I do!" cried Celer, and his plump, pasty face lit up with scholarly fire. "Think of the possibilities, dear Aufidius! Let's say the Hebrews *do* reach Syria Palaestina. They settle themselves permanently, this time, in that hotbed of mystical fertility and harvest cults. Then, many centuries later, someone combines the ferocious religious zeal of the Hebrews with some native Palaestinian belief in rebirth and resurrection derived from the old Aegyptian business about Osiris, and a new religion under an invincible new prophet is born, not in distant Aegyptus but in a province of the Roman Empire much more closely connected with the center of things. And, precisely because Syria Palaestina by this time is a province of the Roman Empire and Roman citizens move freely about from district to district, this cult spreads to Roma itself, as other Eastern cults have done."

"And?" said Aufidius, mystified.

"And it conquers everything, as Cybele and Mithras and Osiris have never been able to do. Its prophets preach a message of universal love, and universal sharing of all wealth—*especially* the sharing of wealth. All property is to be held in common. The poor people of the Empire flock to the churches of this cult in huge droves. Everything is turned upside down. The Emperor himself is forced to recognize it—to convert to it himself, perhaps, for political reasons—this religion comes to dominate everything, and the basic structure of Roman society is weakened by superstition, until the Empire, consumed by the new philosophy, is toppled by the barbarians who forever lurk at its borders—"

"The very thing that Titus Gallius fought to prevent."

"Yes. Therefore in my new book I have postulated a world in which this Hebrew exodus *did* happen, in which this new religion eventually was born, in which it spread uncontrollably throughout the Empire—"

"Well," said Aufidius, suppressing a yawn, "all that is sheer fantasy, you know. None of that happened, after all. And—admit it, Celer—it never *could* have happened."

"Perhaps yes, perhaps no. I find speculating about such possibilities very stimulating."

"Yes," Aufidius said. "I have no doubt that you do. But as for me, I prefer to deal with matters as they really are. No such cult ever infiltrated our beloved Roma, and the Empire is sturdy and sound, and for that, Celer, let us give thanks to nonexistent Jupiter, or to whichever other deity you pretend to believe in. And now, if you will, I'd like to share with you a few discoveries of my own concerning the tax reforms of the Emperor Titus Gallius—"

A.U.C. 1282: WITH CAESAR IN THE UNDERWORLD

The newly arrived ambassador from the Eastern Emperor was rather younger than Faustus had expected him to be: a smallish sort, finely built, quite handsome in what was almost a girlish kind of way, though obviously very capable and sharp, a man who would bear close watching. There was something a bit frightening about him, though not at first glance. He gleamed with the imperviousness of fine armor. His air of sophisticated and fastidious languor coupled with hidden strength made Faustus, a tall, robust, florid-faced man going thick through the waist and thin about the scalp, feel positively plebeian and coarse despite his own lofty and significant ancestry.

That morning Faustus, whose task as an official of the Chancellery it was to greet all such important visitors to the capital city, had gone out to Ostia to meet him at the Imperial pier—the Greek envoy, coming west by way of Sicilia, had sailed up the coast from Neapolis in the south—and had escorted him to the rooms in the old Severan Palace where the occasional ambassadors from the eastern half of the Empire were housed. Now it was the time to begin establishing a little rapport. They faced each other across an onyx-slab table in the Lesser Hall of Columns, which several reigns ago had been transformed into a somewhat oversized sitting-room. A certain amount of preliminary social chatter was required at this point. Faustus called for some wine, one of the big, elegant wines from the great vineyards of Gallia Transalpina.

After they had had a chance to savor it for a little while he said, wanting to get the ticklish part of the situation out in the open right away, "The prince Heraclius himself, unfortunately, has been called without warning to the northern frontier. Therefore tonight's dinner has been canceled. This will be a free evening for you, then, an evening for resting after your long journey. I trust that that'll be acceptable to you."

"Ah," said the Greek, and his lips tightened for an instant. Plainly he was a little bewildered at being left on his own like this, his first evening in Roma. He studied his perfectly manicured fingers. When he glanced up again, there was a gleam of concern in the dark eyes. "I won't be seeing the Emperor either, then?"

"The Emperor is in very poor health. He will not be able to see you tonight and perhaps not for several days. The prince Heraclius has taken over many of his responsibilities. But in the prince's unexpected and unavoidable absence your host and companion for your first few days in Roma will be his younger brother Maximilianus. You will, I know, find him amusing and very charming, my lord Menandros."

"Unlike his brother, I gather," said the Greek ambassador coolly.

Only too true, Faustus thought. But it was a remarkably blunt thing to say. Faustus searched for the motive behind the little man's words. Menandros had come here, after all, to negotiate a marriage between his royal master's sister and the very prince of whom he had just spoken so slightingly. When a diplomat as polished as this finely oiled Greek says something as egregiously undiplomatic as that, there was usually a good reason for it. Perhaps, Faustus supposed, Menandros was simply showing annoyance at the fact that Prince Heraclius had tactlessly managed not to be on hand to welcome him upon his entry into Roma.

Faustus was not going to let himself be drawn any deeper into comparisons, though. He allowed himself only an oblique smile, that faint sidewise smile he had learned from his young friend the Caesar Maximilianus. "The two brothers are quite different in personality, that I do concede. —Will you have more wine, your excellence?"

That brought yet another shift of tone. "Ah, no formalities, no formalities, I pray you. Let us be friends, you and I." And then, leaning forward cozily and shifting from the formal to the intimate form of speech: "You must call me Menandros. I will call you Faustus. Eh, my friend? —And yes, more wine, by all means. What excellent stuff! We have nothing that can match it in Constantinopolis. What sort is it, actually?"

Faustus flicked a glance at one of the waiting servitors, who quickly refilled the bowls. "A wine from Gallia," he said. "I forget the name." A swift flash of unmistakable displeasure, quickly concealed but not quickly enough, crossed the Greek's face. To be caught praising a provincial wine so highly must have embarrassed him. But embarrassing him had not been Faustus's intention. There was nothing to be gained by creating discomfort for so powerful and potentially valuable a personage as the lord of the East's ambassador to the Western court.

This was all getting worse and worse. Hastily Faustus set about smoothing the awkwardness over. "The heart of our production lies in Gallia, now. The Emperor's cellars contain scarcely any Italian wines at all, they tell me. Scarcely any! These Gallian reds are His Imperial Majesty's preference by far, I assure you."

"While I am here I must acquire some, then, for the cellars of His Majesty Justinianus," said Menandros.

They drank a moment in silence. Faustus felt as though he were dancing on swords.

"This is, I understand, your first visit to Urbs Roma?" Faustus asked, when the silence had gone on just a trifle too long. He took care to use the familiar form, too, now that Menandros had started it.

"My first, yes. Most of my career has been spent in Aegyptus and Syria."

Faustus wondered how extensive that career could have been.

This Menandros seemed to be no more than twenty-five or so, thirty at the utmost. Of course, all these smooth-skinned dark-eyed Greeks, buffed and oiled and pomaded in their Oriental fashion, tended to look younger than they really were. And now that Faustus had passed fifty, he was finding it harder and harder to make distinctions of age in any precise way: everybody around him at the court seemed terribly young to him now, a congregation of mere boys and girls. Of those who had ruled the Empire when Faustus himself was young, there was no one left except the weary, lonely old Emperor himself, and hardly anyone had laid eyes on the Emperor in recent times. Of Faustus's own generation of courtiers, some had died off, the others had gone into cozy retirement far away. Faustus was a dozen years older than his own superior minister in the Chancellery. His closest friend here now was Maximilianus Caesar, who was considerably less than half his age. From the beginning Faustus had always regarded himself as a relic of some earlier era, because that was, in truth, what he was, considering that he was a member of a family that had held the throne three dynasties ago; but the phrase had taken on a harsh new meaning for him in these latter days, now that he had survived not just his family's greatness but even his own contemporaries.

It was a little disconcerting that Justinianus had sent so youthful and apparently inexperienced an ambassador on so delicate a mission. But Faustus suspected it would be a mistake to underestimate this man; and at least Menandros's lack of familiarity with the capital city would provide him with a convenient way to glide past whatever difficulties Prince Heraclius's untimely absence might cause in the next few days.

Stagily Faustus clapped his hands. "How I envy you, friend Menandros! To see Urbs Roma in all its splendor for the first time! What an overwhelming experience it will be for you! We who were born here, who take it all for granted, can never appreciate it as you will. The grandeur. The magnificence." Yes, yes, he thought, let Maximilianus march him from one end of the city to the other until Heraclius gets back. We will dazzle him with our wonders and after a time he'll forget how discourteously Heraclius has treated him. "While you're waiting for the Caesar to return, we'll arrange the most

extensive tours for you. All the great temples—the amphitheater—
the baths—the Forum—the Capitol—the palaces—the wonderful
gardens—"

"The grottoes of Titus Gallius," Menandros said unexpectedly.
"The underground temples and shrines. The marketplace of the sorcerers. The catacomb of the holy Chaldean prostitutes. The pool of
the Baptai. The labyrinth of the Maenads. The caverns of the
witches."

"Ah? So you know of those places too?"

"Who doesn't know about the Underworld of Urbs Roma? It's
the talk of the whole Empire." In an instant that bright metallic
façade of his seemed to melt away, and all his menacing poise. Something quite different was visible in Menandros's eyes now, a wholly
uncalculated eagerness, an undisguised boyish enthusiasm. And a
certain roguishness, too, a hint of rough, coarse appetites that belied
his urbane gloss. In a soft, confiding tone he said, "May I confess
something, Faustus? Magnificence bores me. I've got a bit of a taste
for the low life. All that dodgy stuff that Roma's so famous for, the
dark, seamy underbelly of the city, the whores and the magicians, the
freak shows and the orgies and the thieves' markets, the strange
shrines of your weird cults—do I shock you, Faustus? Is this dread-
fully undiplomatic of me to admit? I don't need a tour of the temples. But as long as we have a few days before I have to get down to
serious business, it's the other side of Roma I want to see, the mysterious side, the dark side. We have temples and palaces enough in
Constantinopolis, and baths, and all the rest of that. Miles and miles
of glorious shining marble, until you want to cry out for mercy. But
the true subterranean mysteries, the earthy, dirty, smelly, underground things, ah, no, Faustus, those are what really interest me.
We've rooted all that stuff out, at Constantinopolis. It's considered
dangerous decadent nonsense."

"It is here, too," said Faustus quietly.

"Yes, but you permit it! You revel in it, even! Or so I'm told, on
pretty good authority. —You heard me say I was formerly stationed
in Aegyptus and Syria. The ancient East, that is to say, thousands of
years older than Roma or Constantinopolis. Most of the strange
cults originated there, you know. That was where I developed my in-

terest in them. And the things I've seen and heard and done in places like Damascus and Alexandria and Antioch, well—but nowadays Urbs Roma is the center of everything of that sort, is it not, the capital of marvels! And I tell you, Faustus, what I truly crave experiencing is—"

He halted in midsentence, looking flushed and a little stunned.

"This wine," he said, with a little shake of his head. "I've been drinking it too quickly. It must be stronger than I thought."

Faustus reached across the table and laid his hand gently on the younger man's wrist. "Have no fear, my friend. These revelations of yours cause me no dismay. I am no stranger to the Underworld, nor is the prince Maximilianus. And while we await the return of Prince Heraclius he and I will show you everything you desire." He rose, stepping back a couple of paces so that he would not seem, in his bulky way, to be looming in an intimidating manner over the reclining ambassador. After a bad start he had regained some advantage; he didn't want to push it too far. "I'll leave you now. You've had a lengthy journey, and you'll want your rest. I'll send in your servants. In addition to those who accompanied you from Constantinopolis, these men and women"—he indicated the slaves who stood arrayed in the shadows around the room—"are at your command day and night. They are yours. Ask them for anything. *Anything,* my lord Menandros."

His palanquin and bearers were waiting outside. "Take me to the apartments of the Caesar," Faustus said crisply, and clambered inside.

They knew which Caesar he meant. In Roma the name could be applied to a great many persons of high birth, from the Emperor on down—Faustus himself had some claim to using it—but as a rule, these days, it was an appellation employed only in reference to the two sons of the Emperor Maximilianus II. And, whether or not Faustus's bearers happened to be aware that the elder son was out of town, they were clever enough to understand that their master would in all probability not be asking them to take him to the chambers of the austere and dreary Prince Heraclius. No, no, it was the younger son, the pleasantly dissolute Maximilianus Caesar, whose rooms would surely be his chosen destination: Prince Maximilianus, the friend, the companion, the dearest and most special friend and companion, for all intents and purposes at the present time the *only* true friend and companion, of that aging and ever lonelier minor official of the Imperial court, Faustus Flavius Constantinus Caesar.

Maximilianus lived over at the far side of the Palatine, in a handsome pink-marble palace of relatively modest size that had been occupied by younger sons of the Emperor for the past half dozen reigns or so. The prince, a red-haired, blue-eyed, long-limbed man who was a match for Faustus in height but lean and rangy where Faustus was burly and ponderous, peeled himself upward from a divan as Faustus entered and greeted him with a warm embrace and a tall beaker of chilled white wine. That Faustus had been drinking red with the Greek ambassador for the past hour and a half did not matter now. Maximilianus, in his capacity as prince of the royal blood, had access to the best caves of the Imperial cellars, and what was most pleasing to the prince's palate were the rare white wines of the Alban Hills, the older and sweeter and colder the better. When Faustus was with him, the white wines of the Alban Hills were what Faustus drank.

"Look at these," Maximilianus said, before Faustus had had a chance to say anything whatever beyond a word of appreciation for the wine. The prince drew forth a long, fat pouch of purple velvet and with a great sweeping gesture sent a blazing hoard of jewelry spilling out on the table: a tangled mass of necklaces, earrings, rings, pendants, all of them evidently fashioned from opals set in filigree of gold, opals of every hue and type, pink ones, milky ones, opals of shimmering green, midnight black, fiery scarlet. Maximilianus exultantly scooped them up in both hands and let them dribble through his fingers. His eyes were glowing. He appeared enthralled by the brilliant display.

Faustus stared puzzledly at the sprawling scatter of bright trinkets. These were extremely beautiful baubles, yes: but the degree of Maximilianus's excitement over them seemed excessive. Why was the prince so fascinated by them? "Very pretty," Faustus said. "Are they something you won at the gambling tables? Or did you buy these trinkets as a gift for one of your ladies?"

"Trinkets!" Maximilianus cried. "The jewels of Cybele is what they are! The treasure of the high priestess of the Great Mother! Aren't they lovely, Faustus? The Hebrew brought them just now. They're stolen, of course. From the goddess's most sacred sanctuary. I'm going to give them to my new sister-in-law as a wedding present."

"Stolen? From the sanctuary? Which sanctuary? Which Hebrew? What are you talking about, Maximilianus?"

The prince grinned and pressed one of the biggest of the pendants into the fleshy palm of Faustus's left hand, closing Faustus's fingers tightly over it. He gave Faustus a broad wink. "Hold it. Squeeze it. Feel the throbbing magic of the goddess pouring into you. Is your cock getting stiff yet? That's what should be happening, Faustus. Amulets of fertility are what we have here. Of enormous efficacy. In the sanctuary, the priestess wears them and anyone she touches with the stone becomes an absolute seething mass of procreative energy. Heraclius's princess will conceive an heir for him the first time he gets inside her. It's virtually guaranteed. The dynasty continues. My little favor for my chilly and sexless brother. I'll explain it all to his beloved, and she'll know what to do. Eh? Eh?" Maximilianus amiably patted Faustus's belly. "What are you feeling down there, old man?"

Faustus handed the pendant back. "What I feel is that you may have gone a little too far, this time. Who did you get these things from? Danielus bar-Heap?"

"Bar-Heap, yes, of course. Who else?"

"And where did he get them? Stole them from the Temple of the Great Mother, did he? Strolled through the grotto one dark night and slipped into the sanctuary when the priestesses weren't looking?" Faustus closed his eyes, put his hand across them, blew his breath outward through closed lips in a noisy, rumbling burst of astonishment and disapproval. He was even shocked, a little. That was something of an unusual emotion for him. Maximilianus was the only man in the realm capable of making him feel stodgy and priggish. "In the name of Jove Almighty, Maximilianus, tell me how you think you can give stolen goods as a wedding gift! For a royal wedding, no less. Don't you think there'll be an outcry raised from here to India and back when the high priestess finds out that this stuff is missing?"

Maximilianus, offering Faustus his sly, inward sort of smile, gathered the jewelry back into the pouch. "You grow silly in your dotage, old man. Is it your idea that these jewels were stolen from the sanctuary yesterday? As a matter of fact, it happened during the reign of Marcus Anastasius, which was—what? Two hundred fifty years ago?—and the sanctuary they were stolen from wasn't here at all, it was somewhere in Phrygia, wherever that may be, and they've had at least five legitimate owners since then, which is certainly enough to disqualify them as stolen goods by this time. It happens also that I paid good hard cash for them. I told the Hebrew that I needed a fancy wedding present for the elder Caesar's bride, and he said that this little collection was on the market, and I said, fine, get them for me, and I gave him enough gold pieces to outweigh *two* fat Faustuses, and he went down into the Jewelers' Grotto this very night past and closed the deal, and here they are. I want to see the look on my dear brother's face when I present these treasures to his lovely bride Sabbatia, gifts truly worthy of a queen. And then when I tell him about the special powers they're supposed to have. 'Beloved brother,'" Maximilianus said, in a high, piping tone of savage derision, "'I thought you might need some aid in consummating your marriage, and therefore I advise you to have your bride wear this ring on the wedding night, and to put this bracelet upon her wrist, and also to invite your lady to drape this pendant between her breasts—'"

Faustus felt the beginnings of a headache. There were times when the Caesar's madcap exuberance was too much even for him. In silence he helped himself to more wine, and drank it down in deep, slow, deliberate drafts. Then he walked toward the window and stood with his back toward the prince.

Could he trust what Maximilianus was telling him about the provenance of these jewels? Had they in fact been taken from the sanctuary in antiquity, or had some thief snatched them just the other day? That would be all we need, he thought. Right in the middle of the negotiations for a desperately needed military alliance that were scheduled to follow the marriage of the Western prince and the

Eastern princess, the pious and exceedingly virtuous Justinianus discovers that his new brother-in-law's brother has blithely given the sister of the Eastern Emperor a stolen and sacrilegious wedding gift. A gift that even now might be the object of an intensive police search.

Maximilianus was still going on about the jewels. Faustus paid little attention. A soothing drift of cool air floated toward him out of the twilight, carrying with it a delightfully complex mingling of odors, cinnamon, pepper, nutmeg, roasted meat, rich wine, pungent perfume, the tang of sliced lemons, all the wondrous aromas of some nearby lavish banquet. It was quite refreshing.

Under the benign mellowing influence of the fragrant breeze from outside Faustus felt his little fit of scrupulosity beginning to pass. There was nothing to worry about here, really. Very likely the transaction had been legitimate. But even if the opals *had* just been stolen from the Great Mother's sanctuary, there would be little that the outraged priestesses could do about it, since the police investigation was in no way likely to reach into the household of the Imperial family. And that Maximilianus's gift was reputed to have aphrodisiac powers would be a fine joke on his prissy, tight-lipped brother.

Faustus felt a great sudden surge of love for his friend Maximilianus pass through him. Once again the prince had shown him that although he was only half his age, he was more than his equal in all-around deviltry; and that was saying quite a lot.

"Did the ambassador show you a picture of her, by the way?" Maximilianus asked.

Faustus glanced around. "Why should he? I'm not the one who's marrying her."

"I was just curious. I was wondering if she's as ugly as they say. The word is that she looks just like her brother, you know. And Justinianus has the face of a horse. She's a lot older than Heraclius, too."

"Is she? I hadn't heard."

"Justinianus is forty-five or so, right? Is it likely that he would have a sister of eighteen or twenty?"

"She could be twenty-five, perhaps."

"Thirty-five, more likely. Or even older. Heraclius is twenty-nine. My brother is going to marry an ugly old woman. Who may not even still be of childbearing age—has anyone considered that?"

"An ugly old woman, if that's indeed the case, who happens to be the sister of the Eastern Emperor," Faustus pointed out, "and who therefore will create a blood bond between the two halves of the realm that will be very useful to us when we ask Justinianus to lend us a few legions to help us fend off the barbarians in the north, now that our friends the Goths and the Vandals are chewing on our toes up there again. Whether she's of childbearing age is incidental. Heirs to the throne can always be adopted, you know."

"Yes. Of course they can. But the main thing, the grand alliance—is that so important, Faustus? If the smelly barbarians have come back for another round, why can't we fend them off ourselves? My father managed a pretty good job of that when they came sniffing around our frontiers in '42, didn't he? Not to mention what his grandfather did to Attila and his Huns some fifty years before that."

"Forty-two was a long time ago," Faustus said. "Your father's old and sick, now. And we're currently a little short on great generals."

"What about Heraclius? He might amaze us all."

"Heraclius?" said Faustus. That was a startling thought—the aloof, waspish, ascetic Heraclius Caesar leading an army in the field. Even Maximilianus, frivolous and undisciplined and rowdy as he was, would make a more plausible candidate for the role of military hero than the pallid Heraclius.

With a mock-haughty sniff Maximilianus said, "I remind you, my lord Faustus, that we're a fighting dynasty. We have the blood of mighty warriors in our veins, my brother and I."

"Yes, the mighty warrior Heraclius," Faustus said acidly, and they both laughed.

"All right, then. I yield the point. We do need Justinianus's help, I suppose. So my brother marries the ugly princess, *her* brother helps us smash the savage hairy men of the north for once and all, and the whole Empire embarks upon a future of eternal peace, except perhaps for a squabble or two with the Persians, who are Justinianus's problem, not ours. Well, so be it. In any case, why should I care what Heraclius's wife looks like? *He* probably won't."

"True." The heir to the throne was not notorious for his interest in women.

"The Great Mother's jewels, if their reputation has any substance to it, will help him quickly engender a new little Caesar, let us hope. After which, he'll probably never lay a finger on her again, to her great relief and his, eh?" Maximilianus bounded up from his divan to pour more wine for Faustus, and for himself. "Has he really gone up north to inspect the troops, by the way? That's the tale I've heard, anyway."

"And I," said Faustus. "It's the official story, but I have my doubts. More likely he's headed off to his forests for a few days of hunting, by way of ducking the marriage issue as long as he can." That was the Caesar Heraclius's only known amusement, the tireless, joyless pursuit of stag and boar and fox and hare. "Let me tell you, the Greek ambassador was more than a little miffed when he found out that the prince had chosen the very week of his arrival to leave town. He let it be known very clearly, how annoyed he was. Which brings me to the main reason for this visit, in fact. I have work for you. It becomes your job and mine to keep the ambassador amused until Heraclius deigns to get back here."

Maximilianus responded with a lazy shrug. "Your job, perhaps. But why is it mine, old friend?"

"Because I think you'll enjoy it, once you know what I have in mind. And I've already committed you to it, besides, and you don't dare let me down. The ambassador wants to go on a tour of Roma—but not to the usual tourist attractions. He's interested in getting a look at the Underworld."

The Caesar's eyes widened. "He is? An ambassador, going *there*?"

"He's young. He's Greek. He may be a little on the perverse side, or else he'd simply like to be. I said that you and I would show him temples and palaces, and he said to show him the grottoes and the whorehouses. The marketplace of the sorcerers, the caverns of the witches, that sort of thing. 'I've got a bit of a taste for the low life' is what he told me," Faustus said, in passable imitation of Menandros's drawling tones and Eastern-accented Latin. "'The dark, seamy underbelly of the city' is the very phrase he used. 'All that dodgy stuff that Roma's so famous for.'"

"A tourist," Maximilianus said, with scorn. "He just wants to take a tour that's slightly different from the standard one."

"Whatever. At any rate, I have to keep him entertained, and with your brother hiding out in the woods and your father ill I need to trot forth some other member of the Imperial family to play host for him, and who else is there but you? It's no more than half a day since he arrived in town and Heraclius has succeeded in offending him already, without even being here. The more annoyed he gets, the harder a bargain he's going to drive once your brother shows up. He's tougher than he looks and it's dangerous to underestimate him. If I leave him stewing in his own irritation for the next few days, there may be big trouble."

"Trouble? Of what sort? He can't call off the marriage just because he feels snubbed."

"No, I suppose he can't. But if he gets his jaw set the wrong way, he may report back to Justinianus that the next Emperor of the West is a bumbling fool not worth wasting soldiers on, let alone a sister. The princess Sabbatia quietly goes back to Constantinopolis a few months after the wedding and we get left to deal with the barbarians on our own. I like to think I'll be able to head all that off if I can distract the ambassador for a week or two by showing him a little dirty fun in the catacombs. You can help me with that. We've had some good times down there, you and I, eh, my friend? Now we can take him to some of our favorite places. Yes? Agreed?"

"May I bring along the Hebrew?" Maximilianus asked. "To be our guide. He knows the Underworld even better than we do."

"Danielus bar-Heap, you mean."

"Yes. Bar-Heap."

"By all means," said Faustus. "The more the merrier."

It was too late in the evening by the time he left Maximilianus's to go to the baths. Faustus returned to his own quarters instead and called for a hot bath, a massage, and, afterward, the slave-girl Oalathea, that dusky, lithe little sixteen-year-old Numidian with whom the only language Faustus had in common was that of Eros.

A long day it had been, and a hard, wearying one. He hadn't expected to find Heraclius gone when he came back from Ostia with the Eastern ambassador. Since the old Emperor Maximilianus was in such poor shape, the plan had been for the Greek ambassador to dine with Prince Heraclius on his first evening at the capital; but right after Faustus had set off for Ostia, Heraclius had abruptly skipped out of the city, leaving behind the flimsy inspecting-the-northern-troops excuse. With the Emperor unwell and Heraclius away, there was no one of appropriate rank available to serve as official host at a state dinner except Heraclius's rapscallion brother Maximilianus, and none of the officials of the royal household had felt sufficiently audacious to propose *that* without getting Faustus's approval first. So the state dinner had simply been scrubbed that afternoon, a fact that Faustus had not discovered until his return from the port. By then it was too late to do anything about that, other than to send a frantic message after the vanished prince imploring him to head back to Urbs Roma as quickly as possible. If Heraclius had indeed gone hunting, the message would reach him at his forest lodge in the woods out beyond Lake Nemorensis, and perhaps, perhaps, he would pay heed to it. If he had, against all probability, really gone to the military frontier, he was unlikely to return very soon. And that left only the Caesar Maximilianus, willy-nilly, to do the job. A risky business, that could be.

Well, the ambassador's little confession of a bit of a taste for the low life had taken care of the issue of keeping him entertained, at least for the next couple of days. If slumming in the Underworld was what Menandros was truly after, then Maximilianus would become the solution instead of the problem.

Faustus leaned back in the bath, savoring the warmth of the water, enjoying the sweet smell of the oils floating on the surface. It was while in the bath that proper Romans of the olden days—Seneca, say, or the poet Lucan, or that fierce old harridan Antonia, the mother of the Emperor Claudius—would take the opportunity to slit their wrists rather than continue to endure the inadequacies and iniquities of the society in which they lived. But these were not the olden days, and Faustus was not as offended by the inadequacies and iniquities of society as those grand old Romans had been, and, in any event, suicide as a general concept was not something that held great appeal for him.

Still, it certainly was a sad time for Roma, he thought. The old

Emperor as good as dead, the heir to the throne a ninny and a prude, the Emperor's other son a wastrel, and the barbarians, who were supposed to have been crushed years ago, once again knocking at the gates. Faustus knew that he was no model of the ancient Roman virtues himself—who was, five centuries after Augustus's time?—but, for all his own weaknesses and foibles, he could not help crying out within himself, sometimes, at the tawdriness of the epoch. We call ourselves Romans, he thought, and we know how to imitate, up to a point, the attitudes and poses of our great Roman forebears. But that's all we do: strike attitudes and imitate poses. We merely play at being Romans, and deceive ourselves, sometimes, into accepting the imitation for the reality.

It is a sorry era, Faustus told himself.

He was of royal blood himself, more or less. His very name proclaimed that: Faustus Flavius Constantinus Caesar. Embedded within it was the cognomen of his famous imperial ancestor, Constantinus the Great, and along with it the name of Constantinus's wife Fausta, herself the daughter of the Emperor Maximianus. The dynasty of Constantinus had long since vanished from the scene, of course, but by various genealogical zigs and zags Faustus could trace his descent back to it, and that entitled him to add the illustrious name "Caesar" to his array. Even so he was merely a secondary official in the Chancellery of Maximilianus II Augustus, and his father before him had been an officer of trifling rank in the Army of the North, and his father before him—well, Faustus thought, best not to think of *him*. The family had had some reverses in the course of the two centuries since Constantinus the Great had occupied the throne. But no one could deny his lineage, and there were times when he found himself secretly looking upon the current royal family as mere newcomers to power, jumped up out of nowhere. Of course, the early Emperors, Augustus Caesar and Tiberius and Claudius and such, would have looked even upon Constantinus the Great as a jumped-up newcomer; and the great men of the old Republic, Camillus, for instance, or Claudius Marcellus, would probably have thought the same of Augustus and Tiberius. Ancestry was a foolish game to play, Faustus thought. The past existed here in Roma in layer upon layer, a past that was nearly thirteen hundred years deep, and everyone had been a jumped-up newcomer once upon a time, even the founder Romulus himself.

So the era of the great Constantinus had come and gone, and here was his distant descendant Faustus Flavius Constantinus Caesar, growing old, growing plump, growing bald, spending his days toiling in the middle echelons of the Imperial Chancellery. And the Empire itself seemed to be aging badly, too. Everything had gone soft, here in the final years of the long reign of Maximilianus II. The great days of Titus Gallius and his dynasty, of Constantinus and his, of the first Maximilianus and his son and grandson, seemed already like something out of the legends of antiquity, even if the second Maximilianus still did hold the throne. Things had changed, in the past decade or two. The Empire no longer seemed as secure as it had been. And this year there had been much talk, all up and down the shadowy corridors of the sorcerers' marketplace, of mystic oracular prophecies, lately found in a newly discovered manuscript of the Sibylline Books, that indicated that Roma had entered into its last century, after which would come fire, apocalyptic chaos, the collapse of everything.

If that is so, Faustus thought, let it wait another twenty or thirty years. Then the world can come to an end, for all that I will care.

But it was something new, this talk of the end of eternal Roma. For hundreds of years, now, there had always been some great man available to step in and save things in time of crisis. Three hundred and some years ago, Septimius Severus had been there to rescue the Empire from crazy Commodus. A generation later, after Severus's even crazier son Caracalla had worked all sorts of new harm, it was the superb Titus Gallius who took charge and repaired the damage. The barbarians were beginning to make serious trouble at the Empire's edges by then, but, again and again, strong Emperors beat them back: first Titus Gallius, then his nephew Gaius Martius, and Marcus Anastasius after him, and then Diocletianus, the first Emperor to divide the realm among jointly ruling Emperors, and Constantinus, who founded the second capital in the East, and on and on, down to the present time. But now the throne was to all intents and purposes vacant, and everyone could see that the heir-in-waiting was worthless, and where, Faustus wondered, was the next great savior of the realm to come from?

Prince Maximilianus was right that his own dynasty had been a line of mighty warriors. Maximilianus I, a northerner, not a Roman of Roma at all but a man who could trace his roots back to the long-ago Etruscan race, had founded that line when he made himself the successor to the great Emperor Theodosius on the Imperial throne. As a vigorous young general the first Maximilianus drove back the Goths who were threatening Italia's northern border, and then in the autumn of his years joined with Theodosius II of the Eastern Empire to smash the Hunnish invaders under Attila. Then came Maximilianus's son Heraclius I, who held the line on all frontiers, and when the next wave of Goths and their kinsmen the Vandals began rampaging through Gallia and the Germanic lands, Heraclius's son, the young Emperor Maximilianus II, cut them to pieces with a fierce counterattack that seemed to have ended their threat for all time.

But no: there seemed to be no end of Goths and Vandals and similar nomadic tribes. Here, forty years after Maximilianus II had marched with twenty legions across the Rhenus into Gallia and inflicted a decisive defeat on them, they were massing for what looked like the biggest attack since the days of Theodosius. Now, though, Maximilianus II was old and feeble, very likely dying. The best anyone could say was that the Emperor was dwelling in seclusion somewhere, seen only by his doctors, but there were a great many unreliable stories circulating about his location: perhaps he was here in Roma, perhaps on the isle of Capreae down in the south, or maybe even in Carthago or Volubilis or some other sun-blessed African city. For all Faustus knew, he was already dead, and his panicky ministers were afraid to release the news. It would not be the first time in Roma's history that that had happened.

And after Maximilianus II, what? Prince Heraclius would take the throne, yes. But there was no reason to be optimistic about the sort of Emperor that he would be. Faustus could imagine the course of events only too easily. The Goths, unstoppable, break through in the north and invade Italia, sack the city, slaughter the aristocracy, proclaim one of their kings as monarch of Roma. Meanwhile, off in the west, the Vandals or some other tribe of that ilk lay claim to the rich provinces of Gallia and Hispania, which now become independent kingdoms, and the Empire is dissolved.

"The best and in fact only hope," Faustus had heard the Imperial Chancellor Licinius Obsequens say a month before, "is the royal marriage. Justinianus, for the sake of saving his brother-in-law's throne but also not wanting a pack of unruly barbarian kingdoms springing up along his own borders where the Western Empire used to be, sends an army to back up ours, and with the help of a few competent Greek generals the Goths finally get taken care of. But even that solution solves nothing for us. One can easily see one of Justinianus's generals offering to stay around as an 'adviser' to our young Emperor Heraclius, and next thing you know Heraclius turns up poisoned and the general lets it be known that he will graciously accept the Senate's invitation to take the throne, and from that point on the Western Empire comes completely under the dominance of the East, all our tax money starts to flow toward Constantinopolis, and Justinianus rules the world."

Our best and in fact only hope. I really should slash my wrists, Faustus thought. Make a rational exit in the face of insuperable circumstances, as many a Roman hero has done before me. Certainly there is ample precedent. He thought of Lucan, who calmly recited his own poetry as he died. Petronius Arbiter, who did the same. Cocceius Nerva, who starved himself to death to show his distaste for the doings of Tiberius. "The foulest death," said Seneca, "is preferable to the fairest slavery." Very true; but perhaps I am not a true Roman hero.

He rose from the bath. Two slaves rushed to cover him with soft towels. "Send in the Numidian girl," he said, heading for the bedchamber.

"We will enter," Danielus bar-Heap explained, "by way of the gateway of Titus Gallius, which is the most famous opening into the Underworld. There are many other entrances, but this is the most impressive."

It was midmorning: early in the day, perhaps, for going down below, certainly early in the day for the hard-living Prince Maximilianus to be up and about at all. But Faustus wanted to embark on the excursion as early as possible. Keeping the ambassador amused was his highest priority now.

The Hebrew had very quickly taken charge of the enterprise, doing all of the planning and most of the talking. He was one of the prince's most cherished companions. Faustus had met him more than once before: a big deep-voiced square-shouldered man, with jutting cheekbones and a great triangular beak of a nose, who wore his dark, almost blue-black hair in closely braided ringlets. Though it had been for many years the fashion for men to go clean-shaven in Roma, bar-Heap sported a conspicuous beard, thick and dense, that clung in tight coils to his jaw and chin. Instead of a toga he was clad in a knee-length tunic of rough white linen that was inscribed along its margins with bold lightning-bolt patterns done in bright green thread.

Ambassador Menandros, Easterner though he was, had apparently never met a Hebrew before, and needed to have bar-Heap explained to him. "They are a small tribe of desert folk who settled in Aegyptus long ago," Faustus told him. "Scatterings of them live all over the Empire by now. I dare say you would find a few in Constantinopolis. They are shrewd, determined, rather argumentative people, who don't always have the highest respect for the law, except for the laws of their own tribe, by which they abide under all circumstances in the most fanatic way. I understand they have no belief in the gods, for instance, and only the most grudging allegiance to the Emperor."

"No belief in the gods?" said Menandros. "None at all?"

"Not that I can see," said Faustus.

"Well, they do have some god of their own," Maximilianus put in. "But no one may ever see him, and they make no statues of him, and he has laid down a whole lot of absurd laws about what they can eat, and so forth. Bar-Heap will probably tell you all the details, if you ask him. Or perhaps he won't. Like all his kind, he's a prickly, unpredictable sort."

Faustus had advised the ambassador that it would be best if they dressed simply for the outing, nothing that might indicate their rank. Menandros's wardrobe, of course, ran largely to luxurious

silken robes and other such Eastern splendiferousness, but Faustus
had provided a plain woolen toga for him that had no stripes of rank
on it. Menandros appeared to know how to drape the garment properly around himself. Maximilianus Caesar, who as the son of the
reigning Emperor was entitled to wear a toga bedecked with a purple stripe and strands of golden thread, wore an unmarked one also.
So did Faustus, although, since he too was the descendant of an Emperor, he was permitted the purple stripe as well. Even so, no one
down below was likely to mistake them for anything other than what
they were, Romans of the highest class. But it was never a good idea
to flaunt patrician airs too ostentatiously in the subterranean world
of Roma.

The entrance that the Hebrew had chosen for them was at the
edge of the teeming quarter known as the Subura, which lay east of
the Forum in the valley between the Viminal and Esquiline Hills.
Here, in a district marked by stench and squalor and deafening hubbub, where the common folk of Roma lived jammed elbow to elbow
in shoddy buildings four and five stories high and screeching carts
proceeded with much difficulty through narrow, winding streets, the
Emperor Titus Gallius had begun carving, about the year 980, an
underground refuge in which the citizens of Roma could take shelter
if the unruly Goths, then massing in the north, should break
through Roma's defenses and enter the city.

The Goths, as it happened, were routed long before they got
anywhere near the capital. But by then Titus Gallius had built a
complex network of passageways under the Subura, and he and his
successors went on enlarging it for decades, sending tentacles out in
all directions, creating linkages to the existing labyrinthine chain of
underground galleries and tunnels and chambers that Romans had
been constructing here and there about the city for a thousand years.

And by now that Underworld was a city beneath the city, an entity unto itself down there in the dank and humid darkness. The por-
tals of Titus Gallius lay before them, two ornate stone arches like the
gaping jaws of a giant mouth, rising in the middle of the street where
Imperial forces centuries ago had cleared away a block of ancient
hovels on both sides to make room for the entrance plaza. The opening into the Underground was wide enough to allow three wagons to

pass at the same time. A ramp of well-worn brown brick led downward into the depths.

"Here are your lanterns," bar-Heap said, lighting them and handing them around. "Remember to hold them high, to keep them from going out. The air is heavier down by your knees and will smother the flame."

As they embarked on the ramp the Caesar took the position at the front of the group; Faustus positioned himself next to the Greek; bar-Heap brought up the rear. Menandros had been taken aback to learn that they would be traveling by foot, but Faustus had explained that using porter-born litters would be inconvenient in the tight passageways of the crowded world below. They would not even be accompanied by servants. The Greek seemed delighted to hear that. He was truly slumming today, that was clear. He wanted to travel through the Underworld as an ordinary Roman would, to get right down into all its muck and filth and danger.

Even this early in the day the ramp was crowded, both in the upward and downward directions, a quick, jostling throng. Ahead, all was cloaked in a palpable gloom. Going into the Underworld had always seemed to Faustus like entering the lair of some enormous creature. He was enveloped once again now by the thick, fierce darkness, cool, spicy. He savored its embrace. How often had he and Caesar entered here in search of a night's strange entertainment, and how many times they had found it!

Quickly his eyes began to adapt to the dim murky gleam of the lanterns. By the dull light of distant torches he could see the long ranges of far-off vaults running off on every side. The descent had quickly leveled out into the broad vestibule. Gusts of fetid underground air blew toward them, bearing a host of odors: smoke, sweat, mildew, the smell of animal bodies. It was very busy here, long lines of people and beasts of burden coming and going out of a dozen directions. The wide avenue known as the Via Subterranea stretched before them, and myriad narrower subsidiary passages branched off to right and left. Faustus saw once more the familiar piers and arches and bays, the curving walls of warm golden brick, the heavy rock-hewn pillars and the innumerable alcoves behind them. At once the darkness of this shadowy world seemed less oppressive.

He glanced down at the Greek. Menandros's soft features were alive with excitement. His nostrils were quivering, his lips were drawn back. His expression was like that of a small child who was being taken to the gladiatorial games for the first time. He almost seemed like a child among the three tall men, too, a flimsy, diminutive figure alongside long-limbed Maximilianus and sturdy, deep-chested bar-Heap and fleshy, bulky Faustus.

"What is that?" Menandros asked, pointing to the enormous marble relief of a bearded head, cemented into the wall just ahead of them. From above came a spike of light from one of the openings that pierced the vaulted roof, admitting a white beam that lit up the carved features with an eerie nimbus.

"He is a god," said bar-Heap from behind, with a tincture of contempt in his voice. "An Emperor put him up there, many years ago. Perhaps he is one of yours, or perhaps one from Syria. We call him Jupiter of the Caverns." The Hebrew raised his lantern far over his head to provide an additional burst of illumination for that powerful profile, the great staring eye, the huge all-hearing ear, the ominously parted lips, the massive coiling stone beard thicker even than his own. Everything above the eye was gone, and below the beard there was nothing also: it was a single colossal fragment that looked unthinkably ancient, a brooding relic of some great former age. "Hail, Jupiter!" bar-Heap said in a resonant tone, and laughed. But Menandros paused to examine the immense somber face, and to take note of the marble altar, worn smooth by adoring hands and luminous in the reflected light of candles mounted along its rim, just below it. The charred bones of sacrifices, recent ones, lay in a niche in its side.

Maximilianus beckoned him impatiently onward with quick imperious gestures. "This is only the beginning," the Caesar said. "We have many miles ahead of us."

"Yes. Yes, of course," said the Greek. "But still—it is so new to me, it is so strange—"

After they had gone some two hundred paces down the Via Subterranea, Maximilianus made a sharp left turn into a curving passage where cold damp came stealing down the walls in a steady drip, forming pools beneath their feet. The air had a moist, choking mustiness to it.

It seemed less crowded here. At least there was less foot traffic than in the main avenue. The overhead light-shafts were spaced much farther apart. Fewer torches could be seen ahead. But out of the darkness came unsettling sounds, harsh laughter and blurred incomprehensible whispers and giddy murmurs in unknown tongues and the occasional high, sharp shriek. There were strong odors, too, those of meat roasting over smoky fires, cauliflower stew, tubs of hot peppery broth, fried fish. This was no city of the dead, however dark and grim it might look: it was bursting with secret life, roaring with it, this hidden frenetic underground world. Everywhere around, in chambers and vaults cut from the living rock, an abundance of events was going forward, Faustus knew: the sale of enchantments and the casting of spells, business deals both licit and illicit, the performance of the religious rites of a hundred cults, carnal acts of every kind.

"Where are we now?" Menandros asked.

"These are the grottoes of Titus Gallius," said Caesar. "One of the busiest sectors—a place of general activities, very hard to characterize. One may see anything here, and rarely the same thing twice."

They went from chamber to chamber, following the low-ceilinged winding path that threaded everything together. It was Maximilianus, still, who led the way, hot-eyed now, almost frenzied, pulling them all behind him in his wake, often faster than Menandros wanted to go. Faustus and the Hebrew went along obligingly. This behavior of Caesar's was nothing new to them. It was almost as if some fit came over him when he was here in these tangled grottoes, driving him on from one sight to the next. Faustus had seen this happen many times before down here, the bursting forth of this restless furious hunger of the Caesar's for novelty, this raging inexhaustible curiosity of his.

It was the curse of an idle life, Faustus thought, the poignant anguish of an Emperor's superfluous younger son, vexed by the endless torment of his own uselessness, the mocking powerlessness within great power that was the only thing that his high birth had brought him. It was as if the greatest challenge that Maximilianus faced was the boredom of his own gilded existence, and in the Un-

derworld he warded off that challenge through this quest for the ultimate and the impossible. The Hebrew was a necessary facilitator
for this: more often than not it took a quick word from bar-Heap,
not always speaking Latin, to gain admittance for them to some sector of the caverns normally closed to the uninvited.

Here, under an array of blazing sconces that filled the air with
black smoke, lights that were never extinguished in this place where
no distinction was made between night and day, was a marketplace
where strange delicacies were being sold—the tongues of nightingales and flamingos, lamprey spleen, camel heels, bright yellow
cockscombs, parrot heads, the livers of pikes, the brains of pheas-
ants and peacocks, the ears of dormice, the eggs of pelicans, bizarre
things from every corner of the Empire, everything heaped in big
meaty mounds on silver trays. Menandros, that cosmopolitan Greek,
stared in wonder like any provincial bumpkin. "Do Romans dine on
such things every day?" he asked, and Caesar, smiling that opaque
Etruscan smile of his, assured him that they constantly did, not only
at the Imperial table but everywhere in Roma, even in the humblest
houses, and promised him a meal of nightingales' tongues and peacock brains at the earliest opportunity.

And here was a noisy plaza filled with clowns, jugglers, acrobats,
sword-swallowers, fire-eaters, tightrope-walkers, and performers of
a dozen other kinds, with snarling barkers loudly calling out the
praises of the acts that employed them. Maximilianus tossed silver
coins freely to them, and at his urging Menandros did the same. Beyond it was a colonnaded hallway in which a freak show was being
offered: hunchbacks and dwarfs, three simpering pinheads in elaborate scarlet livery, a man who looked like a living skeleton, another
who must have been nearly ten feet high. "The one with the ostrich
head is no longer here," said bar-Heap, obviously disappointed.
"And also the girl with three eyes, and the twins joined at the waist."
Here, too, they distributed coins liberally, all but bar-Heap, who
kept the strings of his purse drawn tight.

"Do you know, Faustus, who is the greatest freak and monster of
them all?" asked Maximilianus, under his breath, as they walked
along. And when Faustus remained silent the prince offered an answer to his own question that Faustus had not anticipated: "It is the

Emperor, my friend, for he stands apart from all other men, distinct, unique, forever isolated from all honesty and love, from normal feeling of any sort. He is a grotesque thing, an Emperor is. There is no monster so pitiable on this earth as an Emperor, Faustus." The Caesar, gripping the fleshiest part of Faustus's arm with iron force, gave him such a queer look of fury and anguish that Faustus was astounded by its intensity. This was a side of his friend he had never seen before. But then Maximilianus grinned and jabbed him light-heartedly in the ribs, and winked as if to take the sting out of his words.

Farther on was a row of apothecary stalls cluttered one upon the next in a series of narrow alcoves that were part of what looked like an abandoned temple. Lamps were burning before each one. These dealers in medicines offered such things as the bile of bulls and hyenas, the sloughed-off skins of snakes, the webs of spiders, the dung of elephants. "What is this?" the Greek asked, pointing into a glass vial that contained some fine gray powder, and bar-Heap, after making inquiry, reported that it was the excrement of Sicilian doves, much valued in treating tumors of the leg and many other maladies. Another booth sold only rare aromatic barks from the trees of India; another, small disks made of rare red clay from the isle of Lemnos, stamped with the sacred seal of Diana and reputed to cure the bite of mad dogs and the effects of the most lethal poisons. "And this man here," said Maximilianus grandly at the next stall, "purveys nothing but theriac, the universal antidote, potent even for leprosy. It is made mainly from the flesh of vipers steeped in wine, I think, but there are other ingredients, secret ones, and even if we put him to the torture he would not reveal them." And, with a wink to the drug's purveyor, a one-eyed hawk-faced old Aegyptian, "Eh, Ptolemaios, is that not so? Not even if we put you to the torture?"

"It will not come to that, I hope, Caesar," the man replied.

"So they know you here?" Menandros asked, when they had moved onward.

"Some do. This one has several times brought his wares to the palace to treat my ailing father."

"Ah," the Greek said. "Your ailing father, yes. All the world prays for his swift recovery."

Maximilianus nodded casually, as though Menandros had expressed nothing more than a wish for fair weather on the next day.

Faustus felt troubled by the strangeness of the Caesar's mood. He knew Maximilianus to be an unpredictable man who veered constantly between taut control and wild abandon, but it was mere courtesy to offer a grateful word for such an expression of sympathy, and yet he had been unable to bring himself to do it. What, he wondered, does the ambassador think of this strange prince? Or does he think nothing at all, except that this is what one can expect the younger son of a Roman Emperor to be like?

There were no clocks in this subterranean world, nor was there any clue in this sunless place to the hour available from the skies, but Faustus's belly was telling him the time quite unmistakably, now. "Shall we go above to eat," he asked Menandros, "or would you prefer to dine down here?"

"Oh, down here, by all means," said the Greek. "I'm not at all ready to go above!"

They ate at a torchlit tavern two galleries over from the arcade of the apothecaries, sitting cheek by jowl with scores of garlicky commoners on rough wooden benches: a meal of meat stewed in a spicy sauce made from fermented fish, fruits steeped in honey and vinegar, harsh acrid wine not much unlike vinegar itself. Menandros seemed to love it. He must never have encountered such indelicate delicacies before, and he ate and drank with ravenous appetite. The effects of this indulgence showed quickly on him: the sweat-shiny brow, the ruddy cheeks, the glazing eyes. Maximilianus, too, allowed himself course after course, washing his food down with awesome quantities of the dreadful wine; but, then, Maximilianus adored this stuff and never knew when to stop when wine of any kind was within reach. Faustus, not a man of great moderation himself, who loved drinking to excess, loved the dizzy float upward that too much wine brought on, the severing of his soaring mind from his ever more gross and leaden flesh, had to force himself to swallow it. But eventually he took to drinking most of each new pitcher as fast as he could, regardless of the taste, in order to keep the Caesar from overindulging.

He gave much of the rest to the stolid, evidently bottomless bar-Heap, for he knew what perils were possible if the prince, far gone in drunkenness, should get himself into some foolish brawl down here. He could easily imagine bringing Maximilianus back on a board from the caverns some day, with his royal gut slashed from one side to the other and his body already stiffening. If that happened, the best he could hope for himself would be to spend the remainder of his own life in brutal exile in some dismal Teutonic outpost.

When they went onward finally, somewhere late in the afternoon, a subtle change of balance had taken place in the group. Maximilianus, either because he had suddenly grown bored or because he had eaten too much, seemed to lose interest in the expedition. No longer did he sprint ahead, beckoning them on along from corridor to corridor as though racing some unseen opponent from one place to the next. Now it was Menandros, fueled by his heavy input of wine, who seized command, displaying now a hunger to see it all even more powerful than the prince's had been, and rushing them along through the subterranean city. Not knowing any of the routes, he made random turns, taking them now into pitch-black cul-de-sacs, now to the edges of dizzying abysses where long many-runged ladders led to spiraling successions of lower levels, now to chambers with painted walls where rows of cackling madwomen sat in throne-like niches demanding alms.

Most of the time Maximilianus did not seem to be able to identify the places into which Menandros had led them, or did not care to say. It became the task of bar-Heap, whose mastery of the underground city seemed total, to explain what they were seeing. "This place is the underground arena," the Hebrew said, as they peered into a black hole that seemed to stretch for many leagues. "The games are held here at the midnight hour, and all contests are to the death." They came soon afterward to a gleaming marble façade and a grand doorway leading to some interior chamber: the Temple of Jupiter Imperator, bar-Heap explained. That was the cult established by the Emperor Gaius Martius in the hope, not entirely realized, of identifying the father of the gods with the head of the state in the eyes of the common people, who otherwise might wander off

into some kind of alien religious belief that could weaken their loyalty to the state. "And this," said bar-Heap at an adjacent temple
flush against the side of Jupiter's, "is the House of Cybele, where
they worship the Great Mother."

"We have that cult in the East as well," said Menandros, and he
halted to examine with a connoisseur's eye the fanciful mosaic orna-
mentation, row upon row of patterned tiles, red and blue and orange and green and gold, that proclaimed this place the dwelling of
the full-breasted goddess. "How fine this is," the Greek said, "to
build such a wonder underground, where it can barely be seen except by this dirty torchlight, and not well even then. How bold!
How extravagant!"

"It is a very wealthy creed, Cybele's," said Maximilianus, nudg-
ing Faustus broadly as though to remind him of the stolen opals of
the goddess that would be his gift to his brother's Constantinopoli-
tan bride.

Menandros drew them tirelessly on through the dark labyrinth—
past bubbling fountains and silent burial-chambers and frescoed cult-
halls and bustling marketplaces, and then through a slit-like opening
in the wall that took them into a huge, empty space from which a multitude of dusty unmarked corridors radiated, and down one and then
another of those, until, in a place of awkwardly narrow passages,
even bar-Heap seemed uncertain of where they were. A frown furrowed the Hebrew's forehead. Faustus, who by this time was feeling
about ready to drop from fatigue, began to worry, too. Suddenly
there was no one else around. The only sounds here were the sounds
of their own echoing footsteps. Everyone had heard tales of people
roaming the subterranean world who had taken injudicious turns
and found themselves irretrievably lost in mazes built in ancient days
to delude possible invaders, bewilderingly intricate webworks of anarchic design whose outlets were essentially unfindable and from
which the only escape was through starvation. A sad fate for the little
Greek emissary and the dashing, venturesome royal prince, Faustus
thought. A sad fate for Faustus, too.

But this was not a maze of that sort. Four sharp bends, a brief
climb by ladder, a left turn, and they were back on the Via Subterranea, somehow, though no doubt very far from the point where

they had entered the underground metropolis that morning. The vaulted ceiling was pointed, here, and inlaid with rows of coral-colored breccia. A procession of chanting priests was coming toward them, gaunt men whose faces were smeared with rouge and whose eye-sockets were painted brightly in rings of yellow and green. They wore white tunics crisscrossed with narrow purple stripes and towering saffron-colored caps that bore the emblem of a single glaring eye at their summits. Energetically they flogged one another with whips of knotted woolen yarn studded with the knucklebones of sheep as they danced along, and cried out in harsh, jabbering rhythmic tones, uttering prayers in some foreign tongue.

"Eunuchs, all of them," said bar-Heap in disgust. "Worshipers of Dionysus. Step aside, or they'll bowl you over, for they yield place to no one when they march like this."

Close behind the priests came a procession of deformed clowns, squinting hunchbacked men who also were carrying whips, but only pretending to use them on each other. Maximilianus flung them a handful of coins, and Menandros did the same, and they broke formation at once, scrabbling enthusiastically in the dimness to scoop them up. On the far side of them the Hebrew pointed out a chamber that he identified as a chapel of Priapus, and Menandros was all for investigating it; but this time Maximilianus said swiftly, "I think that is for another day, your excellency. One should be in fresh condition for such amusements, and you must be tired, now, after this long first journey through the netherworld."

The ambassador looked unhappy. Faustus wondered whose will would prevail: that of the visiting diplomat, whose whims ought to be respected, or of the Emperor's son, who did not expect to be gainsaid. But after a moment's hesitation Menandros agreed that it was time to go back above. Perhaps he saw the wisdom of checking his voracious curiosity for a little while, or else simply that of yielding to the prince's request.

"There is an exit ramp over there," bar-Heap said, pointing to his right. With surprising speed they emerged into the open. Night had fallen. The sweet cool air seemed, as ever upon emerging, a thousand times fresher and more nourishing than that of the world below. Faustus was amused to see that they were not far from the

Baths of Constantinus, only a few hundred yards from where they had gone in, although his legs were aching fiercely, as though he had covered many leagues that day. They must have traveled in an enormous circle, he decided.

He yearned for his own bath, and a decent dinner, and a massage afterward and the Numidian girl.

Maximilianus, with an Imperial prince's casual arrogance, hailed a passing litter that bore Senatorial markings, and requisitioned its use for his own purposes. Its occupant, a balding man whom Faustus recognized by face but could not name, hastened to comply, scuttling away into the night without protest. Faustus and Menandros and the Caesar clambered aboard, while the Hebrew, with no more farewell than an irreverent offhand wave, vanished into the darkness of the streets.

There was no message waiting at home for Faustus to tell him that Prince Heraclius was heading back to the city. He had been hoping for such news. Tomorrow would be another exhausting day spent underground, then.

He slept badly, though the little Numidian did her best to soothe his nerves.

This time they entered the Underworld farther to the west, between the column of Marcus Aurelius and the Temple of Isis and Sarapis. That was, bar-Heap said, the quickest way to reach the marketplace of the sorcerers, which Menandros had some particular interest in seeing.

Diligent guide that he was, the Hebrew showed them all the notable landmarks along the way: the Whispering Gallery, where even the faintest of sounds traveled enormous distances, and the Baths of Pluto, a series of steaming thermal pools that gave off a foul sulphurous reek but nevertheless abounded in patrons even here at midday, and the River Styx nearby it, the black subterranean stream that followed a rambling course through the underground city until it emerged into the Tiber just upstream from the Cloaca Maxima, the great sewer.

"Truly, the Styx?" Menandros asked, with a credulity Faustus had not expected of him.

"We call it that," said bar-Heap. "Because it is the river of our Underworld, you see. But the true one is somewhere in your own eastern realm, I think. Here—we must turn—"

A jagged, irregularly oval aperture in the passageway wall proved to be the entrance to the great hall that served as the sorcerers' marketplace. Originally, so they said, it had been intended as a storage vault for the Imperial chariots, to keep them from being seized by invading barbarians. When such precautions had turned out to be unnecessary, the big room had been taken over by a swarm of sorcerers, who divided it by rows of pumice-clad arches into a collection of small low-walled chambers. An octagonal light-well, high overhead in the very center of the roof of the hall, allowed pale streams of sunlight to filter down from the street above, but most of the marketplace's illumination came from the smoky braziers in front of each stall. These, whether by some enchantment or mere technical skill, all burned with gaudy many-hued flames, and dancing strands of violet and pale crimson and cobalt blue and brilliant emerald mingled with the more usual reds and yellows of a charcoal fire.

The roar of commerce rose up on every side. Each of the sorcerers' stalls had its barker, crying the merits of his master's wares. Scarcely had the ambassador Menandros entered the room than one of these, a fat, sweaty-faced man wearing a brocaded robe of Syrian style, spied him as a likely mark, beckoning him inward with both arms while calling out, "Eh, there, you dear little fellow: what about a love spell today, an excellent inflamer, the finest of its kind?"

Menandros indicated interest. The barker said, "Come, then, let me show you this splendid wizardry! It attracts men to women, women to men, and makes virgins rush out of their homes to find lovers!" He reached behind him, snatched up a rolled parchment scroll, and waved it in front of Menandros's nose. "Here, friend, here! You take a pure papyrus and write on it, with the blood of an ass, the magical words contained on this. Then you put in a hair of the woman you desire, or a snip of her clothing, or a bit of her bedsheet—acquire it however you may. And then you smear the papyrus with a bit of vinegar gum, and stick it to the wall of her house, and you will marvel! But watch that you are not struck yourself, or you may find yourself bound by the chains of love to some passing drover, or to his donkey, perhaps, or even worse! Three sesterces! Three!"

"If infallible love is to be had so cheaply," Maximilianus said to the man, "why is it that languishing lovers hurl themselves into the river every day of the week?"

"And also why is it that the whorehouses are kept so busy," added Faustus, "when for three brass coins anyone can have the woman of his dreams?"

"Or the man," said Menandros. "For this charm will work both ways, so he tells us."

"Or on a donkey," put in Danielus bar-Heap, and they laughed and passed onward.

Nearby, a spell of invisibility was for sale, at a price of two silver denarii. "It is the simplest thing," insisted the barker, a small lean man tight as a coiled spring, whose swarthy sharp-chinned face was marked by the scars of some ancient knife fight. "Take a night-owl's eye and a ball of the dung of the beetles of Aegyptus and the oil of an unripe olive and grind them all together until smooth, and smear your whole body with it, and then go to the nearest shrine of the lord Apollo by dawn's first light and utter the prayer that this parchment will give you. And you will be invisible to all eyes until sunset and can go unnoticed among the ladies at their baths, or slip into the palace of the Emperor and help yourself to delicacies from his table, or fill your purse with gold from the moneychangers' tables. Two silver denarii, only!"

"Quite reasonable, for a day's invisibility," Menandros said. "I'll have it, for my master's delight." And reached for his purse; but the Caesar, catching him by the wrist, warned him never to accept the quoted first price in a place like this. Menandros shrugged, as though to point out that the price asked was only a trifle, after all. But to the Caesar Maximilianus there was an issue of principle here. He invoked the aid of bar-Heap, who quickly bargained the fee down to four copper dupondii, and, since Menandros did not have coins as small as that in his purse, it was Faustus who handed over the price.

"You have done well," the barker said, giving the Greek his bit of parchment. Menandros, turning away, opened it. "The letters are Greek," he said.

Maximilianus nodded. "Yes. Most of this trash is set out in Greek. It is the language of magic, here."

"The letters are Greek," said Menandros, "but not the words. Listen." And he read out in a rolling resonant tone: " 'BORKE PHOIOUR IO ZIZIA APARXEOUCH THYTHE LAILAM AAAAAA IIII OOOO IEO IEO IEO.' " Then he looked up from the scroll. "And there are three more lines, of much the same sort. What do you make of that, my friends?"

"I think it is well that you didn't read any more of it," said Faustus, "or you might have disappeared right before our noses."

"Not without employing the beetle dung and the owl's eye and the rest," bar-Heap observed. "Nor is that dawn's first light coming down that shaft, even if you would pretend that this is Apollo's temple."

" 'IO IO O PHRIXRIZO EOA,' " Menandros read, and giggled in pleasure, and rolled the scroll and put it in his purse.

It did not appear likely to Faustus that the Greek was a believer in this nonsense, as his earlier eagerness to visit this marketplace had led him to suspect. Yet he was an enthusiastic buyer. Doubtless he was merely looking for quaint souvenirs to bring back to his Emperor in Constantinopolis—entertaining examples of modern-day Roman gullibility. For Menandros must surely have noticed by this time an important truth about this room, which was that nearly all the sorcerers and their salesmen were citizens of the Eastern half of the Empire, which had a reputation for magic going back to the distant days of the Pharaohs and the kings of Babylon, while the customers—and there were plenty of them—all were Romans of the West. Surely spells of this sort would be widely available in the other Empire. This stuff would be nothing new to Easterners. It was an oily place, the Eastern Empire. All the mercantile skills had been invented there. The East's roots went deep down into antiquity, into a time long before Roma itself ever was, and one needed to keep a wary eye out in any dealings with its citizens.

So Menandros was just trying to collect evidence of Roman silliness, yes. Using bar-Heap to beat the prices down for him, he went from booth to booth, gathering up the merchandise. He acquired instructions for fashioning a ring of power that would permit one to get whatever one asks from anybody, or to calm the anger of masters and kings. He bought a charm to induce wakefulness, and another to bring on sleep. He got a lengthy scroll that offered a whole catalog of mighty mysteries, and gleefully read from it to them: " 'You will see the doors thrown open, and seven virgins coming from deep within, dressed in linen garments, and with the faces of asps. They are called the Fates of Heaven and wield golden wands. When you see them, greet them in this manner—' " He found a spell that necromancers could use to keep skulls from speaking out of turn while their owners were using them in the casting of spells; he found one that would summon the Headless One who had created earth and heaven, the mighty Osoronnophris, and conjure Him to expel demons from a sufferer's body; he found one that would bring back lost or stolen property; he went back to the first booth and bought the infallible love potion, for a fraction of the original asking price; and, finally, picked up one that would cause one's fellow drinkers at a drinking party to think that they had grown the snouts of apes.

At last, well satisfied with his purchases, Menandros said he was willing to move on. At the far end of the hall, beyond the territory of the peddlers of spells, they paused at the domain of the soothsayers and augurs. "For a copper or two," Faustus told the Greek, "they will look at the palm of your hand, or the pattern of lines on your forehead, and tell you your future. For a higher price they will examine the entrails of chickens or the liver of a sheep, and tell you your *true* future. Or even the future of the Empire itself."

Menandros looked astonished. "The future of the Empire? Common diviners in a public marketplace offer prophecies of a sort like that? I'd think only the Imperial augurs would deal in such news, and only for the Emperor's ear."

"The Imperial augurs provide more reliable information, I suppose," said Faustus. "But this is Roma, where everything is for sale to anyone." He looked down the row and saw the one who had claimed new knowledge of the Sibylline prophecies and foretold the imminent end of the Empire—an old man, unmistakably Roman, not a Greek or any other kind of foreigner, with faded blue eyes and a lengthy, wispy white beard. "Over there is one of the most audacious of our seers, for instance," Faustus said, pointing. "For a fee he will tell you that our time of Empire is nearly over, that a year is coming soon when the seven planets will meet at Capricorn and the entire universe will be consumed by fire."

"The great *ekpyrosis,*" Menandros said. "We have the same prophecy. What does he base his calculations on, I wonder?"

"What does it matter?" cried Maximilianus, in a burst of sudden unconcealed rage. "It is all foolishness!"

"Perhaps so," Faustus said gently. And, to Menandros, whose curiosity about the old man and his apocalyptic predictions still was apparent: "It has something to do with the old tale of King Romulus and the twelve eagles that passed overhead on the day he and his brother Remus fought over the proper location for the city of Roma."

"They were twelve vultures, I thought," said bar-Heap.

Faustus shook his head. "No. Eagles, they were. And the prophecy of the Sibyl is that Roma will endure for twelve Great Years of a hundred years each, one for each of Romulus's eagles, and one century more beyond that. This is the year 1282 since the founding. So we have eighteen years left, says the long-bearded one over there."

"This is all atrocious foolishness," said Maximilianus again, his eyes blazing.

"May we speak with this man a moment, even so?" Menandros asked.

The Caesar most plainly did not want to go near him. But his guest's mild request could hardly be refused. Faustus saw Maximilianus struggling with his anger as they walked toward the soothsayer's booth, and with some effort putting it aside. "Here is a visitor to our city," said Maximilianus to the old man in a clenched voice, "who wants to hear what you've to say concerning the impending fiery end of Roma. Name your price and tell him your fables."

But the soothsayer shrank back, trembling in fear. "No, Caesar. I pray you, let me be!"

"You recognize me, do you?"

"Who would not recognize the Emperor's son? Especially one whose profession it is to pierce all veils."

"You've pierced mine, certainly. But why do I frighten you so? I mean you no harm. Come, man, my friend here is a Greek from Justinianus's court, full of questions for you about the terrible doom that shortly will be heading our way. Speak your piece, will you?" Maximilianus pulled out his purse and drew a shining gold piece from it. "A fine newly minted aureus, is that enough to unseal your lips? Two? Three?"

It was a fortune. But the man seemed paralyzed with terror. He moved back in his booth, shivering, now, almost on the verge of collapse. The blood had drained from his face and his pale blue eyes were bulging and rigid. It was asking too much of him, Faustus supposed, to be compelled to speak of the approaching destruction of the world to the Emperor's actual son.

"Enough," Faustus murmured. "You'll scare the poor creature to death, Maximilianus."

But the Caesar was bubbling with fury. "No! Here's gold for him! Let him speak! Let him speak!"

"Caesar, I will speak to you, if you like," said a high-pitched, sharp-edged voice from behind them. "And will tell you such things as are sure to please your ears."

It was another soothsayer, a ratty little squint-faced man in a tattered yellow tunic, who now made so bold as to pluck at the edge of Maximilianus's toga. He had cast an augury for Maximilianus just now upon seeing the Caesar's entry into the marketplace, he said, and would not even ask a fee for it. No, not so much as two coppers for the news he had to impart. Not even one.

"Not interested," Maximilianus said brusquely, and turned away.

But the little diviner would not accept the rebuff. With frantic squirrelly energy he ran around Maximilianus's side to face him again and said, with the reckless daring of the utterly insignificant confronting the extremely grand, "I threw the bones, Caesar, and they showed me your future. It is a glorious one. You will be one of Roma's greatest heroes! Men will sing your praises for centuries to come."

Instantly a bright blaze of fury lit Maximilianus's entire countenance. Faustus had never seen the prince so incensed. "Do you dare to mock me to my face?" the Caesar demanded, his voice so thick with wrath that he could barely get the words out. His right arm quivered and jerked as though he were struggling to keep it from lashing out in rage. "A hero, you say! A hero! A *hero!*" If the little man had spat in his face it could not have maddened him more.

But the soothsayer persisted. "Yes, my lord, a great general, who will shatter the barbarian armies like so many empty husks! You will march against them at the head of a mighty force not long after you become Emperor, and—"

That was too much for the prince. "Emperor, too!" Maximilianus bellowed, and in that same moment struck out wildly at the man, a fierce backhanded blow that sent him reeling against the bench where the other soothsayer, the old bearded one, still was cowering. Then, stepping forward, Maximilianus caught the little man by the shoulder and slapped him again and again, back, forth, back, forth, knocking his head from side to side until blood poured from his mouth and nose and his eyes began to glaze over. Faustus, frozen at first in sheer amazement, moved in after a time to intervene. "Maximilianus!" he said, trying to catch the Caesar's flailing arm. "My lord—I beg you—it is not right, my lord—"

He signaled to bar-Heap, and the Hebrew caught Maximilianus's other arm. Together they pulled him back.

There was sudden silence in the hall. The sorcerers and their employees had ceased their work and were staring in astonishment and horror, as was Menandros.

The ragged little soothsayer, sprawling now in a kind of daze against the bench, spat out a tooth and said, in a kind of desperate defiance, "Even so, your majesty, it is the truth: Emperor."

It was all that Faustus and the Hebrew could manage to get the prince away from there without his doing further damage.

This capacity for wild rage was an aspect of Maximilianus that Faustus had never seen. The Caesar took nothing seriously. The world was a great joke to him. He had always let it be known that he cared for nothing and no one, not even himself. He was too cynical and wanton of spirit, too flighty, too indifferent to anything of any real importance, ever to muster the kind of involvement with events that true anger required. Then why had the soothsayer's words upset him so? His fury had been out of all proportion to the offense, if offense there had been. The man was merely trying to flatter. Here is a royal prince come among us: very well, tell him he will be a great hero, tell him even that he will be Emperor some day. The second of those, at least, was not impossible. Heraclius, who soon would have the throne, might well die childless, and they would have no choice but to ask his brother to ascend to power, however little Maximilianus himself might care for the idea.

Saying that Maximilianus would become a great hero, though: that must have been what stung him so, Faustus thought. Doubtless he did not regard himself as having a single iota of the stuff of heroes in him, whatever a flattering soothsayer might choose to say. And must believe also that all Roma perceived him not as a handsome young prince who might yet achieve great things but only as the idle wencher and gambler and dissipated profligate rogue that he was in his own eyes. And so he would interpret the soothsayer's words as mockery of the most inflammatory kind, rather than as flattery.

"We should quickly find ourselves a wineshop, I think," Faustus said. "Some wine will cool your overheated blood, my lord."

Indeed the wine, vile though it was, calmed Maximilianus rapidly, and soon he was laughing and shaking his head over the impudence of the ratty little man. "A hero of the realm! Me! And Emperor, too? Was there ever a soothsayer so far from the truth in his auguries?"

"If they are all like that one," said bar-Heap, "then I think there's no need to fear the coming fiery destruction of the universe, either. These men are clowns, or worse. All they provide is amusement for fools."

"A useful function in the world, I would say," Menandros observed. "There are so many fools, you know, and are they not entitled to amusement also?"

Faustus said very little. The episode among the sorcerers and soothsayers had left him in a mood of uncharacteristic bleakness. He had always been a good-humored man; the Caesar prized him for the jolly companionship he offered; but his frame of mind had grown steadily more sober since the coming to Roma of this Greek ambassador, and now he felt himself ringed round with an inchoate host of despondent thoughts. It was spending so much time in this underground realm of darkness and flickering shadows, he told himself, that had done this to him. He and the prince had found only pleasure here in days gone by, but their time these two days past in these ancient tunnels, this mysterious kingdom of inexplicable noises and visitations, of invisible beings, of lurking ghosts, had made him weary and uncomfortable. This dank sunless underground world, he thought, was the true Roma, a benighted kingdom of magic and terror, a place of omens and dread.

Would the world be destroyed by flame in eighteen years, as the old man said? Probably not. In any case he doubted that he would live to see it. The universe's end might not be approaching, but surely his own was: five years, ten, at best fifteen, and he would be gone, well before the promised catastrophe, the—what had the Greek called it?—the great *ekpyrosis.*

But even if no flaming apocalypse was really in store, the Empire did seem to be crumbling. There were symptoms of disease everywhere. That the man second in line for the throne would react with such fury at the possibility that he might be called upon to serve the realm was a sign of the extent of the illness. That the barbarians might soon be battering at the gates again, only a generation after they supposedly had been put to rout forever, was another. We seem to have lost our way.

Faustus filled his cup again. He knew he was drinking too much too fast: even his capacious paunch had its limits. But the wine eased the pain. Drink, then, old Faustus. Drink. If nothing else, you can allow your body a little comfort.

Yes, he was getting old. But Roma was even older. The immensity of the city's past pressed down on him from all sides. The narrow streets, choked with dunghill rubbish, that gave way to the great plazas and their myriad fountains with their silvery jets, and the palaces of the rich and mighty, and the statues everywhere, the obelisks, the columns taken from far-off temples, the spoils of a hundred Imperial conquests, the shrines of a hundred foreign gods, and the clean old Roma of the early Republic somewhere beneath it all:

level upon level of history here, twelve centuries of it, the present continually superimposing itself upon the past, though the past remains also—yes, he told himself, it has been a good long run, and perhaps, now that we have created so much past for ourselves, we have very little future, and really are wandering toward the finish now, and will disappear into our own softness, our own confusion, our own fatal love of pleasure and ease.

That troubled him greatly. But why, he wondered, did he care? He was nothing but a licentious old idler himself, the companion to a licentious young one. It had been his lifelong pretense never to care about anything.

And yet, yet, he could not let himself forget that he had the blood of the prodigious Constantinus in his veins, one of the greatest Emperors of all. The fate of the Empire had mattered profoundly to Constantinus: he had toiled for decades at its helm, and ultimately he had saved it from collapse by creating a new capital for it in the East, a second foundation to help carry the weight that Urbs Roma itself was no longer capable of bearing alone. Here am I, two and a quarter centuries later, and I am to my great ancestor Constantinus as a plump, sleepy old cat is to a raging lion: but I must care at least a little about the fate of the Empire to which he pledged his life. For his sake, if not particularly for my own. Otherwise, Faustus asked himself fiercely, what is the point of having the blood of an Emperor in my veins?

"You've grown very quiet, old man," Maximilianus said. "Did I upset you, shouting and rioting like that back there?"

"A little. But that's over now."

"What is it, then?"

"Thinking. A pernicious pastime, which I regret." Faustus swirled his cup about and peered glumly into its depths. "Here we are," he said, "down in the bowels of the city, this weird dirty place. I have always thought that everything seems unreal here, that it is all a kind of stage show. And yet right now it seems to me that it's far more real than anything up above. Down here, at least, there are no pretenses. It's every man for himself amidst the fantasies and grotesqueries, and no one has any illusions. We know why we are here and what we must do." Then, pointing toward the world above them:

"Up there, though, folly reigns supreme. We delude ourself into thinking that it is the world of stern reality, the world of Imperial power and Roman commercial might, but no one actually behaves as though any of it has to be taken seriously. Our heads are in the sand, like that great African bird's. The barbarians are coming, but we're doing nothing to stop them. And this time the barbarians will swallow us. They'll go roaring at last through the marble city that's sitting up there above us, looting and torching, and afterward nothing will remain of Roma but this, this dark, dank, hidden, eternally mysterious Underworld of strange gods and ghastly monstrosities. Which I suppose is the true Roma, the eternal city of the shadows."

"You're drunk," Maximilianus said.

"Am I?"

"This place down here is a mere fantasy world, Faustus, as you are well aware. It's a place without meaning." The prince pointed upward as Faustus just had done. "The true Roma that you speak of is up there. Always was, always will be. The palaces, the temples, the Capitol, the walls. Solid, indestructible, imperishable. The eternal city, yes. And the barbarians will never swallow it. Never. *Never.*"

That was a tone of voice Faustus had never heard the prince use before, either. The second unfamiliar one in less than an hour, this one hard, clear, passionate. There was, again, an odd new intensity in his eyes. Faustus had seen that strange intensity the day before, too, when the prince had spoken of Emperors as freaks and monsters. It was as though something new was trying to burst free inside the Caesar these two days past, Faustus realized. And it must be getting very close to the surface now. What will happen to us all, he wondered, when it breaks loose?

He closed his own eyes a moment, nodded, smiled. Let what will come come, he thought. Whatsoever it may be.

They ended their day in the Underworld soon afterward. Maximilianus's savage outburst in the hall of the soothsayers seemed to have placed a damper on everything, even Menandros's previously insatiable desire to explore the infinite crannies of the underground caverns.

It was near sundown when Faustus reached his chambers, having promised Menandros that he would dine with him later at the ambassador's lodgings in the Severan Palace. A surprise was waiting for him. Prince Heraclius had indeed gone to his hunting lodge, not to the frontier, and the message that Faustus had sent to him there had actually reached him. The prince was even now on his way back to Roma, arriving this very evening, and wished to meet with the emissary from Justinianus as soon as possible.

Hurriedly Faustus bathed and dressed in formal costume. The Numidian girl was ready and waiting, but Faustus dismissed her, and told his equerry that he would not require her services later in the evening, either.

"A curious day," Menandros said, when Faustus arrived.

"It was, yes," said Faustus.

"Your friend the Caesar was greatly distressed by that man's talk of his becoming Emperor some day. Is the idea so distasteful to him?"

"It's not something he gives any thought to at all, becoming Emperor. Heraclius will be Emperor. That's never been in doubt. He's the older by six years: he was well along in training for the throne when Maximilianus was born, and has always been treated by everyone as his father's successor. Maximilianus sees no future for himself in any way different from the life he leads now. He's never looked upon himself as a potential ruler."

"Yet the Senate could name either brother as Emperor, is that not so?"

"The Senate could name me as Emperor, if it chose. Or even you. In theory, as you surely know, there's nothing hereditary about it. In practice things are different. Heraclius's way to the throne is clear. Besides, Maximilianus doesn't *want* to be Emperor. Being Emperor is hard work, and Maximilianus has never worked at anything in his life. I think that's what upset him so much today, the mere thought that he somehow would have to be Emperor, some day."

Faustus knew Menandros well enough by now to be able to detect the barely masked disdain that these words of his produced. Menandros understood what an Emperor was supposed to be: a man like that severe and ruthless soldier Justinianus, who held sway from Dacia and Thrace to the borders of Persia, and from the frosty northern shores of the Pontic Sea to some point far down in torrid

Africa, exerting command over everything and everyone, the whole complex crazyquilt that was the Eastern Empire, with the merest flick of an eye. Whereas here, in the ever flabbier West, which was about to ask Justinianus's help in fighting off its own long-time enemies, the reigning Emperor was currently ill and invisible, the heir to the throne was so odd that he was capable of slipping out of town just as Justinianus's ambassador was arriving to discuss the very alliance the West so urgently needed, and the man second in line to the Empire cared so little for the prospect of attaining the Imperial grandeur that he would thrash someone half his size for merely daring to suggest he might.

He sees us of the West as next to worthless, Faustus thought. And perhaps he is correct.

This was not a profitable discussion. Faustus cut it short by telling him that Prince Heraclius would return that very evening.

"Ah, then," said Menandros, "affairs must be settling down on your northern frontier. Good."

Faustus did not think it was his duty to explain that the Caesar couldn't possibly have made the round trip to the frontier and back in so few days, that in fact he had merely been away at his hunting lodge in the countryside. Heraclius would be quite capable of achieving his own trivialization without Faustus's assistance.

Instead Faustus gave orders for their dinner to be served. They had just reached the last course, the fruits and sherbets, when a messenger entered with word that Prince Heraclius was now in Roma, and awaited the presence of the ambassador from Constantinopolis in the Hall of Marcus Anastasius at the Imperial palace.

The closest part of the five-hundred-year-old string of buildings that was the Imperial compound was no more than ten minutes' walk from where they were now. But Heraclius, with his usual flair for the inappropriate gesture, had chosen for the place of audience not his own residential quarters, which were relatively near by, but the huge, echoing chamber where the Great Council of State ordinarily met, far over on the palace's northern side at the very crest of the Palatine Hill. Faustus had two litters brought to take them up there.

The prince had boldly stationed himself on the throne-like seat at the upper end of the chamber that the Emperor used during meetings of the Council. He sat there now with Imperial haughtiness, waiting in silence while Menandros undertook the endless unavoidable ambassadorial plod across the enormous room, with Faustus hulking along irritatedly behind him. For one jarring instant Faustus wondered whether the old Emperor had actually, unbeknownst to him, died during the day, and the reason Heraclius was in Roma was that he had hurried back to take his father's place. But someone surely would have said something to him in that case, Faustus thought.

Menandros knew his job. He knelt before the prince and made the appropriate gesticulation. When he rose, Heraclius had risen also and was holding forth his hand, which bore an immense carnelian ring, to be kissed. Menandros kissed the prince's ring. The ambassador made a short, graceful speech expressing his greetings and the best wishes of the Emperor Justinianus for the good health of his royal colleague the Emperor Maximilianus, and for that of his royal son the Caesar Heraclius, and offered thanks for the hospitality that had been rendered him thus far. He gave credit warmly to Faustus but—quite shrewdly, Faustus thought—did not mention the role of Prince Maximilianus at all.

Heraclius listened impassively. He seemed jittery and remote, more so, even, than he ordinarily was.

Faustus had never felt any love for the Imperial heir. Heraclius was a stiff, tense person, ill at ease under the best of circumstances: a short, slight, inconsequential figure of a man with none of his younger brother's easy athleticism. He was cold-eyed, too, thinlipped, humorless. It was hard to see him as his father's son. The Emperor Maximilianus, in earlier days, had looked much the way the prince his namesake did today: a tall, slender, handsome man with glinting russet hair and smiling blue eyes. Heraclius, though, was dark-haired, where he still had hair at all, and his eyes were dark as coals, glowering under heavy brows out of his pale, expressionless face.

The meeting was inconclusive. The prince and the ambassador both understood that this first encounter was not the time to begin any discussion of the royal marriage or the proposed East-West military alliance, but even so Faustus was impressed by the sheer vacuity of the conversation. Heraclius asked if Menandros cared to attend the gladiatorial games the following week, said a sketchy thing or two about his Etruscan ancestors and their religious beliefs, of which he claimed to be a student of sorts, and spoke briefly of some idiotic Greek play that had been presented at the Odeum of Agrippa Ligurinus the week before. Of the barbarians massing at the border he said nothing at all. Of his father's grave illness, nothing. Of his hope of close friendship with Justinianus, nothing. He might just as well have been discussing the weather. Menandros gravely met immateriality with immateriality. He could do nothing else, Faustus understood. The Caesar Heraclius must be allowed to lead, here.

And then, very quickly, Heraclius made an end of it. "I hope we have an opportunity to meet again very shortly," the prince said, arbitrarily terminating the visit with such suddenness that even the quick-witted Menandros was caught off guard by his blunt dismissal, and Faustus heard a tiny gasp from him. "To my regret, I will have to leave the city again tomorrow. But upon my return, at the earliest opportunity—" And he held forth his ringed hand to be kissed again.

Menandros said, when they were outside and waiting for their litters to be brought, "May we speak frankly, my friend?"

Faustus chuckled. "Let me guess. You found the Caesar to be less than engaging."

"I would use some such phrase, yes. Is he always like that?"

"Oh, no," Faustus said. "He's ordinarily much worse. He was on his best behavior for you, I'd say."

"Indeed. Very interesting. And this is to be the next Emperor of the West. Word had reached us in Constantinopolis, you know, that the Caesar Heraclius was, well, not altogether charming. But—even so—I was not fully prepared—"

"Did you mind very much kissing his ring?"

"Oh, no, not at all. One expects, as an ambassador, to have to show a certain deference, at least to the Emperor. And to his son as well, I suppose, if he requires it of one. No, Faustus, what I was struck by—how can I say this?—let me think a moment—" Menandros paused. He looked off into the night, at the Forum and the Capitol far across the valley. "You know," he said at last, "I'm a relatively young man, but I've made a considerable study of Imperial history, both Eastern and Western, and I think I know what is required to be a successful Emperor. We have a Greek word—*charisma,* do you know it?—it is something like your Latin word *virtus,* but not quite—that describes the quality that one must have. But there are many sorts of charisma. One can rule well through sheer force of personality, through the awe and fear and respect that one engenders—Justinianus is a good example of that, or Vespasianus of ancient times, or Titus Gallius. One can rule through a combination of great personal determination and guile, as the great Augustus did, and Diocletianus. One can be a man of grace and deep wisdom—Hadrianus, say, or Marcus Aurelius. One can win acclaim through great military valor: I think of Trajan here, and Gaius Martius, and your two Emperors who bore the name Maximilianus. But"—and again Menandros paused, and this time he drew in his breath deeply before continuing—"if one has neither grace, nor wisdom, nor valor, nor guile, nor the capability to engender fear and respect—"

"Heraclius will be able to engender fear, I think," said Faustus.

"Fear, yes. Any Emperor can do that, at least for a time. Caligula, eh? Nero. Domitianus. Commodus."

"The four that you name were all eventually assassinated, I think," Faustus said.

"Yes. That is so, isn't it?" The litters were arriving, now. Menandros turned to him and gave him a serene, almost unworldly smile. "How odd it is, Faustus, would you not say, that the two royal brothers are so far from being alike, and that the one who has charisma is so little interested in serving his Empire as its ruler, and the one who is destined to have the throne has so little charisma? What a pity that is: for them, for you, perhaps, even, for the world. It is one of the little jokes that the gods like to play, eh, my friend? But what the gods may find amusing is not so amusing for us, sometimes."

*   *   *

There was no visit to the Underworld the following day. From Menandros came a message declaring that he would remain in his quarters all that day, preparing dispatches to be sent to Constantinopolis. The Caesar Maximilianus likewise sent word to Faustus that his company would not be required that day. Faustus spent it dealing with the copious outpouring of routine documents his own office endlessly generated, holding his regular midweek meeting with the other functionaries of the Chancellery, soaking for several hours at the public baths, and dining with the little bright-eyed Numidian, who watched him wordlessly across the table for an hour and a half, eating very little herself—she had the appetite of a bird, a very small bird—and following him obligingly to the couch when the meal was done. After she had gone he lay in bed reading, at random choice, one of the plays of Seneca, the gory *Thyestes,* until he came upon a passage he would just as soon not have seen that evening: "I live in mighty fear that all the universe will be broken into a thousand fragments in the general ruin, that formless chaos will return and vanquish the gods and men, that the earth and sea will be engulfed by the planets wandering in the heavens." Faustus stared at those words until they swam before his eyes. The next lines rose up before him, then: "Of all the generations, it is we who have been chosen to merit the bitter fate, to be crushed by the falling pieces of the broken sky." That was unappealing bedtime reading. He tossed the scroll aside and closed his eyes.

And so, he thought, passes another day in the life of Faustus Flavius Constantinus Caesar. The barbarians are massing at the gates, the Emperor is dying day by day, the heir apparent is out in the forest poking spears into hapless wild beasts, and old Faustus shuffles foolish official papers, lolls half a day in a great marble tub of warm water, amuses himself for a while with a dusky plaything of a girl, and stumbles upon evil omens as he tries to read himself to sleep.

The next day commenced with the arrival of one of Menandros's slaves, bearing a note telling him that it was the ambassador's pleasure to carry out a third exploration of the subterranean city in mid-afternoon. He had a special interest, Menandros said, in seeing the

chapel of Priapus and the pool of the Baptai, and perhaps the catacomb of the sacred whores of Chaldea. The ambassador's mood, it
seemed, had taken an erotic turn.

Quickly Faustus dashed off a note to the Caesar Maximilianus,
telling him of the day's plans and requesting him to summon
Danielus bar-Heap the Hebrew once more to be their guide. "Let
me know by the sixth hour where you would like us to meet you,"
Faustus concluded. But midday came and went with no reply from
the prince. A second message produced no response either. By now
it was nearly time for Faustus to set out for the Severan Palace to
pick up the ambassador. It was beginning to look as though he
would be Menandros's sole escort on today's expedition. But Faustus realized then that he did not care for that idea: he felt too dour
this morning, too cheerless and morose. He needed Maximilianus's
high-spirited company to get him through the task.

"Take me to the Caesar," he told his bearers.

Maximilianus, unbathed, unshaven, red-eyed, wearing a coarse
old robe with great rents in it, looked startled to see him. "What is
this, Faustus? Why do you come to me unannounced?"

"I sent two notes this morning, Caesar. We are to take the Greek
to the Underworld again."

The prince shrugged. Clearly he hadn't seen either one. "I've
been awake only an hour. And had only three hours of sleep before
that. It's been a difficult night. My father is dying."

"Yes. Of course. We have all been aware of that sad fact for
some time and are greatly grieved by it," said Faustus unctuously.
"Perhaps it will come as a deliverance when His Majesty's long ordeal is—"

"I don't mean simply that he's sick. I mean that he's in his last
hours, Faustus. I've been in attendance on him all night at the
palace."

Faustus blinked in surprise. "Your father is in Roma?"

"Of course. Where do you think he'd be?"

"There were stories that he was in Capreae, or Sicilia, or perhaps
even Africa—"

"All those stories are so much nitwit blather. He's been right
here for months, since he came back from taking the waters at Baiae.

Didn't you know that? —Visited by only a very few, of course, because he's become so feeble, and even the shortest of conversations drains his strength. But yesterday about noon he entered into some sort of crisis. Began vomiting black blood, and there were some tremendous convulsions. The whole corps of doctors was sent for. A whole army of them and every last one of them determined to be the one who saves his life, even if they kill him in the process." In an almost manic way Maximilianus began to list the remedies that had been employed in the last twenty-four hours: applications of lion's fat, potations of dog's milk, frogs boiled in vinegar, dried cicadas dissolved in wine, figs stuffed with mouse liver, dragon's tongue boiled in oil, the eyes of river crabs, and any number of other rare and costly medicines, virtually the whole potent pharmacopeia—enough medication, Faustus thought, to do even a healthy man in. And they had done even more. They had drawn his blood. They had bathed him in tubs of honey sprinkled with powdered gold. They had coated him in warm mud from the slopes of Vesuvius. "And the ultimate preposterous touch, just before dawn," said Maximilianus: "the naked virgin who touches her hand to him and invokes Apollo three times to restrain the progress of his disease. It's a wonder they could even *find* a virgin on such short order. Of course, they could always create one by retroactive decree, I guess." And the prince smiled a savage smile. But Faustus could see that it was mere bravado, a strenuously willed flash of the sort of cool cynicism Faustus was supposed to expect from him: the expression in the Caesar's red-rimmed, swollen eyes was that of a young man pained to the core by his beloved father's suffering.

"Will he die today, do you think?" Faustus asked.

"Probably not. The doctors told me that his strength is prodigious, even now. He'll last at least another day, even two or three, perhaps—but no more than that."

"And is your brother with him?"

"My brother?" Maximilianus said, in a dumbfounded tone. "My brother's at his hunting lodge, you told me!"

"He came back, the night before last. Gave audience to the Greek at the Hall of Marcus Anastasius. I was there myself."

"No," Maximilianus muttered. "No. The bastard! The bastard!"

"The whole meeting lasted perhaps fifteen minutes, I suppose. And then he announced that he would be leaving town again the next morning, but surely, once he found out that your father was so gravely ill—" Faustus, comprehending suddenly, stared in disbelief. "You mean you never saw him at all, yesterday? He didn't go to visit your father at any time during the day?"

For a moment neither of them could speak.

Maximilianus said, finally, "Death frightens him. The sight of it, the smell of it, the thought of it. He can't bear to be near anyone who's ill. And so he's been careful to keep his distance from the Emperor since he took sick. In any case he's never cared a spoonful of spider's piss for my father. It's perfectly in character for him to come to Roma and sleep right under the same roof as the old man and not even take the trouble of making inquiries after his health, let alone going to see him, and then leave again the next day. So he would never have found out that the end was getting very close. As for me, I wouldn't have expected him to bother getting in touch with me while he was here."

"He should be summoned back to Roma again," Faustus said.

"Yes. I suppose he should be. He'll be Emperor in another day or two, you know." Maximilianus gave Faustus a bleary look. He seemed half addled with fatigue. "Will you do it, Faustus? Straight away. Meanwhile I'll bathe and dress. The Greek is waiting for us to take him down below, isn't he?"

Thunderstruck, Faustus said, "You mean you want to go there now—today?—while—while your father—?"

"Why not? There's nothing I can do for the old man right now, is there? And his doctors solemnly assure me that he'll last the day." A kind of eerie iciness had come over the Caesar suddenly. Faustus wanted to back away from the chill that emanated from him.

In a fierce, cold voice Maximilianus said, "Anyway, I'm not the one who's going to become Emperor. It's my brother's responsibility to stand around waiting to pick up the reins, not mine. Send a messenger off to Heraclius to tell him he had better get himself back here as fast as he can, and let's you and I and the Greek go off and have ourselves a little fun. It may be our last chance for a long time."

*   *   *

On such short notice there was no way of finding the Hebrew, so they would have to do without his invaluable assistance for today's outing. Faustus felt edgy about that, because spying on the chapel of Priapus was not without its risks, and he preferred to have the strong, fearless bar-Heap along in case they blundered into any trouble. Maximilianus, though, did not appear to be worried. The prince's mood seemed an unusually impetuous one, even for him, this day. His fury over his brother's absence and the strain of his father's illness had left him very tightly strung indeed, a man who gave every indication of being on the verge of some immense explosion.

But his demeanor was calm enough as he led the way down the winding ramp that entered the Underworld beside the Baths of Constantinus and guided them toward the grotto where the rites of Priapus were enacted. The passageway was low-roofed and moist-walled, with splotchy gray-green fungoid stains clinging to its sides. Menandros, as they neared their goal, displayed such signs of boyish anticipation that Faustus felt both amusement and contempt. Did they no longer have any such shady cults in Constantinopolis? Was Justinianus such a stern master that they had all been suppressed, when Justinianus's own wife Theodora was herself a former actress, said to be of the loosest morality imaginable?

"This way," Maximilianus whispered, indicating an opening in the cavern wall, the merest sliver of an entrance. "It takes us up and over the chapel, where we'll have a very good view. But be absolutely quiet in there. A single sneeze and we're done for, because this is the only way out, and they'll be waiting for us here with hatchets if they find out we've been spying on them."

The passage slanted sharply upward. It was impossible for men as tall as Maximilianus or Faustus to stand upright in it, though Menandros had no difficulty. The nimble young Maximilianus moved easily there, but Faustus, slow and bulky, found every step a challenge. Quickly he was sweating and panting. Once he banged his lantern against the wall and sent a reverberant thump down the length of the passage that drew an angry hiss and a glare from Maximilianus.

Before long came confirmation that a service was in progress: a clash of cymbals, the booming of drums, the hoarse screech of horns, the high jabbing of flutes. When they reached the place from which the scene below could best be viewed, Maximilianus gestured for the lanterns to be laid to one side where they would cast no gleam that could be spied from the shrine, and moved Menandros into position for the best view.

Faustus did not even try to look. He had seen it all too many times before: the wall covered with gaudy erotic murals, the great altar of the god of lust, and the seated figure of Priapus himself with his enormous phallus rising like a pillar of stone from his thighs. Half a dozen naked worshipers, all of them women, were dancing before that fearsome idol. Their bodies were oiled and painted; their eyes had a wild, frantic shine; their nostrils were distended, their lips were drawn back in toothy grimaces, and the dancers' swinging breasts bobbled freely about as they leaped and pranced.

Chanted words came up from below, harsh jabbing rhythms:

"Come to me, great Lord Priapus, as sunlight comes to the morning sky. Come to me, great Lord Priapus, and give me favor, sustenance, elegance, beauty, and delight. Your names in heaven are LAMPTHEN—OUOTH OUASTHEN—OUTHI OAMENOTH—ENTHOMOUCH. And I know your forms: in the east you are an ibis, in the west you are a wolf, in the north you have the form of a serpent, and in the south you are an eagle. Come to me, Lord Priapus—come to me, Lord Priapus, come—"

One by one the women danced up to the great statue, kissed the tip of that great phallus, caressed it lasciviously.

"I invoke you, Priapus! Give me favor, form, beauty! Give me delight. For you are I, and I am you. Your name is mine, and mine is yours."

There was a tremendous demoniacal clatter of drumming. Faustus knew what that meant: one of the worshipers was mounting the statue of the god. Menandros, avidly staring, leaned much too far forward. At this stage of the ceremony there was little risk that any of the impassioned celebrants would look upward and catch a glimpse of him, but there was some danger that he might go tumbling down into the cavern below and land amongst them. It had been known to happen. Death was the penalty for any man caught spying on the rites of the adherents of Priapus. Faustus reached for him; but Maximilianus had already caught him and was tugging him back.

Though covert surveillance of these rites was forbidden, men were not entirely excluded from the chapel. Faustus knew that five or six stalwart slaves were lined up along the wall of the chapel in the shadows behind the statue. Soon the priestess of Priapus would give the signal and the orgy would begin.

They practically needed to drag Menandros away. He crouched by the rim of the aperture like a small boy greedy to discover the intimate secrets of womankind, and even after the event had gone on and on long beyond the point where even the most curious of men should have been sated by the sight, Menandros wanted to see more. Faustus was baffled by this strange hunger of his. He could barely remember a time when any of what was taking place down there had been new and unfamiliar to him, and it was hard to understand Menandros's passionate curiosity over so ordinary a matter as orgiastic copulation. The court of the Emperor Justinianus, Faustus thought, must place an extraordinarily high value on chastity and propriety. But that was not what Faustus had been told.

At last they got the ambassador out of there and they went on to the next place on his list, the pool of the Baptai. "I'll wait for you here," said Faustus, as they arrived at the steep spiraling stairway that led down into the pit of utter blackness where the rites of this cult of immersion occurred. "I'm getting too fat and slow for that much clambering."

It was, he knew, an enchanting place: the smooth-walled rock-hewn chambers bedecked with iridescent glass mosaics in white and red and blue, brightened even further by splashes and touches of vivid golden paint, the scenes of Diana at the hunt, of cooing doves, of cupids swimming among swans, of voluptuous nymphs, of rampant satyrs. But the air was damp and heavy, the interminable downward spiral of the narrow, slippery stone steps would be hard on his aging legs, and the final taxing stage of the long descent, the one that went from the chamber of the mosaics to the fathomless black pool that lay at the lowest level, was beyond all doubt much too much for

him. And of course the mere thought of the ascent afterward was utterly appalling.

So he waited. A tinkling trickle of laughter drifted up to him out
of the darkness. The goddess Bendis of Thrace was the deity worshiped here, a coarse lank-haired demon whose devotees were utterly shameless, and at any hour of the day or night one generally
could find a service in progress, a ritual that involved the usual sort
of orgiastic stuff enlivened by a climactic baptismal plunge into the
icy pool, where Bendis lurked to provide absolution for sins just
committed and encouragement for those yet to come. This was no
secret cult. All were welcome here. But the mysteries of the cult of
Bendis were no longer mysterious to Faustus. He had had baptism
in those freezing waters often enough for one lifetime; he did not
seek it again. And the skillful ministrations of his Numidian playmate Oalathea were gratification enough for his diminishing lusts
these days.

It was a very long time before Menandros and Maximilianus returned from the depths. They said little when they emerged, but it
was clear from the flushed, triumphant look on the little Greek's
face that he had found whatever ecstasies he had been seeking in the
shrine of the Baptai.

Now it was time for the place of the Chaldean whores, far across
the underground city near the welter of caverns below the Circus
Maximus. Menandros seemed to have heard a great deal about these
women, most of it incorrect. "You mustn't call them whores, you
know," Faustus explained. "What they are is prostitutes—sacred
prostitutes."

"This is a very subtle distinction," said the Greek wryly.

"What he means," said the Caesar, "is that they're all women of
proper social standing, who belong to a cult that came to us out of
Babylonia. Some of them are of Babylonian descent themselves,
most are not. Either way, the women of this cult are required at some
point in their lives, between the ages of—what is it, Faustus, sixteen
and thirty?—something like that—to go to the sanctuary of their
goddess and sit there waiting for some stranger to come along and
choose her for the night. He throws a small silver coin into her lap,

and she must rise and go with him, however hideous he is, however repellent. And with that act she fulfills her obligation to her goddess, and returns therewith to a life of blameless purity."

"Some, I understand, are said to go back more than once to fulfill their obligations," Faustus said. "Out of an excess of piety, I suppose. Unless it is for the simple excitement of meeting strangers, of course."

"I must see this," Menandros said. He was aglow with boyish eagerness again. "Virtuous women, you say, wives and daughters of substantial men? And they *must* give themselves? They can't refuse under any circumstances? Justinianus will find this hard to believe."

"It is an Eastern thing," said Faustus. "Out of Babylonian Chaldea. How strange that you have none of this at your own capital." It did not ring true. From all accounts Faustus had heard, Constantinopolis was at least as much a hotbed of Oriental cults as Roma itself. He began to wonder whether there was some reason of state behind Menandros's apparent desire to paint the Eastern Empire as a place of such rigorous piety and virtue. Perhaps it had something to do with the terms of the treaty that Menandros had come here to negotiate. But he could not immediately see what the connection might be.

Nor did they see the holy Chaldean prostitutes that day. They were less than halfway across the Underworld when they became aware of a muddled din of upraised voices coming to them out of the Via Subterranea ahead, and as they drew closer to that broad thoroughfare they began to distinguish some detail of individual words. The shouts still were blurred and confused, but what they seemed to be saying was:

"The Emperor is dead! The Emperor is dead!"

"Can it be?" Faustus asked. "Am I hearing rightly?"

But then it came again, a male voice with the force of the bellowings of a bull rising above all the others: "THE EMPEROR IS DEAD! THE EMPEROR IS DEAD!" There was no possible doubt of the meaning now.

"So soon," Maximilianus murmured, in a voice that could have been that of a dead man itself. "It wasn't supposed to happen today."

Faustus glanced toward the Caesar. His face was chalk white, as though he had spent his whole life in these underground caverns, and his eyes had a hard, frightening glitter to them that gave them the look of brilliantly polished sapphires. Those stony eyes were terrifying to behold.

A man in the loose yellow robes of some Asian priesthood came running toward them, looking half unhinged by fear. He stumbled up against Maximilianus in the narrow hallway and tried to shoulder his way past, but the Caesar, seizing the man by both forearms and holding him immobilized, thrust his face into the other's and demanded to know the news. "His Majesty—" the man gasped, goggle-eyed. He had a thick Syrian lisp. "Dead. They have lit the great bonfire before the palace. The Praetorians have gone into the street to maintain order."

Muttering a curse, Maximilianus shoved the Syrian away from him so vehemently that the man went ricocheting off the wall, and turned his gaze toward Faustus. "I must go to the palace," the Caesar said, and without another word turned and ran, leaving Faustus and Menandros behind as he vanished in furious long-legged strides toward the Via Subterranea.

Menandros looked overwhelmed by the news. "We should not be here either," he said.

"No. We should not."

"Are we to go to the palace, then?"

"It could be dangerous. Anything can happen, when an Emperor dies and the heir apparent isn't on the scene." Faustus slipped his arm through the Greek's. Menandros appeared startled at that, but seemed quickly to understand that it was for the sake of keeping them from being separated in the growing chaos of the underground city. Thus linked, they set out together for the nearest exit ramp.

The news had spread everywhere by now, and hordes of people were running madly to and fro. Faustus, though his heart was pounding from the exertion, moved as quickly as he was able, virtually dragging Menandros along with him, using his bulk to shove anyone who blocked his path out of the way.

"The Emperor is dead!" the endless chorus cried. "The Emperor is dead!" As he came forth blinking into the daylight, Faustus saw the look of stunned shock on every face.

He felt a little stunned himself, though Emperor Maximilianus's passing had not exactly come as a bolt out of the blue to him. But the old man had held the throne for more than forty years, one of the longest reigns in Roman history, longer even than Augustus's, perhaps second only to that of his grandfather the first Maximilianus. These Etruscan Emperors were long-lived men. Faustus had been a slender stripling the last time the Imperial throne had changed hands, and that other time the succession had been handled well, the magnificent young prince who was to become Maximilianus II standing at the side of his dying father in his last moments, and going immediately thereafter to the temple of Jupiter Capitolinus to receive the homage of the Senate and to accept the badges and titles of office.

This was a different situation. There was no magnificent young heir waiting to take the throne, only the deplorable Prince Heraclius, and Heraclius had so contrived matters that he was not even at the capital on the day of his father's death. Great surprises sometimes happened when the throne became vacant and the expected heir was not on hand to claim it. That was how the stammering cripple Claudius had become Emperor when Caligula was assassinated. That was how Titus Gallius had risen to greatness after the murder of Caracalla. For that matter, that was the way the first of the Etruscans had come to power, when Theodosius, having outlived his own son Honorius, had finally died in 1168. Who could say what shifts in the balance of power might be accomplished in Roma before this day reached its end?

It was Faustus's duty now to get Justinianus's ambassador safely back to the Severan Palace, and then to make his own way to the Chancellery to await the developments of the moment. But Menandros did not quite seem to grasp the precariousness of the situation. He was fascinated by the tumult in the streets, and, feckless tourist that he was at heart, wanted to head for the Forum to watch the action at first hand. Faustus had to push the bounds of diplomatic courtesy a little to get him to abandon that foolhardy idea and head for the safety of his own quarters. Menandros agreed reluctantly, but only after seeing a phalanx of Praetorians moving through the street across from them, freely clubbing anyone who seemed to be behaving in a disorderly fashion.

Faustus was the last of the officials of the Chancellery to reach the administrative headquarters, just across the way from the royal palace. The Chancellor, Licinius Obsequens, greeted him sourly. "Where have you been all this while, Faustus?"

"With the ambassador Menandros, touring the Underworld," Faustus replied, just as sourly. He cared very little for Licinius Obsequens, a wealthy Neapolitan who had bribed his way to high office, and he suspected that under the new Emperor neither he nor Licinius Obsequens would continue to hold their posts at the Chancellery, anyway. "The ambassador was very eager to visit the chapel of Priapus, and other such places," Faustus added, with a bit of malice to his tone. "So we took him there. How was I to know that the Emperor was going to die today?"

"*We* took him, Faustus?"

"The Caesar Maximilianus and I."

Licinius's yellowish eyes narrowed to slits. "Of course. Your good friend the Caesar. And where is the Caesar now, may I ask?"

"He left us," said Faustus, "the moment news reached us underground of His Majesty's death. I have no information about where he might be at the present time. The Imperial palace, I would imagine." He paused a moment. "And the Caesar Heraclius, who is our Emperor now? Has anyone happened to hear from him?"

"He is at the northern frontier," Licinius said.

"No. No, he isn't. He's off at his hunting lodge behind Lake Nemorensis. He never went north at all."

Licinius was visibly rocked by that. "You know this for a fact, Faustus?"

"Absolutely. I sent a message to him there, just the other night, and he came back to the city that evening and met with the ambassador Menandros. I was there, as it happens." A look of sickly astonishment came over Licinius's jowly face. Faustus was beginning to enjoy this more than somewhat. "The Caesar then went back to his forest preserve yesterday morning. Early today, when I was informed of His Majesty's grave condition, I sent a second message to him at the lake, once more summoning him to Roma. Beyond that I can tell you nothing."

"You knew that the Caesar was hunting, and not at the frontier, and never reported this to me?" Licinius asked.

Loftily Faustus said, "Sir, I was wholly preoccupied with looking after the Greek ambassador. It is a complicated task. It never occurred to me that you were unaware of the movements of the Caesar Heraclius. I suppose I assumed that when he reached Roma the night before last he would take the trouble to meet with his father's Chancellor and ascertain the state of his father's health, but evidently it didn't occur to him to do that, and therefore—"

Abruptly he cut his words short. Asellius Proculus, the Prefect of the Praetorian Guard, had just shouldered his way into the room. For the Praetorian Prefect to set foot in the Chancellery at all was an unusual event; for him to be here on the day of the Emperor's death verged on the unthinkable. Licinius Obsequens, who was starting to look like a man besieged, gaped at him in consternation.

"Asellius? What—"

"A message," the Praetorian Prefect said hoarsely. "From Lake Nemorensis." He signaled with an upraised thumb and a man in the green uniform of the Imperial courier service came lurching in. He was glassy-eyed and rumpled and haggard, as though he had run all the way from the lake without pausing. Pulling a rolled-up dispatch from his tunic, he thrust it with a trembling hand toward Licinius Obsequens, who snatched at it, opened it, read it through, read it again. When the Chancellor looked up at Faustus his plump face was sagging in shock.

"What does it say?" Faustus asked. Licinius seemed to be having difficulties forming words.

"The Caesar," Licinius said. "His Majesty the Emperor, that is. Wounded. A hunting accident, this morning. He remains at his lodge. The Imperial surgeons have been called."

"Wounded? How seriously?"

Licinius responded with a blank look. "Wounded, it says. That's all: wounded. The Caesar has been wounded, while hunting. The Emperor. —He *is* our Emperor now, is he not?" The Chancellor seemed numb, as though he had had a stroke. To the courier he said, "Do you know any other details, man? How badly is he hurt? Did you see him yourself? Who's in charge at the lodge?" But the courier knew nothing. He had been given the message by a member of the Caesar's guard and told to get it immediately to the capital; that was all he was able to report.

Four hours later, dining with the ambassador Menandros in the ambassador's rooms at the Severan Palace, Faustus said, "The messages continued to come in from the lake all afternoon. Wounded, first. Then, wounded seriously. Then a description of the wound: speared in the gut by one of his own men, he was, some sort of confusion while they were closing in on a boar for the kill, somebody's horse rearing at the wrong moment. Then the next message, half an hour later: the Imperial surgeons are optimistic. Then, the Caesar Heraclius is dying. And then: the Caesar Heraclius is dead."

"The Emperor Heraclius, should you not call him?" Menandros asked.

"It's not certain who died first, the Emperor Maximilianus at Roma or the Caesar Heraclius at Lake Nemorensis. I suppose they can work all that out later. But what difference does it make, except to the historians? Dead is dead. Whether he died as Heraclius Caesar or as Heraclius Augustus, he's still dead, and his brother is our next Emperor. Can you believe it? Maximilianus is going to be Emperor? One moment he's wallowing around with you in some orgy at the pool of the Baptai, and the next he's sitting on the throne. Maximilianus! The last thing he ever imagined, becoming Emperor."

"That soothsayer told him that he would," Menandros said.

A shiver of awe ran through Faustus. "Yes! Yes, by Isis, so he did! And Maximilianus was as furious as though the man had laid a curse on him. Which perhaps he had." Shakily he refilled his wine bowl. "*Emperor!* Maximilianus!"

"Have you seen him yet?"

"No, not yet. It isn't seemly to rush to him so fast."

"You were his closest friend, weren't you?"

"Yes, yes, of course. And doubtless there'll be some benefit to that." Faustus allowed himself a little smirk of pleasure. "Under Heraclius, I'd have been finished, I suppose. Pensioned off, shipped to the country. But it'll be different for me with Maximilianus in charge. He'll need me. He will, won't he?" The thought had only then occurred to him in any coherent way. But the more he examined it, the more it pleased him. "He's never cultivated any of the court officials; he doesn't know them, really, won't know which ones to trust, which to get rid of. I'm the only one who can advise him properly. I might even become Chancellor, Menandros, do you realize that? —But that's exactly why I haven't gone speeding over to see him tonight. He's busy with the priests, anyway, doing whatever religious rites it is a new Emperor is supposed to perform, and then the Senators are calling on him one by one, and so on and so forth. It would be too blatant, wouldn't it, if I turned up there so soon, his bawdy and disreputable old drinking companion Faustus, who by coming around the very first night would be sending an all too obvious signal that he's showing up right away to claim his reward for these years of hearty good fellowship the two of us have shared. No, Menandros, I wouldn't do anything so crass. Maximilianus is not going to forget me. Tomorrow, I suppose, he'll be holding his first *salutatio,* and I can come around then and—"

"His what? I don't know the word."

"*Salutatio?* You must know what that means. In your language you'd say, 'a greeting.' But what it is in Imperial terms is a mass audience with the Roman populace: the Emperor sits enthroned in the Forum, and the people pass before him and salute him and hail him as Emperor. It'll be quite appropriate for me to go before him then, with all the rest. And have him smile at me, and wink, and say, 'Come to me after all this nonsense is over, Faustus, because we have important things to discuss.' "

"This is not a custom we have at Constantinopolis, the *salutatio,*" Menandros said.

"A Roman thing, it is."

"We are Romans also, you know."

"So you are. But you are Greekified Romans, you Easterners— in your particular case, a Romanized Greek, even—with customs that bear the tincture of the old Oriental despots who lie far back in your history, the Pharaohs, the Persian kings, Alexander the Great. Whereas we are Romans of Roma. We once had a Republic here that chose its leaders every year, do you know that?—two outstanding men whom the Senate picked to share power with each other, and at the end of their year they would step down and two others were brought forward. We lived like that for hundreds of years, ruled by our Consuls, until a few problems arose and it became necessary for Augustus Caesar to alter the arrangements somewhat. But we still maintain some traces of that staunch old Republic of the early days. The *salutatio* is one of them."

"I see," Menandros said. He did not sound impressed. He busied himself with his wine for a time. Then, breaking a long silence that had developed between them, he said, "You don't think Prince Maximilianus might have had his brother murdered, do you?"

"*What?*"

"Hunting accidents aren't all that hard to arrange. A scuffle among the horses in the morning fog, an unfortunate little collision, a spear thrust in the wrong place—"

"Are you serious, Menandros?"

"About half, I'd say. These things have been known to happen. Even I could see from the very first what contempt Maximilianus had for his brother. And now the old Emperor is on his last legs. The Empire will go to the unpopular and inadequate Heraclius. So your friend the Caesar, either for the good of the Empire or purely out of the love of power, decides to have Heraclius removed, just as the Emperor is plainly sinking toward his end. The assassin then is slain also, to keep him quiet in case there's an inquest and he's put to the torture, and there you are—Heraclius is gone and Maximilianus III Augustus is in charge. It's not impossible. What became of the man who put the spear into Prince Heraclius, do you by any chance know?"

"He killed himself within an hour of the event, as a matter of fact, out of sheer chagrin. Do you think Maximilianus bribed him to do that, too?"

Menandros smiled faintly and made no reply. This was all just a game for him, Faustus realized.

"The good of the Empire," Faustus said, "is not a concept upon which the Caesar Maximilianus has ever expended much thought. If you were listening closely to much of what he said when he was in our company, you might have perceived that. As for the love of power, here you will have to take my word for it, but I think he has not an atom of that within himself. You saw how enraged he became when that idiot of a soothsayer told him he was going to be a great hero of the Empire? 'You are mocking me to my face,' Maximilianus said, or words to that effect. And then, when the man went on to predict that Maximilianus was going to become Emperor, too—" Faustus laughed. "No, my friend, there was never any conspiracy here. Not even in his dreams did Maximilianus see himself as an Emperor. What happened to Prince Heraclius was mere accident, the gods making sport with us yet again, and my guess is that our new Emperor is having a hard time coming to terms with fate's little prank. I would go so far as to say that he is the unhappiest man in Roma tonight."

"Poor Roma," said Menandros.

A *salutatio,* yes, the very next day. Faustus was correct about that. The line was already forming when he got himself down to the Forum, bathed and shaven and clad in his finest toga, in the third hour after sunrise.

And there was Maximilianus, resplendent in the purple Imperial toga with the border of threads of gold, sitting enthroned in front of the Temple of Jupiter Imperator. A crown of laurel was on his head. He looked magnificent, as a new Emperor should: utterly upright of posture, a calm, graceful figure who displayed in every aspect an almost godlike look of the highest nobility far removed from any expression Faustus had seen him wear during his roistering days. Faustus's bosom swelled with pride at the sight of him sitting like that. What a superb actor the Caesar is, Faustus thought, what a glorious fraud!

But I must not think of him as the Caesar any more. Wonder of wonders, he is the Augustus now, Maximilianus III of Roma.

The Praetorians were keeping the line under careful control. The members of the Senate had already passed through, it seemed, because Faustus saw none of them in evidence. That was appropriate: they should be the first to hail a new Emperor. Faustus was pleased to note that he had arrived just in time to join the line of of-

ficials of the late Emperor's court. He caught sight of Chancellor
Licinius up ahead, and the Minister of the Privy Purse, the Cham-
berlain of the Imperial Bedroom, the Master of the Treasury, the
Master of the Horses, and most of the others, down to such mid-
level people as the Prefect of Works, the Master of Greek Letters,
the Secretary of the Council, the Master of Petitions. Faustus, joining the group, exchanged nods and smiles with a few of them, but
said nothing to anyone. He knew that he was conspicuous among
them, not only because of his height and bulk, but also because they
must all be aware that he was the dearest friend the unexpected new
Emperor had, and was likely to receive significant preferment in the
administration that soon would be taking form. The golden aura of
power, Faustus thought, must already be gathering about his shoulders as he stood here in the line.

The line moved forward at a very slow pace. Each man in turn,
as he came before Maximilianus, made the proper gestures of respect and obeisance, and Maximilianus responded with a smile, a
word or two, an amiable lifting of his hand. Faustus was amazed at
the easy assurance of his manner. He seemed to be enjoying this, too.
It might all be a wondrous pretense, but Maximilianus was making it
seem as though it were he, and not the lamented Prince Heraclius,
who had been schooled all his life for this moment of ascension to
the summit of power.

And at last Faustus himself was standing before the Emperor.

"Your Majesty," Faustus murmured humbly, relishing the
words. He bowed. He knelt. He closed his eyes a moment to savor
the wonder of it all. *Rise, Faustus Flavius Constantinus Caesar, you
who are to be Imperial Chancellor in the government of the third Maximilianus*, is what he imagined the Emperor would say.

Faustus rose. The Emperor said nothing at all. His lean, youthful face was solemn. His blue eyes seemed cold and hard. It was the
iciest look Faustus had ever seen.

"Your Majesty," Faustus said again, in a huskier, more rasping
tone this time. And then, very softly, with a smile, a bit of the old
twinkle: "What an ironic turn of fate this all is, Maximilianus! How
playful destiny is with our lives! —Emperor! Emperor! And I know
what pleasure you will get from it, my lord."

The icy gaze was unrelenting. A quiver of something like impatience, or perhaps it was irritation, was visible on Maximilianus's lips. "You speak as though you know me," the Emperor said. "Do you? And do I know you?"

That was all. He beckoned, the merest movement of the tips of the fingers of his left hand, and Faustus knew that he must move along. The Emperor's words resounded in his mind as he made his way across the front of the temple and up the path that led from the Forum to the Palatine Hill. *Do you know me? Do I know you?*

Yes. He knew Maximilianus, and Maximilianus knew him. It was all a joke, Maximilianus having a little amusement at his expense in this first meeting between them since everything had changed. But some things, Faustus knew, had not changed, and never could. They had seen the dawn in together too many times, the prince and he, for any transformation to come over their friendship now, however strangely and marvelously Maximilianus himself had been transformed by his brother's death.

But still—

Still—

It was a joke, yes, that Maximilianus had been playing on him, but it was a cruel one for all that, and although Faustus knew that the prince could be cruel, the prince had never been cruel to him. Until now. And perhaps not even now. It had been mere playfulness just now, those words of his. Yes. Yes. Mere playfulness, nothing more, Maximilianus's style of humor making itself known even here on the day of his ascent to the throne.

Faustus returned to his lodgings.

For the three days following, he had little company but his own. The Chancellery, like all the offices of the government, would be closed all this week for the double funeral of the old Emperor Maximilianus and the prince his son, and then the ceremonies of installation of the new Emperor Maximilianus. Maximilianus himself was inaccessible to Faustus, as he was to virtually everyone but the highest officials of the realm. During the formal days of mourning the streets of the city were quiet, for once. Not even the Underworld would be stirring. Faustus remained at home, too dispirited to bother summoning his Numidian. When he wandered over to the Severan Palace to see Menandros, he

was told that the ambassador, as the representative in Roma of the new
Emperor's Imperial colleague of the East, the Basileus Justinianus, had
been called into conference at the royal palace, and would be staying at
the palace for the duration of the meetings.

On the fourth day Menandros returned. Faustus saw the litter
bearing him crossing the Palatine and unhesitatingly hurried across
to the Severan to greet him. Perhaps Menandros would bear some
word for him from Maximilianus.

Indeed he did. Menandros handed Faustus a bit of parchment
sealed with the Imperial seal and said, "The Emperor gave me this
for you."

Faustus yearned to open it at once, but that seemed unwise. He
realized he was a little afraid of finding out what Maximilianus had
to say to him, and he preferred not to read the message in Menandros's presence.

"And the Emperor?" Faustus asked. "You found him well?"

"Very well. Not at all troubled by the cares of office, thus far. He
has made an excellent adaptation to the great change in his circumstances. You may have been wrong about him, my friend, when you
said he had no interest in being Emperor. I think he rather likes being Emperor."

"He can be very surprising at times," said Faustus.

"I think that is true. Be that as it may, my task here is done. I
thank you for your good company, friend Faustus, and for your having enabled me to gain the friendship of the former Caesar Maximilianus. A happy accident, that was. The days I spent with the Caesar
in the Underworld greatly facilitated the negotiations I have now
completed with him on the treaty of alliance."

"There is a treaty, is there?"

"Oh, yes, most definitely a treaty. His Majesty will marry the
Emperor Justinianus's sister Sabbatia in the place of his late and
much lamented brother. His Majesty has a gift of some wonderful
jewelry to offer his bride: magnificent gems, opals, quite fine. He
showed them to me himself. And there will be military assistance, of
course. The Eastern Empire will send its finest legions to aid your
Emperor in crushing the barbarians who trouble your borders."
Menandros's cheeks were glowing with pleasure. "It has all gone

very well, I think. I will leave tomorrow. You will send me, I hope, some of that noble wine of Gallia Transalpina that you shared with me on my first day in Roma? And I will have gifts for you as well, my friend. I am deeply grateful to you for everything. In particular," he said, "for the chapel of Priapus, and the pool of the Baptai, eh, friend Faustus?" And he winked.

Faustus lost no time unsealing the Emperor's message once he had escaped from Menandros.

You said you thought our time of greatness was ending, Faustus, that day in the marketplace of the sorcerers. But no, Faustus, you are wrong. We are not ended at all. We are only just begun. It is a new dawn and a new sun rises.
M.

And there below that casually scrawled initial was the formal signature in all its majesty, Maximilianus Tiberius Antoninus Caesar Augustus Imperator.

Faustus's pension was a generous one, and when he and Maximilianus met, as occasionally they did in the early months of Maximilianus's reign, the Emperor was affable enough, with always the amicable word, though they never were intimates again. And in the second year of his reign Maximilianus went north to the frontier, where the legions of his royal colleague Justinianus were assembling to join him, and he remained there, doing battle against the barbarians, for the next seven years, which were the last years of Faustus's life.

The northern wars of Maximilianus III ended in complete triumph. Roma would have no further trouble with invading barbarians. It was a significant turning point in the history of the Empire, which now was free to enter into a time of prosperity and abundance such as it had not known since the great days of Trajan and Hadrianus and Antoninus Pius four centuries before. There had been two mighty Emperors named Maximilianus before him, but men would never speak of the third Maximilianus other than as Maximilianus the Great.

A.U.C. 1365: A HERO OF
THE EMPIRE

H ere I am at last, Horatius, in far-off Arabia, amongst the Greeks and the camels and the swarthy Saracen tribes-men and all the other unpleasant creatures that infest this dreary desert. For my sins. My grievous sins. "Get you to Arabia, serpent!" cried the furious Emperor Julianus, and here I am. *Serpent*. Me. How could he have been so unkind?

But I tell you, O friend of my bosom, I will employ this time of exile to win my way back into Caesar's good graces somehow. I will do something while I am here, *something*, I know not what just yet, that will remind him of what a shrewd and enterprising and alto-gether valuable man I am; and sooner or later he will recall me to Roma and restore me to my place at court. Before many years have passed you and I will stroll together along Tiber's sweet banks again. Of this much I am certain, that the gods did not have it in mind for me that I should spin out all my remaining days in so miserable a sandy wasteland as this.

A bleak forlorn place, it is, this Arabia. A bleak disheartening journey it was to get here, too.

There are, as perhaps you are aware, several Arabias within the vast territory that we know by that general name. In the north lies Arabia Petraea, a prosperous mercantile region bordering on Syria Palaestina. Arabia Petraea has been an Imperial province since the reign of Augustus Caesar, six hundred years ago. Then comes a great deal of emptiness—Arabia Deserta, it is called—a grim, harsh, barren district inhabited mainly by quarrelsome nomads. And on the far side of that lies Arabia Felix, a populous land every bit as happy as its name implies, a place of luxurious climate and easy circumstances, famed for its fertile and productive fields and for the abundance of fine goods that it pours forth into the world's markets, gold and pearls, frankincense and myrrh, balsams and aromatic oils and perfumes.

Which of these places Caesar intended as my place of exile, I did not know. I was told that I would learn that during the course of my journey east. I have an ancient family connection to the eastern part of the world, for in the time of the first Claudius my great ancestor Gnaeus Domitius Corbulo was proconsul of Asia with his seat at Ephesus, and then governor of Syria under Nero, and various other Corbulos since his time have dwelled in those distant regions. It seemed almost agreeable to be renewing the tradition, however involuntary the renewal. Gladly would I have settled for Arabia Petraea if I had to go to Arabia at all: it is a reasonable destination for a highly placed Roman gentleman temporarily out of favor with his monarch. But of course my hopes were centered on Arabia Felix, which by all accounts was the more congenial land.

The voyage from Roma to Syria Palaestina—pfaugh, Horatius! Nightmare. Torture. Seasick every day. Beloved friend, I am no seafaring man. Then came a brief respite in Caesarea Maritima, the one good part, lovely cosmopolitan city, wine flowing freely, complacent pretty girls everywhere, and, yes, Horatius, I must confess it, some pretty boys, too. I stayed there as long as I could. But eventually I received word that the caravan that was to take me down into Arabia was ready to depart, and I had to go.

Let no one beguile you with romantic tales of desert travel. For a civilized man it is nothing but torment and agony.

Three steps to the inland side of Jerusalem and you find yourself in the hottest, driest country this side of Hades; and things only get

worse from there. Every breath you take hits your lungs like a blast
from an oven. Your nostrils, your ears, your lips become coated with
windborne particles of grit. The sun is like a fiery iron platter in the
sky. You go for miles without seeing a single tree or shrub, nothing
but rock and red sand. Mocking phantoms dance before you in the
shimmering air. At night, if you are lucky enough or weary enough
to be able to drop off to sleep for a little while, you dream longingly
of lakes and gardens and green lawns, but then you are awakened by
the scrabbling sound of a scorpion in the sand beside your cheek,
and you lie there sobbing in the stifling heat, praying that you will
die before the coming of the fiery dawn.

Somewhere in the midst of all this dead wilderness the traveler
leaves the province of Syria Palaestina and enters Arabia, though no
one can say precisely where the boundary lies. The first thing you
come to, once across that invisible line, is the handsome city of Petra
of the Nabataeans, an impregnable rock fortress that stands athwart
all the caravan routes. It is a rich city and, aside from the eternal
parching heat, quite a livable one. I would not have greatly minded
serving out my time of exile there.

But no, no, the letter of instruction from His Imperial Majesty
that awaited me in Petra informed me that I needs must go onward,
farther south. Arabia Petraea was not the part of Arabia that he had
in mind for me. I enjoyed three days of civilized urban amusement
there and then I was in the desert again, traveling by camel this time.
I will spare you the horrors of *that* experience. We were heading,
they let me know, for the Nabataean port of Leuke Kome on the
Red Sea.

Excellent, I thought. This Leuke Kome is the chief port of embarkation for travelers sailing on to Arabia Felix. So they must be
sending me to that fertile land of soft breezes and sweet-smelling
blossoms, of spices and precious stones. I imagined myself waiting
out my seasons of banishment in a cozy little villa beside the sea, nibbling tender dates and studying the fine brandies of the place. Perhaps I would dabble a bit in the frankincense trade or do a little
lucrative business in cinnamon and cassia to pass the time.

At Leuke Kome I presented myself to the Imperial legate, a
sleek and self-important young popinjay named Florentius Victor,

and asked him how long it would be before my ship was to leave. He looked at me blankly. "Ship? What ship? Your route lies overland, my dear Leontius Corbulo." He handed me the last of my letters of instruction, by which I was informed that my final destination was a place by the name of Macoraba, where I was to serve as commercial representative of His Imperial Majesty's government, with the special responsibility of resolving any trade conflicts that might arise with such representatives of the Eastern Empire as might be stationed there.

"Macoraba? And just where is that?"

"Why, in Arabia Deserta," said Florentius Victor blandly.

"Arabia Deserta?" I repeated, with a sinking heart.

"Exactly. A very important city, as cities in that part of the world go. Every caravan crossing Arabia has to stop there. Perhaps you've heard of it under its Saracen name. *Mecca*, is what the Saracens call it."

Arabia Deserta, Horatius! Arabia Deserta! For the trifling crime of tampering with the innocence of his unimportant little British cupboy, the heartless vindictive Emperor has buried me in this brutal netherworld of remorseless heat and drifting dunes.

I have been in Macoraba—Mecca, I should say—just three or four days, now. It seems like a lifetime already.

What do we have in this land of Arabia Deserta? Why, nothing but a desolate torrid sandy plain intersected by sharp and naked hills. There are no rivers and rain scarcely ever falls. The sun is merciless. The wind is unrelenting. The dunes shift and heave like ocean waves in a storm: whole legions could be buried and lost by a single day's gusts. For trees they have only scrubby little tamarinds and acacias, that take their nourishment from the nightly dews. Here and there one finds pools of brackish water rising from the bowels of the earth, and these afford a bit of green pasture and sometimes some moist ground on which the date palm and the grapevine can take root, but it is a sparse life indeed for those who have elected to settle in such places.

In the main the Saracens are a wandering race who endlessly

guide their flocks of horses and sheep and camels back and forth across this hard arid land, seeking out herbage for their beasts where they can. All the year long they follow the seasons about, moving from seacoast to mountains to plains, so that they can take advantage of such little rainfall as there is, falling as it does in different months in these different regions. From time to time they venture farther afield—to the banks of the Nile or the farming villages of Syria or the valley of the Euphrates—to descend as brigands upon the placid farmers of those places and extort their harvests from them.

The harshness of the land makes it a place of danger and distress, of rapine and fear. In their own self-interest the Saracens form themselves into little tribal bands under the absolute government of fierce and ruthless elders; warfare between these tribes is constant; and so vehement is each man's sense of personal honor that offense is all too easily given and private blood-feuds persist down through generation after generation, yet ancient offenses never seem to be wiped out.

Two settlements here have come to be dignified with the name of "cities." Cities, Horatius! Mudholes with walls about them, rather. In the northern part of this desert one finds Iatrippa, which in the Saracens' own tongue is named *Medina*. It has a population of fifteen thousand or so, and as Arabian villages go is fairly well provided with water, so that it possesses abundant date groves, and its people live comfortable lives, as comfort is understood in this land.

Then, a ten-day caravan journey to the south, through somber thorny land broken now and then by jutting crags of dark stone, is the town our geographers know as Macoraba, the Mecca of the locals. This Mecca is a bigger place, perhaps twenty-five thousand people, and it is of such ineffable ugliness that Virgil himself would not have been able to conceive of it. Imagine, if you will, a "city" whose buildings are drab hovels of mud and brick, strung out along a rocky plain a mile wide and two miles long that lies at the foot of three stark mountains void of all vegetation. The flinty soil is useless for agriculture. The one sizable well yields bitter water. The nearest pastureland is fifty miles away. I have never seen so unprepossessing a site for human habitation.

You can readily guess, I think, which of the two cities of Arabia Deserta our gracious Emperor chose as my place of exile.

"Why," said I to Nicomedes the Paphlagonian, who was kind enough to invite me to be his dinner guest on my second depressing night in Mecca, "would anyone in his right mind have chosen to found a city in a location of this sort?"

Nicomedes, as his name will have indicated, is a Greek. He is the legate in Arabia Deserta of our Emperor's royal colleague, the Eastern Emperor Maurice Tiberius, and he is, I suspect, the real reason why I have been sent here, as I will explain shortly.

"It's in the middle of nowhere," I said. "We're forty miles from the sea and on the other side there's hundreds of miles of empty desert. Nothing will grow here. The climate is appalling and the ground is mostly rock. I can't see the slightest reason why any person, even a Saracen, would want to live here."

Nicomedes the Paphlagonian, who is a handsome man of about fifty with thick white hair and affable blue eyes, smiled and nodded. "I'll give you two, my friend. One is that nearly all commerce in Arabia is handled by caravan. The Red Sea is a place of tricky currents and treacherous reefs. Sailors abhor it. Therefore in Arabia goods travel mainly by land, and all the caravans have to pass this way, because Mecca is situated precisely at the midpoint between Damascus up north and the thriving cities of Arabia Felix down below us, and it also commands the one passable east-west route across the remarkably dreadful desert that lies between the Persian Gulf and the Red Sea. The caravans that come here are richly laden indeed, and the merchants and hostelkeepers and tax collectors of Mecca do the kind of lively business that middlemen always do. You should know, my dear Leontius Corbulo, that there are a great many very wealthy men in this town."

He paused and poured more wine for us: some wonderful sweet stuff from Rhodes, hardly what I would have expected anyone in this remote outpost to keep on hand for casual guests.

"You said there were two reasons," I reminded him, after a time.

"Oh, yes. Yes." He had not forgotten. He is an unhurried man. "This is also a sacred city, do you see? There is a shrine in Mecca, a sanctuary, which they call the Kaaba. You should visit it tomorrow.

It'll be good for you to get out and about town: it will make the time pass more cheerfully. Look for a squat little cubical building of black stone in the center of a great plaza. It's quite unsightly, but unimaginably holy in Saracen eyes. It contains some sort of lump of rock that fell from heaven, which they think of as a god. The Saracen tribesmen from all over the country make pilgrimages here to worship at the Kaaba. They march round and round it, bowing to the stone, kissing it, sacrificing sheep and camels to it, and afterward they gather in the taverns and hold recitations of war poetry and amorous verses. Very beautiful poetry, in its own barbarous fashion, I think. These pilgrims come here by the *thousands*. There's money in having the national shrine in your town, Corbulo: big money."

His eyes were gleaming. How the Greeks love moneymaking!

"Then, too," he went on, "the chieftains of Mecca have very shrewdly proclaimed that in the holy city all feuds and tribal wars are strictly forbidden during these great religious festivals. —You know about the Saracens and their feuds? Well, you'll learn. At any rate, it's very useful to everybody in this country for one city to be set aside as a place where you don't have to be afraid of getting a scimitar in your gut if you chance to meet the wrong person while crossing the street. A lot of business gets done here during the times of truce between people from tribes that hate each other the rest of the year. And the Meccans take their cut, do you follow me? That is the life of the city: collecting percentages on everything. Oh, this may be a dismal hideous town, Corbulo, but there are men living here who could buy the likes of you and me in lots of two dozen."

"I see." I paused just a moment. "And the Eastern Empire, I take it, must be developing significant business interests in this part of Arabia, or else why would the Eastern Emperor have stationed a high official like you here?"

"We're beginning to have a little trade with the Saracens, yes," the Greek said. "Just a little." And he filled my glass yet again.

The next day—hot, dry, dusty, like every day here—I did go to look at this Kaaba of theirs. Not at all hard to find: right in the center of town, in fact, standing by itself in the midst of an empty square of enormous size. The holy building itself was unimposing, perhaps fifty feet high at best, covered completely by a thick veil of black cloth. I think you could have put the thing down in the courtyard of the Temple of Jupiter Capitolinus or any of Roma's other great temples and it would utterly disappear from view.

This did not seem to be pilgrimage season. There was no one around the Kaaba but a dozen or so Saracen guards. They were armed with such formidable swords, and looked so generally unfriendly, that I chose not to make a closer inspection of the shrine.

My early wanderings through the town showed me very little that indicated the presence of the prosperity that Nicomedes the Paphlagonian had claimed was to be found here. But in the course of the next few days I came gradually to understand that the Saracens are not a people to flaunt their wealth, but prefer instead to conceal it behind unadorned façades. Now and again I would have a peek through a momentarily opened gate into a briefly visible courtyard and got the sense of a palatial building hidden back there, or I would see some merchant and his wife, richly robed and laden with jewels and gold chains, climbing into a shrouded sedan-chair, and I knew from such fitful glimpses that this must indeed be a wealthier city than it looked. Which explains, no doubt, why our Greek cousins have started to find it so appealing.

These Saracens are a handsome people, lean and finely made, very dark of skin, dark hair and eyes as well, with sharp features and prominent brows. They wear airy white robes and the women go veiled, I suppose to protect their skins against the blowing sand. Thus far I have seen more than a few young men who might be of interest to me, and they gave me quick flashing looks, too, that indicated response, though it was far too soon to take any such risks here. The maidens also are lovely. But they are very well guarded.

My own situation here is more pleasing, or at least less displeasing, than I had feared. I feel the pain of my isolation, of course. There are no other Westerners. Greek is widely understood by the better class of Saracens, but I yearn already for the sound of good honest Latin. Still, it has been arranged for me to have a walled villa, of modest size but decent enough, at the edge of town nearest the mountains. If only it had proper baths, it would be perfect; but in a land without water there is no understanding of baths. A great pity, that. The villa belongs to a merchant of Syrian origin who will be spending the next two or three years traveling abroad. I have inherited five of his servants as well. A wardrobe of clothing in the local style has been provided for me.

It all might have been much worse, eh?

But in truth they couldn't simply have left me to shift for myself in this strange land. I am still an official of the Imperial court, after all, even though I happen currently to be in disfavor and exile. I am here on Imperial business, you know. It was not just out of mere pique that Julianus shipped me here, even though I had angered him mightily by getting to his cup-boy before him. I realize now that he must have been looking for an excuse to send someone to this place who could serve unofficially as an observer for him, and I inadvertently gave him the pretext he needed.

Do you understand? He is worried about the Greeks, who evidently have set about the process of extending their authority into this part of the world, which has always been more or less independent of the Empire. My formal assignment, as I have said, is to investigate the possibilities of expanding Roman business interests in Arabia Deserta—*Western* Roman interests, that is. But I have a covert assignment as well, one so covert that not even I have been informed of its nature, that has to do with the growing power of Romans of the other sort in that region.

What I am saying, in ordinary language, is that I am actually a spy, sent here to keep watch over the Greeks.

Yes, I know, it is all one empire that happens to have two emperors, and we of the West are supposed to look upon the Greeks as our cousins and coadministrators of the world, not as our rivals. Sometimes it actually does work that way, I will concede. As in the time of Maximilianus III, for example, when the Greeks helped us put an end to the disturbances that the Goths and Vandals and Huns and other barbarians were creating along our northern frontier. And then again a generation later, when Heraclius II sent Western legions to help the Eastern Emperor Justinianus smash the forces of Persia that had been causing the Greeks such trouble to the east for so many years. Those were, of course, the two great military strokes that eliminated the Empire's enemies for good and laid the foundations for the era of eternal peace and safety in which we live now.

But an excess of peace and safety, Horatius, can bring niggling little problems of its own. With no external enemies left to worry about, the Eastern and Western Empires are beginning to jockey with each other for advantage. Everybody understands that, though no one says it aloud. There was that time, let me remind you, when the ambassador of Maurice Tiberius came to court, bearing a casket of pearls as a gift for Caesar. I was there. "*Et dona ferentes*," said Julianus to me under his breath, as the casket was uncovered. The line every schoolboy knows: *I fear Greeks even when bringing gifts.*

Is the Eastern Empire trying to put a drawstring around the midsection of Arabia, and by so doing to gain control over the trade in spices and other precious exotic merchandise that passes this way? It would not be a good thing for us to become altogether dependent on the Greeks for our cinnamon and our cardamom, our frankincense and our indigo. The very steel of our swords comes westward to us out of Persia by way of this Arabia, and the horses that draw our chariots are Arabian horses.

And so the Emperor Julianus, feigning great wrath and loudly calling me a serpent before all the court when the matter of the little cup-bearer became known, has thrust me into this parched land primarily to find out what the Greeks are really up to here, and perhaps also to establish certain political connections with powerful Saracens myself, connections that he can employ in blocking the Eastern Empire's apparent foray into these regions. Or so I do believe, Horatius. So I *must* believe, and I must make Caesar believe it himself. For it is only by doing some great service for the Emperor that I can redeem myself from this woeful place and win my way back to Roma, to Caesar's side and to yours, my sweet friend, to yours.

The night before last—I have been in Mecca eight days, now— Nicomedes invited me once again for dinner. He was dressed, as I was, in white Saracen robes, and wore a lovely dagger in a jeweled sheath strapped to his waist. I glanced quickly at it, feeling some surprise at being greeted by a host who wore a weapon; but instantly he took the thing off and presented it to me. He had mistaken my concern for admiration, and it is a Saracen custom, I have learned, to bestow upon one's guests anything in one's household that the guest might choose to admire.

We dined this time not in the tiled parlor where he had entertained me previously but in a cool courtyard beside a plashing fountain. The possession of such a fountain is a token of great luxury in this dry land. His servants brought us an array of fine wines and sweetmeats and cool sherbets. I could see that Nicomedes had modeled his manner of living after the style of the leading merchants of the city, and was reveling in that.

I had not been there very long when I got right down to the central issue: that is, what exactly it was that the Greek Emperor hoped to accomplish by stationing a royal legate in Mecca. Sometimes, I think, the best way for a spy to learn what he needs to learn is to put aside all guile and play the role of a simple, straightforward, ingenuous man who merely speaks his heart.

So as we sat over roast mutton and plump dates in warm milk I said, "Is it the Eastern Emperor's hope to incorporate Arabia into the Empire, then?"

Nicomedes laughed. "Oh, we're not so foolish as to think we can do that. No one's ever been able to conquer this place, you know. The Egyptians tried it, and the Persians of Cyrus's time, and Alexander the Great. Augustus sent an expedition in here, ten thousand men, six months to fight their way in and sixty days of horrible retreat. I think Trajan made an attempt, too. The thing is, Corbulo, these Saracens are free men, free *within themselves*, which is a kind of freedom that you and I are simply not equipped to comprehend. They can't be conquered because they can't be governed. Trying to conquer them is like trying to conquer lions or tigers. You can whip a lion or even kill it, yes, but you can't possibly impose your will on it even if you keep it in a cage for twenty years. These are a race of lions here. Government as we understand it is a concept that can never exist here."

"They are organized into tribes, aren't they? That's a sort of government."

He shrugged. "Built out of nothing more than family loyalty. You can't fashion any sort of national administration out of it. Kinsman looks after kinsman and everybody else is regarded as a potential enemy. There are no kings here, do you realize that? Never have been. Just tribal chieftains—*emirs*, they call them. A land without kings is never going to submit to an emperor. We could fill this entire peninsula with soldiers, fifty legions, and the Saracens would simply melt away into the desert and pick us off one by one from a distance with javelins and arrows. An invisible enemy striking at us from a terrain that we can't survive in. They're unconquerable, Corbulo. Unconquerable."

There was passion in his voice, and apparent sincerity. The Greeks are good at apparent sincerity.

I said, "So the best you're looking for is some kind of trade agreement, is that it? Just an informal Byzantine presence, not any actual incorporation of the region into the Empire."

He nodded. "That's about right. Is your Emperor bothered by that?"

"It's drawn his attention, I would say. We wouldn't want to lose access to the goods we obtain from this part of the world. And also those from places like India to the east that normally ship their merchandise westward by way of Arabia."

"But why would that happen, my dear Corbulo? This is a single empire, is it not? Julianus III rules from Roma and Maurice Tiberius rules from Constantinopolis, but they rule jointly for the common good of all Roman citizens everywhere. As has been the case since the great Constantinus divided the realm in the first place three hundred years ago."

Yes. Of course. That is the official line. But I know better and you know better, and Nicomedes the Paphlagonian knew better, too. I had pushed the issue as far as seemed appropriate just then, however. It was time to move on to more frivolous topics.

I found, though, that dropping the matter was not all that easily done. Having voiced my suspicions, I thereby had invited counterargument, and Nicomedes was not finished providing it. I had no choice but to listen while he wove such a web of words about me that it completely captured me into his way of thinking. The Greeks

are damnably clever with words, of course; and he had lulled me
with sweet wines and surfeited me with an abundance of fine food so
that I was altogether unable just then to refute and rebut, and before
he was done with me my mind was utterly spun around on the subject of East versus West.

He assured me in twenty different ways that an expansion of the
Eastern Empire's influence into Arabia Deserta, if such a thing were
to take place, would not in any way jeopardize existing Western Roman trade in Arabian or Indian merchandise. Arabia Petraea just to
the north had long been under the Eastern Empire's administration,
he pointed out, and that was true also of the provinces of Syria
Palaestina and Aegyptus and Cappadocia and Mesopotamia and all
those other sunny eastern lands that Constantinus, at the time of the
original division of the realm, had placed under the jurisdiction of
the Emperor who would sit at Constantinopolis. Did I believe that
the prosperity of the Western Empire was in any way hampered by
having those provinces under Byzantine administration? Had I not
just traveled freely through many of those provinces on my way
here? Was there not a multitude of Western Roman merchants resident in them, and were they not free to do business there as they
wished?

I could not contest any of that. I wanted to disagree, to summon
up a hundred instances of subtle Eastern interference with Western
trade, but just then I could not offer even one.

Believe me, Horatius, at that moment I found myself quite unable to understand why I had ever conceived such a mistrust of
Greek intentions. They are indeed our cousins, I told myself. They
are Greek Romans and we are Roman Romans, yes, but the Empire
itself is one entity, chosen by the gods to rule the world. A gold piece
struck in Constantinopolis is identical in weight and design to one
struck in Roma. One bears the name and face of the Eastern Emperor, one the name and face of the Emperor of the West, but all else
is the same. The coins of one realm pass freely in the other. Their
prosperity is our prosperity; our prosperity is theirs. And so on and
so forth.

But as I thought these things, Horatius, I also realized gloomily
that by so doing I was undercutting in my own mind my one tenuous

hope of freeing myself from this land of burning sands and stark treeless hills. As I noted in my most recent letter, what I need is some way of saying, "Look, Caesar, how well I have served you!" so that he would say in return, "Well done, thou good and faithful servant," and summon me back to the pleasures of the court. For that to occur, though, I must show Caesar that he has enemies here, and give him the way of dealing with those enemies. But what enemies? Who? Where?

We were done with our meal now. Nicomedes clapped his hands and a servitor brought a flask of some rich golden brandy that came, so he said, from a desert principality on the shores of the Persian Gulf. It dazzled my palate and further befogged my mind.

He conducted me, then, through the rooms of his villa, pointing out the highlights of what even in my blurred condition I could see was an extraordinary collection of antiquities and curios: fine Greek bronze figurines, majestic sculptures from Egypt done in black stone, strange wooden masks of barbaric design that had been fashioned, he told me, somewhere in the unknown lands of torrid Africa, and much, much more.

He spoke of each piece with the deepest knowledge. By now I had come to see that my host was not only a devious diplomat but also a person of some power and consequence in the Eastern realm, and a scholar of note besides. I was grateful to him for having reached out so generously to me in these early days of my lonely exile—to the displaced and unhappy Roman nobleman, bereft of all that was familiar to him, a stranger in a strange land. But I knew also that I was *meant* to be grateful to him, that it was his purpose to ensnare me in the bonds of friendship and obligation, so that I would have nothing but good things to say about the Greek legate in Mecca should I ever return to my master the Emperor Julianus III.

Would I ever return, though? That was the question.

That *is* the question, yes. Will I ever see Roma of the green hills and shining marble palaces again, Horatius, or am I doomed to bake in the heat of this oven of a desert forever?

*   *   *

Having no occupation here and having as yet found no friends other than Nicomedes, whose companionship I could not presume to demand too often, I whiled away the days that followed in close exploration of the town.

The shock of finding myself resident in this squalid little place has begun to wear off. I have started to adapt, to some degree, to the change that has come over my existence. The pleasures of Roma are no longer mine to have; very well, I must search out such diversion as is to be found here, for there is no place in the world, humble though it be, that does not offer diversion of some sort to him who has eyes for finding it.

So in these days since my last letter I have roamed from one end of Mecca to the other, up and down the broad though unpaved boulevards and into many of the narrow lanes and byways that intersect them. My presence does not appear to be greatly troublesome to anyone, although from time to time I do become cognizant that I am the object of someone's cold, gleaming stare.

I am, as you know, the only Roman of the West in Mecca, but scarcely the only foreigner. In the various marketplaces I have seen Persians, Syrians, Ethiopians, and of course a good many Greeks. There are numerous Indians here as well, dark lithe people with conspicuous luminous eyes, and also some Hebrews, these being a people who live mainly over in Aegyptus, just on the other side of the Red Sea from Arabia. They have been resident in Aegyptus for thousands of years, though evidently they were originally a desert tribe from some country much like this one, and they are not in any way Aegyptian in language or culture or religion. These Hebrews have in modern times begun to spread from their home along the Nilus into the lands adjacent, and there are more than a few of them here. Nicomedes has spoken of them to me.

They are unusual people, the Hebrews. The most interesting thing about them is that they believe there is only one god, a harsh and austere deity who cannot be seen and who must not be portrayed in images of any sort. They have nothing but contempt for the gods of other races, deeming them wholly imaginary, mere creatures of fable and fantasy that possess no true existence. This may very likely be the case, certainly: who among us has ever laid eyes on Apollo or Mercury or Minerva? Most people, however, have the good sense not to make a mockery of the religious practices of others, whereas the Hebrews apparently cannot keep themselves from trumpeting the virtues of their own odd species of belief while denouncing everybody else most vociferously as idolaters and fools.

As you can readily imagine, this does not make them very popular among their neighbors. But they are an industrious folk, with special aptitudes for the sciences of agriculture and irrigation, and a notable knack, also, for finance and trade, which is why Nicomedes has paid such attention to them. He tells me that they own most of the best land in the northern part of the country, that they are the chief bankers here in Mecca, and that they control the markets in weapons, armor, and agricultural tools everywhere in the land. It seems advantageous for me to get to know one or two important Hebrews of Mecca and I have made attempts to do so, thus far without any success, during the course of my ramblings in the marketplaces.

The markets here are very specialized, each offering its own kind of merchandise. I have visited them all by now.

There is a spice-market, of course: great sacks of pepper both black and white, and garlic and cumin and saffron, sandalwood and cassia, aloes, spikenard, and an aromatic dried leaf that they call malabathron, and hosts of other things I could not begin to name. There is a camel-market, only on certain days of the week, where those strange beasts are bought and sold in heated bargaining that goes to the edge of actual combat. I went up to one of these creatures to see it better and it yawned in my face as though I were the dullest of rogues. There is a market for cloth, which deals in muslins and silks and cotton both Indian and Aegyptian, and a market where crude idols of many kinds are sold to the credulous—I saw a Hebrew man walk past it, and spit and glare and make what I think was a holy sign of his people—and a market for wines, and one for perfumes, and the market of meat and the one of grains, and the market where the Hebrew merchants sell their iron goods, and one for fruits of all kinds, pomegranates and quinces and citrons and lemons and sour oranges and grapes and peaches, all this in the midst of the most forbidding desert you could imagine!

And also there is a market for slaves, which is where I encountered the remarkable man who called himself Mahmud.

The slave-market of Mecca is as bustling as any slave-market
anywhere, which illustrates how great a degree of prosperity lies behind the deceptively shabby façade this city displays to strangers. It
is the great flesh-mart of the land, and buyers sometimes come from
as far away as Syria and the Persian Gulf to check out the slavemon-
gers' latest haul of desirable human exotica.

Though wood is a luxury in this desert country, there is the usual
platform of planks and timbers, the usual awning suspended from a
couple of poles, the usual sorry huddle of naked merchandise waiting to be sold. They were a mix of all races, though with a distinct
Asian and African cast, here: Ethiops dark as night and brawny Nu-
bians even darker, and flat-faced fair-skinned Circassians and Avars
and other sinewy northern folk, and some who might have been Persians or Indians, and even a sullen yellow-haired man who could
have been a Briton or Teuton. The auctions were conducted, quite
naturally, in the Saracen tongue, so that I understood nothing of
what was said, but I suppose it was the customary fraudulent gabble
that fools no one, how this buxom sultry Turkish wench was a king's
daughter in her own land, and this thick-bearded scowling Libyan
had been a charioteer of the highest distinction before his master's
bankruptcy had forced his sale, and so forth.

It so happened that I was passing the auction place at noonday
three days past when three supple tawny-skinned wantons, who
from their shameless movements and smiles must have been very
skilled prostitutes indeed, came up for sale as a single lot, intended
perhaps as concubines for some great emir. They wore nothing but
jingling bracelets of silver coins about their wrists and ankles, and
were laughing and thrusting their breasts from side to side and
winking at the crowd to invite active bidding on behalf of their
seller, who for all I know was their uncle or their brother.

The spectacle was so lively that I paused to observe it a moment.
Hardly had I taken my place in the crowd, though, than the man
standing just to my left surprised me by turning toward me and muttering, in a vibrant tone of intense fury powerfully contained, "Ah,
the swine! They should be whipped and turned out into the desert

for the jackals to eat!" This he said in quite passable Greek, uttering the words in a low whisper that nonetheless was strikingly rich and captivating, one of the most musical speaking voices I have ever heard. It was as though the words had overflowed his soul and he had had no choice but to utter them at once to the man closest at hand.

The power of that extraordinary voice and the violence of his sentiment had the most singular effect on me. It was as though I had been seized by the wrist in an irresistible grip. I stared at him. He was holding himself taut as a bowstring when the archer is at the verge of letting fly, and appeared to be trembling with wrath.

Some sort of response seemed incumbent on me. The best I could do was to say, "The girls, do you mean?"

"The slavemasters," said he. "The women are but chattel. They are not to be held accountable. But it is wrong to put chattel out for pandering, as these criminals do."

And then, relaxing his stance a bit and looking now somewhat abashed at his forwardness, he said in a far less assertive tone of voice, "But you must forgive me for pouring these thoughts into the unwilling ears of a stranger who surely has no interest in hearing such things."

"On the contrary. What you say interests me greatly. Indeed, you must tell me more."

I studied him with no little curiosity. It had crossed my mind immediately that he might be a Hebrew: his horror and rage at the sight of this trifling bit of flesh-peddling seemed to mark him as a kinsman of that dour man who had made such a display of irate piety in the marketplace of idols. You will recall that I had resolved to seek contact with members of that agile-minded race of merchants here. But a moment's closer examination of his look and garb led me now to realize that he must be pure Saracen by blood.

There was tremendous presence and force about him. He was tall and slender, a handsome dark-haired man of perhaps thirty-five years or a little more, with a dense flowing beard, piercing eyes, and a warm and gracious smile that quite contradicted the unnerving ferocity of his gaze. His princely bearing, his eloquent manner of speech, and the fineness of his garments all suggested that he was a man of wealth and breeding, well connected in this city. At once I sensed that he might be even more useful to me than any Hebrew. So I drew him out, questioning him a little on the reasons for his spontaneous outburst against the trade in easy women in this marketplace, and without the slightest hesitation he poured forth a powerful and lengthy tirade, fierce in content although stated in that same captivating musical tone, against the totality of the sins of his countrymen. And what a multitude of sins they were! Mere prostitution was the least of them. I had not expected to encounter such a Cato here.

"Look about you!" he urged me. "Mecca is an utter abyss of wickedness. Do you see the idols that are sold everywhere, and set up piously in shops and homes in places of respect? They are false gods, these images, for the true god, and He is One, cannot be rendered by any image. —Do you observe the flagrant cheating in the marketplaces? —Do you see the men lying shamelessly to their wives, and the wives lying as well, and the gambling and the drinking and the whoring, and the quarreling between brother and brother?" And there was much more. I could see that he held this catalog of outrage pent up in his breast at all times, ready to issue it forth whenever he found some new willing listener. Yet he said all this not in any lofty and superior way, but almost in bewilderment: he was saddened rather than infuriated by the failings of his brethren, or so it seemed to me.

Then he paused, once again changing tone, as though it had occurred to him that it was impolite to remain in this high denunciatory mode for any great length of time. "Again I ask you to pardon me for my excess of zeal. I feel very strongly on these matters. It is the worst of my faults, I hope. —If I am not mistaken, you are the Roman who has come to live among us?"

"Yes. Leontius Corbulo, at your service. A Roman of the Romans, I like to say." I gave him a flourish. "My family is a very ancient one, with historic ties to Syria and other parts of Asia."

"Indeed. I am Mahmud son of Abdallah, who was the son of—" Well, the son of I forget whom, who was the son of so-and-so, the son of someone else. It is the custom of these Saracens to let you have their pedigrees five or six generations back in a single outburst of breath, but it was impossible for me to retain most of the barbarous outlandish names in my mind very long. I do recall his telling me that he was a member of one of the great mercantile clans of Mecca, which is called something like the *Koreish*.

It seemed to me that a strong rapport had arisen between us in just these few moments, and, such was the power of his personality, I was reluctant to leave him. Since it was the time for the midday meal, I proposed that we take it together and invited him to come with me to my villa. But he responded that I was a guest in Mecca and it was not fitting for him to enjoy my hospitality until I had partaken of his. I didn't try to dispute the issue. The Saracens, I had already begun to learn, are most punctilious about this sort of thing. "Come," he said, beckoning. And so it was that for the first time I entered the home of a wealthy merchant of Mecca.

The villa of Mahmud son of Abdallah was not unlike that of Nicomedes, though on a larger scale—walled courtyard, central fountain, bright airy rooms, inlays of vividly colored tile set in the walls. But unlike Nicomedes, Mahmud was no collector of antiquities. He appeared to have scarcely any possessions at all. A prevailing austerity of decoration was the rule in his house. And of course there was no sign anywhere in it of the idols that other Meccans seemed to cherish.

The wife of Mahmud made a fleeting appearance. Her name was something like Kadija, and she seemed considerably older than her husband, a fact soon confirmed from Mahmud's own lips. A couple of daughters passed to and fro in equally brief manner. But he and I dined alone, seated on straw mats in the center of a huge bare room. Mahmud sat crosslegged like a tailor, and appeared to be entirely at ease in that posture. I tried but failed to manage it, and after a time fell into the normal reclining position, wishing mightily that I had a cushion for my elbow, but not willing to give offense by asking for one. The meal itself was simple, grilled meat and a stew of barley and melons, with nothing but water to wash it down. Mahmud did not, it seemed, care for wine.

He spoke of himself with complete openness, as though we were kinsmen from widely distant lands who were meeting for the first time. I learned that Mahmud's father had died before his birth and his mother had lived only a short while thereafter, so he had grown up in impoverished circumstances under the guardianship of an uncle. From his tale I received the impression of a lonely childhood spent wandering the cheerless rocky hills beyond town, pondering from an early age, perhaps, the great questions of eternity and the spirit that plainly have continued to obsess him to this day.

In his twenty-fifth year, said Mahmud, he entered into the service of the woman Kadija, a wealthy widow fifteen years his senior, who soon fell in love with him and asked him to be her husband. This he told me with no trace of embarrassment at all, and I suppose he has no reason to feel any. A look of happiness comes into his eyes when he speaks of her. She has borne him both sons and daughters, though only the daughters have survived. The prosperity that he enjoys today is, I gather, the result of his skillful management of the property that his wife brought to their union.

About Roma, Constantinopolis, or any other place beyond the frontiers of Arabia Deserta, he asked me nothing whatever. Though his intelligence is deep and questing, he did not seem concerned with the empires of this world. It appears that he has scarcely been outside Mecca at all, though he mentioned having made a journey as far as Damascus on one occasion. I would think him a simple man if I did not know, Horatius, how complex in fact he is.

The great preoccupation of his life is his concept of the One God.

This is, of course, the idea famously advocated since antiquity by the Hebrews. I have no doubt that Mahmud has had conversations with the members of that race who live in Mecca, and that their ideas have affected his philosophy. He must surely have heard them express their reverence for their aloof and unknowable god, and their contempt for the superstitions of the Meccans, who cherish such a multitude of idols and talismans and practice a credulous veneration of the sun and the moon and stars and planets and a myriad of demons. He makes no secret of this: I heard him make reference to an ancient Hebrew prophet called Abraham, who is apparently a figure he greatly admires, and also a certain Moses, a later leader of that tribe.

But he lays claim to a separate revelation of his own. He asserts that his special enlightenment came as the result of arduous private prayer and contemplation. He would go up often into the mountains behind the town and meditate in solitude in a secluded cave; and one day an awareness of the Oneness of God was revealed to him as though by a divine messenger.

Mahmud calls this god "Allah." A marvelous transformation comes over him when he begins to speak of him. His face glows; his eyes take on the quality of beacons; his very voice becomes such a thing of music and poetry that you would think you were in the presence of Apollo.

It is impossible, he says, ever to understand the nature of Allah. He is too far above us for that. Other people may regard their gods as personages in some kind of story, and tell lively fanciful tales of their travels throughout the world and their quarrels with their wives and their adventures on the battlefield, and make statues of them that show them as men and women, but Allah is not like that. One does not tell tales about Allah. He cannot be thought of, as we think of Jupiter, as a tall man with a commanding face and a full beard and a host of passions—someone rather like an Emperor, let us say, but on a larger scale—and it is foolishness, as well as blasphemy, to make representations of him the way the ancient Greeks did of such gods of theirs as Zeus and Aphrodite and Poseidon, or we do of Jupiter or Venus or Mars. Allah is the creative force itself, the maker of the universe, too mighty and vast to be captured by any sort of representation.

I asked Mahmud how, if it is blasphemous to imagine a face for his god, it can be acceptable to give him a name. For surely that is a kind of representation also. Mahmud seemed pleased at the sharpness of my question; and he explained that "Allah" is not actually a name, as "Mahmud" or "Leontius Corbulo" or "Jupiter" are names, but is a mere word, simply the term in the Saracen language that means *the god*.

To Mahmud, the fact that there is only one god, whose nature is abstract and incomprehensible to mortals, is the great sublime law from which all other laws flow. This will probably make no more sense to you, Horatius, than it does to me, but it is not our business to be philosophers. What is of interest here is that the man has such a passionate belief in the things he believes. So passionate is it that as you listen to him you become caught up in the simplicity and the beauty of his ideas and the power of his way of speaking of them, and you are almost ready to cry out your belief in Allah yourself.

It is a very simple creed indeed, but enormously powerful in its directness, the way things in this harsh and uncompromising desert land tend to be. He stringently rejects all idol-worship, all fable-making, all notions of how the movements of the stars and planets govern our lives. He places no trust in oracles or sorcery. The decrees of kings and princes mean very little to him either. He accepts only the authority of his remote and all-powerful and inflexible god, whose great stern decree it is that we live virtuous lives of hard work, piety, and respect for our fellow men. Those who live by Allah's law, says Mahmud, will be gathered into paradise at the end of their days; those who do not will descend into the most terrible of hells. And Mahmud does not intend to rest until all Arabia has been brought forth out of sloth and degeneracy and sin to accept the supremacy of the One God, and its scattered squabbling tribes forged at last into a single great nation under the rule of one invincible king who could enforce the laws of that god.

He was awesome in his conviction. I tell you, by the time he was done, I was close to feeling the presence and might of Allah myself. That was surprising and a little frightening, that Mahmud could stir such feelings in me, of all people. I was amazed. But then he had finished his expounding, and after a few moments the sensation ebbed and I was my own self again.

"What do you say?" he asked me. "Can this be anything other than the truth?"

"I am not in a position to judge that," said I carefully, not wishing to give offense to this interesting new friend, especially in his own dining hall. "We Romans are accustomed to regarding all creeds with tolerance, and if you ever visit our capital you will find temples of a hundred faiths standing side by side. But I do see the beauty of your teachings."

"Beauty? I asked about truth. When you say you accept all faiths as equally true, what you are really saying is that you see no truth in any of them, is that not so?"

I disputed that, reaching into my school days for maxims out of Plato and Marcus Aurelius to argue that all gods are reflections of the true godhood. But it was no use. He saw instantly through my Roman indifference to religion. If you claim to believe, as we do, that this god is just as good as that one, what you really mean is that gods in general don't matter much at all, nor religion itself, except where it is needed as a distraction to keep the people of the lower classes from growing too resentful over the miseries of their worldly existence. Our live-and-let-live policy toward the worship of Mithras and Dagon and Baal and all the other deities whose temples thrive in Roma is a tacit admission of that view. And for Mahmud that is a contemptible position.

Sensing the tension that was rising in him, and unwilling to have our pleasant conversation turn acrid, I offered a plea of fatigue and promised to continue the discussion with him at another time.

In the evening, having been invited yet again to dine with Nicomedes the Paphlagonian and with my head still spinning from the thrust of all that Mahmud had imparted to me, I asked him if he could tell me anything about this extraordinary person.

"That man!" Nicomedes said, chuckling. "Consorting with madmen, are you, now, Corbulo?"

"He seemed quite sane to me."

"Oh, he is, he is, at least when he's selling you a pair of camels or a sack of saffron. But get him started on the subject of religion and you'll see a different man."

"As a matter of fact, we had quite a lengthy philosophical discussion, he and I, this very afternoon," I said. "I found it fascinating. I've never heard anything quite like it."

"I dare say you haven't. Poor chap, he should get himself away from this place while he's still got the chance. If he keeps on going the way I understand he's been doing lately, he'll turn up dead out in the dunes one of these days, and no one will be surprised."

"I don't follow you."

"Preaching against the idols the way he does, is what I mean.

You know, Corbulo, they worship three hundred different gods in this city, and each one has his own shrine and his own priesthood and his own busy factory dedicated to making idols for sale to pilgrims, and so on and so forth. If I understand your Mahmud correctly, he'd like to shut all that down. Is that not so?"

"I suppose. Certainly he expressed plenty of scorn for idols and idolaters."

"Indeed he does. Up till now he's simply had a little private cult, though, half a dozen members of his own family. They get together in his house and pray to his particular god in the particular way that Mahmud prescribes. An innocent enough pastime, I'd say. But lately, I'm told, he's been spreading his ideas farther afield, going around to this person and that and testing out his seditious ideas about how to reform Saracen society on them. As he did with you this very day, it seems. Well, it does no harm for him to be talking religion with somebody like you or me, because we Romans are pretty casual about such matters. But the Saracens aren't. Before long, mark my words, he'll decide to set himself up as a prophet who preaches in public, and he'll stand in the main square threatening fire and damnation to anybody who keeps to the old ways, and then they'll have to kill him. The old ways are big business here, and what this town is about is business and nothing but business. Mahmud is full of subversive notions that these Meccans can't afford to indulge. He'd better watch his step." And then, with a grin: "But he is an amusing devil, isn't he, Corbulo? As you can tell, I've had a chat or two with him myself."

If you ask me, Horatius, Nicomedes is half right and half wrong about Mahmud.

Surely he's correct that Mahmud is almost ready to begin preaching his religion in public. The way he accosted me, a total stranger, at the slave-market testifies to that. And his talk of not resting until Arabia has been made to accept the supremacy of the One God: what else can that mean, other than that he is on the verge of speaking out against the idolaters?

Mahmud told me in just so many words, during our lunch together, that the way Allah makes his commandments concerning good and evil known to mankind is through certain chosen prophets, one every thousand years or so. Abraham and Moses of the Hebrews were such prophets, Mahmud says. I do believe that Mahmud looks upon himself as their successor.

I think the Greek is wrong, though, in saying that Mahmud will be killed by his angry neighbors for speaking out against their superstitions. No doubt they'll *want* to kill him, at first. If his teachings ever prevail, they'll throw the whole horde of priests and idol-carvers out of business and knock a great hole in the local economy, and nobody here is going to be very enthusiastic about that. But his personality is so powerful that I think he'll win them over. By Jupiter, he practically had *me* willing to accept the divine omnipotence of Allah before he was done! He'll find a way to put his ideas across to them. I can't imagine how he'll do it, but he's clever in a dozen different ways, a true desert merchant, and somehow he'll offer them something that will make it worthwhile for them to give up their old beliefs and accept his. Allah and no one else will be the god of this place, is what I expect, by the time Mahmud has finished his holy work.

I need to ponder all this very carefully. You don't come upon a man with Mahmud's kind of innate personal magnetism very often. I am haunted by the strength of it, awed by the recollection of how, for the moment, he had managed to win my allegiance to that One God of his. Is there, I wonder, some way that I can turn Mahmud's great power to sway men's minds to the service of the Empire, by which I mean to the service of Julianus III Augustus? So that, of course, I can regain Caesar's good graces and get myself redeemed out of Arabian exile.

At the moment I don't quite see it. Perhaps I could urge him to turn his countrymen against the growing ascendancy of the Greeks in this part of the world, or some such thing. But this week I have plenty of time to think on it, for no company is available to me just now except my own. Mahmud, who travels frequently through the area on business, has gone off to one of the coastal villages to investigate some new mercantile venture. Nicomedes also is away, down into Arabia Felix, where he and his fellow Greeks no doubt are conniving covertly to raise the price of carnelians or aloe-wood or some other commodity currently in great demand at Roma.

So I am alone here but for my servants, a dull lot with whom I can have no hope of companionship. I toyed with the idea of buying myself a lively slave-boy in the bazaar to keep me company of a more interesting kind, but Mahmud, who is so fiery in his piety, might suspect what I had in mind, and I would not at this time want to risk a breach with Mahmud. The idea of such a purchase is very tempting, though.

I think longingly all the time of the court, the festivities at the royal palace, the theater and the games, all that I am missing. Fuscus Salinator: what is he up to? Voconius Rufus? Spurinna? Allifanus? And what of Emperor Julianus himself, he who was my friend, almost my brother, until he turned on me and condemned me to languish like this amidst the sands of Arabia? What times we had together, he and I, until my fall from grace!

And—fear not—I think constantly of you, of course, Horatius. I wonder who you spend your nights with now. Male or female, is it? Lupercus Hector? Little Pomponia Mamiliana, perhaps? Or even the cup-boy from Britannia, whom surely the Emperor no longer would have wanted after I had sullied him. Well, you do not sleep alone, of that much I'm certain.

What, I wonder, would my new friend Mahmud think of our court and its ways? He is so severe and astringent of nature. His hatred for self-indulgence of all sorts seems deep as the bone: a stark prince of the desert, this man, a true Spartan. But perhaps I give him too much credit, you say? Set him up in a villa on the slopes of the Palatine, provide him with a fine chariot and a house full of servants and a cellar of decent wine, let him splash a bit in the Emperor's perfumed pool with Julianus and his giddy friends, and it may be he'll sing another tune, eh?

No. No. I doubt that very greatly. Bring Mahmud to Roma and he will rise up like a modern Cato and sweep the place clean, purging the capital of all the sins of these soft Imperial years. And when he is done with us, Horatius, we shall all be faithful adherents to the creed of Allah.

*   *   *

Five days more of solitude went by, and by the end of it I was ready, I think, to open my veins. There has been a wind blowing here all week that bakes the brain to the verge of madness. The air seemed half composed of sand. People came and went in the streets like phantoms, all shrouded up to the eyes in white. I feared going outside.

For the past two days, though, the air has been calm again. Mahmud yesterday returned from his venture from the coast. I saw him in the main street, speaking with three or four other men. Even though he was some distance away, it was plain that Mahmud was doing nearly all the talking, and the others, caught in his spell, were reduced to mere nods and gestures of the hand. There is wizardry in this man's manner of speech. He casts a powerful spell. You are held; you cannot choose but listen; you find yourself believing whatever he says.

I did not feel it appropriate to approach him just then; but later in the day I sent one of my servants to his house bearing an invitation to dine with me at my villa, and we have spent some hours together this very day. It was a meeting that brought forth a host of startling revelations.

Neither of us chose to plunge back into the theological discussion of our previous conversation, and for a while we made mere idle arm's-length talk in the somewhat uneasy manner of two gentlemen of very different nations who find themselves dining in intimate circumstances and are determined to get through the meal without giving offense. Mahmud's manner was genial in a way I had not seen it before. But as the dishes of the first course were being cleared away the old intensity came back into his eyes and he said somewhat abruptly, "And tell me, my friend, how did it happen, exactly, that you came to our country in the first place?"

It would hardly have been useful to my burgeoning friendship with this man to admit that I had been banished here on account of my pederasty with Caesar's intended plaything. But—you must trust me on this—I had to tell him *something*. There is no easy way of being evasive when the burning eyes of Mahmud son of Abdallah are peering intently into your own. I could lie more readily to Caesar. Or to Jove himself.

And so, on the principle that telling part of the truth is usually more convincing than telling an outright lie, I admitted to him that my Emperor had sent me to Arabia to spy on the Greeks.

"*Your* Emperor who is not *their* Emperor, though it is all one empire."

"Exactly." Mahmud, isolated as he had been all his life from the greater world beyond Arabia's frontiers, seemed to understand the concept of the dual principate. And understood also how little real harmony there is between the two halves of the divided realm.

"And what harm is it that you think the Byzantine folk can cause your people, then?" he asked.

There was a tautness in his voice; I sensed that this was something more than an idle conversational query for him.

"Economic harm," I said. "Too much of what we import from the eastern nations passes through their hands as it is. Now they seem to be drifting down here into the middle of Arabia, where all the key trade routes converge. If they can establish a stranglehold on those routes, we'll be at their mercy."

He was silent for a time, digesting that. But his eyes flashed strange fire. His brain must have been awhirl with thought.

Then he leaned forward until we were almost nose to nose and said, in that low quiet voice of his that seizes your attention more emphatically than the loudest shout, "We share a common concern, then. They are our enemies, too, these Greeks. I know their hearts. They mean to conquer us."

"But that's impossible! Nicomedes himself has told me that no army has ever succeeded in seizing possession of Arabia. And he says that none ever will."

"Indeed, no one can ever take us by force. But that is not what I mean. The Greeks will conquer us by slyness and cunning, if we allow it: playing their gold against our avarice, buying us inch by inch until we have sold ourselves entirely. We are a shrewd folk, but they are much shrewder, and they will bind us in silken knots, and one day we will find that we are altogether owned by Greek traders and

Greek usurers and Greek shipowners. It is what the Hebrews would have done to us, if they were more numerous and more powerful; but the Greeks have an entire empire behind them. Or half an empire, at least." His face was suddenly aflame with that extraordinary animation and excitability, to the point almost of frenzy, that rose in him so easily. He clapped his hand down on mine. "But it will not be. I will not allow it, good Corbulo! I will destroy them before they can ruin us. Tell that to your Emperor, if you like: Mahmud son of Abdallah will take his stand here before the Greeks who would steal this land, and he will march on them, and he will drive them back to Byzantium."

It was a stunning moment. He had told me on the very first day that he intended to bring Arabia under the rule of a single god and of a single invincible king; and now I knew who he expected that invincible king to be.

I was put in mind of Nicomedes's mocking words of the week before: *Consorting with madmen, are you, now, Corbulo?*

This sudden outburst of Mahmud's as we sat quietly together at my table did indeed have the pure ring of madness about it. That an obscure merchant of this desert land should also be a mystic and a dreamer was unusual enough; but now, as though drawing back a veil, he had revealed to me the tumultuous presence of a warrior-king within his breast as well. It was too much. Neither Alexander of Macedon nor Julius Caesar nor the Emperor Constantinus the Great had laid claim to holding so many selves within a single soul, and how could Mahmud the son of Abdallah?

A moment later he had subsided again, and all was as calm as it had been just minutes before.

There was a flask of wine on the table near my elbow, a good thick Tunisian that I had bought in the marketplace the day before. I poured myself some now to ease the thunder that Mahmud's wild speech had engendered in my forehead. He smiled and tapped the flask and said, "I have never understood the point of that stuff, do you know? It seems a waste of good grapes to make it into wine."

"Well, opinions differ on that," said I. "But who's to say who's right? Let those who like wine drink it, and the rest can leave it alone." I raised my glass to him. "This is really excellent, though. Are you sure you won't try even a sip?"

He looked at me as though I had offered him a cup of venom. He will never be a drinker, I guess, will Mahmud son of Abdallah, and so be it. Yea and verily, Horatius, it leaves that much more for the likes of thee and me.

"And how is your friend Mahmud?" asked Nicomedes the Paphlagonian, the next time he and I dined together. "Does he have you bowing down to Allah yet?"

"I am not made for bowing before gods, I think," I told him. And then, warily: "He seems a little troubled about the presence of you people down here."

"Thinks we're going to attempt a takeover, does he? He should know better than that. If Augustus and Trajan couldn't manage to invade this place successfully, why does he think a sensible monarch like Maurice Tiberius would try it?"

"Not a military invasion, Nicomedes. Commercial infiltration is what he fears."

Nicomedes looked unperturbed. "He shouldn't. I'd never try to deny to anybody, Corbulo, that we're looking to increase the quantity of business we do here. But why should that matter to the likes of Mahmud? We won't cut into his slice of the pie. We'll just make the pie bigger for everybody. You know the thing the Phoenicians say—'A rising tide lifts all boats.'"

"Don't they teach rhetoric in Greek schools any more?" I asked. "Pies? Boats? You're mixing your metaphors there, I'd say. And Arabia doesn't have any boats for the tide to raise, or any tides either, for that matter."

"You know what I mean. Tell Mahmud not to worry. Our plans for expansion of trade with Arabia will only be good for everyone involved, and that includes the merchants of Mecca. —Maybe I should have a little talk with him myself, eh? He's an excitable sort. I might be able to calm him down."

"Perhaps it would be best to leave him to me," I said.

*   *   *

It was in that moment, Horatius, that I saw where the true crux of the situation lay, and who the true enemy of the Empire is.

The Emperor Julianus need not fret over anything that the Greeks might plan to do here. The Greek incursion into Arabia Deserta was only to be expected. Greeks are businessmen by second nature; Arabia, though it is outside the Empire, lies within the natural Eastern sphere of influence; they would have come down here sooner or later, and, well, here they are. If they intend to try to build stronger trade connections with these desert folk, we have no reason to get upset about that, nor is there the slightest thing that the West can do about it. As Nicomedes has said, the East already controls Aegyptus and Syria and Libya and a lot of other such places that produce goods we need, and we don't suffer thereby. It really is a single empire, in that sense. The Greeks won't push up prices on Eastern commodities to us for fear that we'll do the same thing to them with the tin and copper and iron and timber that flow to them out of the West.

No. The soft and citified Greeks are no menace to us. The real peril here comes from the desert prince, Mahmud son of Abdallah.

One god, he says. *One Arabian people under one king.* And he says, concerning the Greeks, *I will destroy them before they can ruin us.*

He means it. And perhaps he can do it. Nobody has ever unified these Saracens under a single man's rule before, but I think they have never had anyone like Mahmud among them before, either. I had a sudden vision of him, dear Horatius, as I sat there at Nicomedes's nicely laden table: Mahmud with eyes of fire and a gleaming sword held high, leading Saracen warriors northward out of Arabia into Syria Palaestina and Mesopotamia, spreading the message of the One God as he comes and driving the panicky Greeks before his oncoming hordes. The eager peasantry embracing the new creed everywhere: who can resist Mahmud's persuasive tongue, especially when it is backed by the blades of his ever more numerous followers? Onward, then, into Armenia and Cappadocia and Persia, and then there will come a swing westward as well into Aegyptus and Libya. The warriors of Allah everywhere, inflaming the souls of men with the new belief, the new love of virtue and honor. The old, stale, tired religions of the region melting away before it like springtime snowflakes. The wealth of the temples of the false gods divided among the people. Whole legions of idle parasitic priests butchered like cattle as the superstitions are put to rout. The golden statues of the nonexistent gods melted down. A new commonwealth proclaimed in the world, founded on prayer and and sacred law.

Mahmud can say that he has the true god behind him. His eloquence makes you believe it. We of the Empire have only the statues of our gods, and no one of any intelligence has taken those gods seriously for hundreds of years. How can we withstand the fiery onslaught of the new faith? It will roll down upon us like the lava of Vesuvius.

"You take this much too seriously," said Nicomedes the Paphlagonian, when, much later in the evening and after too many more flasks of wine, I confided my fears to him. "Perhaps you should cover your head when you go out of doors at midday, Corbulo. The sun of Arabia is very strong, and it can do great injury to the mind."

No, Horatius. I am right and he is wrong. Once they are launched, the legions of Allah will not be checked until they have marched on through Italia and Gallia and Britannia to the far shores of the Ocean Sea, and all the world is Mahmud's.

It shall not be.

I will save the world from him, Horatius, and perhaps in so doing I will save myself.

Mecca is, of course, a sanctuary city. No man may lift his hand against another within its precincts, under pain of the most awful penalties.

Umar the idol-maker, who served in the temple of the goddess Uzza, understood that. I came to Umar in his workshop, where he sat turning out big-breasted figurines of Uzza, who is the Venus of the Saracens, and bought from him for a handful of coppers a fine little statuette carved from black stone that I hope to show you one of these days, and then I put a gold piece of Justinianus's time before him and told him what I wanted done; and his only response was to tap his finger two times against Justinianus's nose. Not understanding his meaning, I merely frowned.

"This man of whom you speak is my enemy and the enemy of all who love the gods," said Umar the idol-maker, "and I would kill him for you for three copper coins if I did not have a family to support. But the work will involve me in travel, and that is expensive. It cannot be done in Mecca, you know." And he tapped the nose of Justinianus once again. This time I took his meaning. I laid a second gold piece beside the first one, and the idol-maker smiled.

Twelve days ago Mahmud left Mecca on one of his business trips into the lands to the east. He has not returned. He has met with some accident, I fear, in those sandy wastes, and by now the drifting dunes have probably hidden his body forever.

Umar the idol-maker appears to have disappeared also. The talk around town is that he went out into the desert to collect the black stone that he carves his idols from, and some fellow craftsman with whom he was feuding followed him to the quarry. I think you will agree with me, Horatius, that this was a wise thing to arrange. The disappearance of a well-known man like Mahmud will probably engender some inquiries that could ultimately have led in embarrassing directions, but no one except the wife of Umar will care about the vanishing of Umar the idol-maker.

All of this strikes me as highly regrettable, of course. But it was absolutely necessary.

"He's almost certainly dead by this time," Nicomedes said last night. We still dine together frequently. "How very sad, Corbulo. He was an interesting man."

"A very great one, in his way. If he had lived, I think he would have changed the world."

"I doubt that very much," said Nicomedes, in his airy, ever-skeptical Greek way. "But we'll never know, will we?"

"We'll never know," I agreed. I raised my glass. "To Mahmud, poor devil."

"To Mahmud, yes."

And there you have the whole sad story. Go to the Emperor, Horatius. Tell him what I've done. Place it in its full context, against the grand sweep of Imperial history past and present and especially future. Speak to him of Hannibal, of Vercingetorix, of Attila, of all our great enemies of days gone by, and tell him that I have snuffed out in its earliest stages a threat to Roma far more frightening than any of those. Make him understand, if you can, the significance of my deed.

Tell him, Horatius. Tell him that I have saved all the world from conquest: that I have done for him a thing that was utterly essential to do, something which no one else at all could have achieved on his behalf, for who would have had the foresight to see the shape of things to come as I was able to see them? Tell him that.

Above all else, tell him to bring me home. I have dwelled amidst the sands of Arabia long enough. My work is done; I beg for surcease from the dreariness of the desert, the infernal heat, the loneliness of my life here. This is no place for a hero of the Empire.

A.U.C. 1861: THE SECOND WAVE

T hey were the second wave of the invasion. The first had vanished like water into the sands. But now the Emperor Saturninus had sent another fleet to the New World, far larger than the first, and there would be more to follow if need be. "We will beat against their shores as the ocean does, and in the end we will conquer." So the Emperor had declared, five years before, on the day news of the disaster reached the capital. "For Roma is an ocean, too: immense, inexhaustible, irresistible. They will not stand against our might."

Titus Livius Drusus had been at his father's side that day at the Senate when the Emperor made that speech. He was eighteen, then, a highborn young man of Roma who had not yet settled on his path in life. The Emperor's words had left him profoundly stirred. A far-off new world awaiting conquest—whole unexplored continents far beyond the Pillars of Hercules, brimming with the treasure of mysterious copper-skinned people! And there before the Senate was the towering resplendent figure of the Emperor, magnificent in his robes of Imperial purple, crying out in that wonderfully resonant voice of his for brave men to carry the eagles of Roma's legions to these alien empires.

Here I am, young Drusus thought, focusing every atom of his will on the broad forehead of the Emperor. *I will do it! I am the man! I will conquer this Mexico for you!*

But now five years had passed and the Emperor, true as always to his word, had indeed sent that second expedition across the Ocean Sea to the New World. And Drusus, no longer a starry-eyed boy dreaming of strange new worlds to conquer but an experienced soldier of twenty-three beginning to think of marriage and retirement to a country estate, had been offered a commission in the army of invasion and had accepted it, with rather less enthusiasm than he might have shown earlier. The fate of the first expedition was much on his mind. As he stared out now at the darkness of that enigmatic shore lying just ahead he found himself wondering whether he too might be going to leave his bones in this unknown and very probably hostile land, as so many valiant Romans had done before him.

It was shortly before dawn, the third day of the new year 1861. At home the month of Januarius was the coldest of the year, but if Drusus had needed a reminder that he was far from home, that dry, hot breeze blowing toward him out of the new continent would have provided it. At this time of the year not even the wind out of Africa was as warm as this.

Pale pink strands of first light came up over his shoulder. In the thinning darkness ahead he saw the shadowy outlines of a rocky, inhospitable shore that was crowned on a nearby low hill by a massive white building of impressive height and formidable blocky appearance. The land that stretched off to the west in back of it seemed virtually flat and so densely forested that no sign of habitation was visible.

"What do you think of it, Titus?" asked Marcus Junianus, who had come up quietly on deck beside him. He was two years older than Drusus, a former slave of the family, now a freedman. Free or not, he had chosen to follow Drusus to the New World. They had grown up together; though one was of the ancient Roman nobility and the other the descendant of five hundred years of slaves, they were as close as brothers. Not that anyone would take them for brothers, not ever, for Drusus was tall and pale, with soft straight hair and an aristocrat's fine features and elegant manner of speech, and Marcus Junianus was a short, broad-beamed, swarthy man with a flat nose and thick curling hair, who spoke with the inflections of his class and carried himself accordingly. But between themselves they had never let these distinctions form a barrier: to each other they always had been Marcus and Titus, Titus and Marcus, friends, companions, even brothers, in every important way save one.

"I think it's going to give us a struggle, Marcus. You can smell it in the air." In truth the air itself was unwelcoming: hard, pungent, with an odd sort of spiciness to it that was not at all pleasant. "What do you think that big building is? A fortress or a temple?"

"A temple, wouldn't you say? The Norseman told us that this was a land of great temples. And why would they bother to fortify their coast when it's already defended by thousands of miles of empty sea?"

Drusus nodded. "A good point. Still, I don't think it would be very clever of us to try to make our landfall right below it. Go and tell the captain to look for a safer harbor a couple of miles south of here."

Marcus went off to give the order. Drusus leaned on the rail and watched the land as it came more clearly into visibility. It *did* seem uninhabited. Long stands of unfamiliar-looking trees stood shoulder by shoulder to form a solid black wall with no openings in view. And yet there was that temple. Someone had hewn those rocks and assembled that forbidding building atop this coastal headland. *Someone,* yes.

He had spent eight weeks at sea getting to this place, the longest voyage of his life—or anybody's, so far as he knew. In eight weeks you could sail the Great Sea, the Mare Mediterraneum, from end to end any number of times, from the Syrian coast westward to the Pillars of Hercules in Hispania and back to Syria again. The Great Sea! How wrong the ancients had been to give the Mediterraneum so grandiose a name. The Great Sea was a mere puddle compared to this one that they had just crossed, the vast Ocean Sea that separated the worlds. It had been an easy enough journey through steadily warming waters, lengthy and dull but not in any way difficult. You hoisted your sails, you aimed your nose westward, you picked up a following wind and off you went, and, yes, sure enough, in the fullness of time you found yourself in a gentle blue-green sea dotted with tropical islands where you could replenish your supplies of food and water with no interference from the simple naked natives, and then, continuing onward, you arrived soon afterward at what was unmistakably the shore of some huge continent, which must beyond any doubt be that Mexico of which the Norseman spoke.

Looking at it now, Drusus felt not fear, for fear was an emotion that he did not regard as permissible to feel, but a certain sense of—what, he wondered? Uneasiness? A sense that this expedition might not be a particularly wise idea?

The possibility of meeting fierce military resistance did not trouble him. It was close to six hundred years since Romans had done any serious fighting, not since Maximilianus the Great had finished off the Goths and Justinianus had put down the unruly Persians, but each succeeding generation had yearned for a chance to show that the old warrior tradition still lived, and Drusus was glad that his was the one that finally would get the opportunity. So let whatever might come, come. Nor did he worry much about dying in battle: he owed the gods a death in any event, and it was always deemed glorious to die for the Empire.

But dying a *foolish* death—ah, that was something else again. And there were plenty of people back at the capital who felt that Emperor Saturninus's hunger to turn the New World into a Roman province was the wildest of foolishness. Even the mightiest of empires must admit its limits. The Emperor Hadrianus, a thousand years ago, had decided that the Empire was becoming too unwieldy and had turned away from any conquests east of Mesopotamia. Persia and India, and Khitai and Cipangu farther to the east in Asia Ultima where the yellow-skinned folk lived, had been left as independent lands, though tied to Roma by treaties of trade. And now here was Saturninus going the other way, off into the distant west, with dreams of conquest. He had heard tales of the gold of Mexico and another western land called Peru, the Emperor had, and he hungered for that gold. But could this New World be conquered, across such a distance? And, once conquered, could it be administered? Would it not be more intelligent simply to strike up a mercantile alliance with the people of the new continent, sell them Roman goods in return for their abundance of gold, create new prosperity that would bolster the Western Empire against the competition of its prosperous counterpart of the East? Who did Saturninus think he was, Alexander the Great? Even Alexander had turned back from the conquest of distant lands, finally, after reaching the frontiers of India.

Drusus forced himself to brush these treasonous doubts aside. The grandeur that was Roma admitted of no obstacles, he told himself, and, Hadrianus to the contrary, no limits either. The gods had bestowed the world upon the Romans. It said so right there in the first book of Virgil's great poem, that every schoolboy studied: dominion without end. The Emperor Saturninus had decreed that this place was to be Roman, and Drusus had been sent here to help conquer it in Roma's name, and so it would be.

Dawn had come by the time the fleet had moved far enough down the coast to be out of sight of that hilltop temple. By the harsh light of morning he had a clearer view of the irregular rock-bound shore, the sandy beaches, the thick forests. The trees, Drusus saw now, were palms of some sort, but their curving jagged fronds marked them as different from the ones native to the Mediterranean countries. There was no indication of any settlement here.

Disembarking proved to be a tricky business. The sea was shallow here, and the ships were big ones, specially designed for the long voyage. It was impossible for them to drop anchor very close to shore. So the men had to jump down into the water—it was warm, at any rate—and struggle ashore through the surf, heavily laden with arms and supplies. Three men were swept away by a current that carried them off toward the south, and two of them went under and were lost. Seeing that, some of the others held back from leaving the ship. Drusus himself jumped in and waded ashore to encourage them.

The beach was an eerie white, as though it were made up of tiny particles of powdered bone. It felt stiff to the foot, and crunched when trod upon. Drusus scuffed at it, savoring its strangeness. He thrust his staff of office deep into it, telling himself that he was taking possession of this land in the name of Eternal Roma.

The initial phase of the landing took over an hour, as the Romans established themselves on that narrow strip of sand between the sea and the close-packed palms. Throughout it, Drusus was uncomfortably aware of the tales told by the survivors of the first expedition of Mexican arrows that mysteriously appeared out of nowhere and went straight to the most vulnerable places. But nothing like that happened today. He set the landing party immediately to work cutting down trees and building rafts on which they could transport the rest of the men and equipment and provisions to the camp they would establish here. All up and down the coast, the other commanders were doing the same. The fleet, bobbing out there at anchor, was an inspiring sight: the stout heavy hulls, the high bridges, the great square sails aglow with the Imperial colors.

In the dazzling brightness of the new day the last of Drusus's uncertainties evaporated.

"We have come," he said to Marcus Junianus. "Soon we will see this place. And then we will conquer it."

"You should write those words down," Marcus said. "In future centuries schoolchildren will quote them."

"They are not entirely original with me, I'm afraid," said Drusus.

The Norseman who had enmeshed the Emperor Saturninus in these fantasies of conquest was a certain Haraldus, a gigantic fair-haired mountain of a man who had turned up at the Emperor's winter palace at Narbo in Gallia bearing wild tales of golden kingdoms across the sea. He claimed to have seen at least one of them with his own eyes.

These Norsemen, a savage warlike sort, were common sights in both halves of the Empire. A good many of them had made their way to Constantinopolis, which in their language was called Miklagard, "the mighty city." For a hundred years now the Eastern Emperors had maintained an elite corps of these men—Varangians, they called themselves, "Men of the Pledge"—as their personal bodyguards. Often enough they turned up in the Western capital, too, which they also referred to as Miklagard. Because they reminded Western Romans of their ancient enemies the Goths, to whom they were closely related, the Emperors at Roma had never cared to hire their own force of Varangian guards. But it was interesting to listen to the tales these much-traveled seafarers had to tell.

The homeland of these Norsemen was called Scandia, and they were of three main tribes, depending on whether they came from Svea or Norwegia or the territory of the folk who called themselves Dani. But they all spoke more or less the same uncouth language and all were big, short-tempered people, the men and the women both, resourceful and vengeful and ruthless, who would carry two or three well-honed weapons upon their persons at all times and reached swiftly for their swords or their daggers or their battle-axes whenever they felt offended. Their small sturdy ships traveled freely and fearlessly through the half-frozen waterways of their northern world, carrying them to remote places in the north never visited and scarcely known by Romans, and Norse traders would come down out of those icy lands bearing ivory, furs, seal oil, whale oil, and other such goods much desired in the marketplaces of Europa and Byzantium.

This Haraldus was a Svean who said his travels had taken him to Islandius and Grenelandius, which were the Norse names for two islands in the northern part of the Ocean Sea where they had settled in the past two hundred years. Then he had gone onward even farther, to a place they called Vinilandius, or Wineland, which was on the shore of an enormous body of land—a continent, surely—and then, with a little band of companions, he had set out on a voyage of exploration down the entire coast of that continent.

It was a journey that took him two or three years, he said. From time to time they would go ashore, and when they did they often encountered small villages peopled by naked or half-naked folk of unusual appearance, with dark glossy hair, and skin that was dark also, though not in the way that the skins of Africans are dark, and strong-featured faces marked by jutting cheekbones and beak-like noses. Some of these folk were friendly, some were not. But they were all quite backward, artless people who lived by hunting and fishing and dwelled in little tents fashioned from the hides of animals. Their tiny encampments seemed to have little to offer in the way of opportunities for trade.

But as Haraldus and his companions continued south, things became more interesting. The air was softer and warmer here, the settlements more prosperous-looking. The wandering Norsemen found good-sized villages built beside lofty flat-topped earthen mounds that bore what appeared to be temples at their summits. The people wore elaborate woven garments and bedecked themselves with copper earrings and necklaces made of the teeth of bears. They were a farming folk, who greeted the travelers pleasantly and offered them meals of grain and stewed meats, served in clay vessels decorated with strange images of serpents that had feathers and wings.

The Norsemen worked out an effective method of communicating with these mound-building people by simple sign language, and learned that there were even richer lands farther to the south, lands where the temple mounds were built not of earth but of stone, and where the jewelry was made not of copper but of gold. How distant these places were was unclear: the voyagers just were told, with many gestures of outflung arms, to head down the coast until they reached their destination. And so they did. They went on southward and the land, which had been on their right all the way down from Wineland, dropped away from them so that they were in open sea. The mound people had warned them that that would happen. Some instinct told them to swing westward here and then south again when they picked up signs of an approaching shore, and after a time there was land ahead and they saw the coastline of the unknown western continent once again.

Here they landed and went ashore. And everything that the mound-building people of the northern land had said proved to be true.

"There is a great nation there," Haraldus told the Emperor. "The citizens, who are extremely friendly, wear finely woven robes and they have an astounding abundance of gold, which they use in every imaginable way. Not only do men and women both wear golden jewelry, but even the toys of the children are of gold, and the chieftains take their meals on golden plates." He spoke of colossal stone pyramids like those of Aegyptus, of shining marble temples, of immense statues depicting bizarre gods that looked like monsters. And, best of all, this wealthy land—Yucatan, its people called it— was only the nearest of many rich kingdoms in this remarkable new world across the sea. There was another and even greater one, the Norsemen had been informed, off to the west and north of it. That one was called Mexico, or perhaps Mexico was the name for this entire territory, Yucatan included: that was unclear. Sign language could communicate only so much. And still farther away, some inconceivable distance to the south, was still another land named Peru, so wealthy that it made the wealth of Mexico and Yucatan seem like nothing at all.

Upon hearing this the Norsemen realized that they had stumbled upon something too great for them to be able to exploit by themselves. They agreed to split into two parties. One group, headed by a certain Olaus Danus, would remain in Yucatan and learn whatever they could about these kingdoms. The other, under the command of Haraldus the Svean, would carry the news of their discovery to the Emperor Saturninus and offer to lead a Roman expedition to the New World on a mission of conquest and plunder, in return for a generous share of the loot.

Norsemen are a quarrelsome lot, though. By the time Haraldus and his friends had retraced their coastal path back to Vinilandius in the far north, feuding over rank aboard their little ship had reduced their numbers from eleven to four. One of these four was slain by an angry brother-in-law in Vinilandius; another perished in a dispute over a woman during a stop in Islandius; what happened to the third man, Haraldus did not say, but he alone reached the mainland of Europa to tell the tale of golden Mexico to Saturninus.

"Instantly the Emperor was gripped by an overpowering fascination," said Drusus's father, the Senator Lucius Livius Drusus, who was at court the day Haraldus had his audience. "You could see it happening. It was as though the Norsemen had cast a spell over him."

That very day the Emperor proclaimed the western continent to
be Nova Roma, the new overseas extension of the Empire—the
Western Empire. With a province of such fantastic opulence gathered under its sway, the West would gain permanent superiority in
its rivalry with its increasingly troublesome sister realm, the Empire
of the East. Saturninus raised a veteran general named Valerius
Gargilius Martius to the rank of Proconsul of Mexico and gave him
command of three legions. Haraldus, though not even a Roman citizen, was dubbed a duke of the realm, a station superior to Gargilius
Martius's, and the two men were instructed to cooperate in the venture. For the voyage across the Ocean Sea a fleet of specially designed ships was constructed that had the great size of cargo vessels
but the swiftness of warships. They were powered by sails as well as
oars and were big enough to carry an invading army's full comple-
ment of equipment, including horses, catapults, tents, forges, and all
the rest. "They are not a warlike race, these Mexicans," Haraldus assured the Emperor. "You will conquer them with ease."

Of all the thousands of men who set forth with great fanfare
from the Gallian port of Massilia, just seventeen returned home,
fourteen months later. They were parched and dazed and enfeebled
to the point of collapse from an interminable ocean voyage of terrible hardship in a small open raft. Only three had sufficient strength
even to frame words, and they, like the others, died within a few
days of their arrival. Their stories were barely coherent. They gave
rambling accounts of invisible enemies, arrows emerging out of
nowhere, frightful poisonous insects, appalling heat. The friendli-
ness of the citizens of Yucatan had been greatly overestimated, it
seemed. Apparently the whole expeditionary force but for these seventeen had perished, one way or another. Of the fate of Duke Haraldus the Norseman and of the Proconsul Valerius Gargilius
Martius they could tell nothing. Presumably they were dead too.
The only thing that was certain was that the expedition had been a
total failure.

At the capital, people solemnly reminded one another of the
tale of Quinctilius Varus, the general whom Augustus Caesar had
sent into the Teutonic forests to bring the northern barbarians under control. He too had had three legions under his command,

and through his stupidity and incompetence they were massacred virtually to the last man in an ambush in the woods. The elderly Augustus never entirely recovered from the catastrophe. "Quinctilius Varus, give me back my legions!" he would cry, over and over. And he said no more about sending armies to conquer the wild Teutons.

But Saturninus, young and boundlessly ambitious, reacted differently to the loss of his expedition. Construction of a new and greater invasion fleet began almost immediately. *Seven* legions would be sent this time. The Empire's most capable military men would lead it. Titus Livius Drusus, who had already won distinction for himself in some minor border skirmishes in Africa, where even at this late date wild desert tribes occasionally caused trouble, was among the bright young officers chosen for a high position. "It is madness to go," his father muttered. Drusus knew that his father was growing old and conservative, but still he was a man of profound understanding of events. Drusus also knew, though, that if he refused this commission, which the Emperor himself had offered him, he was dooming himself to a lifetime of border duty in places so dismal that they would make him long most keenly for the comforts of the African desert.

"Well," said Marcus Junianus as he and Drusus stood side by side on the beach, supervising the unloading of the provisions, "so here we are in Yucatan. A strange sort of name for a place that is! What do you think it means, Titus?"

" 'I don't understand you.' "

"Pardon me? I thought I was speaking very clearly, Titus. I said, 'What do you think it means?' I was referring to Yucatan."

Drusus chuckled. "I heard you. And I answered you. You asked a question, and 'I don't understand you' is what I replied. All around the world for centuries now we've been going up to the natives of one far-off place or another and asking them in nice grammatical Latin what that place is called. And since they don't know any Latin, they reply 'I don't understand you' in their own language, and we put that down as the name of the place. In this case it was Norse, I guess, that they don't happen to speak. And so, when Haraldus or one of his friends asked the natives the name of their kingdom, they answered 'Yucatan,' which I'm almost certain isn't the name of the place at all, but merely means—"

"Yes," said Marcus Junianus. "I think I grasp the point."

The immediate task at hand was to set up a camp as quickly as they could, before their arrival attracted the attention of the natives. Once they were secure here at the water's edge they could begin sending scouting expeditions inland to discover the location of the native towns and assess the size of the challenge facing them.

For most of the voyage the fleet had kept close together, but as the ships approached the coast of Yucatan they had fanned out widely, by prearrangement, so that the initial Roman beachhead would cover twenty-five or thirty miles of the shoreline. Three legions, eighteen thousand men, would constitute the central camp, under the command of the Consul Lucius Aemilius Capito. Then there would be two subsidiary camps of two legions apiece. Drusus, who had the rank of legionary legate, would be in command of the northernmost camp, and the southernmost one was to be headed by Masurius Titianus, a man from Pannonia who was one of the Emperor's special favorites, though nobody in Roma could quite understand why.

Drusus stood in the midst of the bustle, watching with pleasure as the camp swiftly came together. Workmen swarmed everywhere. The expedition was well equipped: Saturninus had poured a fortune into it, an amount equal to the total annual revenue of several provinces, so they said. Brawny loggers quickly chopped down dozens of the palm trees that fringed the beach and the carpenters got busy squaring the lumber off to use in constructing the palisades. The surveyors laid out boundaries for the camp along the beach's widest part and marked guidelines for its interior: the central street, the place where the legate's tent would go, the tents of the craftsmen, of the legionaries, of the scribes and recorders, the site of the stables, the workshops, the granary, and all the rest. The horses had to be brought ashore also and given an opportunity to regain their land legs after their long confinement aboard the ships.

As the guide stakes went into the ground, the infantrymen set about erecting the rows of leather tents where they would dwell. Foragers, accompanied by an armed force, made the first ventures inland to find sources of food and water.

These were experienced men. Everyone knew his job. By night-fall, which came on surprisingly early—but this was winter, after all, Drusus reflected, warm though the climate was—the outline of the camp was clearly delineated and the beginnings of a rampart had risen. There did not seem to be any rivers or streams nearby, but, as Drusus had suspected from the presence of so dense a forest, fresh water was readily obtainable even so: the ground, which was ex-ceedingly stony beneath its shallow covering of soil, was honey-combed everywhere with passageways through which underground water came welling up. One of these wells lay not far inland, and a team of engineers started to sketch out the route of a shallow canal that would carry its cool, sweet water the short distance to the camp. The foragers had also found abundant wildlife in the adjacent forest: a multitude of small and apparently fearless deer, herds of what seemed to be little pigs of a kind that had no tails and stiff upright ears, and vast numbers of large, very odd-looking birds with brilliant reddish-green plumage and great fleshy wattles at their throats. So far, so good. The Norseman had said they would have no difficulties finding provisions, and it looked as though he had told the truth about that.

At midday Drusus sent a runner down the beach toward the central camp to bear news of his landing. The man returned a little before sundown with word from the Consul Lucius Aemilius Capito that the main body of men had come ashore as well, and the work of building a camp was under way. To the south, Masurius Titianus had also effected his landing without encountering opposition from the natives.

The first night in the camp was a tense one, but first nights in camp in an unfamiliar place always were. Evening dropped over them like a shroud, with scarcely any interval between sunset and darkness. There was no moon. The stars above the camp were un-usually brilliant, but they were arranged in the strange, unsettling configuration of the southern latitudes. The heat of the day did not abate, and the men in the tents complained of the stifling atmosphere inside. Raucous screeching cries came from the forest. Birds? Monkeys? Who could say? At least they didn't sound like tigers. Clouds of mosquitoes appeared, pretty much similar to those of the Old World, but the humming noise that they made as they swooped in upon one was much nastier, almost jubilant in its intensity, and their stings were maddeningly fierce. At one point Drusus thought he saw a flight of bats passing close overhead. He loathed bats with a powerful loathing that he did not at all understand. Perhaps they are not bats but only owls, he thought. Or some new kind of eagle that flies by night.

Because the camp did not yet have a proper rampart, Drusus tripled the ordinary watch. He spent much of his night strolling among the sentries himself. They were uneasy and would appreciate his presence. They too had heard those tales of arrows whistling out of nowhere, and it heartened them to have their commander sharing their risks on this first and most uncertain of nights.

But the night passed without incident. In the morning, as work on the palisade resumed, Drusus summoned Marcus Junianus, who was serving as his prefect of the camp, and ordered him to begin assembling the scouting party that would attempt to find the location of the nearest Mexican village. Junianus saluted smartly and hurried off.

Later in the day Drusus sent for him again, on another matter. A long while went by; and then the messenger returned with the news that Junianus was not in the camp.

"Not in the camp?" said Drusus, puzzled.

"No, sir. I am told that you sent him out on a scouting mission this morning, sir."

Drusus stared. Anger rose in him like a fountain, and it was all he could do to keep from striking the man. But that would be stupidly misdirected anger, he knew. Marcus was the one at fault, not the messenger. He had never given Marcus any order to go out scouting, just to get a team of scouts together. With the rampart only half finished, it was much too soon to dispatch scouts: the last thing Drusus wanted now was to alert the natives prematurely to their presence, which could easily happen if the scouts stumbled incautiously into one of their villages. And in any case he had never had any intention of sending Marcus himself out with those scouts. Scouts were expendable; Marcus was not.

He realized that this was something he should have foreseen. Marcus, now that he was a freedman, was forever trying to demonstrate his civic valor. More than once he had put himself needlessly in danger when he and Drusus were serving on border patrol in Africa. Sometimes one had to take deliberate risks, yes—Drusus himself, standing watch with his men this night past, had done just that. But there were necessary risks and there were foolish ones. The thought of Marcus blithely misunderstanding his intent so that he could lead the scouting party in person was infuriating.

There was nothing that could be done about it now, though. He would have to take it up with Marcus when the scouting party returned, and forbid him to place himself at risk again.

The problem was that the day passed, and sundown came and deepened swiftly into black night, and the scouts did not return.

Drusus had had no discussion with Marcus about the length of time the scouting mission was supposed to stay out. He had never had it in mind himself to ask the scouts to remain out overnight, not the very first night; but what Marcus had had in mind, Jupiter alone could say. Maybe he planned to keep going until he found something worth finding.

Morning came. No Junianus. At midday, deeply exasperated and more than a little apprehensive, Drusus sent a second band of scouts off to look for the first ones, telling them that under no circumstances were they to remain out after dark. But they returned in less than three hours, and the instant Drusus saw the look on the face of their captain, a Thracian named Rufus Trogus, he knew there was trouble.

"They have been captured, sir," said Trogus without any preamble whatever.

Drusus worked hard to conceal his dismay. "Where? By whom?"

The Thracian told the story quickly and concisely. A thousand paces inland due west and two hundred paces to the north they had come upon signs of a struggle, broken branches, scuffed soil, a fallen

scabbard, a javelin, a sandal. They were able to follow a trail of disturbed undergrowth for another hundred paces or so westward;
then the forest closed over itself and there was no further sign of human presence, not so much as a bent twig. It was as though the attackers, having surprised and very quickly overcome the scouting
party, had in short order melted into the air, and their prisoners also.

"You saw no bodies?"

"None, sir. Nor signs of bloodshed."

"Let's be grateful for that much, I suppose," Drusus said.

But it was a miserable situation. Two days on shore and he had
already lost half a dozen men, his best friend among them. At this
moment the natives might be putting them to the torture, or worse.
And also he had inadvertently sent word to the folk of this land that
an invading army had once again landed on their shores. They
would have found that out sooner or later anyway, of course. But
Drusus had wanted to have some sense of where he was located in
relation to the enemy, first. Not to mention having his camp fully
walled in, his siege engines and other war machinery set up and
ready, the horses of the cavalry properly accustomed to being on
land once again, and all the rest.

Instead it was possible now that they might find themselves under attack at any moment, and not in any real way prepared for it.
How splendid, that Titus Livius Drusus would be remembered
down the ages for having so swiftly placed the second New World
expedition on the path to the same sort of catastrophe that had overwhelmed the first!

It was appropriate, Drusus knew, to send word of what had
happened down the beach to Lucius Aemilius Capito's camp. One
was supposed to keep one's superior officer informed of things like
this. He hated the idea of confessing such stupidity, even if the stupidity had been Marcus Junianus's, not his own. But the responsibility ultimately was his, he knew. He scribbled a note to the effect
that he had sent a scouting party out and it appeared to have been
captured by enemies. Nothing more than that. No apology for having let scouts go out before the camp was completely defended.
Bad enough that the thing had happened; there was no need to

point out to Capito how serious a breach of standard tactics it had been.

From Capito, toward nightfall, came back a frosty memorandum asking to be kept up to date on developments. The implication was there, more in what Capito did not say than in what he did, that if the natives did happen to strike at Drusus's camp in the next day or two, Drusus would be on his own in dealing with it.

No attack came. All the next day Drusus moved restlessly about the camp, urging his engineers onward with the job of finishing the palisade. When new foraging parties went out to hunt for deer and pigs and those great birds, he saw to it that they were accompanied by three times as many soldiers as would ordinarily be deemed necessary, and he worried frantically until they returned. He sent another party of scouts out under Rufus Trogus, too, to investigate the zone just beyond the place where Marcus and his men had been taken and look for clues to their disappearance. But Trogus came back once more with no useful information.

Drusus slept badly that night, plagued by mosquitoes and the unending shrieks and boomings of the jungle beasts and the moist heat that wrapped itself about him with almost tangible density. A bird in a tree that could not have been very far from his tent began to sing in a deep, throbbing voice, a tune so mournful it sounded to Drusus like a funeral dirge. He speculated endlessly about the fate of Marcus. They have not killed him, he told himself earnestly, because if they had wanted to do that, they would have done it in the original ambush in the forest. No, they've taken him in for interrogation. They are trying to get information from him about our numbers, our intentions, our weapons. Then he reflected once more that they were unlikely to get such information out of Marcus without torturing him. And then—

Morning came, eventually. Drusus emerged from his tent and saw sentries of the watch coming down the beach in his direction.

Marcus Junianus was with them, looking weary and tattered, and trailing along behind were half a dozen equally ragged Romans who must have been the scouts he took with him on his venture into the forest.

* * *

Drusus suppressed his anger. There would be time enough for
scolding Junianus later. The flood of relief that surged through him
took precedence over such things, anyway.

He embraced Junianus warmly, and stepped back to study him
for signs of injury—he saw none—and said, finally, "Well, Marcus? I
didn't expect you to stay away overnight, you know."

"Nor I, Titus. A few hours, a little sniffing around, and then
we'd turn back, that was what I thought. But we had hardly gone
anywhere when they fell upon us from the treetops. We fought, but
there must have been a hundred of them. It was all over in moments.
They tied us with silken cord—it felt like silk, anyway, but perhaps it
was some other kind of smooth rope—and carried us away on their
shoulders through the forest. Their city is less than an hour's march
away."

"Their *city*, you say? In the midst of this wilderness, a city?"

"A city, yes. That is the only word for it. I couldn't tell you how
big it is, but it would be a city by anyone's reckoning, a very great
one. It is the size of Neapolis, at the least. Perhaps even the size of
Roma." The forest had been cleared away over an enormous area, he
said, gesturing with both arms. He told of broad plazas surrounding
gleaming temples and palaces of white stone that were greater in
their dimensions than the Capitol in Roma, of towering pyramids
with hundreds of steps leading to the shrines at their summits, of
terraced avenues of the same finely chiseled white stone stretching
off into the jungled distance, with mighty statues of fearsome gods
and monstrous beasts lining them for their entire lengths. The population of the city, Junianus said, was incalculably huge, and its wealth
had to be extraordinary. Even the common folk, though they wore
little more than simple cotton tunics, looked prosperous. The majestic priests and nobles who moved freely among them were magnificent beyond belief. Junianus struggled for words to describe them.
Garbed in the skins of tigers, they were, with green and red capes of
bright feathers on their shoulders, and brilliant feather headdresses
that rose to extravagant, incredible heights. Pendants of smooth

green stone hung from their earlobes, and great necklaces of that same stone were draped about their necks, and around their waists and wrists and ankles they had bangles of shining gold. Gold was everywhere, said Junianus. It was to these people as copper or tin was to Romans. You could not escape the sight of it: gold, gold, gold.

"We were fed, and then we were taken before their king," Junianus told Drusus. "With his own hands he poured out drink for us, using polished bowls of the same smooth green stone that they employ for their jewelry. It was a strong sweet liquor, brewed of honey, I think, with the herbs of this land in it, strange to the taste, but pleasing—and when we had refreshed ourselves he asked us our names, and the purpose for which we had come, and—"

"He *asked* you, Marcus? And you understood what he was saying? But how was that possible?"

"He was speaking Latin," Junianus replied, as though that should have been self-evident. "Not very good Latin, of course, but one can expect nothing better from a Norseman, is that not so? In fact it was very poor Latin indeed. But he spoke it well enough for us to comprehend what he was saying, after a fashion. Naturally I didn't tell him outright that I was a scout for an invading army, but it was clear enough that he—"

"Wait a moment," Drusus said. His head was beginning to spin. "Surely I'm not hearing this right. The king of these people is a *Norseman?*"

"Did I not tell you, Titus?" Junianus laughed. "A Norseman, yes! He's been here for years and years. His name is Olaus Danus, one of those who came down from Vinilandius with Haraldus the Svean on that first voyage long ago, when the Norse discovered this place, and he's lived here ever since. They treat him almost like a god. There he sits on a glistening throne, with a scepter of green stone in his hand and a bunch of golden necklaces around his throat, and wearing a crown of feathers half as tall as I am, and they strew flower petals before him whenever he gets up and walks, and crouch before him and cover their eyes with their hands so he won't blind them with his splendor, and—"

"Their king is a Norseman," Drusus said, lost in astonishment.

"A great hulking giant of a Norseman with a black beard and eyes like a devil's," said Junianus. "Who wants to see you right away. Send me your general, he said. I must speak with him. Bring him to me tomorrow, early in the day. There should not be any soldiers with him. The general must come alone. He told me that I am permitted to accompany you as far as the place in the forest where we were set upon, but then I must leave you, and you must wait by yourself for his men to fetch you. He was very clear on that point, I have to say."

This was rapidly getting beyond the scope of Drusus's official authority. He saw no choice but to take himself down the shore in person and report the whole business to the Consul Lucius Aemilius Capito.

Capito's camp, Drusus was pleased to see, was not nearly as far along in construction as Drusus's own. But the Consul had had his tent, at least, erected—unsurprisingly, it was quite a grand one—and Capito himself, flanked by what looked like a small regiment of clerks, was at his desk, going over a thick stack of inventory sheets and engineering reports.

Looking up, he gave Drusus a bilious glare, as though he regarded a visit from the legionary legate of the northern camp as an irritating intrusion on his contemplation of the inventory sheets. There had never been much amiability between them. Capito, a hard-faced, slab-jawed man of fifty, had evidently had some serious battles with Drusus's father in the Senate, long ago, over the size of military appropriations—Drusus was unsure of the details, and did not want to know—and had never taken the trouble to conceal his annoyance at having had the younger Drusus wished off on him in so high a position of command.

"A problem?" Capito asked.

"It would seem so, Consul."

He set the situation forth in the fewest possible sentences: the safe return of the captured scouts, the discovery of the startling proximity of a major city with its inexplicable Norse king, and the request that Drusus take himself there, alone, as an ambassador to that king.

Capito seemed to have forgotten all about the missing party of scouts. Drusus could see him rummaging through his memory as though their disappearance were some episode out of the reign of Lucius Agrippa. Then at last he fixed his cold gaze on Drusus and said, "Well? What do you intend to do?"

"Go to him, I suppose."

"You suppose? What other option is there? By some miracle this man has made himself king of these copper-skinned barbarians, the gods alone know how, and now he summons a Roman officer to a conference, quite possibly for the sake of concluding a treaty that will convey this entire nation to the authority of His Imperial Majesty, which was the intent of these Norsemen in the first place, I remind you—and the officer hesitates?"

"Well—but if the Norseman has some other and darker intention, Consul—I will be going to him without an escort, I remind you—"

"As an ambassador. Even a Norseman would not lightly take the life of an ambassador, Drusus. But if he does, well, Drusus, I will see to it that you are properly avenged. You have my pledge on that. We will extract rivers of blood from them for every drop of yours that is shed."

And, favoring Drusus with a basilisk smile, the Consul Lucius Aemilius Capito returned his attention to his inventories and reports.

It was well past dark by the time Drusus reached his own camp again. The usual beasts were howling madly in the woods; the usual mysterious flying creatures were flitting by overhead; the mosquitoes had awakened and were seeking their nightly feast. But by now he had spent four nights in this place. He was growing accustomed to it. A little to his own surprise, he passed a good night's sleep, and in the morning made ready for his journey to the city of the copper-skinned folk.

"He will not harm you," said Marcus Junianus gloomily, as they reached the trampled place in the forest where they were supposed to part company. "I'm entirely certain of that." His tone did not carry much conviction. "The Norse are savage with each other, but they'd never lift a hand against a Roman officer."

"I don't expect that he will," Drusus said. "But thank you for your reassurance. Is this the place?"

"This is the place. Titus—"

Drusus pointed back toward the camp. "Go, Marcus. Let's not make a drama out of this. I'll speak to this Olaus, we'll find out how things stand here, and by evening I'll be back, with some idea of the strategy to follow next. Go. Leave me, Marcus."

Junianus gave him a quick embrace and a sad smile and went trudging off. Drusus leaned against the rough trunk of a palm tree and waited for his barbarian guides to arrive.

Perhaps an hour went by. Though it was only an hour past sunrise, the heat was already becoming troublesome. If this is what winter is like here, he thought, I wonder how we will survive a summer. Drusus had chosen to dress formally, greaves and chain mail, the crested helmet, his cloak of office as a legate, his short ceremonial sword. He had wanted to muster as much Roman majesty as he could when he came before the barbaric king of these barbaric people. But it was all a little too much for the warmth of this place, and he was sweating as though he were at the baths. An insect or two had penetrated his armor, too: he was aware of bothersome ticklings along his back. He was beginning to feel a little faint by the time he caught sight of a line of marchers emerging out of the thickets in front of him, moving forward without making a sound.

There were six of them, bare to the waist, dusky-skinned, with tightly set, unsmiling mouths, noses like hatchet blades, and odd sloping foreheads. They were amazingly short, no bigger than small women, but their dignity and gravity of bearing made them seem taller than they were, and also they wore headdresses of jutting green and yellow feathers that rose to an astounding height. Three were armed with spears, three with nasty-looking swords made of some dark, glassy stone, their blades notched like those of saws.

Were these his guides, or his executioners?

Drusus stood motionless as they approached. It was an uneasy moment for him. Of personal fear he had none. As ever, he understood that he owed the gods a death, sooner or later. But, as ever, he did not want it to be a shameful, embarrassing death—walking with his eyes wide open into the clutches of a murderous enemy, for instance. In times of danger he had always prayed that if the time of his death were at hand, let it at least serve some useful purpose for the Empire. There could be no purpose in dying stupidly.

But these men hadn't come here to kill him. They reached his side and took up positions flanking him, three before, three behind, and studied him for a moment with eyes black as night and utterly expressionless. Then one of them signaled with the tips of two fingers, and they led him away into the forest.

The hour was still short of noon when they reached the city. Marcus Junianus had not exaggerated its splendor. If anything he had underestimated its grandeur, not having the command of language that would allow him to describe the place in all its majesty. Drusus had grown up in Urbs Roma, and that was his standard of greatness in a city, eternal Roma, than which there was no city greater, not even, so he had heard, Constantinopolis of the East. But this city seemed just as imposing as Roma, in its very different way. And, he realized, it might not even be the capital city of these people. Once more Drusus began to wonder just how simple the conquest of this New World was going to be.

He was in a plaza of titanic size. It was bordered on each side by vast stone buildings, some rectangular, some pyramidal, all of them alien in style but undeniably grand. There was something strange about them, and after a moment he realized what it was: there were no arches anywhere. These people did not seem to make use of the arch in their construction. And yet their buildings were very large, very solid-looking. Their façades were elaborately carved with geometric designs and painted in brilliant colors. Long rows of stone columns stood before them, engraved with savage, barbaric figures that looked like warriors in full regalia, no two alike. The columns too were painted: red, blue, green, yellow, brown. In the very center of the plaza was a stone altar with the statue of a double-headed tiger on it; to each side of it were curious figures of a reclining man with his knees drawn up and his head turned to one side. Some god, no doubt, for each figure's upturned belly bore a flat stone disk that was covered with offerings of fruit and grain.

Throngs of people were everywhere about, just as Marcus had said, commoners in their skimpy tunics, nobles in their flamboyant headdresses and robes, all of them on foot, as though neither the cart nor the litter was known here. Nor was there a single horse in sight. Whatever had to be carried was being carried by men, even the heaviest of burdens. The creatures must not be found in this New World, Drusus thought.

Nobody seemed to take notice of Drusus as he passed among them.

His guardians marched him to the flat-topped pyramid on the far side of the plaza and up an interminable stone staircase to the colonnaded shrine at the top.

Olaus the Norseman was waiting for him there, enthroned in regal majesty with the scepter of green stone in his hand. Two richly costumed natives, high priests, perhaps, stood beside him. He rose as Drusus appeared and extended the scepter toward him in a gesture of the greatest solemnity.

He was so startling a sight that Drusus felt a sudden momentary weakness of his knees. Not even the Emperor of Roma, the Augustus Saturninus Caesar Imperator himself, had ever stirred any such awe in him. Saturninus, with whom Drusus had had personal audience on more than one occasion, was a tall, commanding-looking figure, majestic, unmistakably royal. For all that, though, you knew he was only a man in a purple robe. But this Olaus, this Norse king of Yucatan, seemed like—what?—a god?—a demon? Something prodigious and frightening, a fantastic, almost unreal being.

His costume itself was terrifying: the tiger pelt around his waist, the necklace and pendant of bear's teeth and massive green stones lying over his bare chest, the long golden armlets, the heavy earrings, the intricate crown of gaudy feathers and blazing gems. But this outlandish garb, nightmarish though it was, formed only a part of the demonic effect. The man himself provided the rest. Olaus was as tall as anyone Drusus ever had seen, better than half a head taller than Drusus himself, and Drusus was a tall man. His body was a massive column, broad through the shoulders, deep through the chest. And his face—

Oh, that face! Square-jawed, with a great outthrust chin, and dark blazing eyes set wide apart in deep, brooding sockets, and a ferocious snarling maw of a mouth. Though most of his countrymen were blond and ruddy, Olaus's hair was black, a wild mane above and a dense, bristling beard covering his cheeks and much of his throat. It was the face of a beast, a beast in human form, cruel, implacable, remorseless, enduring. But the intelligence of a man shone out of those eyes.

Marcus's description had not even begun to prepare him for this man. Drusus wondered if he was expected to salute him by some sort of abasement, kneeling, genuflecting, something like that. No matter: he would not do it. But it seemed almost to be the appropriate thing to do before a man of this sort.

Olaus came forward until he was disturbingly close and said, in bad but comprehensible Latin, "You are the general? What is your name? Your rank?"

"Titus Livius Drusus is my name, son of the Senator Lucius Livius Drusus. I hold the appointment of legionary legate by the hand of Saturninus Augustus."

The Norseman made a low rumbling sound, a kind of bland growl, as though to indicate that he had heard, but was not impressed. "I am Olaus the Dane, who has become king of this land." Indicating the man on his left, a scowling, hawk-nosed individual dressed nearly as richly as he was himself, the Norseman said, "He is Na Poot Uuc, the priest of the god Chac-Mool. This other is Hunac Ceel Cauich, who is the master of the holy fire."

Drusus acknowledged them with nods. Na Poot Uuc, he thought. Hunac Ceel Cauich. The god Chac-Mool. These are not names. These are mere noises.

At another signal from the Norseman, the priest of Chac-Mool produced a bowl of that polished green stone that they seemed to admire so much here, and the master of the holy fire filled it with the same sweet liquor that Marcus had told him of receiving. Drusus sipped it cautiously. It was both sweet and spicy at the same time, and he suspected that it would turn his head if he had very much of it. A few politic sips and he looked up, as though sated. The priest of Chac-Mool indicated that he should drink more. Drusus pretended to do so, and handed the bowl back.

Now the Norseman returned to his throne. He beckoned for some of the honey-wine himself, drank a bowlful of it at a single draught, and, transfixing Drusus with those fiery, fearsome eyes of his, launched abruptly into a rambling tale of his adventures in the New World. The story was difficult to follow, for Olaus's command of Latin had probably never been strong to begin with, and plainly he had not spoken it at all for many years. His grammar was largely guesswork and his sentences were liberally interspersed with phrases from his own thick-sounding northern tongue and, for all Drusus knew, the local lingo as well. But it was possible for Drusus to piece together at least the gist of the story.

Which was that Olaus, after Haraldus and his friends had left him here in Yucatan and sailed off toward Europa to bring the news of the New World to the Emperor, had very quickly established himself as a man of consequence and power among the people of this place, whom he referred to as the Maia. Whether that was their own name for themselves or some invention of Olaus's, Drusus could not tell. He doubted that the word had any relationship to the Roman month of the same name. Nor did he get any clear notion of what had become of the other Norsemen who had stayed behind in the New World with Olaus, and he was shrewd enough not to ask: he knew well enough what a brawling, murderous bunch this race was. Put seven of them in a room and there will be four left alive by morning, and one of those will set fire to the building and leave the other three to burn as he slips away. Surely Olaus's companions all were dead by now.

Olaus, though, through his size and strength and unshakable self-assurance, had managed to make himself first the war leader of these people, and then their king, and, by now, virtually their god. It had all happened because a neighboring city, not long after Olaus's arrival, had chosen to make war against this one. There was no sovereign authority in this land, Drusus gathered: each city was independent, though sometimes they allied themselves in loose confederacies against their enemies. These Maia all were fierce fighters; but when war broke out, Olaus trained the warriors of this city where he was living in military methods of a kind they had never imagined, a combination of Roman discipline and Norse brutality. Under his leadership they became invincible. City after city fell to

Olaus's armies. For the first time in Maian history a kind of empire was formed here in Yucatan.

It seemed to Drusus that Olaus claimed also to have made contact with the other kingdoms of the New World, the one to the west in Mexico and the one to the south that was called Peru. Had he gone to those distant places himself, or simply sent envoys? Hard to tell: the narrative swept along too quickly, and the Norseman's way of speaking was too muddled for Drusus to be certain of what he was saying. But it did appear that the peoples of all these lands had been made aware of the white-skinned, black-bearded stranger from afar who had brought the warring cities of Yucatan together in an empire.

It was the troops of that empire that met the three legions of Saturninus's first expedition, and wiped them out with ease.

The Maian armies had used the knowledge of Roman methods of warfare that Olaus had instilled in them to defend themselves against the legions' attack. And when they made their own response, it was to strike from ambush in a way that Roman military techniques, magnificently effective though they had proven everywhere else, were entirely unsuited to handle.

"And so they all perished," Olaus concluded, "except for a few that I allowed to escape to tell the tale. The same will happen to you and your troops. Pack up now, Roman. Go home, while you still can."

Those eyes, those frightful eyes, were bright with contempt.

"Save yourselves," Olaus said. "Go."

"Impossible," said Drusus. "We are Romans."

"Then it will be war. And you will be destroyed."

"I serve the Emperor Saturninus. He has laid claim to these lands."

Olaus let out a diabolical guffaw. "Let your Emperor claim the moon, my friend! He'll have an easier time of conquering it, I promise you. This land is mine."

"Yours?"

"Mine. Earned by my sweat and, yes, my blood. I am the master here. I am king, and I am their god, even. They look upon me as Odin and Thor and Frey taken all together." And then, seeing

Drusus's uncomprehending look: "Jupiter and Mars and Apollo, I suppose you would say. They are all the same, these gods. I am Olaus. I reign here. Take your army and leave." He spat. *"Romans!"*

Lucius Aemilius Capito said, "What kind of an army do they have, then?"

"I saw no army. I saw a city, peasants, stonemasons, weavers, goldsmiths, priests, nobles," Drusus said. "And the Dane."

"The Dane, yes. A wild man, a barbarian. We'll bring his pelt home and nail it up on a post in front of the Capitol the way one would nail up the pelt of a beast. But where is their army, do you think? You saw no barracks? You saw no drilling grounds?"

"I was in the heart of a busy city," Drusus told the Consul. "I saw temples and palaces, and what I think were shops. In Roma, does one see any barracks in the middle of the Forum?"

"They are only naked savages who fight with bows and javelins," said Capito. "They don't even have a cavalry, it seems. Or crossbows, or catapults. We'll wipe them out in three days."

"Yes. Perhaps we will."

Drusus saw nothing to gain by arguing the point. The older man bore the responsibility for conducting this invasion; he himself was only an auxiliary commander. And the armies of Roma had been marching forth upon the world for thirteen hundred years, now, without encountering a rival who could stand against them. Hannibal and his Carthaginians, the furious Gallic warriors, the wild Britons, the Goths, the Huns, the Vandals, the Persians, the bothersome Teutons—each had stepped forward to challenge Roma and each had been smashed in turn.

Yes, there had been defeats along the way. Hannibal had made a great nuisance of himself, coming down out of the mountains with those elephants and causing all kinds of problems in the provinces. Varus had lost those three legions in the Teutonic woods. The invasion force under Valerius Gargilius Martius had been utterly destroyed right here in Yucatan only a little more than five years ago. But one had to expect to lose the occasional battle. In the long run, mastery of the world was Roma's destiny. How had Virgil said it? "To Romans I set no boundary in space and time."

Virgil hadn't looked into the eyes of Olaus the Dane, though, and neither had the Consul Lucius Aemilius Capito. Drusus, who had, found himself wondering how the seven legions of the second expedition would actually fare against the forces of the bearded white god of the Maia. Seven legions: what was that, forty thousand men? Against an unknown number of Maian warriors, millions of them, perhaps, fighting on their home grounds in defense of their farms, their wives, their gods. Romans had fought against such odds before and won, Drusus reflected. But not this far from home, and not against Olaus the Dane.

Capito's plans involved an immediate assault on the nearby city. The Roman catapults and battering rams would easily shatter its walls, which did not look nearly so strong as the walls of Roman cities. That was odd, that these people would not surround their cities with sturdy walls, when there were enemies on every side. But the enemies must not understand the use of the catapult and the ram.

Once the walls were breached the cavalry would go plunging through the plaza to strike terror in the breasts of the citizenry, who had never seen horses before and would think of them as monsters of some sort. And then an infantry assault from all sides: sack the temples, slaughter the priests, above all capture and slay Olaus the Dane. No business about imprisoning him and bringing him back in triumph to Roma, Capito said: no, find him, kill him, decapitate the empire he had built among these Maia with a single stroke. Once he was gone, the whole political structure would dissolve. The league of cities would fall apart, and the Romans could deal with them one at a time. All military discipline among these people would dissolve, too, without Olaus, and they would become feckless savages again, fighting in their futile helter-skelter way against the formidably disciplined troops of the Roman legions.

The dark fate of the first wave of the invasion indicated nothing that the second wave needed to take into account. Gargilius Martius hadn't understood what sort of general he was facing in Olaus. Capito did, thanks to Drusus; and by making Olaus his prime target he would cut off the source of his enemy's power in the earliest days of the campaign. So he declared: and who was Titus Livius Drusus, only twenty-three years old and nothing more than an auxiliary commander, to say that things would not happen that way?

Intensive preparations for battle began at once in all three Roman camps. The siege machinery was hauled into position at the edge of the forest, and work began on cutting paths through the trees for them. The cavalrymen got their steeds ready for battle. The centurions drilled and redrilled the troops of the infantry. Scouts crept out under cover of night to probe the Maian city's walls for their weakest points.

It was hard work, getting everything ready in this terrible tropical heat, that clung to you like a damp woolen blanket. The stinging insects were unrelenting in their onslaught, night and day, not just mosquitoes and ants, but scorpions also, and other things to which the Romans could give no names. Serpents now were seen in the camps, quick, slender green ones with fiery yellow eyes; a good many men were bitten, and half a dozen died. But still the work went on. There were traditions of many centuries' standing to uphold here. Julius Caesar himself was looking down on them, and the invincible Marcus Aurelius, and great Augustus, the founder of the Empire. Neither scorpions nor serpents could slow the advance of the Roman legions, and certainly not little humming mosquitoes.

Early in the afternoon on the day before the attack was scheduled to begin the clouds suddenly thickened and the sky grew black. The wind, which had been strong all day, now became something extraordinary, furnace-hot, roaring down upon them out of the east, bringing with it such lightning and thunder that it seemed the world was splitting apart, and then, immediately afterward, the torrential rains of a raging storm, a storm such as no man of Roma had ever seen or heard of before, that threatened to scoop them up as though in the palm of a giant's hand and hurl them far inland.

The tents went almost immediately, one after another ripping free of its pegs and whisking away. Drusus, taking refuge with his men under the wagons, watched in amazement as the first row of trees along the beach bent backward under the force of the gale so that their crowns almost touched the ground, and then began to topple as their roots lost their grip. Some did a crazy upside-down dance before they fell. The wagons themselves were shunted about, rising and tipping and crashing down again. The horses set up a weird screaming sound of terror. Someone cried out that the ships were capsizing, and, indeed, many of them had, Drusus saw, knocked over as though by a titan's hand. And then a towering wave came up out of the sea and crashed with devastating strength against the western wall of the palisade, sweeping it away.

The power of the storm seemed almost supernatural. Was Olaus the Dane in league with the gods of this land? It was as though he did not deign to expend his warriors against the invaders, but had sent this terrible tempest instead.

Nor was there any way to hide from it. All they could do was to lie cowering in the midday darkness, pinned down along this narrow strip of beach, while the whirlwinds screamed above them. Lightning cut across the sky like the flash of mighty swords. The boom of thunder mingled with the horrifying wail of the rending winds.

After some hours the rain seemed to slacken, and then it abruptly halted. An eerie stillness descended over the scene. There was something strange, almost crackling, about the quiet air. Drusus rose, stunned, and began to survey the devastation: the ruined walls, the vanished tents, the overturned wagons, the scattered weaponry. But then almost at once the wind and rain returned, sweeping back as if the storm had only been mocking them with that interlude of peace, and the renewed battering went on all night.

When morning came the camp was a shambles. Nothing that they had built still stood. The walls were gone. So was a wide swathe of beachfront trees. There were deep pools all up and down the beach and hundreds of drowned men lay asprawl in them. Many of the ships had disappeared and others were lying on their sides in the water.

The day brought choking heat, air so clogged with moisture it was next to impossible to breathe, and wave upon wave of noxious creatures—snakes, spiders, avalanches of stinging ants, platoons of scorpions, and all manner of other unpleasant things—that the storm appeared to have flushed out of the forest and driven toward the beach. It was like a dream that would not end with the coming of

daybreak. Grimly Drusus marshaled his men and set them to working at cleaning the place up, but it was hard to know where to begin,
and everyone moved as though still adrift in sleep.

For two days they struggled against the chaos that the storm had
left. On the second morning Drusus sent a runner down toward
Capito's camp to find out how things had fared there, but the man
returned in little more than an hour, reporting that a great arc of
beachfront had been washed away not far to the south, cutting the
shoreline route in half, and the forest flanking the coast was such a
maze of fallen trees that he had found that impassable too and had
to turn back.

On the third day came the first Maian offensive: a shower of arrows, descending without warning out of thin air. No archers were in
view: they had to be well back in the forest, sending their shafts aloft
without aiming, using bows of unusual force and carrying power.
Down from the sky the arrows came in the hundreds, in the thousands, even, striking at random in the Roman camp. Fifty men perished within moments. Drusus ordered five squadrons of armored
infantrymen into the forest under the command of Marcus Junianus
in search of the attackers, but they found no signs of anyone.

The next day a ship flying the banner of Lucius Aemilius Capito
appeared in the harbor, with three more behind it. Drusus had himself rowed out to greet the Consul. Capito, looking very much the
worse for wear, told him that the storm had all but destroyed his
camp: he had lost nearly half his men and all his equipment, and the
site itself had been rendered unusable by flooding. These were his
only surviving ships. Unable to make contact with the southern
camp of Masurius Titanus, he had come sailing up the coast, hoping
to find Drusus's camp still reasonably intact.

Drusus had no alternative but to surrender command of the
camp to Capito, although the older man seemed addled and befogged by all that had befallen him. "He is useless," said Marcus
Junianus vehemently, but Drusus shrugged away his friend's objections: Capito was the senior officer, and that was that.

Another attack by archers came the next day, and the day after
that. The arrows came in thicker clouds even than before, falling in
dense barrages from the sky. Drusus understood now that there was

no end to the Maian archers—he imagined thousands of them, millions, standing calmly in row upon row for miles, each row waiting to step forward and discharge its arrows when the one before it had had its turn. This land was full of people and all of them were enemies of Roma. And here the invading force waited in the wreckage of its camp, unable to move fifty feet into that steaming inimical jungle, vulnerable to new storms, venomous crawling creatures, hunger, illness, mosquitoes, arrows. Arrows. It was an impossible situation. Things could not have been worse for Quinctilius Varus who had lost the three legions of Augustus Caesar. But there were *seven* legions at risk here.

After proper consultation with the obviously ailing Capito, Drusus stationed a line of his own archers along the beach, who met the Maian onslaught with shafts of their own, sent blindly into the bush. This had some small effect: a dozen dead Maia were found after the battle. They were wearing armor of a sort, made of quilted cotton. But the Romans had lost twenty more to the arrows falling from the sky in the second attack, and fifteen in the third. The camp was still full of snakes, and they did lethal work also; and other men puffed up and died from the stings of insects, no one knew which.

Fever was the next enemy—the men began sickening by the dozens—and food was beginning to run short, the storm having denuded the nearby forest of its deer and pigs. Marcus Junianus drew Drusus aside and said, "We are beaten, even as the first expedition was. We should get aboard our ships and sail for home." Drusus shook his head, though he knew it was true. Any order to retreat would have to come from Capito, and the Consul was lost in some foggy feverish dream.

So the days passed. Each dawn brought its casualties from disease or hunger or simple weariness, and the sporadic attacks by the Maian archers brought more. "We will smash down the walls of their city," Capito declared in one of his few lucid moments, but Drusus knew there was no possibility of that. It was all they could do to hold their own here at the camp, forage for food and water, drive off the unending waves of archers.

On the twenty-third day a little band of men, perhaps fifty of them, gaunt and ravaged, came staggering up the beach from the south. They were the only survivors of Masurius Titianus's camp, who had cut their way through the forest in search of other remaining Romans. Titianus himself was dead, and all their ships had gone down in the storm.

"We have to leave this place," Drusus told the glassy-eyed Capito. "There's no hope for us here. The archers will pick us off by handfuls every day, and if the rest of us don't die of fever, eventually Olaus the Dane will send an army in here to finish the job."

"The Emperor has sent us to conquer this land," said Capito, rising halfway to a sitting position and glaring around with some desperate semblance of vitality. "Are we not Romans? Do we dare return to His Imperial Majesty with a sorry tale of failure?" And sank back exhausted, muttering in indistinct whispers; but Drusus knew that he must still regard him as the commander.

On the twenty-eighth day several hundred Maian troops appeared on the beach armed with spears, swarthy little men practically naked except for feather headdresses and the quilted-cotton armor. Drusus himself led the counterattack, though he was hard pressed to find enough men capable of withstanding the rigors of battle. The Maia conducted themselves surprisingly well against Roman swords and Roman shields, but finally were driven off, at the cost of thirty Roman lives. A few more battles like this, Drusus thought, and we are finished.

Capito died of his fever the next day.

Drusus saw to it that he had a proper burial, as befitted a Consul who had died in the service of the Empire on a foreign shore. When the last words had been chanted and the last shovelful of sand had been thrown upon the grave, Drusus, taking a deep breath, turned to his lieutenants and said, "Well, we are done with this, now. To the ships, everyone! To the ships!"

This time, of the more than forty thousand men who had gone forth on Roma's second attempt to conquer the New World, six hundred returned. Hundreds more were lost at sea in the return voyage, including those aboard the vessel that Drusus had placed under the command of Marcus Junianus. For Drusus that was the hardest blow of all, losing Marcus on this idiotic adventure in folly. Try as he could to look upon Marcus's death with the dispassionate eye of a Roman of ancient days, he found himself incapable of hiding from the pain of his grief. He owed the gods a death, yes, but he had not owed them Marcus's death, and he knew he would carry the sorrow of that loss, and the guilt of it, to his grave.

The arduous voyage home had left him greatly weakened. He required two weeks of rest at his family estate in Latium before he was strong enough to deliver his report to the Emperor, who received him at the thousand-year-old royal villa at Tibur.

Saturninus seemed to have grown much older since Drusus last had seen him. He was not as tall as Drusus remembered—perhaps he had begun to stoop a little—and his lustrous black hair was touched now with the first gray. Well, everyone gets older, Drusus thought. But something else had gone from the Emperor beside his youthful glow. That aura of irrepressible regal vitality that had made him such an awesome figure seemed to have left him as well. Perhaps it was the passing of time, thought Drusus, or perhaps it was only his own memories of Olaus the Dane, that man of truly boundless force and limitless ferocity, that by comparison had lessened the Emperor in his eyes.

The Emperor asked Drusus, in a distant, somewhat dim way, to tell him of the fate of the second expedition. Drusus replied in a measured, unemotional tone, describing first the land, the climate, the splendor of the one Maian city that he had seen. Then he went on to the calamity itself: there had been great problems, he said, the heat, the serpents and scorpions and the stinging ants, disease, the hostility of the natives, above all a terrible storm. He did not mention Olaus the Dane. It seemed unwise to suggest to the Emperor that a savage Norseman had built an empire in that far-off land that was able to hold Roma at bay: that would only fire Saturninus up with the desire to bring such a man to Roma in chains.

Saturninus listened to the tale in that same remote manner, now and again asking a question or two, but showing a striking lack of real interest. And now Drusus was approaching the most difficult part of his report, the summary of his thoughts about his mission to the New World.

This had to be done carefully. One does not instruct an Emperor, Drusus knew; one merely suggests, one guides him toward the conclusions that one hopes he will reach. One has to be particularly cautious when one has come to the realization that a favorite project of the Emperor's is wrongheaded and impossible.

So he spoke warily at first about the difficulties they had encountered, the challenge of maintaining supply lines over so great a distance, the probable huge native population of the New World, the special complexities posed by climate and disease. Saturninus appeared to be paying attention, but from very far away.

Then Drusus grew more reckless. He reminded the Emperor of his revered predecessor the Emperor Hadrianus, who had built the very villa where they were sitting now: how Hadrianus had come to see, in the end, that Roma could not send her legions to every nation of the world, that there were limits to her grasp, that certain far frontiers had to be left unconquered. Although at first he had not agreed with Hadrianus's thinking, Drusus told the Emperor, his experiences in Yucatan had changed his mind about that.

The Emperor no longer appeared to be listening, though. And Drusus realized that it was very likely that he had not been listening for some while. In sudden desire to break through this glacial remoteness of Saturninus's he found himself on the verge of saying outright, "The thing is impossible, Caesar, we will never succeed, we should give it up as a bad job. For if we continue it will destroy many thousands of our best troops, it will consume our revenues, it will break our spirit."

But before any of those words could pass his lips he heard the Emperor murmur, like an oracle speaking in a trance, "Roma is the ocean, Drusus, immense and inexhaustible. We will beat against their shores as the ocean does." And he realized in shock and horror that the Emperor was already beginning to plan the next expedition.

A.U.C. 1951: WAITING FOR
THE END

T he uglier of the two Praetorians, flat-faced and gruff, with close-cropped red hair and thick Slavic cheekbones, said, "The Emperor wants you, Antipater. Has some work for you, he says."

"Translation work," said the prettier guardsman, a ringleted blond Gaul. "The latest little love note from our friends the Greeks, I guess. Or maybe he wants you to write one for him to them." He gave Antipater a flirtatious little wink-and-wriggle, mock-seductive. The Praetorians all thought Antipater was of that sort, probably because he had such a sleek, well-oiled Levantine look about him, but perhaps merely because he was fluent in Greek. They were wrong, though. He was a slim-hipped, dusky-skinned, dark-haired man of somewhat feline gait and undeniably Eastern appearance, yes, but that was simply an artifact of his ancestry, the heritage of his long-ago Syrian forefathers. His understanding of Greek was a requirement of his job, not an advertisement of his sexual tastes. But he was at least as Roman as either of them. And as for his preference for women's embraces, they need only ask Justina Botaniates, to name just one.

"Where is His Majesty now?" Antipater asked coolly.

"The Emerald Office," replied the Slav. "Greek Letters, he said. Get me the Master of Greek Letters." He glanced at his companion and his broad face writhed in a heavy grin. "We'll all be masters of Greek letters soon enough, won't we, Marius?"

"Those of us who can read and write, at any rate," said the Gaul. "Eh? Eh? —Well, get along with you now, Antipater! Don't keep Caesar waiting!"

They had no respect. They were crude men. Antipater was a high palatine official and they were mere soldiers, and they had no business ordering him about. He glared them down and they backed away, and he gathered up his tablets and stylus and went down the dimly lit halls of the palace annex to the tunnel that led to the main building, and thence to the row of small private offices—Emerald, Scarlet, Indigo, Topaz—clustered along the east side of the Great Hall of Audience. The Emerald Office, the farthest in the series, was the Emperor Maximilianus's favorite, a long narrow windowless room hung with draperies of Indian weave, dark-green in hue, on which scenes of men with spears hunting elephants and tigers and other fantastic creatures were depicted.

"Lucius Aelius Antipater," he told the guard on duty, a vacant-eyed boy of eighteen or so, whom he had never seen before. "Master of Greek Letters to Caesar." The boy nodded him on through, not even bothering with the routine check for concealed weapons.

Antipater wondered about today's assignment. An outgoing letter, he supposed. In these dark days, three or four went out for every one that came in. Yet what was there to write about, with the Greek army on the verge of pouring across the Western Empire's porously defended frontiers? Surely not still another stern ultimatum addressed to Roma's great enemy the Basileus Andronicus, ordering him to cease and desist at once from further military encroachment on the Imperial domain. They had sent the latest in the long series of such ultimatums only last week. The courier most likely was no farther east with it yet than Macedonia, certainly was still a long way from delivering it to the Basileus in Constantinopolis—where it would only be tossed aside with a snort of amusement, like all the rest.

No, Antipater decided. This one had to be something more unusual. A letter from Caesar to some slippery Byzantine lordling on the African coast of the Great Sea, say—the exarch of Alexandria, maybe, or of Carthage—urging him, with the promise of immense bribes, to defect to the Roman side and launch some surprise attack from the rear, one that would distract Andronicus long enough for Roma to recover its balance and mobilize its long overdue counterthrust against the invaders.

A wild stratagem indeed. Nobody but he would ever think of it. "The trouble with you, Lucius Aelius," Justina liked to tell him, "is that you have too much imagination for your own good."

Maybe so. But here he was, just thirty-two years old that year—which was the year 1951 since the founding of the city—and for two years now he had been a member of the high palatinate, the Emperor's inner circle. Caesar had already bestowed a knighthood on him and a seat in the Senate would surely be next. Not bad going for a poor lad from the provinces. A pity that he had achieved his spectacular rise to prominence just as the Empire itself, weakened by its own senseless imprudence, seemed to be about to collapse.

"Caesar?" he said, peering into the Emerald Office.

At first Antipater saw no one. Then, by the smoky light of two dim tapers burning in a far corner of the room, he perceived the Emperor at his desk, the venerable Imperial desk of dark exotic woods that had been occupied in the past by the likes of Aemilius Magnus and Metellus Domitius and Publius Clemens and, for all Antipater knew, by Augustus and Hadrianus and Diocletianus as well. Great Caesars all; but the huge curving desk seemed to swallow their current successor, a pallid wiry little man with a glint of wholly justified worry in his close-set, sea-green, brightly shining eyes. He was wearing a simple gray jerkin and a peasant's red leggings; only the faint thread of pearls running along one shoulder, flanked by a pair of purple stripes, indicated that his rank was anything out of the ordinary.

He bore a grand name, did Maximilianus. It had been Maximilianus III, Maximilianus the Great, who in his short but brilliant reign had beaten the troublesome barbarians of the north into submission once and for all, the Huns and Goths and Vandals and the rest of that unruly shaggy-haired crowd. But that had been almost seven hundred years ago, and *this* Maximilianus, Maximilianus VI, possessed none of his famous namesake's fire and drive. Once again the Empire was at risk, tottering on the brink, in truth, as it had seemed to be in that other Maximilianus's far-off time. But this latter-day Maximilianus was not very likely to be its savior.

"You summoned me, Caesar?"

"Oh, Antipater. Yes. Look at this, Antipater." The Emperor held a yellow vellum scroll out toward him. So what needed translation was an incoming document of some sort, then. Antipater noticed that the Emperor's hand was quivering.

The Emperor, as a matter of fact, seemed to have turned overnight into a palsied old man. There were tics and tremors all over him. And he was only fifty, too. But he had held the throne for twenty grueling years, now, and his reign had been a hard one from its very first hour, when news of his father's death had reached him virtually at the same moment as word of the Greek thrust westward into the African proconsular region. That African invasion was the first major escalation of what had until then been a slow-burning border dispute confined to the province of Dalmatia, a dispute that had blossomed, through subsequent Greek probes along the border separating the two empires, into a full-scale war between East and West that now seemed to be entering its final dismal phase.

Antipater unrolled the scroll and began quickly to scan it.

"This was intercepted at sea by one of our patrols," said the Emperor. "Just south of Sardinia. Greek ship, it was, disguised as a fishing vessel, sailing northward out of Sicilia. I can understand some of what the message says, of course—"

"Yes," Antipater said. "Of course, Caesar." All educated men knew Greek; but it was the Greek of Homer and Sophocles and Plato that was taught in the academies of Roma, not the very different modern-day Byzantine version spoken from Illyricum eastward to Armenia and Mesopotamia. Languages do change. The Latin of Maximilianus VI's Roma wasn't the Latin of Virgil and Cicero, either. It was for his fluency in modern Greek that Antipater had won his place at court.

He moved swiftly through the casually scrawled words. And very quickly he realized why the Emperor was trembling.

"Merciful God defend us!" he muttered, when he was only halfway through.

"Yes," said the Emperor. "Yes. If only he would."

"What it was," said Antipater to Justina that evening in his small but pleasantly situated apartments on the Palatine Hill, "was a dispatch from the Byzantine admiral in Sicilia to the commander of a second Greek fleet that seems to be moored off the western coast of Sardinia, although we didn't know until now that any such fleet was there. The message instructs the commander of the Sardinian naval force to proceed on a northerly route past Corsica toward the mainland and capture our two ports on the Ligurian coast. Antipolis and Nicaea, their names are." He had no business telling her anything of this. Not only was he revealing military secrets, an act that in theory was punishable by death, but she was a Greek, to boot. A daughter of the famed Botaniates family, no less, which had supplied illustrious generals to the Byzantine Emperors for three hundred years. It was fully probable that some of the Greek legions that were marching toward Roma at this very moment were under the command of distant cousins of hers.

But he could withhold nothing from her. He loved her. He trusted her. Justina would never betray him, Greek though she was. A Botaniates, even, although from a secondary and impoverished branch of the family. But just as his own people had given up their allegiance to Byzantium to seek better opportunities in the Western Empire, so had hers. The only difference was that his family had Romanized itself three and a half centuries back and hers had crossed over when she was a little girl. She still felt more comfortable speaking in Greek than in Latin. Yet to her the Byzantines were "the Greeks" and the Romans were "us." That was sufficient for him.

"I was in Nicaea once," she said. "A beautiful little place, mountains behind it, lovely villas all along the coast. The climate is very mild. The mountains shelter it from the north winds that come down out of the middle of Europa. You see palm trees everywhere, and there are plants in bloom all winter long, red, yellow, purple, white. Flowers of every color."

"It isn't as a winter resort that the Basileus wants it," Antipater said. They had just finished dinner: grilled breast of pheasant, baked asparagus, a decent bottle of the smooth sweet golden-hued wine of Rhodes. Even here in wartime fine Greek wines were still available in Roma, if only to the fortunate members of the Imperial elite, though with the eastern ports suffering from the Byzantine blockade the stocks were unlikely to last much longer.

"Here. Look at this, Justina."

He snatched up a tablet and quickly sketched a rough map: the long peninsula of Italia with Sicilia at its tip, the coastline of Liguria curving away along the mainland to the west with the two big islands of Corsica and Sardinia in the sea to the south of it, and that of Dalmatia to the east. With emphatic little dots of his stylus he marked in Antipolis and Nicaea on the coast just to the left of the place where Italia began its southward thrust out of the heart of Europa toward the African shore.

Justina rose and walked around to his side of the table so that she could stand behind him and peer over his shoulder. The fragrance of her perfume drifted toward him, that maddeningly wonderful Arabian myrrh of hers that also could no longer be bought in Roma because of the Greek blockade, and his heart began to pound. He had never known anyone quite like this little Greek. She was a light-boned, delicately built woman: tiny, actually, but with sudden and surprisingly voluptuous curves at hip and bosom. They had been lovers for the past eighteen months and even now, Antipater was convinced, she had not yet exhausted her entire repertoire of passionate tricks.

"All right," he said, compelling himself rigorously to focus on the matter at hand. He gestured toward the lower part of his map. "The Greeks have already come across from Africa, just a short hop, and established a beachhead in Sicilia. It would be child's play for them to cross the strait at Messana and start marching up the peninsula toward the capital. The Emperor expects that some such move is imminent, and he's stationed half the home legions down here in the south, in Calabria, to keep them from getting any closer to us than the vicinity of Neapolis, let alone all the way up to Roma. Now, over here in the northeast"—Antipater indicated the upper right corner of the peninsula, where Italia bordered on the provinces of Pannonia and Dalmatia, which now were fully under Byzantine control—"we have the other half of the home army, guarding the border out back of Venetia against the inevitable push from that direction. The rest of our northern frontier, the territories bordering on Gallia and Belgica, is secure at this time and we aren't anticipating any Greek attempt to break through from that direction. But now, consider this—"

He tapped the stylus against the western shores of Sardinia and Corsica.

"Somehow," he said, "Andronicus seems to have managed to get a fleet up the far side of these two islands, where we haven't expected them to go sniffing around at all. Possibly they marched westward along the African shore and secretly built a bunch of ships somewhere on the Mauritanian coast. However they did it, they're there, apparently, and now they're in a position to outflank us on the west. They sail up past Corsica and seize the Ligurian seacoast, and then they use Nicaea and Antipolis as bases to send an army down the peninsula through Genua and Pisae and Viterbo and right on into Roma, and there's not a thing we can do about it. Not with half our army tied up on the northeast frontier to keep them from moving against us out of Dalmatia and the other half waiting south of Neapolis for an invasion from Sicilia. There isn't any third half to defend the city from a fast attack on our unguarded side."

"Can't the frontier legions be pulled down out of central Gallia to defend the Ligurian ports?" Justina asked.

"Not quickly enough to head off a Greek landing there. And in any case if we yanked troops out of Gallia, the Greeks could simply move their forces westward from Dalmatia, break into Gallia Transalpina themselves, and come down out of the mountains at us the way Hannibal did fifteen hundred years ago." Antipater shook his head. "No, we're boxed in. They've got us on three sides at once, and that's one too many."

"But the message to the Sardinian commander was intercepted

before it got to him," Justina pointed out. "He doesn't know that he's supposed to bring his ships north."

"Do you think they sent only one such message?"

"What if they did, and it was never intended to reach the Sardinian commander in the first place? I mean, what if it was a hoax?"

He stared. "A *hoax,* did you say?"

"Suppose that in fact there's no Greek fleet at all anchored west of Sardinia. But Andronicus wants us to think that there is, and therefore he had this fake message sent out for us to intercept, so that we'd get flustered and move troops toward Liguria to meet the nonexistent invasion force there. Which would open up a hole on one of the other fronts that his forces could stroll right through."

What a bizarre notion! For a moment Antipater was taken aback by the thought that Justina could come up with anything so far-fetched. Far-fetched ideas were supposed to be *his* specialty, not hers. But then he felt a surge of delight and admiration at the fertility of her imagination.

He grinned at her in an access of overflowing love. "Oh, Justina! You really *are* a Greek, aren't you?"

A quick flash of surprise and puzzlement sparkled in the shining black depths of her eyes.

"What?"

"Subtle, I mean. Inscrutable. Dark and devious of thought. The mind that could hatch an idea like that—"

She did not seem flattered. Annoyed, rather: she responded with a quirk of the full lips, a toss of her head. The carefully appointed row of jet-black curls across her forehead was thrown into disarray. She swept them back into place with a crisp peremptory gesture. "If I could hatch it, so could the Basileus Andronicus. So could you, Lucius. It's perfectly obvious. Cook up a false message and deliberately let it be captured, precisely so that Caesar will go into a panic, and start pulling his forces away from places they ought to be and into places where they aren't needed."

"Yes. Of course. But I think the message is genuine, myself."

"Does Caesar? How did he react when you read it to him?"

"He pretended to be calm and cool and completely unruffled."

"Pretended?"

"Pretended, yes. But his hand was shaking when he gave me the scroll. He already knew roughly what it said, and it frightened him."

"He's an old man, Lucius."

"Not really. Not in terms of years, anyway." Antipater rose and went to the window, and stood there staring out into the gathering gray of dusk. The lights of the capital were beginning to gleam on the dark hills all around. A beautiful sight; he never tired of it. His place, well down the hill from the royal palace itself, was far from majestic, but it had a choice location in the quarter of the Palatine reserved for top-level civil servants. From his portico he could see the great grim bulk of the ancient Coliseum where it rose against the horizon, and the lower end of the Forum below it, and the nearby sector of the splendiferous jumbled arc of marbled buildings of all eras that stretched off to the east, awesome structures going back hundreds and hundreds of years: back, some of them, to the time of Augustus and Nero and the first Trajan.

He had been fifteen, a greenhorn from the not very significant city of Salona in the not very significant province of Dalmatia, when he first saw the city of Roma. He had never outgrown the wonder that the capital inspired in him, not even now, when he moved daily among the great men of the realm and had come to understand only too clearly how far from great in truth they were. Yes, of course, they were mere grasping mortals like everyone else. But the *city* was great, the greatest, indeed, that had ever existed in the world, or ever would.

Was all this to be looted and torched now by the triumphant Byzantines, as it had been by the Gauls, so it was said, sixteen hundred years before? Or—what was more likely—would the Greeks just walk in and effortlessly take possession, destroying nothing, simply making themselves the masters of the city out of which their own empire had sprung once upon a time?

Justina came up behind him and pressed herself close. He felt her breasts flattening against his back. Their tips seemed to him to be hard.

Softly she said, "Lucius, what are we going to do now?"

"In the next five minutes, or the next three months?"

"You know what I mean."

"If the Greeks take Roma, you mean?"

"Not if. *When*."

He answered without turning toward her. "I don't actually think that will happen, Justina."

"You just said that there's no way we can defend ourselves against attacks coming from three directions at once."

"I know. But I want to believe that I'm wrong. The Emperor has called a meeting of the Great Council first thing tomorrow, and maybe someone's got a battle plan that I don't know about."

"Or maybe not."

"Even so," Antipater said. "Let's say that the worst happens: that they march against the city and we surrender, and the Greeks take control of the Western Empire. Nothing much should change, if they do. They're civilized people, after all. They might even want to keep the Emperor around as a puppet ruler, if he's willing. In any event they'll still need civil servants who are fluent in both languages. My position should be safe."

"And mine?"

"Yours?"

"You're a Roman citizen, Lucius. You look like a Greek, yes, and why not, considering that your people came originally from Syria—from Antioch, isn't that so? But your family's been living in the Western Empire for centuries and centuries and you were born in a Roman province. Whereas I—"

"You're Roman too."

"Yes, if you believe that Byzantines are Romans just because they say that their country is the Roman Empire and their emperor calls himself King of the Romans. But Greek is what they speak and Greek is what they are. And I'm a Greek, Lucius."

"A naturalized citizen of Roma, though."

"Am I?"

Startled, he swung around to face her. "You are, aren't you?"

"What I am is an Asian Greek. That isn't any secret. My family's from Ephesus, originally. When my father's shipping business went bad we moved to Athens and he started over. When he lost three ships in the same storm he went bankrupt and we left for the Western Empire to escape his creditors. I was three years old then. We lived in Syracusae in Sicilia at first, and then in Neapolis, and after my father died I moved to Roma. But nowhere along the way did I become a Roman citizen."

"I never knew that," Antipater said.

"Well, you do now."

"All the same, what does it matter?"

"It doesn't, maybe, so long as Maximilianus is Emperor. But what happens after the Byzantines take over? Can't you figure that out, Lucius? A Botaniates who sleeps with Romans? They'll punish me as a traitor!"

"Nonsense. Roma's full of Greeks. Always has been. Syrian Greeks, Armenian Greeks, Aegyptian Greeks, Cappadocian Greeks, even Greek Greeks. Once Andronicus's crowd is in charge, they won't care a rat's ass who was sleeping with whom."

But she clung to him, terrified. He had never seen her like this. "How do you know? I'm afraid of what might happen. Let's run away, Lucius. Before they get here."

"And go where?"

"Does it matter? Somewhere. Anywhere. Just so long as it's far from here."

He wondered how he could calm her. She seemed to be in the grip of inordinate unthinking fear. Her face was pale, her eyes had a glassy sheen, her breath was coming in little sobbing gusts.

"Please, Justina. *Please.*"

He took her hands in his for a moment, then slid his fingers up her arms until they rested along her collarbones. Tenderly he kneaded the muscles of her neck, trying to soothe her. "Nothing will happen to us," he said gently. "The Empire hasn't fallen yet, for one thing. It isn't necessarily going to, despite the way everything looks right now. It's survived some pretty bad things in the past and it may well survive this. The Basileus Andronicus might drop dead tomorrow. The sea might swallow his fleet the way it did your father's ships. Or Jupiter and Mars might suddenly appear in front of the Capitol and lead us to a glorious victory. Anything might happen. I don't know. But even if the Empire does fall, it won't be the end of the world, Justina. You and I will be all right." He stared intensely into her eyes. Could he make her believe something that he didn't fully believe himself? "You—and—I—will—be—all—right—"

"Oh, Lucius—"

"We'll be all right. Yes." Antipater folded her small body up against his and held her close until her breathing sounded normal again and he could feel her taut frame beginning to relinquish its tension. And then—a transition so swift that it almost made him want to chuckle—her entire body softened and her hips began to move slowly from side to side. She pressed herself close, wriggling in unmistakable invitation. Her eyes were closed, her nostrils were distended, her tongue flickered like a serpent's between her lips. Yes. Yes. Everything *would* be all right, somehow. They would close the walls in around themselves and ignore all that was going on outside. "Come," he said. He drew her toward the waiting bedchamber.

The Great Council of State assembled at the second hour of morning in the grand velvet-hung chamber known as the Hall of Marcus Anastasius on the northern side of the Imperial palace. Both Consuls were there, and half a dozen senior figures of the Senate, and Cassius Cestianus, the Secretary for Foreign Affairs, and Cocceius Maridianus, the Secretary for Home Affairs, and seven or eight other government ministers as well, and a formidable battery of retired generals and naval officers. So, too, were the key members of the Imperial household: Aurelius Gellius, the Praetorian Prefect, and Domitius Pompeianus, the Master of Latin Letters, and Quintilius Vinicius, the Keeper of the Imperial Treasury, and more. To Antipater's astonishment, even Germanicus Antoninus Caesar, the Emperor's rascally younger brother, had come. His presence was appropriate, since at least in theory he was the heir to the throne; but never had Antipater seen that wastrel prince at any sort of council meeting before, nor, to Antipater's recollection, had Germanicus ever been visible in public at all at such an early hour of the day. When he came sauntering in now, it caused a palpable stir.

The Emperor began the proceedings by asking Antipater to read the captured Greek scroll aloud.

"Demetrios Chrysoloras, Grand Admiral of the Imperial Fleet,

to His Excellency Nicholas Chalcocondyles of Trebizond, Commander of Western Naval Forces, greetings! Be advised by these documents, O Nicholas, of the unanswerable will of His Most Puissant
Imperial Majesty and Supreme Master of All Regions, Andronicus
Maniakes, who by the grace of God holds the exalted title of King of
the Romans and Lord Autocrat of—"

"Will you spare us this Greek foolishness, Antipater, and get to
the essence of the matter?" came a drawling voice from the side of
the chamber.

Antipater, rattled, looked up. His eyes met those of Germanicus
Caesar. It was he who had spoken. The Emperor's brother, lounging
in his chair as though at a banquet, was rouged and pomaded to
gaudy effect, and his purple-edged white robe was rumpled and
stained with wine. Antipater understood now how Germanicus had
managed to be here at this early hour: he had simply come directly
to the palace after some all-night party.

The prince, smirking at him across the room, made a little impatient circling gesture with his hand. Obediently Antipater
skimmed silently through the rest of the flourish of Byzantine pomp
with which the letter opened and began reading again from the
middle of the scroll:

"—to hoist anchor forthwith and undertake the northerly road,
keeping well clear of Corsica isle, so that you journey straightaway to
the Ligurian province of the Western Empire and make yourself the
master of the ports of Antipolis and Nicaea—"

There was murmuring in the chamber already. These people had
no need of maps in order to visualize the maritime movements that
were involved. Or to grasp the nature of the danger to the city of
Roma that the presence of a Greek fleet in those waters would pose.

Antipater closed the scroll and put it down.

The Emperor looked toward him and said, "Would you say, Antipater, that this document is authentic?"

"It's written in good upper-class Byzantine Greek, majesty. I
don't recognize the handwriting, but it's that of a capable scribe, the
sort who'd be attached to an important admiral's staff. And the seal
looks like a genuine one."

"Thank you, Antipater." Maximilianus sat quietly for a moment, staring into the distance. Then he let his gaze travel slowly along the rows of Roma's great leaders. At last it came to bear on the frail figure of Aurelianus Arcadius Ablabius, who had had command of the Tyrrhenian Sea fleet until his retirement to the capital for reasons of health a year before. "Explain to me, Ablabius, how a Byzantine armada could make its way up from Sicilia to the Sardinian coast without our so much as noticing the fact. Tell us about the Empire's naval bases along the west coast of Sardinia, if you will, Ablabius."

Ablabius, a thin, chalk-white man with pale blue eyes, moistened his lips and said, "Majesty, we *have* no significant naval bases on the west coast of Sardinia. Our ports are Calaris in the southeast and Olbia in the northeast. We have small outposts at Bosa and Othoca in the west, nothing more. The island is desolate and unhealthy and we have not seen the need to fortify it greatly."

"Under the assumption, I suppose, that our enemies of the Eastern Empire were not likely to slip around us and attack us from the west?"

"This is so, majesty," said Ablabius, visibly squirming.

"Ah. Ah. So nobody is watching the sea from western Sardinia. How interesting. Tell me about Corsica, now, Ablabius. Do we have a military base somewhere along the western coast of that island, perhaps?"

"There are no good harbors in the west at all, Caesar. The mountains come right down to the sea. Our bases are on the eastern shore, at Aleria and Mariana. It is another wild, useless island."

"So, then, if a Greek fleet should succeed in entering the waters west of Sardinia, it would have clear sailing right on up to the Ligurian coast, is that right, Ablabius? We have no naval force whatsoever guarding that entire sea, is what you're saying?"

"Essentially, yes, your majesty," said Ablabius, in a very small voice.

"Ah. Thank you, Ablabius." The Emperor Maximilianus once more traversed the room with his gaze. This time his eyes did not come to rest, but circled unceasingly about, as though he saw no place to land.

The tense hush was broken at last by Erucius Glabro, the senior Consul, a noble-looking hawk-nosed man who traced his ancestry

back to the earliest years of the Empire. He had had Imperial pretensions himself, once, thirty or forty years back, but he was old now
and generally thought to have become very foolish. "This is a serious
matter, Caesar! If they land an army on the coast and begin marching toward Genua, we'd have no way of keeping them from coming
on all the way down to the city itself."

The Emperor smiled. He looked immensely weary. "Thank you
for stating the obvious, Glabro. I was certain that I could count on
you for that."

"Majesty—"

"Thank you, I said." The senior Consul shriveled back into his
seat. The Emperor, his glinting narrow eyes roaming the group once
more, said, "We have, I think, four choices here. We could transfer
the army under Julius Fronto from the Gallian frontier to the vicinity of Genua, and hope that they'll get there in time to meet any
Greek force coming eastward along the Ligurian coast. But in all
probability they'd be too late. Or we could bring the forces commanded by Claudius Lentulus across from Venetia to hold the Gen-
uan border. That would probably work, but it would leave our
northeastern frontier wide open to the army that Andronicus has in
Dalmatia, and we'd see them in Ravenna or even Florentia before we
knew what was happening. On the other hand, we could call the
army of Sempronius Rufus northward from Calabria to defend the
capital, bring Lentulus south to Tuscia and Umbria, and abandon
the rest of the peninsula to the Greeks. That would put us back to
where we were two thousand years ago, I suppose, but the chances
seem fairly good that we could hold out here in the ancient Roman
heartland for a long time."

There was another long silence.

Then Germanicus Caesar said, in that lazy, offensive drawl of
his, "I think you mentioned that we had *four* choices, brother. You
mentioned only three."

The Emperor did not look displeased. He seemed actually to be
amused. "Very good, brother! Very *good*! There *is* a fourth choice.
Which is to do nothing at all, to ignore this captured message entirely, to sit tight with our defenses in their present configuration and
allow the Greeks to make whatever moves they have in mind."

Antipater heard a few gasps of astonishment; and then there commenced a wild general hubbub. The Emperor, motionless, arms folded across his breast, lips curving into the faintest of smiles, waited for it to die down. As order began to return the voice of the Consul Herennius Capito could be heard clearly asking, "Would that not be the suicide of our nation, Caesar?"

"You might argue that any response at all that we might make at this time would be suicidal," said the Emperor. "Defending ourselves on some new front means leaving some existing front unguarded. Pulling troops from any of our borders now will create a breach through which the enemy can easily move."

"But to take no action whatever, Caesar, while the Greeks are landing an army virtually in our back yard—!"

"Ah, but are they, Capito? What if this message Antipater has just read to us is merely a fraud?"

There was a moment of astounded stillness, after which came a second uproar. "A fraud? A fraud? A fraud?" cried a host of high ministers and Imperial counselors all at once. They seemed stunned. As was Antipater as well, for was this not precisely the idea—implausible, absurd—that Justina had proposed to him in the privacy of his apartments the night before?

Antipater listened in amazement as Maximilianus now set forth the argument that the supposed letter of the Grand Admiral Chrysoloras might have been designed purely as a trap, that its intention was to induce the Romans to draw their forces away from a military front that was in genuine need of defending and move them to a place where no real threat existed.

That was possible, yes. But was it in any way likely?

Not to Antipater. His father had taught him never to underestimate an enemy's cunning, but by the same token never to overestimate it, either. He had seen often enough how easily you could outsmart yourself by trying to think too many moves ahead in a game. It was far more reasonable, he thought, to believe that the Greeks really did have warships out there beyond Sardinia and were at this moment making ready to grab the Ligurian ports than it was to suppose that the Chrysoloras letter was merely a clever ploy in some game of—what was that game the Persians liked to play?— *chess*. A gigantic game of chess.

But no one could tell the Emperor to his face that a position he had put forth was absurd, or even just improbable. Very swiftly the assembled ministers and counselors could be seen bringing themselves around to an acceptance of the argument that it might not be necessary to react to the Grand Admiral's purported orders to the commander of the Sardinian fleet, because there just might not be any Sardinian fleet. Which was the safest way to deal with it, anyway, politically speaking. A decision to do nothing spared them from having to yank Roman legions away from a border point that was quite definitely in danger of imminent attack. Nobody wanted the responsibility for doing that.

In the end, then, the Grand Council voted to take a wait-and-see position; and off went everyone to the Senate House in the Forum to go through the meaningless ritual of presenting the non-decision to the full Senate for its foreordained ratification.

"Stay a moment," said the Emperor to Antipater, as the others headed for their waiting litters.

"Caesar?"

"I saw you shaking your head, there at the end, when the vote was being tallied."

Antipater saw no purpose in offering a reply. He regarded the Emperor with a blank bland subservient stare.

"You think the Admiral's letter is real, don't you, Antipater?"

"Unquestionably the penmanship and the style of phrasing are Byzantine," said Antipater cautiously. "The seal looks right also."

"I don't mean that. I'm talking about the fleet that we're supposed to believe is lying at anchor off western Sardinia. You think it's actually there."

"Caesar, I am in no position to speculate about—"

"I think it's really there, too," Maximilianus said.

"You do, Caesar?"

"Absolutely."

"Then why did you—?"

"Allow them to vote to take no action?" A look of terrible fatigue crossed the Emperor's face. "Because that was the easiest thing, Antipater. It was my duty to bring the letter to their attention. But there's no way we can respond to it, don't you see? Even if the Greeks *are* on their way to Liguria, we don't have any troops to send out there to meet them."

"What will we do, Caesar, if they invade the peninsula?"

"Fight, I suppose," said Maximilianus dully. "What else is there to do? I'll pull Lentulus's army down from the Dalmatian border and bring Sempronius Rufus's men up from the south and we'll hole up in the capital and defend ourselves as well as we can." There was no trace of Imperial vigor in his voice, not a shred of conviction or fire. *He is just striking a pose,* Antipater thought, *and not working very hard at it, either.*

To Antipater the outcome seemed utterly clear.

The Empire is lost, he thought. *All we're doing is waiting for the end.*

Once he had translated the Chrysoloras letter for the benefit of the Senate, there was no need for Antipater to remain for the rest of the debate, nor did he feel any desire to do so. Disdaining the litter-bearers who were waiting outside to take him back to his office at the palace, he set out on foot into the Forum, wandering blindly and purposelessly through the dense crowds, hoping only to soothe the agitation that pounded through his brain.

But the heat and the myriad chaotic sights and smells and sounds of the Forum only made things worse for him. The Empire's present situation seemed all the more tragic to him here amidst the Forum's multitude of glorious gleaming buildings.

Had there ever been an empire like the Roman Empire, in all of history? Or any city like mighty Roma? Surely not, thought Antipater. The greatness of Roma, city and Empire, had been growing steadily with scarcely any check for nearly two thousand years, from the era of the Republic to the coming of the Caesars and then on to the period of grand Imperial expansion that took the eagles of Roma into almost every region of the world. By the time that great age of empire-building had come to its natural end, with as much territory under control as was practical to administer, the power of Roma prevailed from the cool gray island of Britannia in the west to Persia and Babylon in the east.

He was aware that there had been a couple of occasions when that pattern of never-ending growth had suffered interruptions, but those were anomalies of long ago. In the modest early days of the Republic the barbarian Gauls had burst in here and burned the city, such as it had been then, but what had their invasion achieved? Only to strengthen the resolve of Roma never to let such a thing happen again; and the Gauls today were placid provincials, their warrior days long forgotten.

And then the business with Carthago—that affair was ancient history, too. The Carthaginian general Hannibal had caused his little disturbance, true, the thing with the elephants, but his invasion had come to nothing, and Roma had razed Carthago to its foundations and then built it all up again as a Roman colony, and the Carthaginians now were a nation of smiling hotel-keepers and restaurateurs who existed to serve the sun-seeking winter-holiday trade from Europa.

This Forum here, this crowded array of temples and law courts and statues and colonnades and triumphal arches, was the heart and core and nerve center of the whole splendid Empire. For twelve hundred years, from the time of Julius Caesar to the time of the present Maximilianus, the monarchs of Roma had filled these streets with a stunning conglomeration of glistening marble monuments to the national grandeur. Each building was grand in itself; the totality was altogether overwhelming, and, to Antipater just at this moment, depressing in the very fact of its own splendor. It all seemed like a giant memorial display for the dying realm.

Here, today, this sweltering humid blue-skied day in early autumn, Antipater wandered like a sleepwalker under the blazing golden eye of Sol among the innumerable architectural wonders of the Forum. The mammoth Senate House, the lofty temples to Augustus and Vespasianus and Antoninus Pius and half a dozen other early Emperors who had been proclaimed as gods, the colossal tomb of Julius that had been built hundreds of years after his time by some Emperor who had claimed disingenuously to be his descendant. The

arches of Septimius Severus and Constantinus; the five great basilicas; the House of the Vestal Virgins, and on and on and on. There
were richly ornamented buildings everywhere, a surfeit of them, occupying every possible site to north and south and even up the sides
of the Capitoline Hill. Nothing ever was torn down in the Forum.
Each Emperor added his own contribution wherever room could be
found, at whatever cost to rational planning and ease of movement.

At any hour, therefore, the Forum was a noisy, turbulent place.
Antipater, numbed by the fierce heat and his own despair and confusion, was jostled again and again by unthinking common citizens
hurrying blindly on to the shops and marketplaces along the fringes
of the great public buildings. He began to feel a little dizzy. Clammy
sweat soaked his light robe and his forehead was throbbing.

I must be somewhat ill, he decided.

Then, suddenly bewildered, he staggered and lurched and it was
all he could do to keep from falling to the ground. He knew that he
had to pause and rest. A high-domed eight-sided temple with massive ochre walls loomed up before him. Antipater lowered himself
carefully to the bottommost of its broad stone steps and huddled
there with his face in his hands, surprised to find himself shivering in
this great warmth. Exhaustion, he thought. Exhaustion, stress, perhaps a little touch of fever.

"Thinking of making an offering to Concordia, are you, Antipater?" a cool mocking voice from above asked him.

He looked blearily up into the dazzling glare of the midday sunlight. A long smirking angular face, fashionably pale, caked with
cracking makeup, hovered before him. Shining sea-green eyes, eyes
precisely the color of the Emperor's, but these were bloodshot and
crazed.

Germanicus Caesar, it was, the royal heir, the profligate, sybaritic
younger brother.

He had descended from a litter right in front of Antipater and
stood rocking back and forth before him, grinning lopsidedly as if
still drunk from the night before.

"Concordia?" Antipater asked muzzily. "Concordia?"

"The temple," Germanicus said. "The one you're sitting in
front of."

"Ah," Antipater said. "Yes."

He understood. The steps on which he had taken refuge, he saw now, were those of the magnificent Temple of Concordia. There was rich irony in that. The Temple of Concordia, Antipater knew, had been a gift to the city of Roma from the celebrated Eastern Emperor Justinianus, six hundred fifty years earlier, by way of paying homage to the spirit of fraternal harmony that existed between the two halves of the Roman Empire. And here was the Eastern Empire now, no longer so touchingly fraternal, about to invade Italia and subjugate as much of the senior Roman realm as it could manage to conquer, up to and including the city of Roma itself. So much for Concordia. So much for the harmony of the two empires.

"What's the matter with you?" Germanicus demanded. "Drunk?"

"The heat—the crowds—"

"Yes. That could make anybody sick. What are you doing walking around by yourself here, anyway?" Germanicus leaned forward. His breath, stinking of wine and overripe anchovies, was like a blast out of Hades. Nodding toward his litter, he said, "My chair's big enough for two. Come on: I'll give you a ride home."

That was the last thing Antipater wanted, to be cooped up with this foul-smelling lascivious prince inside a covered litter, even for the quarter of an hour it would take to cross the Forum to the Palatine. He shook his head. "No—no—"

"Well, get out of the sun, at least. Let's go into the temple. I want to talk to you, anyway."

"You do?"

Helplessly Antipater allowed himself to be tugged to his feet and herded up the dozen or more steps of Justinianus's temple. Within, behind the great bronze door, all was cool and dark. The place was deserted, no priests, no worshipers. A brilliant shaft of light descending from an opening high overhead in the dome illuminated a marble slab above the altar that proclaimed, in fiery letters of gold, the Emperor Justinianus's eternal love for his kinsman and royal counterpart of the West, His Imperial Roman Majesty Heraclius II Augustus.

Germanicus laughed softly. "Those two should only know what's going on now! Could it ever have worked, d'ye think—divid-

ing the Empire and expecting the two halves to live together peacefully forever after?"

Antipater, still dizzied and faint, felt little wish to discuss history
with Prince Germanicus just now.

"Perhaps, in an ideal world—" he began.

Germanicus laughed again, this time a harsh cackle. "An ideal
world, yes! Very good, Antipater! Very good! But we happen to live
in the real one, is that not so? And in the real world there was no
way that an empire the size of the one we once had could have been
maintained intact, so it had to be divided. But once the first Constantinus divided it, Antipater, war between the two halves was inevitable. The wonder of it is that it took so long to happen."

A discourse on history from the Emperor's drunken dissolute
brother, here in Justinianus's serene temple. How strange, Antipater
thought. And was there any truth in the point Germanicus was
making, Antipater wondered? The war between East and West—
inevitable?

He doubted that Constantinus the Great, who had split the unwieldy Roman world in half by setting up a second capital far to the
east of Roma at Byzantium on the Bosporus, ever had thought so.
Beyond question Constantinus had supposed that his sons would
share power peacefully, one reigning over the eastern provinces
from the new capital of Constantinopolis, one in Italia and the
Danubian provinces, a third in Britannia and Gallia and Hispania.
Hardly was Constantinus in his grave, though, than the divided Empire was embroiled in war, with one of the sons attacking another
and seizing his realm; and for sixty years after that all was in flux,
until the great Emperor Theodosius had brought about the final administrative division of the Roman world, separating its Greek-
speaking territories from the Latin-speaking ones.

But Theodosius hadn't accepted the inevitability of East-West
war either. By his decree the two Emperors, the Eastern one and the
Western one, were supposed to consider themselves colleagues,
joint rulers of the entire realm, consulting each other on all high
matters of state, each even having the power to name a successor
for an Imperial colleague that died. It hadn't worked out that way,
of course. The two nations had drifted apart, though some measure

of cooperation did continue for hundreds of years. And now—the friction of the past half century, culminating in the present slowly escalating war of East against West—the foolish, needless, ghastly war that was about to burst in all its fury upon this greatest of all cities—

"Look at this stuff!" Germanicus cried. He had left Antipater's side to go roaming about in the deserted temple, peering at the paintings and mosaics with which Justinianus's Byzantine craftsmen had bedecked the sides of the building. "I hate the Greek style, don't you? Flat and stiff and creaky—you'd think they didn't understand a damned thing about perspective. If I had been Heraclius, I'd have covered the walls over with plaster the moment Justinianus's people were out of town. Too late for all that now, though." Germanicus had reached the far side, and peered up for a moment at the vast regal portrait of solemn scowling Justinianus, done in gleaming golden tile, that loomed out from the belly of the dome like Jupiter himself glowering down. Then he whirled to face Antipater. "But what am I saying?" he bellowed through the echoing dimness. "You're a Greek yourself! You love this kind of art!"

"I am a Roman citizen born, sir," said Antipater quietly.

"Yes. Yes, of course. That's why you speak Greek so well, and why you look the way you do. And that hot little dark-eyed lady you spend your nights with—she's Roman, too, right? Where are you from, anyway, Antipater? Alexandria? Cyprus?"

"I was born in Salona in Dalmatia, sir. It was Roman territory at the time."

"Salona. Yes. The palace of Diocletianus is there, isn't it? And nobody would say that Diocletianus wasn't a Roman. Why do you look so damnably Greek, though? Come over here, Antipater. Let me look at you. *Antipater.* What a fine Roman name that is!"

"My family was Greek originally. We were from Antioch, but that was many hundreds of years ago. If I am Greek, then Romans are Trojans, because Aeneas came from Troia to found the settlement that became Roma. And where is Troia today, if not in the territory of the Greek Emperor?"

"Oh-ho! Oh-ho! A wise man! A sophist!" Briskly Germanicus returned to Antipater's side and grasped at the front of his robe, clutching it into a tight bunch. Antipater expected a stinging slap. He lifted one hand to protect his face. "Don't cower like that," the prince said. "I won't hit you. But you're a traitor, aren't you? A Greek and a traitor. Who consorts nightly with the enemy. I'm speaking of that Greek wench of yours, the little bosomy spy. When the Basileus comes in triumph to Roma, you'll go rushing to his side and tell him you were loyal to him all along."

"No, sir. By your leave, sir, none of that is true, sir."

"Not a traitor?"

"No, sir," said Antipater desperately. "Nor is Justina a spy. We are Romans of Roma, faithful to the West. I serve your royal brother the Caesar Maximilianus Augustus and no one else."

That appeared to be effective. "Ah. Good. Good. I'll accept that. You seem sincere." Germanicus winked and released him with a light shove, and spun away to stand with his back toward Antipater. In a much less manic tone, sounding almost subdued, he said, "You stayed at the meeting after the rest of us left. Did Caesar have anything interesting to say to you?"

"Why—why—he merely—"

Antipater faltered. What kind of loyalty to Caesar would it be to betray his private conversations to another, even Caesar's own brother?

"He said nothing of significance, sir. Just a bit of recapitulation of the meeting, was all."

"Just a bit of recapitulation."

"Yes, sir. Nothing more."

"I wonder. You're very thick with him, Antipater. He trusts you, you know, shifty little Greek that you are. Emperors always trust their secretaries more than they do anybody else. It doesn't matter to him that you're a Greek. He tells you things that he doesn't tell others." Germanicus swung round again. The sea-green eyes drilled with sudden ferocity into Antipater's. "I wonder," he said once more. "Was he speaking the truth, when he said that we don't need to do anything about this fleet off Sardinia? Does he actually and truly believe that?"

Antipater felt his cheeks growing hot. He was grateful for the faintness of the light in here, and for his own swarthy skin, that would hide his embarrassment from the prince. It seemed odd to him that the famously idle Germanicus, who had never to Antipater's knowledge demonstrated a shred of interest in public affairs, should be so concerned now with his Imperial brother's military intentions. But perhaps the imminence of a Greek invasion of the capital had aroused even this roguish, lackadaisical, irresponsible lordling to some alarm. Or, perhaps, all this was just some passing whim of his. No matter which, Antipater could not evade a reply this time.

Carefully he said, "I would not presume to tell anyone what I imagined the Emperor was thinking, sir. My understanding of his position, though, is that he sees that there's very little we can really do against the Basileus—that we are hemmed in on two sides already and that we are unable to protect ourselves against an attack on some new front."

"He's absolutely right," said Germanicus. "Our goose, as the Britannians say, is cooked. The question is what kind of sauce will go on the dish, eh? Eh, Antipater?" And then, abruptly, Antipater found himself being seized once again and swept forward into a hard, crushing embrace. Germanicus's bristly cheek rubbed across his with stinging force. The reek of the young prince brought a new surge of dizziness to him. He is crazy, Antipater thought. *Crazy.* "Ah, Antipater, Antipater, you know I mean you no harm! I do love you, man, for your devotion to my brother. Poor Maximilianus! What a burden it must be to him to be Emperor at a time like this!" Letting go of Antipater once more, he stepped back and said, in yet another new tone of voice, somber now and oddly earnest, "You will not speak a word of this meeting to my brother, will you, eh? I think I've disturbed your tranquility, and I wouldn't want him thinking ill of me for that. He's terribly fond of you. He relies on you so very much. —Come, Antipater, will you let me take you home, now? That hot little Greek of yours very likely has a sizzling noontime surprise for you, and it would be rude to keep her waiting."

*　*　*

He said nothing to Justina of his strange encounter with the Emperor's brother. But the episode stayed in his mind.

Beyond much doubt the prince was mad. And yet, yet, there had seemed to be some undertone of seriousness in his discourse—a side of Germanicus Caesar that Antipater had never seen before, nor, perhaps, anyone else either.

Germanicus's belief that the original Empire, the one that had spanned the world from Britannia to the borders of India, had been too large to govern from a single capital—well, yes, nobody would dispute that issue. Even in Diocletianus's time the job had been so big that several Emperors reigning jointly had been needed to handle it, not that that had worked particularly well; and a generation later the great Constantinus had found governing the entire thing impossible even for him. And so had come the formal division of the realm, which under Theodosius had become permanent.

But what about the other point, the inevitability of war between East and West?

Antipater had no love for that line of thinking. Yet he knew that the historical record provided strong support for it. Even in the era of supposed East-West concord, that time when Justinianus reigned in Constantinopolis and his nephew Heraclius in Roma, great trade rivalries had sprung up, each Empire trying to outflank the other, Latin Romans reaching out around Byzantium toward remote India and even more remote Khitai and Cipangu where the yellow-faced men live, and Greek Romans seeking influence to the south in black Africa and to the far frozen northern territories that lay behind the homeland of the half-savage Goths.

That had all been sorted out by treaty; perhaps, thought Antipater, Justinianus's temple in Roma had been erected in commemoration of some such agreement. But the frictions had continued, the jockeying for prime position in the world's commerce.

And then, beginning eighty or ninety years ago, the West's big mistake, the colossally foolish expedition to the New World—what a calamity that had been! Certainly it was exciting to discover that two great continents lay beyond the Ocean Sea, and that mighty nations—Mexico, Peru—existed there, strange lands rich in gold and silver and precious stones, inhabited by multitudes of copper-skinned people ruled by lordly monarchs who lived in pomp and opulence worthy of Caesar himself. But what lunacy had possessed the megalomaniac Emperor Saturninus to try to *conquer* those nations, instead of simply to enter into trade relations with them? Decades of futile overseas expeditions—millions of sesterces wasted, whole legions sent out by that obstinate and perhaps insane Emperor to die under the searing sun of the inhospitable continents that Saturninus had optimistically named Nova Roma—the pride of the Western Empire's military destroyed by the spears and arrows of unstoppable torrents of demonic wild-eyed warriors with painted faces, or swept away by the overwhelming force of great tropical storms—hundreds of ships lost in those perilous alien waters—the spirit of the Empire broken by the unfamiliar experience of defeat after defeat, and the ultimate grim capitulation and evacuation of the final batch of shattered Roman troops—

That ill-advised adventure had, as Antipater and everyone else recognized now, drained the economic resources of the Western Empire in a terrible way, and, perhaps, weakened its military power beyond repair. Two entire generations of the most gifted generals and admirals had perished on the shores of Nova Roma. And then, the idiotically arrogant Emperor Julianus IV compounding the error by evicting a Greek mercantile mission from the island of Melita, a trifling dot in the sea between Sicily and the African coast that both Empires long had laid claim to. To which Leo IX of Byzantium had retaliated not only by landing troops on Melita and taking control of it, but by unilaterally redrawing the ancient dividing line of the two empires that ran through the province of Illyricum, so that the Dalmatian coast, with its valuable ports on the Adriatic Sea, now came under Byzantine rule.

That was the beginning of the end. The Western Empire, already badly overextended by its doomed project in the New World, could not resist the takeover with any real force. Which had encouraged Leo and his successors in the East, first Constantinus XI and then Andronicus, to reach deeper and deeper into Western territory, until by now the capital itself was in jeopardy and the West seemed certain to fall into Byzantine control for the first time in history.

Still, Antipater wondered whether it all had been, as Germanicus maintained, inevitable from the start.

Rivalry, yes. Friction and occasional outright conflict, yes. But the conquest of one Empire by the other? There was nothing in the divided-Empire schemes of Constantinus and Theodosius that had made it obligatory for the West to undertake a stupid and ruinous overseas campaign, one that no Caesar would abandon until the Empire had crippled itself. Nor anything requiring the crippled Empire to have wantonly given its eastern rival provocation for attacking it, on top of the previous folly. Under wiser Emperors, Roma would have remained Roma for all eternity. But now—

"You brood too much," Justina told him.

"There's much to brood about."

"The war? I tell you again, Antipater: we need to flee before it gets here."

"And I answer you again: go where?"

"Some place where no fighting is going to happen. Some place far to the east, where the sun is always bright and the weather is warm. Syria or Aegyptus. Cyprus, maybe."

"Greek places, all of them. I'm a Roman. They'll say I'm a spy."

Justina laughed indelicately. "We don't fit in anywhere, is what you say! The Romans think you're a Greek. Now you don't want to fly to the East because they'll say you're a Roman. How will they be able to tell, anyway? You look and sound as Greek as I do."

Antipater stared at her gloomily. "The truth is, Justina, we *don't* fit in anywhere. Not really. But the main point, completely aside from whatever I may look and sound like, is that I'm an official of the Western Imperial court. I've signed my name to endless pieces of diplomatic correspondence that are on file in Constantinopolis."

"Who's to know? Who would care? The Western Empire is a dead thing. We escape to Cyprus; we raise sheep, we grow some grapes; you earn some money, perhaps, by working as a Latin translator. You tell people you lived for a time in the West, if anybody wonders where you came from. What of it? Nobody will accuse you of being a spy for the Western Empire when the Western Empire doesn't exist any more."

"But it still does exist," he said.

"Only for the time being," said Justina.

He had to admit that the idea was tempting. He was being overly apprehensive, perhaps, in thinking that anyone would hold his service under Maximilianus Caesar against him if he ran away to the East. No one would care a fig for that, back there in the sunny, sleepy, sea-girt lands of the Greek world. He and Justina could start new lives together.

But still—still—

He didn't see how he could desert his post while the government of Maximilianus was still intact. That seemed a vile deed to him. Unmanly. Treacherous. *Greek.* He was a Roman; he would stay at his post until the end came. And then—

Well, who knew what would happen then?

"I can't leave," he told Justina. "Not now."

The days passed. The bright skies of early autumn gave way to gray, dreary ones that betokened the oncoming rainy season. Justina said little to him about the political situation, now. She said little about anything. The Roman winter was a difficult time for her. She had lived nearly all her life in the Western Empire, yes, but she was Greek to the core, a child of the south, of the sun. A life down in Neapolis or, even better, Sicilia, might have been warm and bright enough for her, but not Roma, where the winters were wet and chilly. Antipater often wondered, as he made his way homeward from his duties at the palace under the darkening skies, whether he would discover, some afternoon, that she had packed up and vanished. Already it was possible to detect signs that a small abandonment of the capital might be getting under way: the crowds in the streets seemed more sparse, and every day he noticed another shop or two closed and boarded up. But Justina remained by his side.

His palace duties became more pointless day by day. No more ultimatums went forth to the Basileus Andronicus. What was the use? The end was in sight. Antipater's work consisted now mainly in translating the reports that came in from the spies that Caesar still

had posted all around the perimeter of the Greek world. Troop
movements in Dalmatia—reinforcements of the already huge Greek
army sitting up there opposite the northeastern end of the peninsula
within striking distance of the Roman outpost at Venetia. Another
Greek army on the march down in Africa, heading westward along
the shore from Aegyptus toward Carthago and the other ports of the
Numidian coast: backup forces, no doubt, for the troops already in
Sicilia. And still other shufflings about of the apparently infinite
Byzantine military power were going on to the north: a legion of
Turks supposedly being sent up into Sarmatia, along the German
border, presumably for the purpose of stretching the already thin
Roman lines of defense even further.

Punctiliously Antipater read all these dispatches to the Emperor,
but Maximilianus only occasionally seemed to pay attention. The
Emperor was moody, remote, distracted. One day Antipater entered
the Emerald Office and found him poring over a huge book of history, open to the page that bore the long list of past Caesars. He was
running his finger down the list from the beginning, Augustus,
Tiberius, Gaius Caligula, Claudius, Nero, and onward through
Hadrianus, Marcus Aurelius, Septimius Severus, Titus Gallius, into
the time of the division of the realm, and beyond that to medieval
times and the modern era. The list, just the Western Emperors now,
stretched on and on beyond his pointing finger, scores of names great
and small, Clodianus, Claudius Titianus, Maximilianus the Great, all
the Heracliuses, all the Constantinuses, all the Marcianuses.

Antipater watched as Maximilianus drew his quivering fingertip
down into recent time: Trajan VI, Julianus IV, Philippus V, and
Maximilianus's own father, Maximilianus V. There the list had originally stopped. It had been compiled before the commencement of
the present reign. But someone had written in at the bottom, in a
different hand, the name of Maximilianus VI. Maximilianus's finger,
tracing its way downward, halted there. His own name. He began
slowly to shake his head from side to side. Antipater understood at
once what was passing through the Emperor's mind. Staring at that
great list, encompassing it from top to bottom, he was recapitulating
all the long flow of the river of Roman time, from the Empire's grand

inauguration under the immortal Augustus to . . . its end . . . its *end* . . . under the inconsequential, insignificant Maximilianus VI.

He closed the book, and looked up at Antipater, and smiled a bleak, chilly little smile. Antipater had no difficulty in reading the Emperor's thoughts. *The last of all that great list! What a distinction, Antipater! What an extraordinary distinction!*

That night Antipater dreamed of wild-eyed drunken Greek soldiers in bulky blue-green linen jerkins running jubilantly through the streets of Roma, laughing and shouting, looting stores, pulling women into alleyways. And then the Emperor Andronicus riding in glory down the Via Flaminia into the city, resplendent in his purple *chlamys*, his robe of authority, with his great mane of golden hair flowing behind him and his enormous yellow beard tumbling over his chest. Throngs of Roman citizens lined the great highway to pelt him with flower petals and cheer him on, crying out enthusiastically in praise of their new master, hailing him in his own language, calling him *Basileus Romaion,* "King of the Romans." Spurning the use of a chariot, the conquering monarch sat astride a colossal white horse bedecked with jewels; he wore the shining Greek crown crested with peacock feathers and carried in one hand the eagle-headed scepter of rule, and with the other he waved magnanimously to the crowds. And went on toward the Forum, where he dismounted and looked around in satisfaction. And, sauntering on into the avenue running below the Capitoline Hill, paused there and gestured to a member of his entourage with a broad sweeping movement of his hand, as though to indicate where he intended to erect the triumphal arch marking his victory.

The next day—a day of endless pelting driving rain—a messenger arrived at the palace bearing word that Greek forces had landed on the Ligurian shore. The ports of Antipolis and Nicaea had fallen to them without a battle, and the Greeks were presently en route along the coastal highway toward the city of Genua. In the afternoon came a second runner, half dead on his feet, who carried news from the south that a tremendous military engagement was under way in Calabria, where the Roman army was hard pressed and slowly retreating, while a second Greek force out of Sicilia had unexpectedly

landed farther up the peninsula, had captured the harbor of Neapolis, and was laying siege to that essential southern city, whose fall was
imminent.

The only piece missing, thought Antipater, was an attack on the
northeastern frontier by the Byzantine forces in Dalmatia. "Perhaps
we'll get news of that invasion too, before long," he said to Justina.
"But it hardly matters, does it?" The soldiers of Andronicus were already moving through the Italian peninsula toward Roma from both
the north and the south. "The goose is cooked, as Germanicus
would say. The game is lost. The Empire's finished."

"You will take a letter to the Basileus Andronicus," said the Emperor.

They were in the little Indigo Office, next door to the Emerald
one. In dank, rainy weather it was a little warmer there than in the
Emerald. This was the fourth day of rain, now. Neapolis had fallen,
and the Greek army of the south, having polished off most of the
southern Roman garrison, was moving steadily up the Via Roma toward the capital. The only difficulties it was encountering were from
mudslides blocking the roads. The second Greek force, the one
coming down from Liguria, was somewhere in Latium, it seemed,
perhaps as far south as Tarquinii or Caere. Apparently it, too, was
meeting no resistance other than from the weather. Caere was just
thirty miles north of Roma. There had also been a Byzantine break-
through on the Venetian front out of Dalmatia.

Maximilianus cleared his throat. " 'To His Royal Splendor Andronicus Maniakes, Autocrat and Imperator, by the grace of God
King of Kings, King of the Romans and Supreme Master of All Regions'—you have all that, Antipater?—"

" 'Basileus basileion,' " Antipater murmured. "Yes, majesty." He
gave Maximilianus a carefully measured glance. "Did you say
'Supreme Master of All Regions'?"

"So he styles himself, yes," said Maximilianus, a little irritably.

"But, begging your pardon, the implication, sire—"

"Let us just continue, Antipater. 'And Supreme Master of All
Regions. From his cousin Maximilianus Julianus Philippus Romanus

Caesar Augustus, Imperator and Grand Pontifex, Tribune of the People, et cetera, et cetera'—you know all the titles, Antipater; put them in—'Greetings, and may the benevolence of all the gods be upon you forever and ever, world without end.' " Again the Emperor paused. He took two or three deep breaths. " 'Whereas it has been the pleasure of the gods to permit me to occupy the throne of the Caesars these past twenty years, it has lately begun to seem to me that the favor of heaven has been withdrawn from me, and that it is the will of the most divine gods that I lay down the responsibilities that were placed upon me long ago by the command of my royal father, His Most Excellent Majesty the Divine Imperator Maximilianus Julianus Philippus Claudius Caesar Augustus. Likewise it is evident to me that the favor of heaven has fallen upon my Imperial cousin His Most Puissant Majesty the Basileus Andronicus Maniakes, Autocrat and Imperator, et cetera, et cetera,'—give his full titles all over again, will you, Antipater?—"

Antipater was on to his second wax tablet by this time, and he had scarcely written down anything but strings of royal titles. But the sense of the message was already quite clear. He felt his heart beginning to thump as the meaning of what the Emperor was dictating to him sank in.

It was a document of abdication.

Maximilianus was handing the Empire over to the Greeks.

Well, of course, the Greeks had grabbed the Empire already, essentially, everything but the capital itself and a few miserable miles of territory surrounding it. But still, was this proper Roman behavior? There was hardly any precedent for the capitulation of a Roman Emperor to a foreign conqueror, and that was what Andronicus was, a Greek, a foreigner, whatever pretense the Byzantines might make toward being a legitimate half of the original Roman Empire. Rulers had been deposed before, yes. There had been civil wars in ancient times, Octavianus versus Marcus Antonius, and the squabble over the succession to Nero, and the battle for the throne after the assassination of Commodus. But Antipater couldn't recall any instances of a defeated Emperor supinely resigning the throne to his conqueror. The usual thing was to fall on your sword, wasn't it, as the troops of the victorious rival drew near? But what had been usual a thousand years ago might no longer be considered appropriate behavior, Antipater decided.

And Maximilianus was still speaking in a steady flow, every sentence constructed with a careful sense of style and precise in its grammar, as though he had begun drafting this letter many weeks back, revising it again and again in his mind until it was perfect, and nothing remained now but for him to express it aloud so that Antipater could render it into Byzantine Greek.

Definitely, a document of abdication. To Antipater's astonishment, Maximilianus was indeed not merely giving up his throne, he was designating Andronicus as his legally valid successor, the true and lawful wielder of the Imperial power.

There was, of course, the problem that Maximilianus had not managed to produce any children, and the official heir to the throne, Germanicus, was hardly suitable for the job. But Maximilianus was basically handing Andronicus clear title to the crown, not just by right of conquest but by the explicit decree of the outgoing monarch. In effect he was reuniting the two halves of the ancient Empire. Was it really necessary for him to carry the thing so far? If he didn't plan to kill himself, Antipater thought, and who could blame him for that, couldn't he simply acknowledge his defeat with a curt letter of surrender and go off into history with a certain degree of dignity intact?

But Maximilianus was still speaking, and suddenly Antipater realized that there was another, and deeper, purpose to this document.

" 'I have grown old in office' "—not true; he was hardly more than fifty—" 'and the burden of power wearies me, and I seek only now to live a quiet life of reading and meditation in some corner of Your Imperial Majesty's immense domain. I cite the precedent of the Caesar Diocletianus of old, who, after having reigned exactly twenty years, as I have, voluntarily yielded up his tremendous powers and took up residence in the province of Dalmatia, in the city of Salona, where the palace of his retirement stands to this day. It is the humble request of Maximilianus Caesar, my lord, that I be permitted to follow the path of Diocletianus, and, in fact, if it should be pleasing to you, that I even be allowed to occupy the palace at

Salona, where I spent a number of nights during the years of my reign, and which is to me an agreeable residence to which I could gladly retire now—' "

Antipater knew the palace at Salona well. He had grown up virtually in its shadow. It was quite a decent sort of palace, practically a small town in itself, right on the sea, with enormous fortified walls and, no doubt, the most luxurious accommodations within. Many a Caesar had used it as a guest house while visiting the lovely Dalmatian coast. Perhaps Andronicus had stayed in it himself, inasmuch as Dalmatia had been under Byzantine control the past couple of decades.

And here was Maximilianus asking for it—no, *begging* for it, the fallen Emperor making a "humble request," addressing Andronicus suddenly as "my lord," using a phrase like "if it should be pleasing to you." Turning over legal title to the Empire to Andronicus on a silver platter, asking nothing more in return than to be allowed to go off and hide himself behind the gigantic walls of Diocletianus's retirement home for the rest of his life.

Dishonorable. Disgraceful. Disgusting.

Antipater looked hastily away. He did not dare let Caesar see the blaze of contempt that had come into his eyes.

The Emperor was still speaking. Antipater had missed a few words, but what did that matter? He could always fill in with something appropriate.

" '—I remain, I assure you, dear cousin Andronicus, yours in the deepest gratitude, offering herewith the highest regard for your wisdom and benevolence and my heartfelt felicitations on all the glorious achievements of your reign—cordially, Maximilianus Julianus Philippus Romanus Caesar Augustus, Imperator and Grand Pontifex, et cetera, et cetera—' "

"Well," Justina said, when Antipater summarized the abdication document for her the next evening after he had spent much of yet another rainy day copying it out prettily on a parchment scroll, "Andronicus doesn't have to give Maximilianus anything, does he? He can simply cut his head off, if he likes."

"He won't do that. This is the year 1951. The Byzantines are civilized folk. Andronicus doesn't want to look like a barbarian. Besides, it's bad politics. Why make a martyr out of Maximilianus, and set him up as a hero for whatever anti-Greek resistance movement is likely to come into being in the rougher provinces of the West, when he can simply give him a kiss on the cheek and pack him off to Salona? The whole Western Empire's his, regardless. He might just as well make a peaceful start to his reign here."

"So Andronicus will accept the deal, do you think?"

"Oh, yes. Yes, of course. If he has any sense at all."

"And then?"

"Then?"

"Us," said Justina. "What of us?"

"Oh. Yes. Yes. The Emperor had a few things to say about that, too."

Justina drew her breath in sharply. "He did?"

Uneasily Antipater said, "When he was finished dictating the letter, he turned to me and asked me if I would come with him to Salona, or wherever else Andronicus allowed him to go. 'I'll still need a secretary, even in retirement,' he said. 'Especially if I wind up in the Greek-speaking part of the Empire, and that's surely where Andronicus will want to put me, so that he can keep me under his thumb. Marry your little Greek and come along with me, Antipater.' That's exactly what he said. 'Marry your little Greek. Come along with me.'"

Instantly Justina's eyes were glowing. Her face was flushed, her breasts were rising and falling quickly. "Oh, Antipater! How wonderful! You accepted, naturally!"

In fact he had not, not exactly. Not at all, as a matter of fact. Nor had he refused, exactly, either. Not at all. He had given Caesar no real answer of any sort.

In some discomfort he said, "You know that I'd be delighted to marry you, Justina."

She looked perplexed. "And the part about following Caesar to Dalmatia?"

"Well—" he said. "I suppose—"

"You *suppose*? What other choice do we have?"

Antipater hesitated, fumbling in the air with his outspread hands. "How can I say this, Justina? But let me try. What Caesar is asking is, well—cowardly. Shameful. Un-Roman."

"Perhaps so. And if it is, so what? Better to stay here and die like a Roman, do you think?"

"I've already told you, Andronicus would never put him to death."

"I'm talking about us."

"Why would anyone harm *us*, Justina?"

"We've been through all this. As you yourself pointed out last week, you're an official of the court. I'm a Greek citizen who's been consorting with Romans. Surely there'd be a purge of the old bureaucracy. You wouldn't be executed, I guess, but you'd certainly be given a hard time. So would I. A worse time than you, I'd think. You'd be reassigned to some grubby menial job, maybe. But they'd find some very nasty uses for someone like me. Conquering soldiers always do."

It was hard for him to meet the implacable fury of her eyes.

All yesterday afternoon since he'd taken his leave of Caesar in the Indigo Office, and most of today as well, his head had been swirling with ringing heroic phrases—*in the end, one must comport oneself as a Roman must, or be seen to be nothing at all—our great heroic traditions demand—history will never forgive—a time comes when a man must proclaim himself to be a man, or else he is nothing more than—how shameful, how unutterably and eternally shameful, it would be to affiliate myself with the court of so despicable a coward, an Emperor who—*and much more in the same vein, all leading up to his grand repudiation of the invitation to accompany Maximilianus into a cozy Dalmatian retirement. But now he saw only too clearly that all that was so much nonsense.

Our great heroic traditions demand, do they? Perhaps so. But Maximilianus Caesar was no hero, and neither was Lucius Aelius Antipater. And if the Emperor himself could not bring himself to behave like a Roman, why should his Master of Greek Letters? A man who was no sort of warrior, only a clerk, a man of books, and not all that much of a Roman, either, not so that Cicero or Seneca or Cato the Censor would have believed. They would have laughed at his pretensions. You, a Roman? You with your oily Greek hair and your little snub nose and your ballet-dancer way of walking? Anybody can call himself a Roman, but only a Roman can *be* a Roman.

The time of Seneca and Cato and Cicero was long over, anyway. Things were different today. The enemy was at the gates of Roma, and what was the Emperor doing? Serenely falling on his sword? Calmly slitting his wrists? No. No. Why, the Emperor was busy composing a letter that pleaded abjectly for a soft safe withdrawal to a big palace on the Dalmatian coast. Was the Master of Greek Letters supposed to stand at the bridge facing the foe with a blade in each hand like some indomitable hero of old, while the Emperor he served was blithely running out of town the back way?

"Look," Justina said. She had gone to the window. "Bonfires out there. A big one on the Capitoline Hill, I think."

"We can't see the Capitoline from that window."

"Well, some other hill, then. Three, four, five bonfires on the hills out there. And look down there, in the Forum. Torches all along the Sacra Via. The whole city's lit up. —I think they're here, Antipater."

He peered out. The rain had stopped, and torches and bonfires indeed were blazing everywhere. He heard distant shouts in the night, but was unable to make out any words. Everything was vague, blurry, mysterious.

"Well?" Justina asked.

He let his tongue slide back and forth across his upper lip a couple of times. "I think they're here, yes."

"And now? It's too late for us to run, isn't it? So we stand our ground and await our fates, you and I and the Emperor Maximilianus, like the stoic Romans that we are. Isn't that so, Antipater?"

"Andronicus won't harm the Emperor. No harm will come to you or me, either."

"We'll find that out soon enough, won't we?" said Justina.

The next day was a day like none before it in the long history of Roma. The Greeks had come in the night before just as darkness was falling, thousands of them, entering through four of the city's gates at once; and they had met with no opposition whatever. Evidently the Emperor had sent out word to the commanders of the home guard that no attempts at resistance were to be made, for they surely would be futile and would only lead to great loss of life and widespread destruction within the city. The war was lost, said the Emperor; let the Greeks come in without prolonging the agony. Which was either a wise and realistic attitude, thought Antipater, or else a despicably fainthearted one, and he knew what he believed. But he kept his opinions to himself.

The rain, which had halted for most of the night on the evening of the conquest, returned in the morning, just as the Basileus Andronicus was making his triumphal entrance into the city from the north, along the Via Flaminia. The scene was almost as Antipater had seen it in his dream, except that the weather was bad, and there were no flower petals being thrown, and the people lining the road looked stunned rather than jubilant and no one hailed the new Emperor in Greek. But Andronicus did ride a huge white horse and looked rather splendid, even in the rain with his great mass of golden hair pasted together in strings and his beard a soggy mop. He went not to the Forum, as Antipater had dreamed he would, but straight to the Imperial palace, where, the conqueror had been told, he would be presented with the document of abdication that the Emperor had dictated to Antipater the previous day.

The entire Great Council was present at the ceremony. It took place in the glittering Hall of the Hunting Mosaics, built by one of the later Heracliuses, where the Emperor usually received delegations from distant lands under showy depictions in glowing red and green and purple tiles of the spearing of lions and elephants by valiant men in ancient Roman costume. Today, though, instead of seating himself on the throne, Maximilianus stood meekly at the left side of it, facing the Byzantine monarch, who stood just opposite him at a distance of some eight or ten paces. Behind Maximilianus were arrayed the members of the Council; behind Andronicus, half a dozen Greek officials who had traveled with him in the parade down the Via Flaminia.

The contrast between the two monarchs was instructive. The Emperor seemed dwarfed beside Andronicus, a giant of a man, by

far the tallest and burliest in the room, who had thick heavy features and the coarse unruly yellow hair of a Celt or a Briton tumbling far down his back. Everything about him, his broad
shoulders, his massive chest, his long drooping mustaches, his jutting jaw and vast beard, radiated a sense of bull-like, almost brutish,
strength. But there was a look of cold intelligence in his small piercing gray-violet eyes.

Antipater, standing at Maximilianus's side, served as interpreter.
At a nod from the Emperor he handed the scroll to some high magistrate of Andronicus's court, a man with a tonsured head and a
richly brocaded robe inset with what looked like real rubies and
emeralds; and the magistrate, giving it only the merest glance,
solemnly rolled it up and passed it on to the Basileus. Andronicus
unrolled it, quickly ran his eyes along the first two or three lines in a
nonchalantly cursory way, and let it roll closed again. He handed it
back to the tonsured magistrate.

"What does this thing say?" he asked Antipater brusquely.

Antipater found himself wondering whether the King of the Romans could be unable to read. With some astonishment he heard
himself reply, "It is a document of abdication, your majesty."

"Give it here again," said Andronicus. His voice was deep and
hard and rough-edged, and his Greek was not in the least melliflu-
ous: more a soldier's kind of Greek, or even a farmer's kind of
Greek, than a king's. An affectation, most likely. Andronicus came
from one of the great old Byzantine families. You would never know
it, though.

With a grandiose gesture the tonsured magistrate returned the
scroll to the Basileus, who once more made a show of unrolling it,
and again seemingly reading a little, another line or two, and then
closing it a second time and casually tucking it under his arm.

The room was very quiet.

Antipater, uncomfortably conscious of his place much too close
to the center of the scene, glanced about him at the two Consuls, the
assembled Ministers and Secretaries, the great generals and admirals, the Praetorian Prefect, the Keeper of the Imperial Treasury. Unlike the Emperor Maximilianus, who bore himself now with no sign
whatever of self-importance, a small man who knew he was about to

be diminished even further, they were all holding themselves bolt upright, standing with ferocious military rigidity. Did any of them realize what was in the letter? Probably not. Not the Salona part, anyway. Antipater's eye met that of Crown Prince Germanicus, who looked remarkably fresh for the occasion, newly bathed and spotless in a brilliant white robe edged with purple. Germanicus too had adopted today's general posture of martial erectness, which seemed notably inappropriate on him. But he seemed almost to be smiling. What, Antipater wondered, could there be to smile about on this terrible day?

To Antipater the Basileus Andronicus said, "The Emperor resigns his powers unconditionally, does he not?"

"He does, your majesty."

From members of the Great Council here and there around the room came little gasping sounds, more of shock than surprise. They could not be surprised, surely, Antipater thought. But the blunt acknowledgment of the reality of the situation had an unavoidable impact even so.

Prince Germanicus's demeanor did not change, though: the same lofty stance, the same calm, cool half-smile at the corner of his lips. His elder brother had just signed away for all time the throne that Germanicus might one day have inherited; but had Germanicus ever really expected to occupy that throne, anyway?

Andronicus said, "And are there any special requests?"

"Only one, majesty."

"And that is?"

All eyes were on Antipater. He wished he could sink into the gleaming stone floor. Why was it necessary for *him* to be the one to speak the damning words out loud before the great men of Roma?

But there was no escaping it. "Caesar Maximilianus requests, sire," said Antipater in the steadiest voice he could muster, "that he be permitted to withdraw with such members of his court as may care to accompany him to the palace of the Emperor Diocletianus in Salona in the province of Dalmatia, where he hopes to spend the rest of his days in contemplation and study."

There. Done. Antipater stared into the air before him, looking at nothing.

The hard gray-violet eyes of the Basileus flickered shut for half an instant; and something like a scornful smirk was visible just as briefly at a corner of the Byzantine Emperor's mouth. "We see no reason why the request cannot be granted," he said, after a time. "We accept the terms of the document as proposed." Yet again he unrolled it; and, taking a pen from the magistrate beside him, he scrawled a huge capital A at the bottom. His signature, evidently. "Is there anything else?"

"No, your majesty."

Andronicus nodded. "Well, then. Inform the former Emperor that it is our pleasure to spend this night in our camp beside the river, among our men. Tomorrow we intend to take up residence in this palace, from which nothing is to be removed without our permission. Tomorrow, also, we will present to you our brother Romanos Caesar Stravospondylos, who is to reign over the Western Empire as its Emperor thenceforth. Tell all this to the former Emperor, if you will." He beckoned to his men, and they strode in a stiff phalanx from the room.

Antipater turned toward Maximilianus, who stood completely still, like a man transformed into a stone statue of himself.

"The Basileus says, Caesar, that he—"

"I understood what the Basileus said, thank you, Antipater," said Maximilianus, in a voice that seemed to come from the tomb. He smiled. It was a death's-head smile, the merest quick flashing of his teeth. Then he, too, went from the room. The members of the Great Council, most of them looking dazed and disbelieving, followed him in twos and threes.

So this is how empires fall in the modern era, Antipater thought.

No bloodshed, no executions. A parchment scroll passing back and forth a couple of times from conqueror to conquered, a scrawled letter A, a change of occupants for the royal apartments. And so it will go down in history. *Lucius Aelius Antipater, the defeated Emperor's Master of Greek Letters, presented the statement of abdication to the Basileus Andronicus, who gave it the most perfunctory of glances and then—*

"Antipater?"

It was Germanicus Caesar. He alone remained in the great room with the Master of Greek Letters.

The prince beckoned to him. "A word with you on the portico, Antipater. Now."

Outside, strolling together down the long enclosed porch that ran along this wing of the palace, with the rain clattering on the wooden roof overhead, Germanicus said, "What can you tell me about this Romanos Caesar, Antipater? I thought the Basileus's brother was named Alexandros."

There was something strange about his voice. Antipater realized after a moment that the prince's indolent drawl was gone. His tone was crisp, business-like, curt.

"There are several brothers, I believe. Alexandros is the best-known one. A warrior like his brother, is Alexandros. Romanos is very likely of a different sort. The name '*Stravospondylos*' means 'crook-back.' "

Germanicus's eyes widened. "Andronicus has picked a *cripple* to be Emperor of the West?"

"It would seem so from the name, sir."

"Well. His little joke. So be it, I suppose." Germanicus smiled, but he did not look amused. "One thing's clear, anyway: there'll still be two Emperors. Andronicus isn't going to try to rule the whole united Empire from Constantinopolis, because it can't be done. Which is what I told you, Antipater, in the Forum that day, at the Temple of Concordia."

Antipater found himself still amazed by the abrupt change in Germanicus, this new seriousness of his, this no-nonsense manner. Even his posture was different. Gone was the easy aristocratic slouch, the loose-limbed ease. Suddenly he was holding himself like a soldier. Antipater had not noticed before how much taller Germanicus was than his brother the Emperor.

"How long," Germanicus asked, "do you imagine that this Western Greek Empire will last, Antipater?"

"Sir?"

"How long? Five years? Ten? A thousand?"

"I have no way of knowing, sir."

"Give it some thought. Andronicus marches west, knocks over our pitiful defenses with two flicks of his fingers, sets up his deformed little brother as our Emperor, and goes back to the good life in Constantinopolis. Leaving a dozen or so legions of Greek troops to occupy the entire immensity of the Western Empire: Hispania, Germania, Britannia, Gallia, Belgica, on and on and on, not to mention Italia itself. For what purpose has he conquered us? Why, so our taxes will flow eastward and wind up in the Byzantine treasury. Are the farmers of Britannia going to be happy about that? Are the wild whiskery men up there in Germania? You know the answer. Andronicus has captured Roma, but that doesn't mean he's gained control of the whole Empire. They don't want Greeks running things, out there in the provinces. They won't put up with it. They're Romans, those people, and they want to be ruled by Romans. Sooner or later there'll be active resistance movements flourishing all over the place, and I say it'll be sooner rather than later. The assassination of Greek tax collectors and magistrates and municipal procurators. Local rebellions. Eventually, wide-scale uprisings. Andronicus will decide that it's not worthwhile, trying to maintain supply lines over such long distances. He'll simply shrug and let the West slide. He's not going to come out here twice in one lifetime to fight with us. Either we'll kill all the Greek occupiers, or, more likely, we'll simply swallow them up and turn them into Romans. Two or three generations in the West and they won't remember how to speak Greek."

"I dare say you're right, sir."

"I dare say I am. —I'll be leaving Roma tomorrow evening, Antipater."

"Going to Dalmatia, are you? With the Emp—with your brother?"

Germanicus spat. "Don't be a fool. No, I'm going the other way." He leaned close to Antipater and said, in a low, hard-edged voice, "There's a ship waiting at Ostia to take me to Massalia in Gallia. I'll make my capital there or at Lugdunum, I'm not yet sure which."

"Your—capital?"

"The Emperor has abdicated. You wrote the document yourself, didn't you? So I'm Emperor now, Antipater. Emperor-in-exile, maybe, but Emperor none the less. I'll proclaim myself formally the moment I land in Massalia."

If Germanicus had said that a week ago, Antipater thought, it would have sounded like madness, or drunken folly, or some derisive joke. But this was a different Germanicus.

The prince's sea-green eyes bore down on him mercilessly. "You're a dead man if you say a word of this to anyone before I'm gone from Roma, of course."

"Why tell me in the first place, then?"

"Because I think that in your weird shifty Greek way you're a trustworthy man, Antipater. I told you that at the Temple of Concordia, too.—I want you to come with me to Gallia."

The calmly spoken sentence struck Antipater like a thunderbolt. "What, sir?"

"I need a Master of Greek Letters, too. Someone to help me communicate with the temporary occupying authorities in Roma. Someone to decipher the documents that my spies in the East will be sending me. And I want you as an adviser, too, Antipater. You're a timid little man, but you're smart, and shrewd as well, and you're a Greek and a Roman both at the same time. I can use you in Gallia. Come with me. You won't regret it. I'll rebuild the army and push the Greeks out of Roma within your lifetime and mine. You can be a Consul, Antipater, when I come back here to take possession of the throne of the Caesars."

"Sir—sir—"

"Think about it. You have until tomorrow."

Justina's expression was entirely unreadable as Antipater finished telling the tale. Whatever was going on behind those dark glistening eyes was something he could not guess at all.

"It surprised me more than I can tell you," he said, "to find out how much deeper a man Germanicus is than anybody knew. How strong he really is, despite that foppish attitude he found it useful to affect. How truly Roman, at the core."

"Yes," she said. "It must have been quite a surprise."

"It's a noble romantic idea, I have to admit, this business of proclaiming himself Emperor-in-exile and leading a resistance movement from Gallia. And his invitation to be part of his government, I confess, was very flattering. —But of course I couldn't possibly go with him." He would not go, Antipater knew, because Justina surely would not; and if one thing was clear in his mind just now amidst all the chaos of the suddenly whirling world, it was that wherever Justina wanted to go, that was where they would go. She was more important to him than politics, than empires, than all such abstract things. He understood that now as never before: for him it all came down to Justina and Lucius, Lucius and Justina, and let other men fret over the burdens of empire.

"Will he succeed, do you think, in overthrowing the Greeks?" she asked.

"He stands a good chance," said Antipater. "Everyone knows that the Empire's too big to be governed from one capital off in the East, and appointing a Greek Emperor for the West won't work for long either. The West is Roman. It thinks Roman. For the time being the Greeks have the advantage over us, because we weakened ourselves so much through our own imbecility in the past fifty years that they were able to come in and take us over, but it won't last. We'll recover from what's just happened to us, and we'll return to being what we once were." He had a sudden vivid sense of the river of time flowing in two directions at once, the past returning even as it departed. "The gods intended that Roma should govern the world. We did for a thousand years or more, and did it damned well. We will again. Destiny's on Germanicus's side. Mark my words, there'll be Latin-speaking Emperors in this city again in our lifetime."

It was a long speech. Justina greeted it with a spell of silence that lasted almost as long.

Then she said, "It gets very cold in Gallia in the winter, does it not?"

"Rather cold, yes, so I'm told. Colder than here, certainly."

Too cold for her, that much he knew. Why would she even ask? It was unthinkable that she would want to go there. She would hate it there.

"It's very strange," he said, since she was saying nothing. "The Emperor is worthless and the brother that I thought was worthless turns out actually to be a bold and courageous man. If there's such a thing as a Roman soul, and I think there is, it goes westward with Germanicus tomorrow."

"And you, Lucius? Which way do you go?"

"We're Greeks, you and I. We'll be going the other way, Justina. Toward the East. Toward the sun. To Dalmatia, with Caesar."

"You're a Roman, Lucius."

"More or less, yes. What of it?"

"Roma goes west. The coward Maximilianus goes east. Do you truly want to go with the coward, Lucius?"

Antipater gaped at her, stunned, unable to speak.

"Tell me, Lucius, how cold does it really get in Gallia in the winter? Is there very much snow?"

He found his voice, finally. "What are you trying to say, Justina?"

"What are *you* trying to say? Suppose I didn't exist. Which way would you go tomorrow, east or west?"

He paused only an instant. "West."

"To follow the Emperor's brother into the snow."

"Yes."

"The brother that you thought was worthless."

"The Emperor is worthless. Not so the brother, I begin to think. If you weren't in the equation, I'd probably go with him." Was it so, he wondered? Yes. Yes. It was so. "I'm a Roman. I'd want to act like a Roman, for once."

"Then go. Go!"

He felt the room rocking, as if in an earthquake. "And you, Justina?"

"I don't have to act like a Roman, do I? I could stay here, and continue to be a Greek—"

"No, Justina!"

"Or I could follow you and your new Emperor into the snow, I suppose." She wrapped her arms around her body and shivered, as though white flakes were already falling, here in their snug room. "Or, on the other hand, we still have the option, both of us, of going east with the other Emperor. The cowardly one who gave his throne away to be safe."

"I'm not very brave myself, you know."

"I know that. Yet you would go with Germanicus, if I were not here. So you just said. There's a difference between not being very brave and being a coward. Which is worse, I wonder, to walk through the snow once in a while, or to live in warmth among cowards? How can you live among cowards, unless you're a coward yourself?"

He had no answer. His head was throbbing. She had him outflanked on every front. He understood only that he loved her, he needed her, he would make whatever choice she wanted him to make.

From outside came shouting again, raucous, jubilant. He could hear what sounded like screams, also. Antipater glanced toward the window and saw new fires burning on the hills. The conquest was beginning in earnest, now. The victors were raking in their spoils.

Well, that was only to be expected, Antipater thought. It made no difference to him. The one question that mattered was which way to go: eastward with the fallen Emperor, westward with his brother.

He looked to Justina. Waited for her to speak.

She was still holding herself against the imagined cold of an imagined winter, but she was smiling now. The cold was imaginary; the smile was real. "And so," she said. "A Roman, I will be. With you, in the snow, in Gallia. Is that a crazy thing, Lucius? Well, then. We can be crazy together. And try to keep each other warm wherever we go. —We should start packing, love. Your new Emperor is sailing for Massalia tomorrow, is that not what you said?"

A.U.C. 2206: AN OUTPOST OF
THE REALM

You know your enemy from the first moment you see him. I saw mine on a gleaming spring day almost a year ago, when I had gone down to the Grand Canal as I usually do in the morning to enjoy the breezes. A flotilla of ornate Roman barges was moving along the water, shouldering our gondolas aside as though they were so much flotsam. In the prow of the foremost barge stood a sturdy dark-bearded young Imperial proconsul, grinning in the morning sunshine, looking for all the world like some new Alexander taking possession of his most recently conquered domain.

I was watching from the steps of the little Temple of Apollo, just by the Rialto. The proconsul's barge bore three great poles from which the eagle standard fluttered, and they were too tall to pass. The drawbridge, for some reason, was slow to open. As he looked impatiently around his gaze fell on me and his bright, insolent eyes met mine. They rested there a moment, comfortably, presumptuously. Then he winked and waved, and cupped his hand to his lips and called something to me that I could not make out.

"What?" I said, automatically, speaking in Greek.

"Falco! Quintus Pompeius Falco!"

Then the bridge opened and his barge passed through and was gone, swiftly heading down the canal. His destination, I soon would learn, was the Palace of the Doges on the great plaza, where he was going to take up residence in the house where the princes of Venetia formerly had dwelled.

I glanced at Sophia, my waiting-maid. "Did you hear him?" I asked. "What was that he said?"

"His name, lady. He is Pompeius Falco, our new master."

"Ah. Of course. Our new master."

How I hated him in that first moment! This hairy-faced garlic-eating Italian boy, making his swaggering way into our serene and lovely city to be our overlord—how could I not detest him? Some crude soldier from Neapolis or Calabria, jumped up out of sweaty obscurity to become proconsul of Venetia as a reward, no doubt, for his bloodthirstiness on the battlefield, who now would fill our ears with his grating Latin crudities and desecrate the elegance of our banquets with his coarse Roman ways—I loathed him on sight. I felt soiled by the cool, casual glance he had bestowed on me in that moment before his barge passed under the drawbridge. Quintus Pompeius Falco, indeed! What could that ugly name possibly mean to me? I, a highborn woman of Venetia, Byzantine to the core, who could trace her ancestry to the princes of Constantinopolis, who had mingled since childhood with the great ones of the Greek world?

It was no surprise that the Romans were here. For months I had felt the Empire seeping into our city the way the bitter ocean tides slip past our barrier islands into our quiet lagoon. That is the way it is in Venetia: we shelter ourselves as best we can from the sea, but in time of storm it prevails over everything and comes surging in upon us, engulfing us and flooding us. There is no sea in all the world more powerful than the Empire of Roma; and now it was about to sweep over us at last.

We were a defeated race, after all. Five, eight, ten years had passed, already, since the Basileus Leo XI and the Emperor Flavius Romulus had signed the Treaty of Ravenna by which the Eastern and Western Empires were reunited under Roman rule and all was as it had been so many centuries ago in the time of the earliest Caesars. The great Greek moment was over. We had had our time of glory, two hundred years of it, but the Romans had prevailed in the end. Piece by piece the whole independent Byzantine world had returned to Roman control, and it was our turn to be swallowed up now, Venetia, the westernmost outpost of the fallen realm. Roman barges sailed our canals. A Roman proconsul had come here to live in the Palace of the Doges. Roman soldiers strutted in our streets. Fifty years of bloody civil war, two hundred years of Greek ascendancy after that, and now it was all nothing but history. We did not even have an Emperor of our own. For a thousand years, since the time of Constantinus, we of the East had had that. But now we would have to bend our knees to the Caesars as we did in ancient times. Do you wonder that I hated Caesar's man on sight, as he proudly made his entry into our conquered but not humbled city?

Scarcely anything changed at first. They did not reconsecrate the Temple of Zeus as a temple of Jupiter. Our fine Byzantine coins, our solidi and miliaresia, continued to circulate, though I suppose there were Roman aurei and sesterces among them now. We spoke the language we had always spoken. Official documents now bore the Roman date—it was their year 2206—instead of using the Greek numbering, which ran from the founding of Constantinopolis. But who among us paid attention to official documents? For us it was still the year 1123.

We saw Roman officials occasionally in the plaza, or in the shops of the Rialto, or journeying in gondolas of state along the main canals, but they were few in number and they seemed to take care not to intrude on our lives. The great men of the city, the members of the old patrician class from whose ranks the Doges once had been drawn, went about in proper pomp and majesty as usual. There was no Doge, of course, but there had been none for a long time.

My own existence was as it had been. As the daughter of Alexios Phokas and the widow of Heraclios Cantacuzenos I had wealth and privilege. My palace on the Grand Canal was a center for the high-born and cultured. My estate to the east in warm and golden Istria yielded a rich bounty of figs, olives, oats, and wheat, and afforded me a place of diversion when I wearied of the watery charms of

Venetia. For as much as I love Venetia I find the city's dank winters and sweltering miasmic summers very much of a burden on my spirit, and must escape from it when those times come.

I had my lovers and my suitors, who were not necessarily the same men. It was generally assumed that I would marry again: I was still only thirty, childless and wealthy and widely hailed for my beauty, and of high family with close connection to the Byzantine imperial dynasty. But although my mourning time was over, I was in no hurry for a new husband. I had been too young when I was married to Heraclios, and had had insufficient experience of the world. The accident that had robbed me of my lord so early had given me the opportunity to make up for my past innocence, and so I had done. Like Penelope, I surrounded myself with suitors who would gladly have taken a daughter of the Phokases to wife, widow that she might be. But while these ambitious grandees, most of them ten years older than I or more, buzzed about me bringing their gifts and murmuring their promises, I amused myself with a succession of less distinguished gentlemen of greater vigor—gondoliers, grooms, musicians, a soldier or two—to the great enhancement of my knowledge of life.

I suppose it was inevitable that I would encounter the Roman proconsul sooner or later. Venetia is a small city; and it was incumbent upon him to ingratiate himself with the local aristocracy. For our part we were obliged to be civil with him: among the Romans all benefits flow downward from the top, and he was the Emperor's man in Venetia. When lands, military rank, lucrative municipal offices became available, it was Quintus Pompeius Falco who would distribute them, and he could, if he chose, ignore the formerly mighty of the city and raise new men to favor. So it behooved those who had been powerful under the fallen government to court him if they hoped to maintain their high positions. Falco had his suitors just as I had mine. On feast days he was seen at the Temple of Zeus, surrounded by Venetian lords who fawned on him as though he were Zeus himself come to visit. He had the place of honor at many banquets; he was invited to join in the hunt at the estates of the great noblemen; often, as the barges of the wealthy traveled down our canals, there was Pompeius Falco among them on deck, laughing and sipping wine and accepting the flattery of his hosts.

As I say, I could not help but encounter him eventually. From time to time I saw him eyeing me from afar at some grand occasion of state; but I never gave him the satisfaction of returning his glance. And then came an evening when I could no longer avoid direct contact with him.

It was a banquet at the villa of my father's younger brother, Demetrios. With my father dead, Demetrios was the head of our family, and his invitation had the power of a command. What I did not know was that Demetrios, for all his sacks of gold and his many estates in the hinterland, was angling for a political post in the new Roman administration. He wished to become Master of the Cavalry, not a military position at all—for what sort of cavalry could seaborne Venetia have?—but simply a sinecure that would entitle him to a share of the city's customs revenues. Therefore he was cultivating the friendship of Pompeius Falco and had invited him to the banquet. And, to my horror, he had seated me at the proconsul's right hand at the dinner table. Was my uncle willing to play the pimp for the sake of gaining a few extra ducats a year? So it would appear. I was ablaze with fury. But there was nothing I could do now except go through with my part. I had no wish to cause a scandal in my uncle's house.

Falco said to me, "We are companions this evening, it would seem. May I escort you to your seat, Lady Eudoxia?"

He spoke in Greek, and accurate Greek at that, though there was a thick-tongued barbarian undercurrent to his speech. I took his arm. He was taller than I had expected, and very broad through the shoulders. His eyes were alert and penetrating and his smile was a quick, forceful one. From a distance he had seemed quite boyish but I saw now that he was older than I had thought, at least thirty-five, perhaps even more. I detested him for his easy, confident manner, for his proprietarial air, for his command of our language. I even detested him for his beard, thick and black: beards had not been in fashion in the Greek world for several generations now. His was a short, dense fringe, a soldier's beard, that gave him the look of an emperor on one of the old Roman coins. Very likely that was its purpose.

Platters of grilled fish came, and cool wine to go with it. "I love your Venetian wine," he said. "So much more delicate than the heavy stuff of the south. Shall I pour, lady?"

There were servants standing around to do the pouring. But the proconsul of Venetia poured my wine for me, and everyone in the room noticed it.

I was the dutiful niece. I made amiable conversation, as though Pompeius Falco were a mere guest and not the agent of our conqueror; I pretended that I had utterly accepted the fall of Byzantium and the presence of Roman functionaries among us. Where was he from? Tarraco, he said. That was a city far in the west, he explained: in Hispania. The Emperor Flavius Romulus was from Tarraco also. Ah, and was he related to the Emperor, then? No, said Falco, not at all. But he was a close friend of the Emperor's youngest son, Marcus Quintilius. They had fought side by side in the Cappadocian campaign.

"And are you pleased to have been posted to Venetia?" I asked him, as the wine came around again.

"Oh, yes, yes, lady, very much. What a beautiful little city! So unusual: all these canals, all these bridges. And how civilized it is here, after the frenzy and clamor of Roma."

"Indeed, we are quite civilized," I said.

But I was boiling within, for I knew what he really meant, which was, *How quaint your Venetia is, how sweet, a precious little bauble of a place. And how clever it was of you to build your pretty little town in the sea as you did, so that all the streets are canals and one must get about by gondola instead of by carriage. And what a relief it is for me to spend some time in a placid provincial backwater like this, sipping good wine with handsome ladies while all the local lordlings scurry around me desperately trying to curry my favor, instead of my having to make my way in the cutthroat jungle that surrounds the Imperial court in Roma.* And as he went on praising the beauties of the city I came to hate him more and more. It is one thing to be conquered, and quite another to be patronized.

I knew he intended to seduce me. One didn't need the wisdom of Athena to see that. But I resolved then and there to seduce him first: to seize such little control as I could over this Roman, to humble him and thus to defeat him. Falco was an attractive enough animal, of course. On a sheer animal level there surely was pleasure to be had from him. And also the other pleasure of the conqueror conquered, the pursuer made the pursued: yes. I was eager for that. I was no longer the innocent of seventeen who had been given as bride to the radiant Heraclios Cantacuzenos. I had wiles, now. I was a woman, not a child.

I shifted the conversation to the arts, to literature, to philosophy, to history. I wanted to show him up as the barbarian he was; but he turned out to be unexpectedly well educated, and when I asked if he had been to the theater to see the current play, which was the *Nausicaa* of Sophocles, he said that he had, but that his favorite play of Sophocles was the *Philoctetes,* because it so well defined the conflict between honor and patriotism. "And yet, Lady Eudoxia, I can see why you are partial to the *Nausicaa,* for surely that kind princess must be a woman close to your heart." More flattery, and I loathed him for it; but in truth I had wept at the theater when Nausicaa and Odysseus had loved and parted, and perhaps I did see something of her in myself, or something of myself in her.

At the evening's end he asked me to take the midday meal with him at his palace two days hence. I was prepared for that and coolly begged a prior engagement. He proposed dinner, then, the first of the week following. Again I invented a reason for declining. He smiled. He understood the nature of the game we had entered into.

"Perhaps another time, then," he said, and gracefully left me for my uncle's company.

I meant to see him again, of course, but at a time and a place of my own choosing. And soon I found the occasion. When traveling troupes of musicians reach Venetia, they find a ready welcome at my home. A concert was to be held; I invited the proconsul. He came, accompanied by a stolid Roman retinue. I gave him the place of honor, naturally. Falco lingered after the performance to praise the quality of the flutes and the poignance of the singer; but he said nothing further about my joining him for dinner. Good: he had abdicated in my favor. From this point on I would define the nature of the chase. I offered him no further invitations either but allowed him a brief tour of the downstairs rooms of my palace before he left, and he admired the paintings, the sculptures, the cabinet of antiquities, all the fine things that I had inherited from my father and my grandfather.

The next day a Roman soldier arrived with a gift for me from the proconsul: a little statuette in highly polished black stone, showing a woman with the head of a cat. The note from Falco that accompanied it said that he had obtained it while serving in the province of Aegyptus some years ago: it was an image of one of the Aegyptian gods, which he had purchased at a temple in Memphis, and he thought I might find some beauty in it. Indeed it was beautiful, after a fashion, but also it was frightening and strange. In that way it was very much like Quintus Pompeius Falco, I found myself thinking, to my own great surprise. I put the statuette on a shelf in my cabinet— there was nothing like it there; I had never seen anything of its kind—and I resolved to ask Falco to tell me something of Aegyptus the next time I saw him, of its pyramids, its bizarre gods, its torrid sandy wastes.

I sent him a brief note of thanks. Then I waited seven days and invited him to join me for a holiday at my Istrian estate the following week.

Unfortunately, he replied, that week the cousin of Caesar would be passing through Venetia and would have to be entertained. Could he visit my estate another time?

The rejection caught me off guard. He was a better player of the game than I had suspected; I broke into hot tears of rage. But I had enough sense not to answer immediately. After three days I wrote again, telling him that I regretted being unable to offer him an alternate date at present, but perhaps I would find myself free to entertain him later in the season. It was a risky ploy: certainly it jeopardized my uncle's ambitions. But Falco seemingly took no offense. When our gondolas passed on the canal two days later, he bowed grandly to me and smiled.

I waited what seemed to be the right span of time and invited him again; and this time he accepted. A ten-man bodyguard came with him: did he think I meant to murder him? But of course the Empire must proclaim its power at every opportunity. I had been warned he would bring an entourage, and I was prepared for it, lodging his soldiers in distant outbuildings and sending for girls of the village to amuse and distract them. Falco himself I installed in the guest suite of my own dwelling.

He had another gift for me: a necklace made from beads of some strange green stone, carved in curious patterns, with a blood-red wedge of stone at its center.

"How lovely," I said, although I thought it frightening and harsh.

"It comes from the land of Mexico," he told me. "Which is a great kingdom in Nova Roma, far across the Ocean Sea. They worship mysterious gods there. Their festivals are held atop a great pyramid, where priests cut out the hearts of sacrificial victims until rivers of blood run in the streets of the city."

"And you have been there?"

"Oh, yes, yes. Six years past. Mexico and another land called Peru. I was in the service of Caesar's ambassador to the kingdoms of Nova Roma then."

It stunned me to think that this man had been to Nova Roma. Those two great continents on the other side of the Ocean—they seemed as remote as the face of the moon to me. But of course in this great time of the Empire under Flavius Romulus the Romans have carried their banners to the most remote parts of the world.

I stroked the stone beads—the green stone was smooth as silk and seemed to burn with an inner fire—and put the necklace on.

"Aegyptus—Nova Roma—" I shook my head. "And have you been everywhere, then?"

"Yes, very nearly so," he said, laughing. "The men who serve Flavius Caesar grow accustomed to long journeys. My brother has been to Khitai and the islands of Cipangu. My uncle went far south in Africa, beyond Aegyptus, to the lands where the hairy men dwell. It is a golden age, lady. The Empire reaches out boldly to every corner of the world." Then he smiled and leaned close and said, "And you, lady? Have you traveled very much?"

"I have seen Constantinopolis," I said.

"Ah. The great capital, yes. I stopped there on my way to Aegyptus. The races in the Hippodrome—nothing like it, even in Urbs

Roma itself! I saw the royal palace: from the outside, of course. They say it has walls of gold. I think not even Caesar's house can equal it."

"I was in it, once, when I was a child. When the Basileus still ruled, I mean. I saw the golden halls. I saw the lions of gold that sit beside the throne and roar and wave their tails, and the jewelled birds on the gold and silver trees in the throne-chamber, who open their beaks and sing. The Basileus gave me a ring. My father was his distant relative, you know. I am of the Phokas family. Later I married a Cantacuzenos: my husband too had royal connections."

"Ah," he said, as though greatly impressed, as though the names of the Byzantine aristocracy might possibly mean something to him.

But in fact I knew he was still condescending to me. A dethroned emperor is no emperor at all; a fallen aristocracy merits little awe.

And what did it matter to him that I had been once to Constantinopolis—he who had been there too, in passing, on his way to fabulous Aegyptus? The one great journey I had taken in my life was a mere stopover to him. His cosmopolitanism humbled me, as I suppose it was meant to do. He had been to other continents: other worlds, really. Aegyptus! Nova Roma! He could find things to praise about our capital, yes, but it was clear from his effusive tone that he really regarded it as inferior to the city of Roma, and inferior perhaps to the cities of Mexico and Peru as well, and other exotic places that he had visited in Caesar's name. The breadth and scope of his travels dazzled me. Here we Greeks were, penned up in our ever-shrinking realm that now had collapsed utterly. Here was I, daughter of one minor city on the periphery of that fallen realm, pathetically proud of my one visit long ago to our formerly mighty capital. But he was a Roman; all the world was open to him. If mighty Constantinopolis of the golden walls was just one more city to him, what was our little Venetia? What was I?

I hated him more violently than ever. I wished I had never invited him.

But he was my guest. I had had a wondrous banquet prepared, with the finest of wines, and delicacies that even a far-traveled Roman might not have met with before. He was obviously pleased. He drank and drank and drank, growing flushed though never losing control, and we talked far into the night.

I must confess that he amazed me with the scope and range of his mind.

He was no mere barbarian. He had had a Greek tutor, as all Romans of good family had had for over a thousand years. A wise old Athenian named Eukleides, he was, who had filled the young Falco's head with poetry and drama and philosophy, and drilled him in the most obscure nuances of our language, and taught him the abstract sciences, at which we Greeks have always excelled. And so this proconsul was at home not just in Roman things like science and engineering and the art of warfare, but also in Plato and Aristoteles, in the playwrights and poets, in the history of my race back to Agamemnon's time—indeed, he was able to discourse on all manner of things that I myself knew more by name than by their inner meaning.

He talked until I had had all the talking I could bear, and then some. And at last—it was the middle hour of the night, and the owls were crying in the darkness—I took him by the hand and led him to my bed, if only to silence that flow of words that came from him like the torrents of Aegyptus's Nilus itself.

He lit a taper in the bedchamber. Our clothes dropped away as though they had turned to mist.

He reached for me and drew me down.

I had never been loved by a Roman before. In the last moment before he embraced me I had a sudden fresh burst of fiery contempt for him and all his kind, for I was certain that his innate brutality now would come to the fore, that all his philosophic eloquence had been but a pose and now he would take possession of me the way Romans for fifteen hundred years had taken possession of everything in their path. He would subjugate me; he would colonize me. He would be coarse and violent and clumsy, but he would have his way, as Romans always did, and afterward he would rise and leave without a word.

I was wrong, as I had been wrong about everything else concerning this man.

His touch indeed was Roman, not Greek. That is to say, instead of insinuating himself into me in some devious, cunning, left-handed manner, he was straightforward and direct. But not clumsy, not at all. He knew what to do, and he set about doing it; and where there were things he had to learn, as any man must when it is his first time with a new woman, he knew what they were and he knew how to learn them. I understood now what was meant when women said that Greek men make love like poets and Romans like engineers. What I had never realized until that moment was that engineers have skills that many poets never have, and that an engineer could be capable of writing fine poetry, but would you not think twice about riding across a bridge that had been designed or built by a poet?

We lay together until dawn, laughing and talking when we were not embracing. And then, having had no sleep, we rose in our nakedness and walked through the halls to the bath-chamber, and in great merriment washed ourselves, and, still naked, walked out into the sweet pink dawn. Side by side we stood, saying nothing, watching the sun come up out of Byzantium and begin its day's journey onward toward Roma, toward the lands along the Western Sea, toward Nova Roma, toward far-off Khitai.

We dressed and had a breakfast of wine and cheese and figs, and I called for horses and took him on a tour of the estate. I showed him the olive groves, the fields of wheat, the mill and its stream, the fig trees laden with fruit. The day was warm and beautiful; the birds sang, the sky was clear.

Later, as we took our midday meal on the patio overlooking the garden, he said, "This is a marvelous place. I hope that when I'm old I can retire to a country estate like this."

"Surely there must be one in your family," I said.

"Several. But not, I think, as peaceful as this. We Romans have forgotten how to live peacefully."

"Whereas we, since we are a declining race, can allow ourselves the luxury of a little tranquility?"

He looked at me strangely. "You see yourselves as a declining race?"

"Don't be disingenuous, Quintus Pompeius. There's no need to flatter me now. Of course we are."

"Because you're no longer an imperial power?"

"Of course. Once ambassadors from places like Nova Roma and Baghdad and Memphis and Khitai came to us. Not here to Venetia, I mean, but to Constantinopolis. Now the ambassadors go only to Roma; what the Greek cities get is tourists. And Roman proconsuls."

"How strange your view of the world is, Eudoxia."

"What do you mean?"

"You equate the loss of the Imperium with being in decline."

"Wouldn't you?"

"If it happened to Roma, yes. But Byzantium isn't Roma." He was staring at me very seriously now. "The Eastern Empire was a folly, a distraction, a great mistake that somehow endured a thousand years. It should never have been. The burden of ruling the world was given to Roma: we accept it as our duty. There was never any need for an Eastern Empire in the first place."

"It was all some terrible error of Constantinus's, you say?"

"Exactly. It was a bad time for Roma, then. Even empires have their fluctuations; even ours. We had overextended ourselves, and everything was shaking. Constantinus had political problems at home, and too many troublesome sons. He thought the Empire was unwieldy and impossible to hold together, so he built the eastern capital and let the two halves drift apart. The system worked for a while—no, I admit it, for hundreds of years—but as the East lost sight of the fact that its political system had been set up by Romans and began to remember that it was really Greek, its doom became inevitable. A Greek Imperium is an anomaly that can't sustain itself in the modern world. It couldn't even sustain itself very long in the ancient world. The phrase is a contradiction in terms, a Greek Imperium. Agamemnon had no Imperium: he was only a tribal chief, who could barely make his power felt ten miles from Mycenae. And how long did the Athenian Empire last? How long did Alexander's kingdom hold together, once Alexander had died? No, no, no, Eudoxia, the Greeks are a marvelous people, the whole world is in their debt for any number of great achievements, but building and sustaining governments on a large scale isn't one of their skills. And never has been."

"You think so?" I said, with glee in my voice. "Then why was it that we were able to defeat you in the Civil War? It was Caesar Maximilianus who surrendered to the Basileus Andronicus, is that not so, West yielding to East, and not the other way around. For two hundred years we of the East were supreme in the world, may I remind you."

Falco shrugged. "The gods were teaching Roma a lesson, that's all. It was another fluctuation. We were being punished for having allowed the Empire to be divided in the first place. We needed to be humbled for a little while, so we'd never make the same mistake again. You Greeks beat us very soundly in Maximilianus's time, and you had a couple of hundred years of being, as you say, supreme, while we discovered what it felt like to be a second-rate power. But it was an impossible situation. The gods *intend* Roma to rule the world. There's simply no doubt of that. It was true in the time of Carthago and it's true today. And so the Greek Empire fell apart without even the need for a second Civil War. And so here we are. A Roman procurator sits in the royal palace at Constantinopolis. And a Roman proconsul in Venetia. Although at the moment he happens to be at the country estate of a lovely Venetian lady."

"You're serious?" I said. "You really believe that you are a chosen people? That Roma holds the Imperium by the will of the gods?"

"Absolutely."

He was altogether sincere.

"The Pax Romana is Zeus's gift to humanity? Jupiter's gift, I should say."

"Yes," he said. "But for us, the world would fall into chaos. Gods, woman, do you think we *want* to spend our lives being administrators and bureaucrats? Don't you think I'd prefer to retire to some estate like this and spend my days hunting and fishing and farming? But we are the race that understands how to rule. And therefore we have the obligation to rule. Oh, Eudoxia, Eudoxia, you think we're simple brutal beasts who go around conquering everybody for the sheer joy of conquest, and you don't realize that this is our task, our burden, our *job.*"

"I will weep for you, then."

He smiled. "Am I a simple brutal beast?"

"Of course you are. All Romans are."

He stayed with me for five days. I think we slept perhaps ten hours in all that time. Then he begged leave of me, saying that it was necessary that he return to his tasks in Venetia, and he went away.

I remained behind, with plenty to think about.

I could not, of course, accept his thesis that Greeks were incapable of governing anyone and that Roma had some divine mandate to run the world. The Eastern Empire had spread over great segments of the known world in its first few hundred years—Syria, Arabia, Aegyptus, much of eastern Europa even as far as Venetia, which is little more than a good stone's throw from Urbs Roma itself—and we had thrived and prospered mightily, as the wealth of the great Byzantine cities still attests. And in later years, when the Romans had begun to find that their Greek cousins were growing uncomfortably powerful and had attempted to reassert the supremacy of the West, we had fought a fifty-year Civil War and had beaten them quite handily. Which had led to two centuries of Byzantine hegemony, hard times for the West while Byzantine merchant ships traveled to the rich cities of Asia and Africa. I suppose ultimately we had overreached ourselves, as all empires eventually do, or perhaps we simply went soft with too much prosperity, and so the Romans awakened out of their sleep of centuries and shook our empire apart. Maybe they are the great exception: maybe their Imperium really will go on and on and on through the ages to come, as it has done for the last fifteen hundred years, with only minor periods of what Falco would call "fluctuations" to disrupt its unbroken span of command. And therefore our territories have been reduced by the inexorable force of the imperial destiny of Roma to the status of Roman provinces again, as they were in the time of Augustus Caesar. But we had had our time of grandeur. We had ruled the world just as well as the Romans ever did.

Or so I told myself. But even as I thought it, I knew it wasn't so. We Greeks could understand grandeur, yes. We understand splendor and imperial pomp. But the Romans know how to do the day-by-day work of governing. Maybe Falco was right after all: maybe our pitiful few centuries of Imperium, interrupting the long Roman sway, had been just an anomaly of history. For now the Eastern Empire was only a memory and the Pax Romana was once again in force across thousands of miles, and from his hilltop in Roma the great Caesar Flavius Romulus presided over a realm such as the world had never before known, Romans in remotest Asia, Romans in India, Roman vessels traveling even to the astonishing new continents of the far western hemisphere, strange new inventions coming forth—printed books, weapons that hurl heavy missiles great distances, all sorts of miracles—and we Greeks are reduced to contemplation of past glories as we sit in our conquered cities sipping our wine and reading Homer and Sophocles. For the first time in my life I saw my people as a minor race, elegant, charming, cultivated, unimportant.

How I had despised my handsome proconsul! And how he had revenged himself on me for that!

I stayed in Istria two more days and then I returned to the city. There was a gift waiting for me from Falco: a sleek piece of carved ivory that showed a house of strange design and a woman with delicate features sitting pensively beside a lake under a tree with weeping boughs. The note from him that accompanied it said that it was from Khitai, that he had obtained it in the land of Bactria, on India's borders. He had not told me that he had been to Bactria too. The thought of his travels on behalf of Roma dizzied me: so many voyages, such strenuous journeys. And I imagined him gathering little treasures such as these wherever he went, and carrying them about with him to bestow on his ladies in other lands. That thought so angered me that I nearly hurled the ivory piece away. But I reconsidered and put it in my cabinet of curios next to the stone goddess from Aegyptus.

It was his turn now to invite me to dine with him at the palace of the Doges, and—I assumed—to spend the night in the bed where the Doges and their consorts once had slept. But I waited a week and then a second week, and the invitation did not come. That seemed out of keeping with my new awareness of him as a man of great attainment. Perhaps I had overestimated him, though. He was, after all, a Roman. He had had what he wanted from me; now he was on to other adventures, other conquests.

I was wrong about that, too.

When my impatience had darkened once again into anger toward him and my fury over having let him use me this way had obliterated all the regard for him that had developed in me during his visit to my estate, I went to my uncle Demetrios and said, "Have you seen this Roman proconsul of ours lately? Has he been ill, do you think?"

"Why, is he of any concern to you, Eudoxia?"

I glowered at him. Having pushed me into Falco's arms to serve his own purposes, Demetrios had no right to mock me now. Sharply I said, "He owes me the courtesy of an invitation to the palace, uncle. Not that I would accept it—not now. But he should know that he has given offense."

"And I am supposed to tell him that?"

"Tell him nothing. *Nothing!*"

Demetrios gave me a knowing smirk. But I was sure he would keep silent. There was nothing for him to gain from humiliating me in the eyes of Pompeius Falco.

The days went by. And then at last came a note from Falco, in elegant Greek script as all his notes were, asking if he might call on me. My impulse was to refuse. But one did not refuse such requests from a proconsul. And in any case I realized that I wanted to see him again. I wanted very much to see him again.

"I hope you will forgive me, lady, for my inattentiveness," he said. "But I have had a great deal on my mind in these recent weeks."

"I'm certain that you have," I said drily.

Color came to his face. "You have every right to be angry with me, Eudoxia. But this has been a time of unusual circumstances. There have been great upheavals in Roma, do you know? The Emperor has reshuffled his Cabinet. Important men have fallen; others have risen suddenly to glory."

"And how has this concerned you?" I asked him. "Are you one of those who has fallen, or have you risen to glory? Or should I not ask you any of this?"

"One of those who has risen," he said, "is Gaius Julius Flavillus." The name meant nothing to me.

"Gaius Julius Flavillus, lady, had held the post of Third Flamen. Now he is First Tribune. Which is a considerable elevation, as you may know. It happens that Gaius Flavillus is a man of Tarraco, like the Emperor, like myself. He is my father's cousin. He has been my patron throughout my career. And so—messengers have been going back and forth between Venetia and Roma for all these weeks—I too have been elevated, it seems, by special favor of the new Tribune."

"Elevated," I said hollowly.

"Indeed. I have been transferred to Constantinopolis, where I am to be the new procurator. It is the highest administrative post in the former Eastern Empire." His eyes were glittering with self-satisfaction. But then his expression changed. A kind of sadness came into them, a kind of tenderness. "Lady, you must believe me when I tell you that I greeted the news with a mixture of feelings, not all of them pleasant ones. It is a great honor for me. And yet I would not have left Venetia so quickly of my own choosing. We have barely begun to know each other; and now, to my immense regret, we must part."

He took my hands in his. He seemed almost to be at the edge of tears. His sincerity seemed real; or else he was a better actor than I suspected.

A kind of numbness spread through me.

"When do you leave?" I asked.

"In three days, lady."

"Ah. Three days."

"Three very busy days."

You could always take me with you to Constantinopolis, I found myself thinking. There would surely be room for me somewhere in the vast palace of the former Basileus where you now will make your home.

But of course that could never be. A Roman rising as swiftly as he was would never want to encumber himself with a Byzantine wife. A Byzantine mistress, perhaps. But mistresses of any sort were no longer what he needed. Now was the time for him to make an auspicious marriage and undertake the next stage of his climb. The procurator's seat at Constantinopolis would detain him little longer than his proconsulship in Venetia had; his path would lead him before very long back to Roma. He would be a flamen, a tribune, perhaps Pontifex Maximus. If he played his cards right he might some day be Emperor. I might be summoned then to Roma to relive old times, perhaps. But I would not see him again before then.

"May I stay this night with you?" he asked, with a strange new note of uncertainty in his voice, as though expecting that I might refuse.

But of course I did not refuse. That would have been crass and petty; and in any case I wanted him. I knew that this was the last chance.

It was a night of wine and poetry, of tears and laughter, of ecstasy and exhaustion.

And then he was gone, leaving me mired in my petty little provincial life while he went on to Constantinopolis and glory. A grand procession of gondolas followed him down the canal as he made his way to the sea. A new Roman proconsul, so they say, will be arriving in Venetia any day now.

From Falco I had one parting gift: the plays of Aeschylus, in a finely bound volume that had been produced on the printing press, which is one of those new inventions of which they are so proud in Roma. My first reaction was one of scorn, that he should give me this machine-made thing instead of a manuscript indited by hand. And then, as I had done so many times in the days of my involvement with this difficult man, I was forced to reconsider, to admire what at first sight I had seen as cheap and vulgar. The book was beautiful, in its way. More than that: it was a sign of a new age. To deny that new age, or turn my back on it, would be folly.

And so I have learned at first hand of the power of Roma and of the insignificance of the formerly great. Our lovely Venetia was only a way station for him. Constantinopolis of Imperial grandeur will be the same. It was a powerful lesson: I have been thoroughly educated in the ways of Roma and the Romans, to my own great cost, for I see now as I never could have seen before that they are everything and we, polished and refined as we may be, are nothing at all.

I had underestimated Quintus Pompeius Falco at every turn; I had underestimated his race the same way. As had we all, which is why they once again rule the world, or most of it, and we smile and bow and hope for their favor.

He has written to me several times. So I must have made a strong impression on him. He speaks fondly, if guardedly, of our times together. He says nothing, though, about hoping that I will pay a visit to Constantinopolis to see him.

But perhaps I will, one of these days, nevertheless. Or perhaps not. It all depends on what the new proconsul is like.

A.U.C. 2543: GETTING TO KNOW THE DRAGON

I reached the theater at nine that morning, half an hour before the appointed time, for I knew only too well how unkind the Caesar Demetrius could be to the unpunctual. But the Caesar, it seemed, had arrived even earlier than that. I found Labienus, his personal guard and chief drinking companion, lounging by the theater entrance; and as I approached, Labienus smirked and said, "What took you so long? Caesar's been waiting for you."

"I'm half an hour early," I said sourly. No need to be tactful with the likes of Labienus—or Polykrates, as I should be calling him, now that Caesar has given us all new Greek names. "Where is he?"

Labienus pointed through the gate and turned his middle finger straight upward, jabbing it three times toward the heavens. I limped past him without another word and went inside.

To my dismay I saw the figure of Demetrius Caesar right at the very summit of the theater, the uppermost row, his slight figure outlined sharply against the brilliant blue of the morning sky. It was less than six weeks since I had broken my ankle hunting boar with the Caesar in the interior of the island; I was still on crutches, and walk-

ing, let alone climbing stairs, was a challenge for me. But there he
was, high up above.

"So you've turned up at last, Pisander!" he called. "It's about
time. Hurry on up! I've got something very interesting to show you."

Pisander. It was last summer when he suddenly bestowed the
Greek names on us all. Julius and Lucius and Marcus lost their good
honest Roman praenomina and became Eurystheos and Idomeneos
and Diomedes. I who was Tiberius Ulpius Draco was now Pisander.
It was the latest fashion at the court that the Caesar maintained—at
his Imperial father's insistence—down here in Sicilia, these Greek
names: to be followed, we all supposed, by mandatory Greek hair-
styles and sticky pomades, the wearing of airy Greek costumes, and,
eventually, the introduction on an obligatory basis of the practice of
Greek buggery. Well, the Caesars amuse themselves as they will; and
I might not have minded it if he had named me something heroic,
Agamemnon or Odysseus or the like. But Pisander? Pisander of
Laranda was the author of that marvelous epic of world history,
Heroic Marriages of the Gods, and it would have been reasonable
enough for Caesar to name me for him, since I am an historian also.
And also there is the earlier Pisander, Pisander of Camirus, who
wrote the oldest known epic of the deeds of Herakles. But there was
yet another Pisander, a fat and corrupt Athenian politician who
comes in for some merciless mockery in the *Hyperbolos* of Aristophanes, and I happen to know that play is one of Caesar's special favorites. Since the other two Pisanders are figures out of antiquity,
obscure except to specialists like me, I cannot help but think that
Caesar had Aristophanes's character in mind when coining my
Greek name for me. I am neither fat nor corrupt, but the Caesar
takes great pleasure in vexing our souls with such little pranks.

Forcing a cripple to climb to the top of the theater, for example.
I went hobbling painfully up the steep stone steps, flight after flight
after flight, until I emerged at last at the very highest row. Demetrius
was staring off toward the side, admiring the wonderful spectacle of
Mount Etna rising in the west, snow-capped, stained by ashes at its
summit, a plume of black smoke coiling from its boiling maw. The
views that can be obtained up here atop the great theater of Tau-

romenium are indeed breathtaking; but my breath had been taken sufficiently by the effort of the climb, and I was in no mood just then to appreciate the splendor of the scenery about us.

He was leaning against the stone table in the top-row concourse where the wine sellers display their wares during intermission. An enormous scroll was laid out in front of him. "Here is my plan for the improvement of the island, Pisander. Come take a look and tell me what you think of it."

It was a huge map of Sicilia, covering the entire table. Drawn practically to full scale, one might say. I could see great scarlet circles, perhaps half a dozen of them, marked boldly on it. This was not at all what I was expecting, since the ostensible purpose of the meeting this morning was to discuss the Caesar's plan for renovating the Tauromenium theater. Among my various areas of expertise is a certain knowledge of architecture. But no, no, the renovation of the theater was not at all on Demetrius's mind today.

"This is a beautiful island," he said, "but its economy has been sluggish for decades. I propose to awaken it by undertaking the most ambitious construction program Sicilia has ever seen. For example, Pisander, right here in our pretty little Tauromenium there's a crying need for a proper royal palace. The villa where I've been living these past three years is nicely situated, yes, but it's rather modest, wouldn't you say, for the residence of the heir to the throne?" Modest, yes. Thirty or forty rooms at the edge of the steep cliff overlooking town, affording a flawless prospect of the sea and the volcano. He tapped the scarlet circle in the upper right-hand corner of the map surrounding the place that Tauromenium occupies in northeastern Sicilia. "Suppose we turn the villa into a proper palace by extending it down the face of the cliff a bit, eh? Come over here, and I'll show you what I mean."

I hobbled along behind him. He led me around to a point along the rim where his villa's portico was in view, and proceeded to describe a cascading series of levels, supported by fantastic cantilevered platforms and enormous flaring buttresses, that would carry the structure down the entire face of the cliff, right to the shore of the Ionian Sea far below. "That would make it ever so much simpler for me to get to the beach, wouldn't you say? If we were to build a track of some sort that ran down the side of the building, with a car suspended on cables? Instead of having to take the main road down, I could simply descend within my own palace."

I stared the goggle-eyed stare of incredulity. Such a structure, if it could be built at all, would take fifty years to build and cost a billion sesterces, at the least. Ten billion, maybe.

But that wasn't all. Far from it.

"Then, Pisander, we need to do something about the accommodations for visiting royalty at Panormus." He ran his finger westward across the top of the map to the big port farther along the northern shore. "Panormus is where my father likes to stay when he comes here; but the palace is six hundred years old and quite inadequate. I'd like to tear it down and build a full-scale replica of the Imperial palace on Palatine Hill on the site, with perhaps a replica of the Forum of Roma just downhill from it. He'd like that: make him feel at home when he visits Sicilia. Then, as a nice place to stay in the middle of the island while we're out hunting, there's the wonderful old palace of Maximianius Herculeus near Enna, but it's practically falling down. We could erect an entirely new palace—in Byzantine style, let's say—on its site, being very careful not to harm the existing mosaics, of course. And then—"

I listened, ever more stupefied by the moment. Demetrius's idea of reawakening the Sicilian economy involved building unthinkably expensive royal palaces all over the island. At Agrigentum on the southern coast, for example, where the royals liked to go to see the magnificent Greek temples that are found there and at nearby Selinunte, he thought that it would be pleasant to construct an exact duplicate of Hadrianus's famous villa at Tibur as a sort of tourist lodge for them. But Hadrianus's villa is the size of a small city. It would take an army of craftsmen at least a century to build its twin at Agrigentum. And over at the western end of the island he had some notion for a castle in rugged, primordial Homeric style, or whatever he imagined Homeric style to be, clinging romantically to the summit of the citadel of Eryx. Then, down at Syracusae—well, what he had in mind for Syracusae would have bankrupted the Empire. A grand new palace, naturally, but also a lighthouse like the one in Alexandria, and a Parthenon twice the size of the real one, and a dozen or so pyramids like those in Aegyptus, only perhaps a little bigger, and a bronze Colossus on the waterfront like the one that used to stand in the harbor at Rhodos, and—I'm unable to set down the entire list without wanting to weep.

"Well, Pisander, what do you say? Has there ever been a building program like this in the history of the world?"

His face was shining. He is a very handsome man, is Demetrius Caesar, and in that moment, transfigured by his own megalomaniac scheme, he was a veritable Apollo. But a crazy one. What possible response could I have made to all that he had just poured forth? That I thought it was the wildest lunacy? That I very much doubted there was enough gold in all his father's treasury to underwrite the cost of such an absurd enterprise? That we would all be long dead before these projects could be completed? The Emperor Lodovicus his father, when assigning me to the service of the Caesar Demetrius, had warned me of his volatile temper. A word placed wrongly and I might find myself hurled sprawling down the very steps up which I had just clambered with so much labor.

But I know how to manage things when speaking with royalty. Tactfully but not unctuously I said, "It is a project that inspires me with awe, Caesar. I am hard pressed to bring its equal to mind."

"Exactly. There's never been anything like it, has there? I'll go down in history. Neither Alexander nor Sardanapalus nor Augustus Caesar himself ever attempted a public-works program of such ambitious size. —You, of course, will be the chief architect of the entire project, Pisander."

If he had kicked me in the gut I would not have been more thoroughly taken aback.

I smothered a gasp and said, "I, Caesar? You do me too much honor. My primary field these days is historical scholarship, my lord. I've dabbled a bit in architecture, but I hardly regard myself as qualified to—"

"Well, I do. Spare me your false modesty, will you, Draco?" Suddenly he was calling me by my true name again. That seemed very significant. "Everyone knows just how capable a man you are. You hide behind this scholarly pose because you think it's safer that way, I would imagine, but I'm well aware of your real abilities, and when I'm Emperor I mean to make the most of them. That's the mark of a great Emperor, wouldn't you say—to surround himself with men who are great themselves, and to inspire them to rise to their full potentiality? I do expect to be a great Emperor, you know, ten years from now, twenty, whenever it is that my turn comes. But I'm already beginning to pick out my key men. You'll be one of them." He winked at me. "See to it that that leg heals fast, Draco. I mean to start this project off by building the Tauromenium palace, which I want you to design for me, and that means that you and I are going to be scrambling around on the face of that cliff looking for the best possible site. I don't want you on crutches when we do that. —Isn't the mountain beautiful today, Pisander?"

In the space of three breaths I had become Pisander again.

He rolled up his scroll. I wondered if we were finally going to discuss the theater-renovation job. But then I realized that the Caesar, his mind inflamed by the full magnificence of his plan for transforming every major city of the island, was no more interested just now in talking about a petty thing like replacing the clogged drainage channel running down the hillside adjacent to this theater than a god would be in hearing about somebody's personal health problems, his broken ankle, say, when his godlike intellect is absorbed with the task of designing some wondrous new plague with which he intends to destroy eleven million yellow-skinned inhabitants of far-off Khitai a little later in the month.

We admired the view together for a while, therefore. Then, when I sensed that I had been dismissed, I took my leave without bringing up the topic of the theater, and slowly and uncomfortably made my way down the steps again. Just as I reached the bottom I heard the Caesar call out to me. I feared for one dreadful moment that he was summoning me back and I would have to haul myself all the way up there a second time. But he simply wanted to wish me a good day. The Caesar Demetrius is insane, of course, but he's not really vicious.

* * *

"The Emperor will never allow him to do it," Spiculo said, as we sat late that night over our wine.

"He will. The Emperor grants his crazy son his every little wish. His every big one, too."

Spiculo is my oldest friend, well named, a thorny little man. We are both Hispaniards; we went to school together in Tarraco; when I took up residence in Roma and entered the Emperor's service, so did he. When the Emperor handed me off to his son, Spiculo followed me loyally to Sicilia, too. I trust him as I trust no other man. We utter the most flagrant treason to each other all the time.

"If he begins it, then," said Spiculo, "he'll never go through with anything. You know what he's like. Six months after they break ground for the palace here, he'll decide he'd rather get started on his Parthenon in Syracusae. He'll erect three columns there and go off to Panormus. And then he'll jump somewhere else a month after that."

"So?" I said. "What business is that of mine? He's the one who'll look silly if that's how he handles it, not me. I'm only the architect."

His eyes widened. "What? You're actually going to get involved in this thing, are you?"

"The Caesar has requested my services."

"And are you so supine that you'll simply do whatever he tells you to, however foolish it may be? Piss away the next five or ten years of your life on a demented young prince's cockeyed scheme for burying this whole godforsaken island under mountains of marble? Get your name linked with his for all time to come as the facilitator of this lunatic affair?" His voice became a harsh mocking soprano. "*'Tiberius Ulpius Draco, the greatest man of science of the era, foolishly abandoned all his valuable scholarly research in order to devote the remaining years of his life to this ill-conceived series of preposterously grandiose projects, none of which was ever completed, and finally was found one morning, dead by his own hand, sprawled at the base of the unfinished Great Pyramid of Syracusae—'* No, Draco! Don't do it! Just shake your head and walk away!"

"You speak as though I have any choice about it," I said.

He stared at me. Then he rose and stomped across the patio toward the balcony. He is a cripple from birth, with a twisted left leg and a foot that points out to the side. My hunting accident angered him, because it caused me to limp as well, which directs additional attention to Spiculo's own deformity as we hobble side by side through the streets, a grotesquely comical pair who might easily be thought to be on their way to a beggar's convention.

For a long moment he stood scowling at me without speaking. It was a night of bright moonlight, brilliantly illuminating the villas of the wealthy all up and down the slopes of the Tauromenian hillside, and as the silence went on and on I found myself studying the triangular outlines of Spiculo's form as it was limned from behind by the chilly white light: the broad burly shoulders tapering down to the narrow waist and the spindly legs, with the big out-jutting head planted defiantly atop. If I had had my sketchpad I would have begun to draw him. But of course I have drawn him many times before.

He said at last, very quietly, "You astound me, Draco. What do you mean, you don't have any choice? Simply resign from his service and go back to Roma. The Emperor needs you there. He can find some other nursemaid for his idiot princeling. You don't seriously think that Demetrius will have you thrown in jail if you decline to take on the job, do you? Or executed, or something?"

"You don't understand," I said. "I *want* to take the job on."

"Even though it's a madman's wet dream? Draco, have you gone crazy yourself? Is the Caesar's lunacy contagious?"

I smiled. "Of course I know how ridiculous the whole thing is. But that doesn't mean I don't want to give it a try."

"Ah," Spiculo said, getting it at last. "Ah! So that's it! The temptation of the unthinkable! The engineer in you wants to pile Pelion on Ossa just to find out whether he can manage the trick! Oh, Draco, Demetrius isn't as crazy as he seems, is he? He sized you up just perfectly. There's only one man in the world who's got the *hybris* to take on this idiotic job, and he's right here in Tauromenium."

"It's piling Ossa on Pelion, not the other way around," I said. "But yes. Yes, Spiculo! Of course I'm tempted. So what if it's all craziness? And if nothing ever gets finished, what of it? At least things will be started. Plans will be drawn; foundations will be dug. Don't you think I want to see how an Aegyptian pyramid can be built? Or how to cantilever a palace thousands of feet down the side of this cliff here? It's the chance of a lifetime for me."

"And your account of the life of Trajan VII? Only the day before yesterday you couldn't stop talking about the documents that are on their way to you from the archive in Sevilla. Speculating half the night about the wonderful new revelations you were going to find in them, you were. Are you going to abandon the whole thing just like that?"

"Of course not. Why should one project interfere with another? I'm quite capable of working on a book in the evening while designing palaces during the day. I expect to continue with my painting and my poetry and my music too. —I think you underestimate me, old friend."

"Well, let it not be said that you've ever been guilty of doing the same."

I let the point pass. "I offer you one additional consideration, and then let's put this away, shall we? Lodovicus is past sixty and not in wonderful health. When he dies, Demetrius is going to be Emperor, whether anybody likes that idea or not, and you and I will return to Roma, where I will be a key figure in his administration and all the scholarly and scientific resources of the capital will be at my disposal. —Unless, of course, I irrevocably estrange myself from him while he's still only heir apparent by throwing this project of his back in his face, as you seem to want me to do. So I will take the job. As an investment leading to the hope of future gain, so to speak."

"Very nicely reasoned, Draco."

"Thank you."

"And suppose, when Demetrius becomes Emperor, which through some black irony of the gods he probably will before too long, he decides he'd rather keep you down here in Sicilia finishing the great work of filling this island with second-hand architectural splendors instead of transferring you to the court in Roma, and here you'll stay for the rest of your life, plodding around this backwater of a place supervising the completely useless and unnecessary construction of—"

I had had about enough. "Look, Spiculo, that's a risk I'm willing
to take. He's already told me in just that many words that when he's
Emperor he plans to make fuller use of my skills than his father ever
chose to do."

"And you believe him?"

"He sounded quite sincere."

"Oh, Draco, Draco! I'm beginning to think you're even crazier
than he is!"

It was a gamble, of course. I knew that.

And Spiculo might well have been speaking the truth when he
said that I was crazier than poor Demetrius. The Caesar, after all,
can't help being the way he is. There has been madness, real madness, in his family for a hundred years or more, serious mental insta-
bility, some defect of the mind leading to unpredictable outbreaks of
flightiness and caprice. I, on the other hand, face each day with clear
perceptions. I am hardworking and reliable, and I have a finely
tuned intelligence capable of succeeding at anything I turn it to.
This is not boasting. The solidity of my achievements is a fact not
open to question. I have built temples and palaces, I have painted
great paintings and fashioned splendid statues, I have written epic
poems and books of history, I have even designed a flying machine
that I will some day build and test successfully. And there is much
more besides that I have in mind to achieve, the secrets that I write
in cipher in my notebooks in a crabbed left-handed script, things
that would transform the world. Some day I will bring them all to
perfection. But at present I am not ready to do so much as hint at
them to anyone, and so I use the cipher. (As though anyone would
be able to comprehend these ideas of mine even if they could read
what is written in those notebooks!)

One might say that I owe all this mental agility to the special
kindness of the gods, and I am unwilling to contradict that pious
thought; but heredity has something to do with it, too. My superior
capacities are the gift of my ancestors just as the flaws of Demetrius
Caesar's mind are of his. In *my* veins courses the blood of one of the
greatest of our Emperors, the visionary Trajan VII, who would have

been well fit to wear the title that was bestowed sixteen centuries ago on the first Emperor of that name: Optimus Princeps, "best of princes." Who, though, are the forefathers of Demetrius Caesar? Lodovicus! Marius Antoninus! Valens Aquila! Why, are these not some of the feeblest men ever to have held the throne, and have they not led the Empire down the path of decadence and decline?

Of course it is the fate of the Empire to enter into periods of decadence now and then, just as it is its supreme good fortune to find, ever and always, a fresh source of rebirth and renewal when one is needed. That is why our Roma has been the preeminent power in the world for more than two thousand years and why it will go on and on to the end of time, world without end, eternally rebounding to new vigor.

Consider. There was a troubled and chaotic time about eighteen hundred years ago, and out of it Augustus Caesar gave us the Imperial government, which has served us in good stead ever since. When the blood of the early Caesars ran thin and such men as Caligula and Nero came disastrously to power, redemption was shortly at hand in the form of the first Trajan, and after him Hadrianus, succeeded by the equally capable Antoninus Pius and Marcus Aurelius.

A later period of troubles was put to right by Diocletianus, whose work was completed by the great Constantinus; and when, inevitably, we declined yet again, seven hundred years later, falling into what modern historians call the Great Decadence, and were so easily and shamefully conquered by our Greek-speaking brothers of the East, eventually Flavius Romulus arose among us to give us our freedom once more. And not long after him came Trajan VII to carry our explorers clear around the globe, bringing back incalculable wealth and setting in motion the exciting period of expansion that we know as the Renaissance. Now, alas, we are decadent again, living through what I suppose will some day be termed the Second Great Decadence. The cycle seems inescapable.

I like to think of myself as a man of the Renaissance, the last of my kind, born by some sad and unjust accident of fate two centuries out of his proper time and forced to live in this imbecilic decadent age. It's a pleasant fantasy and there's much evidence, to my way of thinking, that it's true.

That this is a decadent age there can be no doubt. One defining symptom of decadence is a fondness for vast and nonsensical extravagance, and what better example of that could be provided than the Caesar's witless and imprudent scheme for reshaping Sicilia as a monument to his own grandeur? The fact that the structures he would have me construct for him are, almost without exception, imitations of buildings of earlier and less fatuous eras only reinforces the point.

But also we are experiencing a breakdown of the central government. Not only do distant provinces like Syria and Persia blithely go their own way most of the time, but also Gallia and Hispania and Dalmatia and Pannonia, which are practically on the Emperor's own home turf, are behaving almost like independent nations. The new languages, too: what has become of our pure and beautiful Latin, the backbone of our Empire? It has degenerated into a welter of local dialects. Every place now has its own babbling lingo. We Hispaniards speak Hispanian, and the long-nosed Gallians have the nasal honking thing called Gallian, and in the Teutonic provinces they have retreated from Latin altogether, reverting to some primitive sputtering tongue known as Germanisch, and so on and so on. Why, even in Italia itself you find Latin giving way to a bastard child they call Roman, which at least is sweetly musical to the ear but has thrown away all the profundity and grammatical versatility that makes Latin the master language of the world. And if Latin is discarded entirely (which has not been the fate of Greek in the East), how will a man of Hispania be understood by a man of Britannia, or a Teuton by a Gallian, or a Dalmatian by anyone at all?

Surely this is decadence, when these destructive centrifugalities sweep through our society.

But is it really the case that I am a man of the Renaissance stranded in this miserable age? That's not so easy to say. In common speech we use the phrase "a Renaissance man" to indicate someone of unusual breadth and depth of attainment. I am certainly that. But would I have truly felt at home in the swashbuckling age of Trajan VII? I have the Renaissance expansiveness of mind; but do I have the flamboyant Renaissance temperament as well, or am I in truth just as timid and stodgy and generally piddling as everyone I see about me? We must not forget that they were medievals. Could I have carried a sword in the streets and brawled like a legionary at the slightest provocation? Would I have had twenty mistresses and fifty bastard sons? And yearned to clamber aboard a tiny creaking ship and sail off beyond the horizon?

No, I am probably not much like them. Their souls were large. The world was bigger and brighter and far more mysterious to them than it seems to us, and they responded to its mysteries with a romantic fervor, a ferocious outpouring of energy, that may be impossible for any of us to encompass today. I have taken on this assignment of Caesar's because it stirs some of that romantic fervor in me and makes me feel renewed kinship with my great world-girdling ancestor Trajan VII, Trajan the Dragon. But what will I be doing, really? Discovering new worlds, as he did? No, no, I will be building pyramids and Greek temples and the villa of Hadrianus. But all that has been done once already, quite satisfactorily, and there is no need to do it again. Am I, therefore, as decadent as any of my contemporaries?

I wonder, too, what would have happened to great Trajan if he had been born into this present era of Lodovicus Augustus and his crackbrained son Demetrius? Men of great spirit are at high risk at a time when small souls rule the world. I myself have found shrewd ways of fitting in, of ensuring my own security and safety, but would he have done the same? Or would he have gone noisily swaggering around the place like the true man of the Renaissance that he was, until finally it became necessary to do away with him quietly in some dark alley as an inconvenience to the royal house and to the realm in general? Perhaps not. Perhaps, as I prefer to think, he would have risen like a flaming arrow through the dark night of this murky epoch and, as he did in his own time, cast a brilliant light over the entirety of the world.

In any case here was I, undeniably intelligent and putatively sane, voluntarily linking myself with our deranged young Caesar's project, simply because I was unable to resist the wonderful technical challenge that it represented. A grand romantic gesture, or sim-

ply a mad one? Very likely Spiculo *was* right in saying by accepting
the job I demonstrated that I was crazier than Demetrius. Any gen-
uinely sane man would have run screaming away.

One did not have to be the Cumaean Sibyl to be able to foresee that
a long time would go by before Demetrius mentioned the project to
me again. The Caesar is forever flitting from one thing to another; it
is a mark of his malady; two days after our conversation in the theater he left Tauromenium for a holiday among the sand dunes of
Africa, and he was gone more than a month. Since we had not yet
done so much as chosen a location for the cliffside palace, let alone
come to an understanding about such things as a design and a construction budget, I put the whole matter out of my mind pending his
return. My hope, I suppose, was that he would have forgotten it entirely by the time he came back to Sicilia.

I took advantage of his absence to resume work on what had
been my main undertaking of the season, my study of the life of Trajan VII.

Which was something that had occupied me intermittently for
the past seven or eight years. Two things had led me back to it at this
time. One was the discovery, in the dusty depths of the Sevilla maritime archives, of a packet of long-buried journals purporting to be
Trajan's own account of his voyage around the world. The other was
the riding mishap during the boar hunt that had left me on crutches
for the time being: a period of enforced inactivity that gave me, for
lack of any other option, a good reason to assume the scholar's role
once more.

No adequate account of Trajan's extraordinary career had ever
been written. That may seem strange, considering our long national
tradition of great historical scholarship, going back to the misty figures of Naevius and Ennius in the time of the Republic, and, of
course, Sallust and Livius and Tacitus and Suetonius later on, Ammianus Marcellinus after them, Drusillus of Alexandria, Marcus
Andronicus—and, to come closer to modern times, Lucius Aelius
Antipater, the great chronicler of the conquest of Roma by the
Byzantines in the time of Maximilianus VI.

But something has gone awry with the writing of history since Flavius Romulus put the sundered halves of Imperial Roma back together in the year 2198 after the founding of the city. Perhaps it is that in a time of great men—and certainly the era of Flavius Romulus and his two immediate successors was that—everyone is too busy making history to have time to write it. That was what I used to believe, at any rate; but then I broke my ankle, and I came to understand that in any era, however energetic it may be, there is always someone who, from force of special circumstances, be it injury or illness or exile, finds himself with sufficient leisure to turn his hand to writing.

What has started to seem more likely to me is that in the time of Flavius Romulus and Gaius Flavillus and Trajan the Dragon, publishing any sort of account of those mighty Emperors would not have been an entirely healthy pastime. Just as the finest account of the lives of the first twelve Caesars—I speak of Suetonius's scathing and scabrous book—was written during the relatively benign reign of the first Trajan and not when such monsters as Caligula or Nero or Domitianus were still breathing fire in the land, so too may it have seemed unwise for scholars in the epoch of the three Hispaniard monarchs to set down anything but a bare-bones chronicle of public events and significant legislation. To analyze Caesar is to criticize him. That is not always safe.

Whatever the reason, no worthwhile contemporary books on the remarkable Flavius Romulus have come down to us, only mere factual chronicles and some fawning panegyrics. Of the inner nature of his successor, the shadowy Gaius Julius Flavillus, we know practically nothing, only such dry data as where he was born—like Flavius Romulus, he came from Tarraco in Hispania, my own native city—and which governmental posts he held during his long career before attaining the Imperial throne. And for the third of the three great Hispaniards, Trajan VII—whose surname happened by coincidence to be Draco but who earned by his deeds as well, throughout the world, the name of Trajan the Dragon—we have, once again, just the the most basic annals of his glorious reign.

That no one has tackled the job of writing his life in the two centuries since his death should come as no surprise. One can write safely about a dead Caesar, yes, but where was the man to do the job? The glittering period of the Renaissance gave way all too quickly to the dawning age of industrial development, and in that dreary, smoky time the making of money took priority over everything else, art and scholarship included. And now we have our new era of decadence, in which one weakling after another has worn the Imperial crown and the Empire itself seems gradually to be collapsing into a congeries of separate entities that feel little or no sense of loyalty to the central authority. Such vigor as our masters can manage to muster goes into inane enterprises like the construction of gigantic pointy-headed tombs in the Pharaonic style here in this isle of Sicilia. Who, in such an age, can bear to confront the grandeur of a Trajan VII?

Well, I can.

And have a thick sheaf of manuscript to show for it. I have taken advantage of my position in the Imperial service to burrow in the subbasements of the Capitol in Roma, unlocking cabinets that have been sealed for twenty centuries and bringing official papers into the light of day whose very existence had been forgotten. I have looked into the private records of the deliberations of the Senate: no one seemed to mind, or to care at all. I have read memoirs left behind by high officials of the court. I have pored over the reports of provincial excise collectors and tax commissioners and inspectors of the public markets, which, abstract and dull though they may seem, are in fact the true ore out of which history is mined. From all of this I have brought Trajan the Dragon and his era back into vivid reality—at least in my own mind, and on the pages of my unfinished book.

And what a figure he was! Throughout the many years of his long life he was the absolute embodiment of strength, vision, implacable purpose and energy. He ranks with the greatest of Emperors. With Augustus Caesar who founded the Empire, with Trajan I and Hadrianus who carried its boundaries to the ends of the earth, with Constantinus who established efficient rule over that far-flung domain, with Maximilianus III who conquered the barbarians once and for all, with his own countryman and predecessor Flavius Romulus. I have spent these years getting to know him—getting to know the Dragon!—and the contact with his great soul that I have enjoyed during these years of research into his life has ennobled and enlightened my days.

Well, then, what do I know of him, this great Emperor, this Dragon of Roma, this distant ancestor of mine?

That he was born illegitimately, for one thing. I have combed very carefully through the records of marriages and births in Tarraco and surrounding regions of Hispania for the entire period from A.U.C. 2215 to 2227, which should have been more than sufficient, and although I have found a number of Dracos entered in the tax rolls for those years, Decimus Draco and Numerius Draco and Salvius Draco, not one of them seems to have been married in any official way or to have brought forth progeny that warranted enumeration in the register of births. So his parents' names must remain unknown. All I can report is that one Trajan Draco, a native of Tarraco, is listed as enrolling in military service in the Third Hispanic Legion in the year 2241, from which I conclude that he was born somewhere between A.U.C. 2220 and 2225. In that period it was most usual to enter the army at the age of eighteen, which would place his date of birth at 2223, but, knowing Trajan Draco as I do, I would hazard a guess that he went in even younger, perhaps when he was sixteen or only fifteen.

The Empire was still under Greek rule at that time, technically; but Hispania, like most of the western provinces, was virtually independent. The Emperor at Constantinopolis was Leo XI, a man who cared much more about filling his palace with the artistic treasures of ancient Greece than he did about what might be going on in the Europan territories. Those territories were nominally under the control of the Western Emperor, anyway, his distant cousin Nicephoros Cantacuzenos. But the Western Emperors during the era of Greek domination were invariably idle puppets, and Nicephoros, the last of that series, was even more idle than most. They say he was never even to be seen in Roma but spent all his days in comfortable retreat in the south, near Neapolis.

The rebellion of the West, I am proud to say, began in Hispania, in my very own native city of Tarraco. The bold and dynamic Flavius

Romulus, a shepherd's son who may have been illiterate, raised an army of men just as ragged as he, overthrew the provincial government, and proclaimed himself Emperor. That was in the year 2193; he was twenty-five or thirty years old.

Nicephoros, the Western Emperor, chose to regard the Hispanic uprising as an insignificant local uproar, and it is doubtful that news of it reached the Basileus Leo XI in Constantinopolis at all. But very shortly the nearby province of Lusitania had sworn allegiance to the rebel banner, and the isle of Britannia, and Gallia next; and piece by piece the western lands fell away from their fealty to the feckless government in Roma, until finally Flavius Romulus marched into the capital, occupied the Imperial palace, and sent troops south to arrest Nicephoros and carry him into exile in Aegyptus. By the year 2198 the Eastern Empire had fallen also. Leo XI made his famous somber pilgrimage from Constantinopolis to Ravenna to sign a treaty recognizing Flavius Romulus not only as Emperor of the West but as monarch of the eastern territories, too.

Flavius ruled another thirty years. Not content with having reunited the Empire, he distinguished himself by a second astonishing exploit, a voyage around the tip of Africa that took him to the shores of India and possibly even to the unknown lands beyond. He was the first of the Maritime Emperors, setting a noble example for that even more extraordinary traveler, Trajan VII, two generations later.

We Romans had made journeys overland to the Far East, Persia and even India, as far back as the time of the first Augustus. And in the era of the Eastern Empire the Byzantines had often sailed down Africa's western coast to carry on trade with the black kingdoms of that continent, which had led a few of the more venturesome Emperors of the West to send their own expeditions all the way around Africa and onward to Arabia, and from there now and then to India. But these had been sporadic adventures. Flavius Romulus wanted permanent trade relations with the Asian lands. On his great voyage he carried thousands of Romans with him to India by the African route and left them there to found mercantile colonies; and thereafter we were in constant commercial contact with the dark-skinned folk of those far-off lands. Not only that, he or one of his captains—

it is not clear—sailed onward from India to the even more distant realms of Khitai and Cipangu, where the yellow-skinned people live. And thus began the commercial connections that would bring us the silks and incense, the gems and spices, the jade and ivory of those mysterious lands, their rhubarb and their emeralds, rubies and pepper, sapphires, cinnamon, dyes, perfumes.

There were no bounds to Flavius Romulus's ambitions. He dreamed also of new westward voyages to the two continents of Nova Roma on the other side of the Ocean Sea. Hundreds of years before his time, the reckless Emperor Saturninus had undertaken a foolhardy attempt to conquer Mexico and Peru, the two great empires of the New World, spending an enormous sum and meeting with overwhelming defeat. The collapse of that enterprise so weakened us, militarily and economically, that it was an easy matter for the Greeks to take control of the Empire within fifty years. Flavius knew from that sorry precedent that we could never achieve the conquest of those fierce nations of the New World, but he hoped at least to open commercial contact with them, and from the earliest years of his reign he made efforts to that end.

His successor—he had outlived all his sons—was another Hispaniard of Tarraco, Gaius Julius Flavillus, a man of nobler birth than Flavius whose family fortunes may have underwritten the original Flavian rebellion. Gaius Flavillus was a forceful man in his own right and an admirable Emperor, but, reigning between two such mighty figures as Flavius Romulus and Trajan Draco, he seems more of a consolidator than an innovator. During his time on the throne, which covered the period from 2238 to 2253, he continued the maritime policy of his predecessor, though placing more emphasis on voyages to the New World than toward Africa and Asia, while also striving to create greater unity between the Latin and Greek halves of the Empire itself, something to which Flavius Romulus had devoted relatively little attention.

It was during the reign of Gaius Flavillus that Trajan Draco rose to prominence. His first military assignments seem to have been in Africa, where he won early promotion for his heroism in putting down an uprising in Alexandria, and then for suppressing the depre-

dations of bandits in the desert south of Carthago. How he came to
the attention of Emperor Gaius is unclear, though probably his Hispanic birth had something to do with it. By 2248, though, we find
him in command of the Praetorian Guard. He was then only about
twenty-five years old. Soon he had acquired the additional title of
First Tribune, and shortly Consul too, and in 2252, the year before
his death, Gaius formally adopted Trajan as his son and proclaimed
him as his heir.

It was as though Flavius Romulus had been born again, when
Trajan Draco, soon afterward, assumed the purple under the name
of Trajan VII. In the place of the aloof patrician Gaius Flavillus
came a second Hispaniard peasant to the throne, full of the same
boisterous energy that had catapulted Flavius to greatness, and the
whole world echoed to the resonant sound of his mighty laughter.

Indeed, Trajan was Flavius redone on an even grander scale.
They were both big men, but Trajan was a giant. (I, his remote descendant, am quite tall myself.) He wore his dark hair to the middle
of his back. His brow was high and noble; his eyes flashed like an eagle's; his voice could be heard from the Capitoline Hill to the Ja-
niculum. He could drink a keg of wine at a sitting with no ill effect.
In the eighty years of his life he had five wives—not, I hasten to add,
at the same time—and innumerable mistresses. He sired twenty legitimate children, the tenth of whom was my own ancestor, and such
a horde of bastards that it is no unusual thing today to see the hawk-
faced visage of Trajan Draco staring back at one in the streets of almost any city in the world.

He was a lover not only of women but of the arts, especially
those of statuary and music, and of the sciences. Such fields as math-
ematics and astronomy and engineering had fallen into neglect during the two hundred years of the West's subservience to the soft,
luxury-loving Greeks. Trajan sponsored their renewal. He rebuilt
the ancient capital at Roma from end to end, filling it with palaces
and universities and theaters as though such things had never existed there before; and, perhaps for fear that that might seem insufficient, he moved on eastward into the province of Pannonia, to the
little city of Venia on the River Danubius, and built himself what was
essentially a second capital there, with its own great university, a host

of theaters, a grand Senate building, and a royal palace that is one of the wonders of the world. His reasoning was that Venia, though darker and rainier and colder than sunny Roma, was closer to the heart of the Empire. He would not allow the partition of the Empire once again into eastern and western realms, immense though the task of governing the whole thing was. Placing his capital in a central location like Venia allowed him to look more easily westward toward Gallia and Britannia, northward into the Teuton lands and those of the Goths, and eastward to the Greek world, while maintaining the reins of power entirely in his own hands.

Trajan did not, however, spend any great portion of his time at the new capital, nor, for that matter, at Roma either. He was constantly on the move, now presenting himself at Constantinopolis to remind the Greeks of Asia that they had an Emperor, or touring Syria or Aegyptus or Persia, or darting up into the far north to hunt the wild shaggy beasts that live in those Hyperborean lands, or revisiting his native Hispania, where he had transformed the ancient city of Sevilla into the main port of embarkation for voyages to the New World. He was a tireless man.

And in the twenty-fifth year of his reign—A.U.C. 2278—he set out on his greatest journey of all, the stupendous deed for which his name will be forever remembered: his voyage around the entirety of the world, beginning and ending at Sevilla, and taking into its compass almost every nation both civilized and barbaric that this globe contains.

Had anyone before him conceived of such an audacious thing? I find nothing in all the records of history to indicate it.

No one has ever seriously doubted, of course, that the world is a sphere, and therefore is open to circumnavigation. Common sense alone shows us the curvature of the Earth as we look off into the distance; and the notion that there is an edge somewhere, off which rash mariners must inevitably plunge, is a fable suited for children's tales, nothing more. Nor is there any reason to dread the existence of an impassable zone of flame somewhere in the southern seas, as simple folk used to think: it is twenty-five hundred years since ships first sailed around the southern tip of Africa and no one has seen any walls of fire yet.

But even the boldest of our seamen had never even thought of sailing all the way around the world's middle, let alone attempting it, before Trajan Draco set out from Sevilla to do it. Voyages to Arabia and India and even Khitai by way of Africa, yes, and voyages to the New World also, first to Mexico and then down the western coast of Mexico along the narrow strip of land that links the two New World continents until the great empire of Peru was reached. From that we learned of the existence of a second Ocean Sea, one that was perhaps even greater than the one that separates Europa from the New World. On the eastern side of that vast ocean were Mexico and Peru; on its western side, Khitai and Cipangu, with India farther on. But what lay in between? Were there other empires, perhaps, in the middle of that Western Sea—empires mightier than Khitai and Cipangu and India put together? What if there were an empire somewhere out there that put even Imperial Roma into the shade?

It was to the everlasting glory of Trajan VII Draco that he was determined to find out, even if it cost him his life. He must have felt utterly secure in his throne, if he was willing to abandon the capital to subordinates for so long a span of time; either that, or he did not care a fig about the risk of usurpation, so avid was he to make the journey.

His five-year expedition around the world was, I think, one of the most significant achievements in all history, rivaling, perhaps, the creation of the Empire by Augustus Caesar and its expansion across almost the whole of the known world by Trajan I and Hadrianus. It is the one thing, above all else that he achieved, that drew me to undertake my research into his life. He found no empires to rival Roma on that journey, no, but he did discover the myriad island kingdoms of the Western Sea, whose products have so greatly enriched our lives; and, moreover, the route he pioneered through the narrow lower portion of the southern continent of the New World has given us permanent access by sea to the lands of Asia from either direction, regardless of any opposition that we might encounter from the ever-troublesome Mexicans and Peruvians on the one hand or the war-like Cipanguans and the unthinkably multitudinous Khitaians on the other.

But—although we are familiar with the general outlines of Trajan's voyage—the journal that he kept, full of highly specific detail, has been lost for centuries. Which is why I felt such delight when one of my researchers, snuffling about in a forgotten corner of the Office of Maritime Affairs in Sevilla, reported to me early this year that he had stumbled quite accidentally upon that very journal. It had been filed all that time amongst the documents of a later reign, buried unobtrusively in a pack of bills of lading and payroll records. I had it shipped to me here in Tauromenium by Imperial courier, a journey that took six weeks, for the packet went overland all the way from Hispania to Italia—I would not risk so precious a thing on the high sea—and then down the entire length of Italia to the tip of Bruttium, across the strait by ferry to Messana, and thence to me.

Was it, though, the richly detailed narrative I yearned for, or would it simply be a dry list of navigators' marks, longitudes and latitudes and ascensions and compass readings?

Well, I would not know that until I had it in my hands. And as luck would have it, the very day the packet arrived was the day the Caesar Demetrius returned from his month's sojourn in Africa. I barely had time to unseal the bulky packet and run my thumb along the edge of the thick sheaf of time-darkened vellum pages that it contained before a messenger came to me with word that I was summoned to the Caesar's presence at once.

The Caesar, as I have already said, is an impatient man. I paused only long enough to look beyond the title page to the beginning of the text, and felt a profound chill of recognition as the distinctive backhanded cursive script of Trajan Draco rose to my astonished eyes. I allowed myself one further glimpse within, perhaps the hundredth page, and found a passage that dealt with a meeting with some island king. Yes! Yes! The journal of the voyage, indeed!

I turned the packet over to the major-domo of my villa, a trustworthy enough Sicilian freedman named Pantaleon, and told him exactly what would happen to him if any harm came to a single page while I was away.

Then I betook myself to the Caesar's hilltop palace, where I found him in the garden, inspecting a pair of camels that he had brought back with him from Africa. He was wearing some sort of

hooded desert robe and had a splendid curving scimitar thrust
through his belt. In the five weeks of his absence the sun had so
blackened the skin of his face and hands that he could have passed
easily for an Arab. "Pisander!" he cried at once. I had forgotten that
foolish name in his absence. He grinned at me and his teeth gleamed
like beacons against that newly darkened visage.

I offered the appropriate pleasantries, had he had an enjoyable
trip and all of that, but he swept my words away with a flick of his
hand. "Do you know what I thought of, Pisander, all the time of my
journey? Our great project! Our glorious enterprise! And do you
know, I realize now that it does not go nearly far enough. I have decided, I think, to make Sicilia my capital when I am Emperor. There
is no need for me to live in the cool stormy north when I can so easily be this close to Africa, a place that I now see I love enormously.
And so we must build a Senate House here, too, in Panormus, I
think, and great villas for all the officials of my court, and a library—
do you know, Pisander, there's no library worthy of the name on this
whole island? But we can divide the holdings of Alexandria and
bring half here, once there's a building worthy of housing them. And
then—"

I will spare you the whole of it. Suffice it to say that his madness
had entered an entirely new phase of uninhibited grandiosity. And I
was the first victim of it, for he informed me that he and I were going to depart that very night on a trip from one end of Sicilia to the
other, searching out sites for all the miraculous new structures he
had in mind. He was going to do for Sicilia what Augustus Caesar
had done for the city of Roma itself: make it the wonder of the age.
Forgotten now was the plan to begin the building program with the
new palace in Tauromenium. First we must trek from Tauromenium
to Lilybaeum on the other coast, and back again from Eryx to Syracusae to here, pausing at every point in between.

And so we did. Sicilia is a large island; the journey occupied two
and a half months. The Caesar was a cheerful enough traveling companion—he is witty, after all, and intelligent, and lively, and the fact
that he is a madman was only occasionally a hindrance. We traveled
in great luxury and the half-healed state of my ankle meant that I
was carried in a litter much of the time, which made me feel like

some great pampered potentate of antiquity, a Pharaoh, perhaps, or Darius of Persia. But one effect of this suddenly imposed interruption in my studies was that it became impossible for me to examine the journal of Trajan VII for many weeks, which was maddening. To take it with me while we traveled and study it surreptitiously in my bedchamber was too risky; the Caesar can be a jealous man, and if he were to come in unannounced and find me diverting my energies to something unconnected to his project, he would be perfectly capable of seizing the journal from me on the spot and tossing it into the flames. So I left the book behind, turning it over to Spiculo and telling him to guard it with his life; and for many a night thereafter, as we darted hither and yon across the island in increasingly more torrid weather, summer having now arrived and Sicilia lying as it does beneath the merciless southern sun, I lay tossing restlessly, imagining the contents of the journal in my fevered mind, devising for myself a fantastic set of adventures for Trajan to take the place of the real ones that the Caesar Demetrius had in his blithe selfishness prevented me from reading in the newly discovered journal. Though I knew, even then, that the reality, once I had the chance to discover it, would far surpass anything I could imagine for myself.

And then I returned at last to Tauromenium; and reclaimed the book from Spiculo and read its every word in three astonishing days and nights, scarcely sleeping a moment. And found in it, along with many a tale of wonder and beauty and strangeness, many things that indeed I would not have imagined, which were not so pleasing to find.

Though it was written in the rougher Latin of medieval days, the text gave me no difficulties. The Emperor Trajan VII was an admirable writer, whose style, blunt and plain and highly fluent, reminded me of nothing so much as that of Julius Caesar, another great leader who could handle a stylus as well as he did a sword. He had, apparently, kept the journal as a private record of his circumnavigation, very likely not meaning to have it become a public document at all, and its survival in the archives seems to have been merely fortuitous.

His tale began in the shipyards of Sevilla: five vessels being readied for the voyage, none of them large, the greatest being only of 120 tons. He gave detailed listings of their stores. Weapons, of course, sixty crossbows, fifty matchlock arquebuses (this weapon having newly been invented then), heavy artillery pieces, javelins, lances, pikes, shields. Anvils, grindstones, forges, bellows, lanterns, implements with which fortresses could be constructed on newly discovered islands by the masons and stonecutters of his crew; drugs, medicines, salves; six wooden quadrants, six metal astrolabes, thirty-seven compass needles, six pairs of measuring compasses, and so forth. For use in trading with the princes of newly discovered kingdoms, a cargo of flasks of quicksilver and copper bars, bales of cotton, velvet, satin, and brocades, thousands of small bells, fishhooks, mirrors, knives, beads, combs, brass and copper bracelets, and such. All this was enumerated with a clerk's finicky care: reading it taught me much about a side of Trajan Draco's character that I had not suspected.

At last the day of sailing. Down the River Baetis from Sevilla to the Ocean Sea, and quickly out to the Isles of the Canaria, where, however, they saw none of the huge dogs for which the place is named. But they did find the noteworthy Raining Tree, from whose gigantic swollen trunk the entire water supply of one island was derived. I think this tree has perished, for no one has seen it since.

Then came the leap across the sea to the New World, a journey hampered by sluggish winds. They crossed the Equator; the pole-star no longer could be seen; the heat melted the tar in the ships' seams and turned the decks into ovens. But then came better sailing, and swiftly they reached the western shore of the southern continent where it bulges far out toward Africa. The Empire of Peru had no sway in this place; it was inhabited by cheerful naked people who made a practice of eating human flesh, "but only," the Emperor tells us, "their enemies."

It was Trajan's intention to sail completely around the bottom of the continent, an astounding goal considering that no one knew how far south it extended, or what conditions would be encountered at its extremity. For that matter, it might not come to an end in the south at all, and so there would be no sea route westward whatever, but only a continuous land mass running clear down to the southern pole and blocking all progress by sea. And there was always the possibility of meeting with interference by Peruvian forces somewhere along the way. But southward they went, probing at every inlet in the hope that it might mark the termination of the continent and a connection with the sea that lay on the other side.

Several of these inlets proved to be the mouths of mighty rivers, but wild hostile tribes lived along their banks, which made exploration perilous; and Trajan feared also that these rivers would only take them deep inland, into Peruvian-controlled territory, without bringing them to the sea on the continent's western side. And so they continued south and south and south along the coast. The weather, which had been very hot, swiftly worsened to the south, giving them dark skies and icy winds. But this they already knew, that the seasons are reversed below the Equator, and winter comes there in our summer, so they were not surprised by the change.

Along the shore they found peculiar black and white birds that could swim but not fly; these were plump and proved good to eat. There still appeared to be no westerly route. The coast, barren now, seemed endless. Hail and sleet assailed them, mountains of ice floated in the choppy sea, cold rain froze in their beards. Food and water ran low. The men began to grumble. Although they had an Emperor in their midst, they began to speak openly of turning back. Trajan wondered if his life might be in danger.

Soon after which, as such wintry conditions descended upon them as no man had ever seen before, there came an actual mutiny: the captains of two ships announced that they were withdrawing from the expedition. "They invited me to meet with them to discuss the situation," Trajan wrote. "Plainly I was to be killed. I sent five trusted men to the first rebel ship, bearing a message from me, with twenty more secretly in another boat. When the first group came aboard and the rebel captain greeted them on deck, my ambassadors slew him at once; and then the men of the second boat came on board." The mutiny was put down. The three ringleaders were executed immediately, and eleven other men were put ashore on a frigid island that had not even the merest blade of grass. I would not have expected Trajan Draco to treat the conspirators mildly, but the calm words in which he tells of leaving these men to a terrible death were chilling indeed.

The voyagers went on. In the bleak southern lands they discovered a race of naked giants—eight feet tall, says Trajan—and captured two to bring back to Roma as curiosities. "They roared like bulls, and cried out to the demons they worshiped. We put them on separate ships, in chains. But they would take no food from us and quickly perished."

Through storms and wintry darkness they proceeded poleward, still finding no way west, and even Trajan began now to think they would have to abandon the quest. The sea now was nearly impassable on account of ice: they found another source of the fat flightless birds, though, and set up winter camp on shore, remaining for three months, which greatly depleted their stores of food. But when in weather that was fairer, though still quite inhospitable, they decided finally to go on, they came almost at once to what is now known as the Strait of Trajan near the continent's uttermost point. Trajan sent one of his captains in to investigate, and he found it narrow but deep, with a strong tidal flow, and salty water throughout: no river, but a way across to the Western Sea!

The trip through the strait was harrowing, past needle-sharp rocks, through impenetrable mists, over water that surged and boiled from one wall of the channel to another. But green trees now appeared, and the lights of the natives' campfires, and before long they emerged in the other sea: "The sky was wondrously blue, the clouds were fleecy, the waves were no more than rippling wavelets, burnished by the brilliant sun." The scene was so peaceful that Trajan gave the new sea the name of Pacificus, on account of its tranquility.

His plan now was to sail due west, for it seemed likely to him then, entering into this uncharted sea, that Cipangu and Khitai must lie only a short distance in that direction. Nor did he desire to venture northward along the continent's side because that would bring him to the territory of the belligerent Peruvians, and his five ships would be no match for an entire empire.

But an immediate westward course proved impossible because of contrary winds and eastward-bearing currents. So northward he went anyway, for a time, staying close to shore and keeping a wary eye out for Peruvians. The sun was harshly bright in the cloudless sky, and there was no rain. When finally they could turn to the west again, the sea was utterly empty of islands and looked vast beyond all imagining. By night strange stars appeared, notably five brilliant ones arranged like a cross in the heavens. The remaining food supply dwindled rapidly; attempts at catching fish proved useless, and the men ate chips of wood and mounds of sawdust, and hunted down the rats that infested the holds. Water was rationed to a single sip a day. The risk now was not so much another mutiny as out-and-out starvation.

They came then to some small islands, finally: poor ones, where nothing grew but stunted, twisted shrubs. But there were people there too, fifteen or twenty of them, simple naked people who painted themselves in stripes. "They greeted us with a hail of stones and arrows. Two of our men were slain. We had no choice but to kill them all. And then, since there was no food to be found on the island except for a few pitiful fishes and crabs that these people had caught that morning and nothing of any size or substance was to be had off shore, we roasted the bodies of the dead and ate those, for otherwise we would surely have died of hunger."

I cannot tell you how many times I read and reread those lines, hoping to find that they said something other than what they did. But they always were the same.

In the fourth month of the journey across the Pacificus other islands appeared, fertile ones, now, whose villagers grew dates of some sort from which they made bread, wine, and oil, and also had yams, bananas, coconuts, and other such tropical things with which we are now so familiar. Some of these islanders were friendly to the mariners, but most were not. Trajan's journal becomes a record of atrocities. "We killed them all; we burned their village as an example to their neighbors; we loaded our ships with their produce." The same phrases occur again and again. There is not a word of apology or regret. It was as if by tasting human flesh they had turned into monsters themselves.

Beyond these islands was more emptiness—Trajan saw now that the Pacificus was an ocean whose size was beyond all comprehension, compared with which even the Ocean Sea was a mere lake—

and then, after another disheartening trek of many weeks, came the discovery of the great island group that we call the Augustines, seven thousand islands large and small, stretching in a huge arc across more than a thousand miles of the Pacificus. "A chieftain came to us, a majestic figure with markings drawn on his face and a skirt of cotton fringed with silk; he carried a javelin and a dagger of bronze encrusted with gold, a shield that also sparkled with the yellow metal, and he wore earrings, armlets, and bracelets of gold likewise." His people offered spices—cinnamon, cloves, ginger, nutmeg, mace—in exchange for the simple trinkets the Romans had brought, and also rubies, diamonds, pearls, and nuggets of gold. "My purpose was fulfilled," Trajan wrote. "We had found a fabulous new empire in the midst of this immense sea."

Which they proceeded to conquer in the most brutal fashion. Though in the beginning the Romans had peaceful relations with the natives of the Augustines, demonstrating hourglasses and compasses to them and impressing them by having their ships' guns fired and by staging mock gladiatorial games in which men in armor fought against men with tridents and nets, things quickly went wrong. Some of Trajan's men, having had too much of the date wine to drink, fell upon the island women and possessed them with all the zeal that men who have not touched a woman's breasts for close upon a year are apt to show. The women, Trajan relates, appeared willing enough at first; but his men treated them with such shameful violence and cruelty that objections were raised, and then quarrels broke out as the island men came to defend their women (some of whom were no more then ten years old), and in the end there was a bloody massacre, culminating in the murder of the noble island chieftain.

This section of the journal is unbearable to read. On the one hand it is full of fascinating detail about the customs of the islanders, how pigs are sacrificed by old women who caper about blowing reed trumpets and smear the blood of the sacrifice on the foreheads of the men, and how males of all ages have their sexual organs pierced from one side to the other with a gold or tin bolt as large as a goose quill, and so on and on with many a strange detail that seems to have come from another world. But interspersed amongst all this is the tale of the slaughter of the islanders, the inexorable destruction of them under one pretext or another, the journey from isle to isle, the Romans always being greeted in peace but matters degenerating swiftly into rape, murder, looting.

Yet Trajan appears unaware of anything amiss here. Page after page, in the same calm, steady tone, describes these horrors as though they were the natural and inevitable consequence of the collision of alien cultures. My own reactions of shock and dismay, as I read them, made it amazingly clear to me how different our era is from his, and how very little like a Renaissance man I actually am. Trajan saw the crimes of his men as unfortunate necessities at the worst; I saw them as monstrous. And I came to realize that one profound and complex aspect of the decadence of our civilization is our disdain for violence of this sort. We are Romans still; we abhor disorder and have not lost our skill at the arts of war; but when Trajan Draco can speak so blandly of retaliating with cannons against an attack with arrows, or of the burning of entire villages in retribution for a petty theft from one of our ships, or the sating of his men's lust on little girls because they were unwilling to take the time to seek out their older sisters, I could not help but feel that there is something to be said in favor of our sort of decadence.

During these three days and nights of steady reading of the journals I saw no one, neither Spiculo nor the Caesar nor any of the women with whom I have allayed the boredom of my years in Sicilia. I read on and on and on, until my head began to swim, and I could not stop, horrified though I often was.

Now that the empty part of the Pacificus was behind them, one island after another appeared, not only the myriad Augustines, but others farther to the west and south, multitudes of them; for although there is no continent in this ocean, there are long chains of islands, many of them far larger than our Britannia and Sicilia. Over and over I was told of the boats ornamented with gold and peacock feathers bearing island chieftains offering rich gifts, or of horned fish and oysters the size of sheep and trees whose leaves, when they fall to the ground, will rise on little feet and go crawling away, and kings called rajahs who could not be addressed face to face, but only through speaking tubes in the walls of their palaces. Isles of spices, isles of gold, isles of pearls—marvel after marvel, and all of them now seized and claimed by the invincible Roman Emperor in the name of eternal Roma.

Then, finally, these strange island realms gave way to familiar territory: for now Asia was in sight, the shores of Khitai. Trajan made landfall there, exchanged gifts with the Khitaian sovereign, and acquired from him those Khitaian experts in the arts of printing and gunpowder-making and the manufacture of fine porcelains whose skills, brought back by him to Roma, gave such impetus to this new era of prosperity and growth that we call the Renaissance.

He went on to India and Arabia afterward, loading his ships with treasure there as well, and down one side of Africa and up the other. It was the same route as all our previous far voyages, but done this time in reverse.

Trajan knew once he had rounded Africa's southernmost cape that the spanning of the globe had been achieved, and he hastened onward toward Europa, coming first to Lusitania's southwestern tip, then coasting along southern Hispania until he returned with his five ships and their surviving crew to the mouth of the River Baetis and, soon after, to the starting point at Sevilla. "These are mariners who surely merit an eternal fame," he concluded, "more justly than the Argonauts of old who sailed with Jason in search of the golden fleece. For these our wonderful vessels, sailing southwards through the Ocean Sea toward the Antarctic Pole, and then turning west, followed that course so long that, passing round, we came into the east, and thence again into the west, not by sailing back, but by proceeding constantly forward: so compassing about the globe of the world, until we marvelously regained our native land of Hispania, and the port from which we departed, Sevilla."

There was one curious postscript. Trajan had made an entry in his journal for each day of the voyage. By his reckoning, the date of his return to Sevilla was the ninth day of Januarius in 2282; but when he went ashore, he was told that the day was Januarius the tenth. By sailing continuously westward around the world, they had lost a day somewhere. This remained a mystery until the astronomer Macrobius of Alexandria pointed out that the time of sunrise varies by four minutes for each degree of longitude, and so the variation for a complete global circuit of three hundred sixty degrees would be 1,440 minutes, or one full day. It was the clearest proof, if anyone had dared to doubt Trajan's word, that the fleet had sailed entirely around the world to reach the strange new isles of that unknown sea. And by so doing had unlocked a treasure chest of wonders that the great Emperor would fully exploit in the two decades of absolute power that remained to him before his death at the age of eighty.

And did I, having gained access at last to the key document of the reign of Trajan VII, set immediately about the task of finishing my account of his extraordinary life?

No. No. And this is why.

Within four days of my finishing my reading of the journal, and while my head was still throbbing with all I had discovered therein, a messenger came from Italia with news that the Emperor Lodovicus Augustus had died in Roma of an apoplexy, and his son the Caesar Demetrius had succeeded to the throne as Demetrius II Augustus.

It happened that I was with the Caesar when this message arrived. He showed neither grief over his father's passing nor jubilation over his own ascent to the highest power. He simply smiled a small smile, the merest quirking of the corner of his mouth, and said to me, "Well, Draco, it looks as if we must pack for another trip, and so soon after our last one, too."

I had not wanted to believe—none of us did—that Demetrius would ever become Emperor. We had all hoped that Lodovicus would find some way around the necessity of it: would discover, perhaps, some hitherto unknown illegitimate son, dwelling in Babylon or Londinium all these years, who could be brought forth and given preference. It was Lodovicus, after all, who had cared so little to witness the antics of his son and heir that he had packed Demetrius off to Sicilia these three years past and forbidden him to set foot on the mainland, though he would be free to indulge whatever whim he fancied in his island exile.

But that exile now was ended. And in that same instant also was ended all the Caesar's scheme to beautify Sicilia.

It was as though those plans had never been. "You will sit among my high ministers, Draco," the new Emperor told me. "I will make you Consul, I think, in my first year. I will have the other Consulship myself. And you will also have the portfolio of the Ministry of Public Works; for the capital beyond all doubt is in need of beautification. I have a design for a new palace for myself in mind, and then perhaps we can do something about improving the shabby old Capitol, and there are some interesting foreign gods, I think, who would appreciate having temples erected in their honor, and then—"

If I had been Trajan Draco, I would perhaps have assassinated our crazy Demetrius in that moment and taken the throne for myself, both for the Empire's sake and my own. But I am only Tiberius Ulpius Draco, not Trajan of the same cognomen, and Demetrius has become Emperor and you know the rest.

And as for my book on Trajan the Dragon: well, perhaps I will complete it some day, when the Emperor has run short of projects for me to design. But I doubt that he ever will, and even if he does, I am not sure that it is a book I still want to give to the public, now that I have read Trajan's journal of the circumnavigation. If I were to tell the story of my ancestor's towering achievement, would I dare to tell the whole of it? I think not. And so I feel only relief at allowing my incomplete draft of the book to gather dust in its box. It was my aim, in this research of mine, to discover the inner nature of my great royal kinsman the Dragon; but I delved too deeply, it seems, and came to know him a little too well.

A.U.C. 2568: THE REIGN
OF TERROR

T he Emperor," said Quintus Cestius, "dined last night on fish and mushrooms sprinkled with powdered pearls, on lentils with onyx, on turnips with amber. He has the stomach of an ox and the mind of a madman."

"Ah, do you think he's mad, then?" Sulpicius Silanus asked. A mischievous twinkle came into his eyes. "I don't. I think he's merely playful."

"Playful," Cestius said somberly. "Yes. Feeds his dogs on goose liver. Sleeps on couches of solid silver, with mattresses stuffed with rabbit fur or partridge feathers. Covers his furniture with cloth of gold. Yes, very playful indeed."

"Has buckets of saffron dumped into the palace swimming pool before he'll dip a toe in," Silanus said.

"Cooking-pots of silver."

"Wine flavored with poppy juice."

"All his food tinted blue one night, green the next, scarlet the night after that."

"Drove a chariot pulled by four elephants down the concourse in front of the Vatican Palace."

"And one drawn by four camels, the week before. It'll be dogs next week, I suppose, and lions the week after that."

"A madman," said Cestius.

"Merely very playful," Silanus said. And they both laughed, though each of them knew only too well that the Emperor Demetrius II's mounting extravagance was not any laughing matter; for Cestius was the Prefect of the Fiscus Imperialis, the Emperor's private purse, and Silanus, his counterpart on the other side of the Roman treasury, was Prefect of the Fiscus Publicus, out of which all governmental expenditures came. In some reigns, those two great pots of money had been kept rigidly segregated. In others, the Emperors had been not unwilling to dip into their private funds to pay for such popular things as the rebuilding of aqueducts and bridges, the underwriting of gladiatorial games, and the construction of grand new public buildings. But the Emperor Demetrius had never seemed to see any distinction at all between Fiscus Imperialis and Fiscus Publicus. He spent as he pleased, and left it up to Silanus and Cestius to find the money in one department of the treasury or the other. And in the last few years the problem had been growing steadily worse.

It was the first day of the new month, when the two treasurers customarily lunched together in the dining room that was provided for high governmental officials in the Senatorial office building just in back of the Senate House. They made a curious couple: the perpetually gloomy Quintus Cestius was round as a barrel, a big, fleshy-cheeked man of florid complexion, and the ever-exuberant Sulpicius Silanus was small and lean and spare, a taut little hatchet of a man who could easily have been tucked in a stray fold of Cestius's vast toga. The lunches that they favored were always the same, a plate of raw vegetables and apples for Cestius, and a gluttonous procession of soups, porridges, stewed meats, and aromatic cheeses soaked in honey for little Silanus. Cestius, plump from childhood though he had never had much of a fondness for food, often wondered where Silanus managed to store all that he was capable of consuming at a single sitting.

As he worked on a great haunch of boar Silanus said, without looking up, "I have had a letter from my brother in Hispania. He tells me the Count Valerian Apollinaris has finished the reconquest there and will be returning to the capital soon."

"Wonderful," said Cestius darkly. "A great triumphal feast will be in order, then. A million and a half sesterces scattered at a single throw to pay for it: flamingo brains, mullets baked on a bed of hyacinths shipped up from Sicilia, venison of the giant stag of the far northlands, wines a hundred years old, and all the rest. All of it wasted on Apollinaris, who will disapprove of the expense, and who will sit there stiff as one of those stone gods from Aegyptus, merely nibbling at this dish and that one. But I'll have to find the money for it all the same. Or you will, I suppose."

"My brother says," Silanus continued, as though Cestius had not spoken at all, "that the thrifty Count Valerian Apollinaris is deeply disturbed by the shortfall in military funds that made his work of reconquest so much more complicated than it needed to be, and intends to speak vigorously with His Majesty concerning a tighter domestic budget."

"The Count would be well advised not to try."

"Would anyone, even the Emperor, dare to lay a finger on the Count Valerian Apollinaris, the hero of the War of Reunification?"

"I don't mean that he'd be in any danger," said Cestius. "Only that the Emperor will pay no attention. Just the other day the equally thrifty Larcius Torquatus took the very same matter up with the Emperor at the palace. I wasn't there, but I heard. If anything, Torquatus has become more ferocious on the subject of the Emperor's wastefulness than Apollinaris ever was, now that he's part of the government himself. So there they were, the Consul and the Emperor, the Consul ranting and shouting, the Emperor laughing and laughing."

"And he would laugh at us as well. You and I are the only two officials in the entire government who care at all about his level of expenditures. Other than Apollinaris and Torquatus, of course."

"Yes. All the rest are fools or weaklings, or else just as mad as the Emperor himself."

"And you and I are the ones who have to find the funds to pay the bills, somehow. We are the ones who bear the burden of the Emperor's lunacy," said Silanus.

"Indeed."

"And has the Emperor dismissed Torquatus, then, for shouting at him?"

"Oh, no, not at all. As ever, the Emperor is untroubled about such things. After Torquatus left the palace, I'm told, Demetrius sent him a little gift as a peace offering: the beautiful harlot Eumenia, stark naked and covered all over with gold dust, sitting in a jeweled carriage drawn by the black horses of Arabia that cost a hundred thousand sesterces apiece. They say that Torquatus nearly had a stroke when he saw it arrive."

"Well, then," said Silanus, "you'd better start putting money aside for a present for Apollinaris."

The Count Valerian Apollinaris, just then, was hundreds of miles away in the great Hispanian city of Tarraco, the final stopping point on his whirlwind military tour of the Empire's rebellious western provinces. One by one he had subjugated them with a minimal expenditure of force and bloodshed: first Sicilia, where all the trouble had begun back in 2563, then Belgica and Gallia, and finally Hispania. His technique had been the same in each place, arriving with a small hand-picked army of tough, grim legionaries, demanding of the local governors an immediate renewal of the oath of allegiance to the Emperor, and then the swift seizure and public execution of eight or ten insurrectionist leaders as an example to the others. The idea was to remind the provincials that Roma was still Roma, that the Imperial army was as efficient and ruthless now as it had been in the days of Trajan and Hadrian and Marcus Aurelius seventeen centuries before, and that he, Count Valerian Apollinaris, was the living embodiment of all the ancient Roman virtues that had made the Empire the immortal globe-spanning entity that it was.

And it had worked. In a series of quick, bloody strokes, Apollinaris had put an end—for all time, he hoped—to the slow, steady process of crumbling that had afflicted the Empire for nearly a century, during this era of foolishness and wanton waste that was beginning to be known as the Second Decadence.

Now, coming to the end of his fourth term of office as Consul, he was ready to return to Roma and enter into private life once more. Power for its own sake had never interested him, nor great wealth, or enormous luxury. Wealth was something he had been born to, and he took it for granted; power had accrued to him almost by default from his early manhood on, and because he had never hungered for it he never abused it; and as for enormous luxury, he left that to those who craved it, such as that hapless idiot, the Emperor Demetrius II.

Demetrius, of course, was an unending problem. The craziest Emperor of a largely crazy dynasty, he had held the throne for more than twenty years of ever-increasing madness, and it was small wonder that the Empire seemed to be spinning centrifugally apart. Only the devoted work, behind the scenes, of a small group of staunchly disciplined men like Apollinaris and his Consular counterpart back in Roma, Marcus Larcius Torquatus, had kept the regime from collapsing entirely.

There had been difficulties in the outlying provinces for nearly a century. Some of that was inherent in the Imperial system: the Empire was really too big to be governed from a central authority. That much had been understood from earliest Imperial times, which was why no serious attempt had ever been made to bring such far-off places as India and the lands that lay beyond it under direct Roman administration. Even a one-capital system had proven unworkable, and so Constantinopolis had been founded in the East and the Empire had been divided.

But then, after Saturninus—another of the crazy Emperors—had practically bankrupted the Western Empire in his hopeless attempt to conquer the New World, and set it drifting off into the pathetic era later to be called the Great Decadence, the Eastern realm had taken advantage of the West's weakness to invade it and then had come the two hundred years of Eastern rule, until the invincible Flavius Romulus restored the Western Empire's independence. Determined never to allow the East to regain the upper hand, Flavius Romulus had stripped Constantinopolis of its status as a capital city and reunited the severed halves of the Empire a thousand years after their first separation.

But it would take a Flavius Romulus to govern so great a stretch of territory single-handedly, and very few of his successors had been up to the mark. Within a century after his death the throne was in the possession of Demetrius of Vindonissa, a wealthy provincial patrician who just happened to have a streak of hereditary insanity in his family. Both Demetrius's son Valens Aquila and his grandson Marius Antoninus were notably eccentric Emperors; Marius's son Lodovicus had been reasonably stable, but he had blithely handed the throne on to *his* son, the present Emperor Demetrius, who by easy stages had come to make the citizens of Roma believe that they were being ruled once again by Caligula, or Commodus, or Caracalla.

Demetrius II was, at least, not murderous, as those three had been. But his reign, which by now had gone on longer than any of theirs, had been marked by a similar wildness of inspiration. Though he had not, like Caligula, tried to declare himself a god or appoint his horse to the Senate, he had given banquets at which six hundred ostriches were slaughtered at a time, and ordered the sinking of fully laden merchant ships in the harbor at Ostia to demonstrate the Empire's prodigious wealth. Unlike Commodus he had not amused himself by posing as a surgeon and operating on hapless subjects, but he did, now and then, set tame lions and leopards loose in the guest rooms of the palace to terrify his sleeping friends. He did not, like Caracalla, have his brother and other members of his own family murdered, but he did stage lotteries that all members of his court were required to enter at great expense, in which one man might win ten pounds of gold and another ten dead dogs or a dozen spoiled cabbages.

In the days of the indifferent Valens Aquila and the witless Marius Antoninus such far-off provinces as Syria and Persia began running themselves with very small regard for the decrees of the central government. That in itself caused little alarm in Roma, so long as the exotic goods that those lands exported to the capital continued to arrive. But then, in Lodovicus's reign, the two provinces of Dalmatia and Pannonia, just east of the Italian heartland of the Empire, also tried to break free, and had to be reined in by force. And then, soon after Demetrius II came to power, Sicilia, always a troublesome island of malcontents, chose to cease paying taxes to the Imperial tax collectors. When Demetrius took no action, the movement spread to Belgica and Gallia and Hispania and declarations of independence quickly followed. That, of course, could not be tolerated, even by the likes of Demetrius.

Apollinaris was Consul then, his third time in the office, sharing the Consulship with the feckless drunkard Duilius Eurupianus. Since the time of Maximilianus the Great, at least, the Consulship had been a basically meaningless post, a mere honorific, with nothing like the virtually royal powers it had had in the ancient days of the Republic. As Epictetus had said long ago, the Consulship under the Emperors, having lost nearly all its functions, had degenerated into a post that allowed you nothing more than the privilege of underwriting the games of the Circus and giving free dinners to a lot of undeserving flatterers.

But a crisis now was at hand. Firm action was required. Apollinaris, resigning his Consulship, called upon Eurupianus to do the same, making it clear to him that if he chose to remain in office it would have adverse effects on his health. Then Apollinaris prevailed upon the Emperor, who was preoccupied at the time with forming a collection of venomous serpents from the farthest reaches of the realm, to reappoint him to the Consulship in collaboration with an equally public-spirited citizen, the dour and austere Larcius Torquatus. At Apollinaris's urgent behest the Emperor agreed that he and Torquatus would be granted emergency powers far beyond any that the Consuls had had for hundreds of years, and would remain in office indefinitely, instead of serving one-year terms at the pleasure of the Emperor. Torquatus would attempt to restore some sanity on the home front; Apollinaris, an experienced soldier, would march through the rebellious provinces, bringing them one after another to heel.

Which had been achieved. Here in Tarraco, Apollinaris was packing up, getting ready to go home.

Tiberius Charax, his aide-de-camp, a slender, narrow-eyed Greek from Ionia who had served at his side for many years, entered and said, "A letter for you from Roma, from the Consul Larcius Torquatus, Count Valerian. Also Prince Laureolus has arrived and is waiting outside to see you."

Taking the letter from Charax, Apollinaris said, "Send him in."

He broke the seal and quickly glanced over the text. His fellow Consul, concise as ever, had written, "I have told the Emperor of your successes in the field, and he responds with the usual childishness. As for affairs here at Roma, the problems grow worse all the time. If his spending continues at the present pace the treasury will soon be down to its last denarius. I am planning to take severe measures." And, with an elaborate flourish, the signature, nearly the size of the text itself: *M. Larcius Torquatus, Consul.*

Looking up, Apollinaris became aware that Prince Laureolus was in the room.

"Bad news, sir?" the prince asked.

"Infuriating news," said Apollinaris. He made no effort to hide his smoldering anger. "A letter from Torquatus. The Emperor is running the treasury dry. What did he pay, I wonder, for that mountain of snow he had them set up in his garden last summer? Or for that tunic of plates of gold, studded with diamonds and pearls? And what little expenses are coming next? I fear to guess."

"The Emperor," Laureolus said quietly, and a derisive flicker appeared for a moment at one corner of the younger man's mouth. "Ah! The Emperor, yes." He needed to say no more.

Apollinaris had come to like the prince a great deal. They were men built to the same general design, short, compact, muscular, though there was little else in the way of physical resemblance, Apollinaris being a man of dark, almost swarthy complexion with a broad triangular nose, a generous mouth, and deep-set coal-black eyes beneath a dense, shaggy brow, while Laureolus was pale, with chilly aristocratic features, a long, narrow high-bridged nose, a thin-lipped mouth, ice-cold eyes of the palest blue. He came from ancient Imperial lineage, tracing his ancestry in some fashion to the Emperor Publius Clemens, who had reigned a hundred years or so before the Byzantine conquest of the Western Empire. Disgusted with the profligate ways of Demetrius II, he had withdrawn five years back to his family's property in the country to occupy himself with the study of early Roman history and literature. That was how Apollinaris, whose own country home was nearby and who shared Laureolus's antiquarian interests, had come to meet him. He saw quickly that Laureolus, who was ten years his junior, had the same nostalgia for the strict ethical rigor of the long-vanished Roman Republic that he himself had, and Larcius Torquatus, and virtually no one else in modern Roma.

When he embarked on the War of Reunification Apollinaris had chosen the prince to be his second in command, sending him shuttling from one newly pacified province to another to see to it that the process of restoring full Imperial control went smoothly forward in each of them. Lately Laureolus had been in northern Gallia, where there had been some minor disturbances at a place called Bononia, on the coast along the channel that divided Gallia from Britannia. Thinking that this renewal of the troubles might spread across the channel to the previously unrebellious Britannia, he had repressed it rigorously. Now, with all resistance to the Imperial government at last wiped out, he had come to Tarraco to present Apollinaris with his final report on the state of the provinces.

Apollinaris leafed quickly through it and set it aside. "All is well, I see. I need stay here no longer."

Laureolus said, "And when you return to the capital, sir, will you attempt to get Demetrius to restrain himself a little?"

"I? Don't be silly. I know better than to try to tell an Emperor what he ought to do. History is full of tales of the sad fates of those who tried it. Go back and reread your Suetonius, your Tacitus, your Ammianus Marcellinus. No, Laureolus, I'm going back to my estate in the country. Four Consulships is quite enough for me. Anyway, my fellow Consul Marcus Larcius has the responsibility for affairs in Urbs Roma." He tapped Torquatus's letter. "He tells me here that he's going to take severe measures to clean things up. Good for him, if he can do it."

"Can he do it single-handedly?" Laureolus asked.

"No. No, probably not." He shot a glance at the prince. "How would you like to be Consul, Laureolus?"

"*Me,* sir?" Laureolus's eyes were wide with astonishment.

"You, yes." Then Apollinaris shook his head. "No, I suppose not. Demetrius would never allow it. You're of royal blood, after all. He'd see it as the prelude to his own overthrow." Smiling, he said, "Well, it was just a thought. You and Torquatus, between you, might just be able to do the job. But it's probably safer for your health to

stay out of the capital, anyway. You go back to your estate, too. We'll
get together once a week and have a good meal and discuss ancient
history, and let Torquatus worry about the mess in Roma. Eh, Laureolus? We've worked hard out here in the provinces for five whole
years. I think we deserve a rest, don't you?"

In his wood-paneled office at the top of the nine-story Consular
building at the eastern end of the Forum the Consul Larcius Torquatus stacked and restacked the pile of documents on his desk, tidying
their edges with a fastidiousness that one might not have expected in
a man of so massive and heavy-set a build. Then he stared fiercely up
at the two prefects of the Fiscus, who had delivered these papers an
hour ago and now were sitting uneasily in front of him. "If I've read
these correctly, and I think I have, then there's no single department
of the Imperial government that even came close to staying within its
budget in the last fiscal year. That's correct, isn't it, Silanus?"

The Prefect of the Fiscus Publicus nodded unhappily. His famously buoyant spirits were nowhere in evidence just now. "This is
so, Consul."

"And you, Cestius," Torquatus said, turning his glare in the direction of the Prefect of the Fiscus Imperialis. "You tell me here that
the Emperor overdrew his personal funds last year by thirty-one million sesterces, and you made the deficit good by borrowing the
money from Silanus?"

"Yes, sir," big round-bellied Cestius said in the smallest of
voices.

"How could you? Where's your sense of responsibility to the nation, to the Senate, to your own conscience? The Emperor squan-
ders thirty-one million on top of what he's already got on hand for
squandering, which must be immense, and you simply grab it out of
the funds with which we're supposed to be repairing the bridges and
sweeping the dung out of the stables and paying Apollinaris's soldiers? I ask you again: how *could* you?"

A flicker of defiance glowed in Cestius's eyes. "You'd do better
to ask, how *couldn't* I, Consul. Would you have me tell the Emperor
to his face that he's spending too much? How long, do you think,

would it take him to find a new Prefect of the Fiscus Imperialis? And how long would it take me to find a new head?"

Torquatus responded with a snort. "Your responsibility, Cestius, what about your responsibility? Even if it *does* cost you your head, it's your job to prevent the Emperor from overspending. Otherwise why do we have a Prefect of the Fiscus at all?—And you, Silanus? By what right did you grant Cestius's request for those thirty-one million? You weren't being asked to confront the Emperor here, only to say no to Cestius. But you didn't do it. Is saving your friend's neck more important to you than the financial welfare of the Empire, which you are sworn to defend?"

Silanus, shamefaced, offered no reply.

Torquatus said, finally, "Shall I ask for your resignations?"

"You can have mine at any time," said Cestius.

"And mine, sir," Silanus said.

"Yes. Yes. And then I replace you with—whom? You two are the only worthwhile men in the whole administration, and neither of you is worth very much at all. But at least you keep honest accounts. —You *do* keep honest accounts, don't you? The deficit isn't even bigger than these documents of yours claim it is?"

"The accounts are accurate ones, sir," said Silanus stiffly.

"The gods be thanked for small mercies, then. —No, keep your jobs. But I want reports of a different sort from you both from now on. I want the names of the spenders. A detailed list: department heads, the ones who encourage the Emperor in his folly, those who sign the vouchers authorizing the payouts that you two are so ready to approve. And not just the department heads but anyone in the chain of command who is in a position to say no to spending requests and conspicuously fails to do so."

The two prefects were staring at him, horrified.

"Names, sir?" Cestius asked. "Of all such people?"

"Their names, yes."

"So that they can be reprimanded?"

"So that they can be removed from office," said the Consul. "The entire pack of them will go, the worst ones first, but every last one of them, eventually. Since the Emperor can't be controlled, we'll control the men who serve him. I want the first lists by tomorrow afternoon." Torquatus waved them from the room. "No. Tomorrow morning," he said, when they were at the door.

But he did not intend to wait even that long to begin making a list of his own. He knew who the first victims of the purge would have to be: the entourage of the Emperor's own household, the little cluster of parasitical lickspittles and sycophants and leeches who hovered about him day and night, egging foolish Demetrius on to ever greater triumphs of grotesque improvidence and lining their own pockets with the pieces of gold that went spilling away on all sides.

He knew the names, most of them. The officials of the cubiculo, the Emperor's intimate attendants, his grooms and pimps and butlers, many of them men of immense wealth in their own right, who went home from the royal palace every night to pleasant palaces of their own: there was Polybius, there was Hilarion—two Greeks, he thought, clamping his lips in displeasure—and the Hebrew, Judas Antonius Soranus, and the private secretary, Statius, and the royal cobbler, Claudius Nero, who made the fabulous jewel-encrusted shoes that Demetrius would never wear twice, and the court physician who prescribed such costly rarities as medicines for the monarch, taking his own percentage from the suppliers—what was his name, Mallo, Trallo, something like that?—and the architect, Tiberius Ulpius Draco, who as Minister of Public Works had built all those useless new palaces for the Emperor, and then had torn them down and built even grander ones on their sites—

No, Draco had died a year or two ago, probably of shame over his own misdeeds, for as Torquatus remembered him he was fundamentally an honorable man. But there were plenty of others to go on the list. Gradually, over the next hour, Torquatus added name after name, until he had fifty or sixty of them. A good beginning, that. His fury mounted as he contemplated their sins. A cold fury, it was, for he was by nature a frosty man.

After twenty years it was time, and long past time, to put a stop to Demetrius's imbecilic prodigality, before he brought the Empire down about him. Whatever the risks, Torquatus meant to place himself in the Emperor's way. It was in his blood, his loyalty to the Empire. A Torquatus had been Consul in the time of Marcus Aurelius, and another in the reign of Diocletianus, and there had been other great Torquati along the way, and now he was the Torquatus of the era, the Consul Marcus Larcius Torquatus, adding distinction to his line. Those other Torquati looked down on him out of history. He knew he must save Roma for them.

This Roma, he thought, this Empire, to which we have devoted so much loyalty, so great a part of our lives, for these two thousand years past—

For a moment he supposed that the best tactic would be to round up five or six of the Emperor's henchmen at a time, extracting them piecemeal from the Emperor's proximity so that Demetrius might not notice what was going on, but then he saw that that was precisely the wrong approach. Get them all, right away, a single bold sweep, the way Apollinaris had handled things in the provinces. Out of the palace, into the prisons: bring the situation to immediate resolution. Yes. That was the way.

He imagined the conversation with the Emperor that would follow.

"Where are my beloved friends? Where is Statius? Where is Hilarion? What has become of Claudius Nero?"

"All of them under arrest, your majesty. Crimes against the state. We have reached such a precarious position that we can no longer afford the luxury of having such people in your household."

"My doctor! My cobbler!"

"Dangerous to the welfare of the nation, Caesar. Dangerous in the extreme. I have had spies out among the people in the taverns, and they are talking revolution. They are saying that the streets and bridges and public buildings are going unrepaired, that there is no money available for distribution to the populace, that the war in the provinces is likely to break out again at any moment—and that the Emperor must be removed before things get even worse."

"*Removed?* The Emperor? Me?"

"They cry out for a return to the Republic."

Demetrius would laugh at that. "The Republic! People have been crying out for a return to the Republic for the last eighteen hundred years! They were saying it in Augustus's time, ten minutes after he threw the Republic overboard. They don't mean it. They know the Emperor is the father of the country, their beloved prince, the one essential figure who—"

"No, your majesty, this time they mean it." And Torquatus would sketch for the Emperor a vivid, terrifying picture of what a revolution would mean, laying it on as thickly as he knew how, the uprising in the streets, Senators hunted down, some of them slaughtered in their beds, and, above all, the massacre of the royal family, blood flowing, the Imperial museums looted, the burning of palaces and governmental buildings, the desecration of temples. The Emperor himself, Demetrius II Augustus Caesar, crucified in the Forum. Better yet: crucified head downward, hanging there dizzy with agony, while the jeering populace threw rocks or perhaps hurled spears—

Yes. Ten minutes of that and he would have Demetrius cowering in his golden sandals, wetting his purple robe in fear. He would retreat into his palace and hide himself there among his toys and his mistresses and his tame lions and tigers. Meanwhile the trials would go forward, the miscreants would rapidly be found guilty of their embezzlements and malfeasances, sent into exile in the remote provinces of the realm—

Exile?

Exile might be too risky, Torquatus thought. Exiles sometimes find their way home—seek vengeance—

Something more permanent than exile might be a wiser idea, he told himself.

He scratched away with his stylus. The list grew and grew. Apollinaris would be proud of him. Constantly quoting ancient history at him, telling him how much better things had been under the Republic, when staunch stoic men like Cato the Elder and Furius Camillus and Aemilius Paulus set examples of self-denial and discipline for all the nation. "The Empire is in profound need of purification," Apollinaris liked to say: Torquatus had heard him say it a thousand times. So it was. And by the time the Count got back from Gallia or Lusitania or wherever he was right now, he would discover that that profoundly needed purification was already under way.

They will all die, he told himself: these parasites who surround the Emperor, these caterpillars who devour the commonwealth.

*   *   *

That something strange was going on at Roma began to become apparent to Apollinaris in the first minutes after the merchant vessel that had brought him from Tarraco had reached the harbor at Ostia. The familiar ritual in which the customs officials of the port came aboard, received their bribes, and presented a perfunctory bill of duty payable did not take place. Instead there was an actual search, six men in the black-and-gold uniforms of the Imperial treasury poking through the ship's hold and making a formal tally of the cargo, item by item.

In theory all merchandise shipped into Italia from the provinces for resale was subject to customs duties. In practice, the customs inspectors, having paid stiff bribes to the secretariat of their department to get their jobs, skimmed off most of the customs revenue and allowed only a fraction of the legitimate amount to dribble through to the Imperial Treasury. Everyone knew it, but no one seemed to care. Apollinaris himself disliked the arrangement, even though he did not see why transfers of merchandise from one part of the Empire to another should be subject to customs charges in the first place. But the bribing of customs officials in lieu of paying duty was only one out of myriad practices of the Imperial regime that cried out for reform, and in any event the affairs of merchants and shippers had never been anything to which he had devoted much attention.

Today's process, though, caused unusual delays in disembarking. After a time he sent for the ship's captain, a genial black-bearded Carthaginian, and asked what was going on.

The captain, who was livid with dismay and indignation, wasn't sure. New procedures, he said. Some sort of shakeup in the Department of Customs, that was all he knew.

Apollinaris guessed at first that it might have something to do with the revenue shortfall about which Torquatus had written him: the Emperor, running low on cash, had instructed his officials to start increasing governmental revenues. Then he realized how little sense that notion made. Demetrius had never shown any awareness that there was a relationship between governmental income and

Imperial expenditure. No, this must be the doing of Torquatus himself, Apollinaris decided: one of the "severe measures" that his co-Consul had said he would be taking in order to set things to rights.

From Ostia, Apollinaris went straight to the suburban villa that he maintained along the Via Flaminia, just north of the city wall. It had been in the care of his younger brother, Romulus Claudius Apollinaris, during the five years of his absence, and Apollinaris was pleased to discover that Romulus Claudius, although he too had been absent from Roma most of that time and was living up in Umbria right now, had had the place kept up as though his brother might require its use at any moment.

His homeward route took him through the heart of the city. It was good to be back in Roma, to see the ancient buildings again, two thousand years of history standing forth on every street, the marble walls of temples and government offices, some as old as Augustus and Tiberius, mellowed by time despite centuries of ongoing repair, and the medieval buildings, solid and a little coarse, their ornate façades throbbing in the hot sunlight, and then the new buildings of the Decadence, all strange parapets and soaring flying buttresses and sudden startling cantilevered wings, like those of some great beetle, leaping off into space. How glad he was to see it all! Even the heat stirred some gladness in him. It was the month of Julius, hot and humid, a time when the river ran very low, turbid, choked with yellow silt. The day's heat held the city in its tight grip. Far away, lightning sounded—a dry crack, lightning without rain, the sinister thunder of the absent-minded gods. There was a malarious stench in the air. He had forgotten how Roma stank in the summer, during all those years he had spent off in the lesser cities of the western provinces. Roma was the grandest city that ever was or would be, but there was no escaping the truth of its odor this time of year, the effluvia of a million people, their discarded rotting food, their wastes, the sweat of those million bodies. He was a fastidious man. He disliked the heat, the stench, the dirt. And yet, yet—this was Roma, and there was no city like it!

When Apollinaris reached his villa he sent word to Torquatus that he had returned and would be pleased to meet with him as soon as possible, and at once a messenger came back from Torquatus inviting him to dine at his house that evening.

That was a doubtful pleasure. Apollinaris, for all his scholarly interest in the stoic virtues of Republican Roma, was a civilized and cultivated man who appreciated fine wines and imaginative cooking. His colleague in the Consulship was of another kind entirely, very much an Old Roman in his distaste for comfort and luxury—a ponderous, wintry-souled sort who showed little interest in food or wine or literature or philosophy, indeed whose only pleasurable pursuit, so far as Apollinaris knew, was to hunt wild boar in the snow-choked forests of the northern provinces.

But this night Torquatus's table was set for a person of Apollinaris's tastes, with any number of wines and sherbets and a splendid main course of spiced venison. There was no entertainment—dancers and musicians would not be appropriate for such a meeting—and just the two of them were at the table. Apollinaris had never married and Torquatus's wife, who was seldom seen in public, made no appearance even in her own home this evening.

He had indeed made changes in the customs procedures, he told Apollinaris. He had made other changes as well. The whole depraved crew that surrounded the Emperor had been rounded up and taken away. There would be no more wild spending sprees on Demetrius's part. Torquatus had instituted reforms on every level of the government, as well. Corrupt officials had been removed. Regulations that had been on the books for decades but never enforced were now being applied. All governmental departments had been ordered to draw up new budgets and they would be required to live within them.

"And the Emperor?" Apollinaris asked, when Torquatus finally paused in his recitation. "How has he taken your dismissal of his coterie of flunkies? I see your head is still on its shoulders, so you must have found some way of pacifying him, but what could it have been?"

"His Majesty is not in any position to order executions these days," said Torquatus. "His Majesty is currently under house arrest."

Apollinaris felt a stab of amazement.

"Do you seriously mean that? Yes, yes, of course you do. You always seriously mean it. —Penned up in his own palace, is he?"

"In the palace guest-house, actually. That new building, the weird-looking one with those bizarre mosaics. I have troops posted on duty around it twenty-four hours a day."

"But surely the Praetorian Guard wouldn't have allowed—"

"I took the precaution of having the Prefect of the Praetorian Guard removed from office, and replaced him with a man of my own staff, a certain Atilius Rullianus. The Praetorians have received a generous payment and have willingly taken an oath of allegiance to their new prefect."

"Yes. They usually do, if paid well enough."

"And so we keep Demetrius well supplied with women and food, but otherwise he is completely isolated. He has no contact with any of the officials of his court, or with the members of the Senate. Naturally I stay away from him also. You will, I hope, keep your distance from him yourself, Apollinaris. Essentially you and I, jointly, are the Emperor, now. All governmental decrees flow from the Consular office; all governmental officials report to us."

Apollinaris gave Torquatus a keen, close look. "So you intend to keep the Emperor a prisoner for the rest of his life? You know there'll be problems with that, man. Crazy or not, the Emperor is expected to present himself before the people at certain times of the year. The New Year festival, the opening of the new Senate session, the first day of the season's games at the Colosseum—you can't just hide him away indefinitely, you know, without arousing a little curiosity about where he is."

"For the moment," said Torquatus, "it has been announced that His Majesty is ill. I think we can leave it at that for the time being. How fast he recovers—well, we can deal with that issue later. There are other problems."

"Such as?"

"The Senate, for one. You may or may not be aware that a goodly number of Senators have been quite comfortable with Demetrius's way of doing things. The general corruption spills over to them as well. With no real Emperor to hold them accountable, they do as they please, and plenty of them live like little Demetriuses themselves. The kind of orgiastic existences that Roma was famous for in Nero's time, I mean. We can't allow a return to that kind of thing. The Senate is in need of some reform itself. If it doesn't get it, many of its members will try to obstruct our program."

"I see," Apollinaris said. "Are you talking about removing certain Senators from office, then?"

"That might be necessary."

"But only an Emperor can do that."

"We will do it in the name of the Emperor," said Torquatus. "As we do everything else that must be done."

"Ah," Apollinaris said. "I see. In the name of the Emperor."

For the first time he noticed how tired Torquatus looked. Torquatus was a big man, of formidable physical strength and legendary endurance; but his eyes, Apollinaris saw, were reddened with fatigue, and his heavy-jowled face was drawn and sallow.

"There's even more to deal with," Torquatus went on.

"More than dismissing the whole court, imprisoning the Emperor, and purging the Senate?"

"I refer to the possibility of a general uprising of the people," Torquatus said portentously.

"Because of the reforms you've been instituting, you mean?"

"On the contrary. My reforms are the salvation of the Empire, and sooner or later everyone will see that—if we can hold things together until that point. But the people may not allow us enough time to explain things to them. You've been away these five years and you don't know what's been happening here. I want you to come with me to the Subura tomorrow."

"The Subura," Apollinaris said. He pressed his hands together and brought the tips of his fingers to his lips. The Subura, as he recalled, was an ancient slum district of the capital, a filthy, smelly place of dark alleys and crooked streets that led nowhere. Every few hundred years some civic-minded Emperor would order it cleaned out and rebuilt, but its innate nature was unconquerable and the pestilential nature of the place always managed to reassert itself in a couple of generations. "The Subura is restless, is it? A few truckloads of free bread and wine can fix that, I'd think."

"Wrong. Those people have plenty to eat as it is. For all of Demetrius's excesses, this is still a prosperous land. And, whatever you think, revolutions don't spring up because of poverty. It's the

passion for novelty, the pursuit of excitement, that does it. Revolution is the fruit of idleness and leisure, not of poverty."

"The idleness and leisure of the slum-dwellers of the Subura,"
Apollinaris said, gazing thoughtfully at the other man. It was an interesting concept, marvelous in its complete absurdity.

But it appeared that Torquatus found a certain logic in it. "Yes.
Amid the general breakdown of law and order, this thing that some
people call the Decadence, they've come to see that nobody's really
in charge of anything any more. And so they want to get themselves
a bigger share of the loot. Overthrow the monarchy, butcher all the
patricians, divide up the wealth among themselves. I've been in their
taverns, Apollinaris. I've listened to their harangues. You come with
me tomorrow and sit down next to them and you'll hear the same
things yourself."

"Two Consuls, going freely and unguarded into slum taverns?"

"They'll have no idea who we are. I'll show you how to dress."

"It would be interesting, I suppose. But, thank you, no. I'll take
your word for it: there's restlessness in the Subura. But we still have
an army, Torquatus. I've just spent five years pacifying the provinces.
I can pacify the Subura too, if I have to."

"Turn the Roman army against the citizens of the capital? Think
about it, my friend. The agitators in the Subura must be dealt with
before the real trouble breaks out. —I agree, a great deal for you to
consider on your first day back. But there's no time to waste. We
face a very big job." Torquatus signaled to a slave who was waiting
nearby to refill their glasses. "Enough of this talk for the moment, all
right? What do you think of this wine? Forty-year-old Falernian, it
is. From the Emperor's own cellars, I should tell you. I had some
brought here especially for this occasion."

"Quite splendid," said Apollinaris. "But age has made it a trifle
bitter. Would you pass me the honey, Torquatus?"

Charax said, "This is the list so far, sir."

Apollinaris took the sheet of paper from his aide-de-camp and
ran quickly down the names. "Statius—Claudius Nero—Judas Antonius Soranus—who are these people, Charax?"

"Lucius Status is the Emperor's private secretary. Soranus is a Hebrew who is said to import unusual animals from Africa for his collection. I have no information about Claudius Nero, sir, but he is probably a craftsman to the court."

"Ah." Apollinaris turned his attention back to the list. "Hilarion and Polybius, yes. The personal attendants. I remember those two. Oily little bastards, both of them. Glitius Agricola. Gaius Callistus. Marco Cornuto—what kind of name is that, 'Marco Cornuto?' "

"A Roman name, sir. I mean, it's Roman in language, not Latin."

That puzzled him. "Latin—Roman—what's the difference?"

"The lower classes speak some rough new kind of language now that they call 'Roman,' a dialect—the dialect of the people, it's called. Derived from Latin, the way the languages of the provinces are. It's like an easier, sloppier form of Latin. They've begun translating their own names into it, I hear. This Marco Cornuto is probably one of the Emperor's coachmen, or a stable groom, something along those lines."

Apollinaris made a face. He very much disliked the custom, of late so prevalent out in the provinces, of speaking local dialects that were coarse, vulgar versions of Latin mixed with primitive regional words: one way of speaking in Gallia, another in Hispania, another in Britannia, and still another, very different from the others, in the Teutonic provinces. He had suppressed the use of those languages, those dialects, wherever he had encountered it. So now it was happening here, too? "What sense does that make, a new dialect of Latin used right here in Roma? In the provinces, those dialects are a way of signifying independence from the Empire. But Roma can't secede from itself, can it?"

Charax merely smiled and shrugged.

Apollinaris remembered now what Torquatus had told him about the restlessness in the slums, the likelihood of some kind of uprising among the plebeians. Was a new bastard form of Latin beginning to establish itself among the poor, a private language of their own, setting them apart from the hated aristocrats? It was worth investigating. He knew from his experiences in the provinces what power language could have in fomenting political unrest.

He looked once more at the list of those whom Torquatus had arrested.

"Matius—Licentius—Licinius—Caesius Bassius—" He looked up. "What do these little red marks next to some of the names mean?"

"Those are the ones who have already been executed," Charax said.

"Did you say 'executed'?" Apollinaris asked, startled.

"Put to death, yes," said Charax. "You seem surprised. I thought you knew, sir."

"No," Apollinaris said. "I haven't heard anything about executions."

"At the far end of the Forum, in the little plaza in front of the Arch of Marcus Anastasius: he's had a platform set up there, and every afternoon there have been executions all week, four or five a day."

" 'He'?"

"Larcius Torquatus, sir," Charax said, in the tone of one who was explaining something to a child.

Apollinaris nodded. This was the tenth day since his return to Roma, and they had been busy days. Torquatus had never given him a chance, at their first meeting in Torquatus's home, to explain that it was his intention to give up his Consulship and retire to private life. And once he had heard what Torquatus had been up to—putting the Emperor under house arrest, throwing His Majesty's playmates into prison, issuing a raft of stringent new decrees designed to cleanse the government of corruption—Apollinaris had realized that his notion of retiring was an impossible one. Torquatus's program, commendable though it was, was so radical that he could not be left to carry it out alone. That would make him, in effect, dictator of Roma, and Apollinaris knew from his readings in history that the only kind of dictators Roma would tolerate were those who, like Augustus Caesar, were able to conceal their dictatorial ways behind a façade of constitutional legitimacy. A mere appointive Consul, ruling on his own after overthrowing the Emperor, would not be able to sustain himself in power unless he assumed the Imperial powers himself. Apollinaris did not want to see Torquatus do that. Maintaining the Consular system was essential now. And Torquatus must have a legitimate Consular colleague if he wanted his reforms to have any success.

So Apollinaris had put all thought of retirement aside and had spent his first days back reestablishing his presence at the capital, setting up his office in the Consular building, renewing his connections with the important men of the Senate, and otherwise resuming his life at the center of power. He had met daily with his colleague Torquatus, who assured him that the work of purging the commonwealth of idlers and parasites was moving along smoothly, but up until now Apollinaris had not pressed him for details. That had been a mistake, he realized now. Torquatus's policy of ending the drain on the public treasury that the Emperor's huge mob of hangers-on had created was one that he had applauded, of course. But it had never occurred to Apollinaris that his co-Consul was having them killed. And his travels around the city since his return had not taken him anywhere near that little plaza of Marcus Anastasius, the place of execution where heads rolled in the dust by order of M. Larcius Torquatus.

"Perhaps I should have a little talk with Torquatus about this," Apollinaris said, rising and tucking the list of the arrested men into a fold of his robe.

Torquatus's office was one floor above Apollinaris's in the Consular building. In the old days the two Consuls had divided the ninth floor between themselves: that was how it had been in Apollinaris's first three terms as Consul, certainly. The first time, as junior Consul, he had used the office on the eastern side of the building, looking down into Trajan's Forum. During his second and third terms, when he now was senior Consul, he had moved over to the somewhat more imposing rooms on the western side of the top floor. But during Apollinaris's long absence in the provinces Torquatus had expanded his own Consular domain into the part of the floor that had previously been his, and had set up a secondary office for his colleague on the building's eighth floor. "The Consul's tasks have increased so greatly since we reconstituted the post," Torquatus explained, a little shamefacedly, when Apollinaris, having returned, had showed up to reclaim his old office. "You were away fighting in Sicilia and probably wouldn't be back for two or three years, and I needed more room close at hand for the additional staff members that now were required, et cetera, et cetera—"

The new arrangement rankled more than a little, but this was not the moment, Apollinaris felt, to start quarreling with his co-Consul about office space. There would be time to express concern over matters of precedence and status once things were a little more stable at the capital.

Torquatus was busily signing papers when Apollinaris arrived. He seemed unaware, for a moment, that his fellow Consul had entered the room. Then he looked up and offered Apollinaris a quick apologetic smile. "So much paperwork—"

"Signing more death warrants, are you?"

Apollinaris had meant the statement to sound neutral, even bland. But Torquatus's frowning response told him that he had not quite succeeded.

"As a matter of fact, Apollinaris, I am. Does that trouble you?"

"A little, perhaps. I don't think I understood that you were actually going to have Demetrius's people put to death."

"I thought we had discussed it."

"Not in so many words. You said you were 'removing' them, I think. I don't recall your explicitly explaining what you meant by that." Already a defensive iciness was visible in Torquatus's eyes. Apollinaris brought forth the list of prisoners that Charax had procured for him and said, "Do you think it's wise, Torquatus, to inflict such severe penalties on such trivial people? The Emperor's barber? The Emperor's clown?"

"You've been away from the capital many years," Torquatus said. "These men are not such simple innocents as you may think. I send no one lightly to his death."

"Even so, Torquatus—"

Smoothly Torquatus cut him off. "Consider our choices, if you will. Strip them of office but let them go free? Then they remain among us, stirring up trouble, conniving to get themselves back to their high positions in the palace. We merely imprison them? Then we must maintain them at public expense, perhaps for the rest of their lives. Send them into exile? Then they take their illicitly gained wealth with them, which otherwise we could recapture for the treasury. No, Apollinaris, getting rid of them once and for all is the only solution. If we allow them to live, sooner or later they'll manage to get access to His Majesty again and begin working him up to over-throw us."

"So we put them to death to minimize the risks to ourselves?"

"The risks to the Empire," Torquatus said. "Do you think I care that much about my own life? But if we fall, the Empire falls with us. These men are the enemies of the commonwealth. You and I are all that stand between them and the reign of chaos. They have to go. I thought we had already come to full agreement on that point."

In no way was that statement true, Apollinaris knew. Yet he saw the validity of the argument. The Empire stood, not for the first time, at the brink of anarchy. The disturbances in the provinces had given early warning of that. Augustus had created the Imperium by dint of military force, and it was the army that had sustained the Em-perors on their thrones all these centuries. But Emperors ruled, ulti-mately, by the consent of the governed. No army was strong enough to compel the populace to accept the authority of a wicked or crazy Emperor indefinitely: that had been shown again and again, from the time of Caligula and Nero on up through history. Demetrius was plainly crazy; most of the government officials were demonstrably corrupt; if Torquatus was right that the plebeians were muttering about a revolution, and it was altogether possible that he *was* right about that, then a fierce purge of the corruption and craziness might be the only way of heading off calamity. And to allow Demetrius's minions to live, and to regroup, and to regain the Emperor's ear, was to invite that very calamity.

"Very well," said Apollinaris. "How far do you intend to carry this, though?"

"As far as the situation demands," Torquatus said.

The month of Julius gave way to the month of Augustus, and the worst summer in Roma's long history went grinding on, intolerable heat, choking humidity, low ominous clouds hiding the sun, light-ning in the hills but never any rain, tensions rising, tempers snap-ping everywhere as the daily procession of carts bearing the latest batches of the condemned rolled onward toward the executioner's block. Great throngs came to watch each day, commoners and patri-

cians alike, looking toward the headsman and his victims in the fascinated way one stares at a weaving serpent making ready to strike.
The spectacle of horror was terrifying but no one could stay away.
The reek of blood hung over Roma. With each passing day the city
grew more pure, and much more frightened, paralyzed by fear and
suspicion.

"Five weeks now," said Lactantius Rufus, who was the presiding
magistrate of the Senate, "and the killing has spread into our own
House itself."

"Pactumeius Pollio, tried and found guilty," Julius Papinio said.
He stood closest to Rufus among the little group of men on the portico of the Senate this sizzling, steamy morning.

"Likewise Marcus Florianus," said the rotund Terentius Figulus.

"And Macrinus," said Flavius Lollianus.

"And Fulpianus."

"That's it, I think. Four all together."

"Four Senators, yes," said Lactantius Rufus. "So far. But who's
next, I ask you? You? Me? Where does it stop? Death is king in
Roma these days. This whole House is endangered, my friends."
He was a great sickle of a man, enormously tall, stoop-shouldered,
his back curving in a wide arc, his face in profile a jagged blade of
angular features. For more than thirty years he had been a prominent member of the Senate: a confidant of the late Emperor
Lodovicus, a close adviser to the present Emperor Demetrius, a
three-time holder of the Consulship. "We must find a way of pro-
tecting ourselves."

"What do you suggest?" Papinio asked. "Shall we call upon the
Emperor to remove the Consuls?"

It was said in a halfhearted way. Papinio and all the others knew
how ludicrous a suggestion that was. "Let me remind you," Lactantius said anyway, "that the Emperor is a prisoner himself."

"So he is," Papinio conceded. "All power lies with the Consuls
now."

"Quite true," Rufus said. "And therefore our task must be to
drive a wedge between them. We should go, three or four of us, or
perhaps five, as a delegation to Apollinaris. He's a reasonable man.
Surely he sees the damage Torquatus is doing, the risk that these

purges, if they continue, will get out of hand and run through Roma like a wildfire. We ask him to remove Torquatus from office and name a new colleague."

"To remove Torquatus from office—!" said Terentius Figulus, astounded. "You make it sound so easy! But could he do it?"

"Apollinaris has just reconquered four or five whole provinces without any serious difficulty. Why would he have any trouble overcoming one man?"

"What if he doesn't want to?" Papinio asked. "What if he *approves* of what Torquatus has been doing?"

"Then we remove them both," replied Rufus. "But let's keep that for a last resort. Which of you will come with me to Apollinaris?"

"I," said Papinio immediately. But no one else spoke out.

Rufus looked about at the others. "Well?" he said. "Figulus? Lollianus? What about you, Priscus? Salvius Julianus?"

In the end Rufus managed to collect just two companions for his mission, the ever-ambitious Julius Papinio and another Senator named Gaius Lucius Frontinus, a younger man whose family had enormous wine-producing properties in southern Italia. Though these were busy times in the Consular office—the Consuls' days were consumed by the task of purification, making out arrest orders, attending trials, authorizing the executions of those found guilty, which was nearly everyone placed on trial—they had surprisingly little difficulty gaining an audience with the Consul Valerian Apollinaris. But winning his support was not quite so easy.

"What you're asking is treasonous, as you surely must know," said Apollinaris calmly. He had remained seated behind his desk; the others stood before him. "By suggesting that one constitutionally appointed Consul should depose his colleague, you're inviting me to join the conspiracy that you apparently have formed to overthrow the legitimate government of the Empire. That in itself is a capital offense. I could have you whisked off to prison this very minute. Before the end of the week you'd be staring at the headsman's axe. Eh, Rufus? Papinio? Frontinus?"

It was impossible to tell whether he meant it as a threat or as a joke. Lactantius Rufus, steadfastly meeting the Consul's coolly appraising gaze, said, "You'd probably follow us there in the next

week or two, Count Apollinaris. Certainly you, of all people, must
understand how dangerous Torquatus is to everybody's welfare, certainly to ours and yours, perhaps even to his own."

"Dangerous to yours, yes. But why to mine? I've backed
Torquatus in all of his actions, haven't I? So why would my respected Consular colleague turn against me?"

"Because the way things are going," said Rufus, "the removal of
Emperor Demetrius will become a political necessity somewhere
down the line, more likely sooner than later. And the Emperor has
no sons. The heir to the throne is his addlepated and utterly incapable brother Marius, who sits quietly giggling to himself in his
palace on Capreae. He can never reign. You and Torquatus are the
only plausible successors to Demetrius in sight. But you can't both
become Emperor. Do you see my logic, Apollinaris?"

"Of course I do. But I have no intention of having the Emperor
killed, and I doubt that Torquatus does either, or he'd have done it
already."

Rufus sighed. "Unless he's simply biding his time. But let that be
as it may: perhaps you don't feel that you're in any danger, dear
Apollinaris, but we certainly do. Four members of the Senate are
dead already. Others are probably on the proscribed list. Torquatus
is drunk with power, killing people as quickly as he can, scores of
them. Some of them very much deserved their fate. In other cases
Torquatus is simply settling old personal accounts. To claim that the
Senator Pactumeius Pollio was an enemy of the realm—or Marcus
Florianus—"

"To save your skins, then, you want me to lift my hand against
my colleague in violation of my oaths. And if I refuse?"

"The Senate, with the Emperor indisposed, has the power to
strip you and Torquatus both of your Consulships."

"Do you think so? And if you can manage to bring it off, who
will our replacements be? You, Rufus? Young Frontinus here? And
would the people ever accept you as their leaders? You know perfectly well that Torquatus and I are the only men left in this rotting
Empire who have the strength to keep things from falling apart."
Apollinaris smiled and shook his head. "No, Rufus. You're just
bluffing. You have no candidates to take our places."

"Agreed," Rufus said, without any hesitation. "This is certainly so. But if you refuse us, you'll leave us no choice but to try to strike Torquatus down ourselves, and we may very well fail, which will plunge everything into disorder and turmoil as he takes his revenge. You and you alone can save Roma from him. You must remove him and take sole command, and make an end to this reign of terror before a river of Senatorial blood runs in the streets."

"You want me to be Emperor, then?"

This time Rufus, taken by surprise, did hesitate before replying. "Do you want to be?"

"No. Never. If I take sole command, though, I would be acting essentially as an Emperor. Before long, as you correctly foresee, I *would* be Emperor. But the throne has no appeal for me. The most I want is to be Consul."

"Be Consul, then. Get rid of Torquatus and appoint some congenial partner, anyone you like. But you have to stop him before he devours us all. Yourself included, I warn you, Apollinaris."

When the three Senators had left his office Apollinaris sat quietly for a time, replaying the discussion in his mind. There was no denying the truth of anything Rufus had said.

Rufus was grasping and manipulative, of course, as anyone of his great wealth and long occupation of a position close to the centers of Imperial power could be expected to be. But he was not really evil, as powerful men went, and he was certainly no fool. He saw very clearly, and Apollinaris saw it as well, how unlikely it was that there would be any end to Torquatus's frenzied purification of the realm, that not only were prominent Senators like Lactantius Rufus in obvious danger but that it would go on and on until the list of victims included Count Valerian Apollinaris himself.

That was inevitable. Apollinaris, though he had approved from the start of the need to call a halt to the Emperor Demetrius's excesses and purge the court of its parasites, had seen Torquatus's zealousness growing day by day. And he was far from comfortable with the extreme nature of Torquatus's methods—midnight arrests, secret trials, verdict within an hour, execution the next day.

Now that Torquatus had succeeded in establishing death as a valid penalty for undermining the moral fiber of the Empire, the list of potential victims of the purge had become almost infinite, too. Demetrius's clump of odious hangers-on, some of them truly vicious and some mere witless buffoons, was gone now. So were dozens of the most corrupt members of the bureaucracy and four of their facilitators in the Senate. And, yes, just as Rufus had guessed, many more indictments were pending. Torquatus's concentration was focused now on the unrest in the Subura, where the ordinary theft and vandalism had given way to rioting and anarchic outcries against the government. Soon Torquatus would be executing plebeians, too. If left unchecked he would purge Roma from top to bottom.

That a cleansing of the commonwealth had been in order was something that Apollinaris did not question. Despite his reservations he had made no attempt to interfere in what Torquatus had been doing these five weeks past. But it was clear to him now that Torquatus had begun ruling almost as a dictator, a murderous one at that, and that as Torquatus's Consular colleague he was expected to continue to join him in that role, or else face the possibility of becoming a victim of Torquatus's zeal himself. For a time would come—if it was not already at hand—when it would be necessary to say to Torquatus, "Things have gone far enough, now. This is where we should stop the killings." And what if Torquatus disagreed?

Very likely the name of Valerian Apollinaris would be the next one added to the roster of the condemned, in that case. And, though Apollinaris had never been greatly concerned about his personal safety, he saw now that in the present situation he must preserve his life for the sake of the Empire. There was no other bulwark but him against the encroaching chaos.

Best to face the issue immediately, Apollinaris decided.

He went to see Torquatus.

"The Senate is growing very uneasy," he said. "These four executions—"

"They were traitors," Torquatus said sharply. Sweat was rolling down his fleshy face in the dense, humid atmosphere of the room, but for some reason unfathomable to Apollinaris the man was wearing a heavy winter toga. "They wallowed in Demetrius's iniquities to their own enormous profit."

"No doubt they did. But we need the Senate's continued support if we're to carry through our program."

"Do we? The Senate's just an antiquarian vestige, something left over from the ancient Republic. Just as the Consuls were, before you and I revived the office. Emperors functioned perfectly well for at least a thousand years without sharing any power at all with the Senate or the Consuls. We can get along without the Senate, too. Who's been talking to you? Lactantius Rufus? Julius Papinio? I know who the malcontents are. And I'll take them down, one by one, until—"

"I beg you, Torquatus." Apollinaris wondered whether he had ever uttered those words before in his life. "Show some moderation, man. What we're trying to achieve is a very difficult thing. We can't simply dispense with the backing of the Senate."

"Of course we can. The axe awaits anyone who stands in our way, and they all know it. What was Caligula's famous line? 'Oh, that these annoying Romans had only a single neck'—something like that. That's how I feel about the Senate."

"Caligula is not, I think, the philosopher you ought to be quoting just now," said Apollinaris. "I urge you again, Torquatus, let us be more moderate from here on. Otherwise, what I fear is that you and I are lighting a fire in Roma that may prove to be extremely difficult to put out, a fire that may easily consume you and me as well before it's over."

"I'm not convinced that moderation is what we need at this point," said Torquatus. "And if you fear for your life, my friend, you have the option of resigning your Consulship." His gaze now was cold and uncompromising. "I know that you've often spoken of returning to private life, your studies, your country estate. Perhaps the time has come for you to do just that."

Apollinaris summoned the most pleasant smile he could find. "Not just yet, I think. Despite the objections I've just put to you, I still share your belief that there's much work for us to do in Roma, and I intend to stand with you while it's being carried out. You and

I are colleagues in this to the end, Marcus Larcius. We may have dis-
agreements along the way, but they'll never be permitted to come
between us in any serious way."

"You mean that, do you, Apollinaris?"

"Of course I do."

A look of enormous relief appeared on Torquatus's heavy-
featured, deeply furrowed face. "I embrace you, colleague!"

"And I you," said Apollinaris, standing and offering his hand to
the bigger man, but making no move to let the talk of embraces be
anything more than metaphorical.

He returned quickly to his headquarters on the floor below and
called Tiberius Charax to him.

"Take ten armed men—no, a dozen," he told the aide-de-camp,
"and get yourself upstairs to Marcus Larcius's office. Tell his bodyguards, if you encounter any, that you're there at my orders, that a
matter concerning the Consul Torquatus's security has come up and
I have instructed you to place these men at the Consul's disposal at
once. I doubt that they'll try to stop you. If they do, kill them. Then
grab Torquatus, tell him that he's under arrest on a charge of high
treason, bundle him out of the building as fast as you can, and place
him under tight guard in the Capitoline dungeons, where no one is
to be allowed to see him or send messages to him."

It was to Charax's great credit, Apollinaris thought, that not the
slightest evidence of surprise could be detected on his face.

The problem now was choosing a new co-Consul, who would aid
him in the continuing work of reconstruction and reform without in
any way presenting serious opposition to his programs. Apollinaris
was adamant in his desire not to rule by sole command. He lacked
the temperament of an Emperor and he disliked the idea of trying to
reign dictatorially, as a kind of modern-day Sulla. Even after twenty
centuries the memory of Sulla was not beloved by Romans. So a co-
operative colleague was needed, quickly. There was no question in
Apollinaris's mind that the task that he and Torquatus had begun
needed to be seen through to completion, and that at this moment it
was very far from being complete.

He hoped it could be done without many more executions, though. Certainly Torquatus in his Old Roman rigor had allowed the process of purgation to go too far. The first spate had been sufficient to eliminate the worst of the ones Torquatus had referred to, rightly, as the caterpillars of the commonwealth. But then he had begun his cleansing of the Senate, and by now everyone of any consequence in the realm seemed to be denouncing everybody else. The prisons were filling up; the headsman's arm was growing weary. Apollinaris meant to check the frantic pace of the killings, and eventually to halt them altogether.

He was pondering how he was going to reach that goal, three days after Torquatus had been taken into custody, when Lactantius Rufus came to him and said, "Well, Apollinaris, I hope your soul is at peace and your will is up to date. We are scheduled to be assassinated the day after tomorrow, you and I, and some fifty of the other Senators, and Torquatus also, and the Emperor too, for that matter. The whole regime swept away in one grand sweep, in other words."

Apollinaris shot a look of bleak displeasure at the wily old Senator. "This is no time for jokes, Rufus."

"So you see me as a comedian, do you? The joke will be on you, then. Here: look at these papers. The entire plot's spelled out for you in them. It's Julius Papinio's work."

Rufus handed a sheaf of documents across the desk. Apollinaris riffled hastily through them: lists of names, diagrammatic maps of the governmental buildings, a step-by-step outline of the planned se- quence of events. It had occurred to Apollinaris that Rufus's purpose in coming to him with these charges was simply to get rid of an annoyingly ambitious young rival, but no, no, this was all too thorough in its detail to be anything but authentic.

He considered what little he knew of this Papinio. A red-haired, red-faced man, old-line Senatorial family. Young, greedy, shifty-eyed, quick to take offense. Apollinaris had never seen much to admire in him.

Rufus said, "Papinio wants to restore the Republic. With himself as Consul, of course. I suspect he thinks he's the reincarnation of Junius Lucius Brutus."

Apollinaris smiled grimly. He knew the reference: a probably

mythical figure out of the very distant past, the man who had ex-
pelled the last of the tyrannical kings who had ruled Roma in its earliest days. It was this Brutus, supposedly, who had founded the
Republic and established the system of Consuls. Marcus Junius Brutus, the assassin of Julius Caesar, had claimed him as an ancestor.

"A new Brutus among us?" Apollinaris said. "No, I don't think
so. Not Papinio." He glanced through the papers once more. "The
day after tomorrow. Well, that gives us a little time."

With Torquatus locked away, the task of dealing with this was
entirely his. He ordered Papinio arrested and interrogated. The interrogation was swift and efficient: at the first touch of the torturer's
tongs Papinio provided a full confession, naming twelve co-
conspirators. The trial was held that evening and the executions
took place at dawn. So much for the new incarnation of Junius Lucius Brutus.

There were great ironies here, Apollinaris knew. He had put
Torquatus away in the hope of halting the torrent of killings, and
now he had ordered a whole new series of executions himself. But
he knew he had had no choice. Papinio's plot would surely have
brought the whole Imperial system down if the man had managed to
live another two days.

With that out of the way, he took up the matter of the increasing
troubles in the slum districts. The rioters were breaking statues,
looting shops. Troops had been sent in and hundreds of plebeians
had been killed, yet each day brought new violence.

Apollinaris's agents brought him pamphlets that the agitators in
the Subura were passing out in the streets. Like the late Julius Papinio, these men were calling for the overthrow of the government
and the restoration of the Republic of olden times.

The return of the Republic, Apollinaris thought, might actually
not be such a bad thing. The Imperial system had produced some
great rulers, yes, but it had also brought the Neros and Saturninuses
and Demetriuses to the throne. Sometimes it seemed to him that
Roma had endured this long despite most of its Emperors, rather
than because of them. Reverting now to the way things had been in
antiquity, the Senate choosing two highly qualified men to serve as
Consuls, supreme magistrates ruling in consultation with the Senate,

holding office not for life but only for brief terms that they would voluntarily relinquish when the time came—there was more than a little merit in that idea.

But what he feared was that if the monarchy were overthrown Roma would pass instantly through the stage of a republic to that of a democracy—the rule of the mob, is what that meant, giving the government over to the man who promised the greatest benefits to the least worthy segments of society, buying the support of the crowd by stripping the assets of the productive citizens. That was not to be tolerated: democracy in Roma would bring madness even worse than that of Demetrius. Something had to be done to prevent that. Apollinaris ordered his men to seek out and arrest the ring-leaders of the Subura anarchy.

Meanwhile Torquatus himself, safely tucked away in the Imperial dungeons, lay under sentence of death. The Senate, with Lactantius Rufus presiding over the trial, had been quick to indict him and find him guilty. But Apollinaris had not been able to bring himself, thus far, to sign the death warrant. He knew that he would have to deal with it sooner or later, of course. Torquatus, once imprisoned, could never be freed, not if Apollinaris intended to remain alive himself. But still—actually to send the man to the block—

Apollinaris left the matter unresolved for the moment and returned to the issue of the new co-Consul.

He went through the list of Senators but found no one who might be acceptable. They were all tainted in one way or another by ambition, by corruption, by laziness, by foolishness, by any of a dozen sins and flaws. But then the name of Laureolus Caesar came to mind.

Of royal blood. Intelligent. Youthful. Presentable. A student of history, familiar with the errors of Roma's turbulent past. And a man without enemies, because he had wisely kept himself far from the capital during the most deplorable years of Demetrius's reign. They would work well together as Consular colleagues, Apollinaris was sure.

Apollinaris had sounded Laureolus out about the Consulship once already, back in Tarraco. But he had withdrawn the suggestion as soon as he had made it, realizing that the Emperor would probably see young Laureolus as a potential rival for the throne and reject the nomination. That problem was no longer a factor.

Well, then. Summon Laureolus from his country retreat, let him know that Torquatus had been removed from office, tell him that his duty as a Roman required him to accept the Consulship in Torquatus's place. Yes. Yes.

But before Apollinaris could call Tiberius Charax in to dictate the message to him Charax came running into his office unbidden, flushed, wild-eyed. Apollinaris had never seen the little Greek so flustered-looking before.

"Sir—sir—"

"Easy, man! Catch your breath! What's happened?"

"The—Emperor—" Charax could barely get the words out. He must have sprinted all the way across the Forum and up the eight flights of stairs. "Has bribed—his way—out of his confinement. Is— back in the palace. Is under—the protection—of the former Praetorian Prefect, Leo Severinus." He paused to collect himself. "And has named a completely new set of governmental ministers. Many of whom are dead, but he doesn't know that yet."

Apollinaris muttered a curse. "What is he saying about the Consuls?"

"He has sent a letter to the Senate, sir. Commanding that yourself and Torquatus be dismissed."

"Well, at least I've taken care of the second part of that for him already, eh, Charax?" Apollinaris gave the aide-de-camp a grim smile. This was a maddening development, but he had no time for anger now. Action, quick and decisive, was the only remedy. "Get me the same dozen men you used when you arrested Torquatus. And half a dozen more of the same quality. I want them assembled outside this building ten minutes from now. I'm going to have to pay a little visit to the Praetorians. —Oh, and send word to Prince Laureolus that I want him here in Roma as soon as he can get here. Tomorrow, at the latest. No: tonight."

The headquarters of the Praetorian Guard had been located since the time of Tiberius in the eastern part of the city. By now, nearly eighteen centuries later, the Praetorians, the Emperor's elite personal military force, had come to occupy a huge forbidding block there, a dark, ugly building that was meant to frighten, and did. Apollinaris understood the risks he was running by presenting himself at that menacing garrison. The little squad of armed men accompanying him had purely a symbolic value: if the Praetorians chose to attack, there would be no withstanding their much greater numbers. But there were no options here. If Demetrius had really regained control, Apollinaris was a dead man already, unless he succeeded in winning the Praetorians over.

Luck was with him, though. The mystique of the Consular emblem, the twelve bundles of birchwood rods with the axe-heads jutting through, opened the gates of the building for him. And both of the Praetorian Prefects were on the premises, the Emperor's man Leo Severinus and the replacement whom Torquatus had appointed, Atilius Rullianus. That was a good stroke, finding them both. He had expected to find Rullianus; but Severinus was the key player at the moment, and it had been more likely that he would be at the palace.

They might have been stamped from the same mold: two big pockmarked men, greasy-skinned, hard-eyed. The Praetorians had certain expectations about what their commanders were supposed to be like, and it was good policy to see that those expectations were met, which almost always was the case.

Severinus, the former and present prefect, had served under Apollinaris as a young officer in the Sicilian campaign. Apollinaris was counting on the vestiges of Severinus's loyalty to him to help him now.

And indeed Severinus looked bewildered, here in the presence not only of his rival for command of the Guard but also of his own onetime superior officer. He stood gaping. "What are you doing here?" Apollinaris asked him immediately. "Shouldn't you be with your Emperor?"

"I—sir—that is—"

"We needed to confer," Rullianus offered. "To work out which one of us is really in charge."

"So you asked him to come, and he was madman enough to do it?" Apollinaris laughed harshly. "I think you've spent too much time around the Emperor, Severinus. The lunacy must be contagious."

"In fact it was my idea to come," said Severinus stolidly. "The situation—the two of us holding the same post, Rullianus and I—"

"Yes," Apollinaris said. "One of you appointed by an Emperor who has lost his mind, and the other one appointed by a Consul who has lost his job. —You do know that Torquatus is in the dungeons, don't you, Rullianus?"

"Of course, sir." It was hardly more than a whisper.

"And you, Severinus. Surely you understand that the Emperor is insane."

"It is very bad, yes. He was foaming at the mouth, sir, when I left him an hour ago. Nevertheless—His Majesty ordered me—"

"Give me no neverthelesses," Apollinaris snapped. "Orders coming from a crazy man have no value. Demetrius is unfit to rule. His years on the throne have brought the Empire to the point of collapse, and you two are the men who can save it, if you act quickly and courageously." They stood before him as though frozen, so profoundly awed they did not seem even to be breathing. "I have tasks for you both, which I want you to carry out this very morning. You will have the gratitude of the Empire as your reward. And also the gratitude of the new Emperor, and of his Consuls." He transfixed them, each in his turn, with an implacable stare. "Do I make myself clear? The men who make Emperors reap great benefit from their deeds. This is your moment in history."

They understood him. There was no doubt about that.

He gave them their instructions and returned to the Consular building to await results.

It would be a long and difficult day, Apollinaris knew. He barricaded himself within his office, with his little group of guardsmen stationed in front of his door, and passed the hours reading here and there in Lentulus Aufidius's account of the reign of Titus Gallius, in the *Histories* of Sextus Asinius, in Antipater's great work on the fall of Roma to the Byzantines, and other chronicles of troubled times. In particular he lingered over Sextus Asinius's account of Cassius Chaerea, the colonel of the Guards who had slain the mad Emperor Caligula, even though it meant his own doom when Claudius followed his nephew Caligula to the throne. Cassius Chaerea had known what needed to be done, aware that it might cost him his life, and he had done it, and it had. Apollinaris read Asinius's account of Chaerea twice through and gave it much thought.

Late afternoon brought a great crack of thunder and a flash of lightning that seemed to split the skies, and then torrential rainfall, the first rain the city had had in the many weeks of this ferociously hot summer. Apollinaris took it as an omen, a signal from the gods in whom he did not believe that the miasma of the hour was about to be swept away.

Rullianus was admitted to his presence only minutes afterward, drenched by the sudden downpour. The execution of the former Consul Marcus Larcius Torquatus, Rullianus reported, had been duly carried out, secretly, in the dungeons, as ordered. Virtually on his heels came Severinus, with the news that in accordance with Count Apollinaris's instructions the late Emperor Demetrius had been smothered in his own pillows, the body weighted with rocks, thrown into the Tiber at the place where such things usually were done.

"You'll return to your barracks immediately and say nothing about this to anyone," Apollinaris told them both, and they gave him brisk, enthusiastic salutes and left.

To Charax he said, "Follow them and have them taken into custody. Here are the orders for their arrests."

"Very good, sir. The prince Laureolus is outside, sir."

"And still almost an hour before nightfall. He must have borrowed the wings of Mercurius to get here this fast!"

But the prince's appearance showed not the least sign that he had hurried unduly to the capital. He looked as cool as ever, calm, self-possessed, an aristocrat to the core, his chilly blue eyes betraying no trace of concern at the disarray that was apparent all over the city.

"I regret to tell you," Apollinaris began at once, in his most exaggeratedly solemn tone, "that this is a day of great sorrow for the Empire. His Majesty Demetrius Augustus is dead."

"A terrible loss indeed," said Laureolus, in that same tone of mock solemnity. But then—clearly his quick mind needed only a fraction of an instant to leap to the right conclusion—a look of something close to horror came into his eyes. "And his successor is to be—"

Apollinaris smiled. "Hail, Laureolus Caesar Augustus, Emperor of Roma!"

Laureolus held his hands up before his face. "No. No."

"You must. You are the savior of the Empire."

Only this morning—it seemed years ago—Apollinaris had thought to invite Laureolus to join him in the Consulship. But Demetrius's unexpected brief escape from his confinement in the royal guest-house had ended all that. Apollinaris knew that he could make Charax Consul now, or Sulpicius Silanus, the thrifty Prefect of the Fiscus Publicus, or anyone else he pleased. It would not matter. The role that needed filling this day was that of Emperor. And, very quickly, Laureolus had seen that, too.

Color had come to his face. His eyes were bright with anger and shock.

"My quiet life of retirement, Apollinaris—my work as a scholar—"

"You can read and write just as well in the palace. The Imperial library, I assure you, is the finest in the world. Refusing is not an option. Would you have Roma tumble into anarchy? You are the only possible Emperor."

"What about yourself?"

"I was bred to be a military man. An administrator. Not an Emperor. —No, there's no one else but you, Caesar. No one."

"Stop calling me 'Caesar'!"

"I must. And *you* must. I'll be beside you, your senior Consul. I had thought to retire also, you know, but that too will have to wait. Roma demands this of us. We have had madness upon madness in this city, first the madness of Demetrius, then the different sort of madness that Torquatus brought. And there are men in the Subura threatening yet another kind of madness. Now all that must end, and you and I are the only ones who can end it. So I say it once again: 'Hail, Laureolus Caesar Augustus!' We will present you to the Senate tomorrow, and the day after that to the people of the city."

"Damn you, Apollinaris! Damn you!"

"For shame! What way is that, Caesar, to speak to the man who has placed you on the throne of the great Augustus?"

Lactantius Rufus himself, as the presiding magistrate of the Senate, presented the motion that awarded Laureolus the titles of Princeps, Imperator, Pontifex Maximus, Tribune of the People, and all the rest that went with being First Citizen, Emperor of Roma, and, as the Senators got quickly to their feet to shout their approval, lost no time in declaring that the vote was unanimous. The Count Valerian Apollinaris was confirmed immediately afterward as Consul once again, and the eighty-three-year-old Clarissimus Blossius, the eldest member of the Senate, won quick confirmation also as Apollinaris's new colleague in the Consulship.

"And now," said Apollinaris that night at the palace, "we must begin the task of restoring the tranquility of the realm."

It was a good glib phrase, but converting it from rhetoric into reality posed a greater challenge than even Apollinaris had realized. Charax had built a network of agents who traversed the city day and night to detect unrest and subversion, and they reported, to a man, that the poison of democratic ideas had spread everywhere in the capital. The people, the plebeians, those without rank or property of any kind, had not been in any way distressed to see mass executions of Imperial courtiers in the plaza of Marcus Anastasius, nor did it trouble them when the Consuls were sending packs of Senators to the scaffold, nor when they learned of the virtually simultaneous deaths of the Consul Torquatus and the Emperor Demetrius. So far as they were concerned it would be just as well to arrest the entire class of men who were qualified to wear the toga of free-born citizenship, and their wives and children as well, and send them off for execution, and divide their property among the common folk for the welfare of all.

Apollinaris decreed the formation of a Council of Internal Security to investigate and control the spread of such dangerous ideas in the capital. He was its chairman. Charax and Lactantius Rufus were the only other members. When Laureolus protested being omitted from the group, Apollinaris named him to it also, but saw to it that its meetings always were held when the new Emperor was otherwise occupied. Many unpleasant things needed to be done just now, and Laureolus was, Apollinaris thought, too proper and civilized a cavalier to approve of some of the bloody tasks ahead.

So am I, Apollinaris thought, a proper and civilized cavalier, and yet these weeks past I have waded through rivers of blood for the sake of sparing our Empire from even greater calamity. And I have come too far now for turning back. I must go onward, on to the other shore.

The ringleader of the rioting in the Subura had now been identified: a certain Greek named Timoleon, a former slave. Charax brought Apollinaris a pamphlet in which Timoleon urged the elimination of the patrician class, the abolition of all the existing political structures of the Empire, and the establishment of what he called the Tribunal of the People: a governing body of a thousand men, twenty from each of the fifty districts of the capital city, chosen by popular vote of all residents. They would serve for two years and then would have to step down so that a new election could be held, and no one could hold membership in the Tribunal twice in the same decade. Men of the old Senatorial and knightly ranks would not be permitted to put themselves forth as candidates.

"Arrest this Timoleon and two or three dozen of his noisiest followers," Apollinaris ordered. "Put them on trial and see to it that justice is swift."

Shortly Charax returned with the news that Timoleon had disappeared into the endless caverns of the Underworld, the ancient city beneath the city, and was constantly moving about down there, keeping well ahead of the agents of the Council of Internal Security.

"Find him," Apollinaris said.

"We could search for him in there for five hundred years and not succeed in finding him," said Charax.

"Find him," Apollinaris said again.

The days went by, and Timoleon continued to elude capture.

Other plebeian revolutionaries were not as clever, or as lucky, and arrested agitators were brought in by the cartload. The pace of executions, which had fallen off somewhat during the period of official mourning following the announcement of Emperor Demetrius's death and the ceremonies accompanying Emperor Laureolus's accession, now quickened again. Before long there were as many each day as there had been toward the end of Torquatus's time; and then the daily toll came to surpass even that of Torquatus.

Apollinaris had never been one to indulge in self-deception. He had removed Torquatus in the interests of peace, and here he was following the same bloody path as his late colleague. But he saw no alternative. There was necessity here. The commonwealth had become a fragile one. A hundred years of foolish Emperors had undermined its foundations, and now they had to be rebuilt. And since it appeared unavoidable that blood must be mixed into the mortar, so shall it be, Apollinaris thought. So shall it be. It was his duty, painful though it sometimes was. He had always understood that word, "duty," as meaning nothing more complicated than "service": service to the Empire, to the Emperor, to the citizens of Roma, to his own sense of his obligations as a Roman. But he had discovered in these apocalyptic days that it was more complex than that, that it entailed a heavy weight of difficulty, conflict, pain, and necessity.

Even so, he would not shirk it.

During this time the Emperor Laureolus was rarely seen in public. Apollinaris had suggested to him that it would be best, in this transitional period, if he let himself be perceived as a remote figure sequestered in the palace, floating high above the carnage, so that when the time of troubles finally ended he would not seem unduly stained with the blood of his people. Laureolus seemed willing to follow this advice. He kept to himself, attending no Senate sessions, taking part in none of the public rituals, issuing no statements. Several times a week Apollinaris visited him at the palace but those visits were Laureolus's only direct contact with the machinery of the government.

Somehow he was aware, though, of the hectic activities in the plaza of execution.

"All this bloodshed troubles me, Apollinaris," the Emperor said. It was the seventh week of his reign. The intolerable heat of summer had given way to the chill of an unnaturally cold and rainy autumn. "It's a bad way to begin my reign. I'll be thought of as a heartless monster, and how can a heartless monster expect to win the love of his people? I can't be an effective Emperor if the people hate me."

"In time, Caesar, they'll be brought to understand that what is happening now is for the good of our whole society. They'll give thanks to you for rescuing the Empire from degradation and ruin."

"Can we not revive the old custom of sending our enemies into exile, Apollinaris? Can we not show a little clemency now and then?"

"Clemency will only be interpreted as weakness just now. And exiles return, more dangerous than ever. Through these deaths we guarantee the peace of future generations."

The Emperor remained unconvinced. He reminded Apollinaris that the brunt of punishment now was falling on the common people, whose lives had always been hard even in the best of times. The contract that the Emperors had made with the people, said Laureolus, was to offer stability and peace in return for strict obedience to Imperial rule; but if the Emperor made the bonds too tight, the populace would begin turning toward the fantasy of a happier life in some imaginary existence beyond death. There had always been religious teachers in the East, in Syria, in Aegyptus, in Arabia, who had tried to instill such concepts in the people, and it had always been necessary to stamp such teachings out. A cult that promised salvation in the next world would inevitably weaken the common folk's loyalty to the state in this one. But that loyalty had to be won, over and over again, through the benevolence of the rulers. Thus the need for judicious relaxation, from time to time, of governmental restraint. The present campaign of executing the people's leaders, said Laureolus, flew in the face of wisdom.

"This man Timoleon, for example," the Emperor said. "Must you make such a great thing of searching him out? You don't seem to be able to find him, and you're turning him into an even bigger popular hero than he already was."

"Timoleon is the greatest danger the Empire has ever faced, Caesar. He is a spear aimed straight at the throne."

"You are too melodramatic sometimes, Apollinaris. I urge you: let him go free. Show the world that we can tolerate even a Timoleon in our midst."

"I think you fail to understand just how dangerous—"

"Dangerous? He's just a ragged rabble-rouser. What I don't want to do is make him into a martyr. We could capture him and crucify him, yes, but that would give the people a hero, and they would turn the world upside down in his name. Let him be."

But Apollinaris saw only peril in that path, and the search for Timoleon went on. And in time Timoleon was betrayed by a greedy associate and arrested in one of the Underworld's most remote and obscure caverns, along with dozens of his most intimate associates and several hundred other followers.

Apollinaris, on his own authority as head of the Council of Internal Security and without notifying the Emperor, ordered an immediate trial. There would be one more climactic spate of executions, he told himself, and then, he swore, the end of the time of blood would finally be at hand. With Timoleon and his people gone, Laureolus at last could step forth and offer the olive branch of clemency to the citizenry in general: the beginning of the time of reconciliation and repair that must follow any such epoch as they had all just lived through.

For the first time since his return to Roma from the provinces Apollinaris began to think that he was approaching the completion of his task, that he had brought the Empire safely through all its storms and could retire from public responsibility at long last.

And then Tiberius Charax came to him with the astonishing news that the Emperor Laureolus had ordered an amnesty for all political prisoners as an act of Imperial mercy, and that Timoleon and his friends would be released from the dungeons within the next two or three days.

"He's lost his mind," Apollinaris said. "Demetrius himself would not have been guilty of such insanity." He reached for pen and paper. "Here—take these warrants of execution to the prison at once, before any releases can be carried out—"

"Sir—" said Charax quietly.

"What is it?" Apollinaris asked, not looking up.

"Sir, the Emperor has sent for you. He asks your attendance at the palace within the hour."

"Yes," he said. "Just as soon as I've finished signing these warrants."

*   *   *

The moment Apollinaris entered the Emperor's private study he understood that it was his own death warrant, and not Timoleon's, that he had signed this afternoon. For there on Laureolus's desk was the stack of papers that he had given Charax less than an hour before. Some minion of Laureolus's must have intercepted them.

There was a coldness beyond that of ice in the Emperor's pale blue eyes.

"Were you aware that we ordered clemency for these men, Consul?" Laureolus asked him.

"Shall I lie to you? No, Caesar, it's very late for me to take up the practice of lying. I was aware of it. I felt it was a mistake, and countermanded it."

"Countermanded your Emperor's orders? That was very bold of you, Consul!"

"Yes. It was. Listen to me, Laureolus—"

"Caesar."

"*Caesar.* Timoleon wants nothing less than the destruction of the Imperium, and the Senate, and everything else that makes up our Roman way of life. He *must* be put to death."

"I've already told you: any fool of an Emperor can have his enemies put to death. He snaps his fingers and the thing is done. The Emperor who's capable of showing mercy is the Emperor whom the people will love and obey."

"I'll take no responsibility for what happens, Caesar, if you insist on letting Timoleon go."

"You will not be required to take responsibility for it," said Laureolus evenly.

"I think I understand your meaning, Caesar."

"I think you do, yes."

"I fear for you, all the same, if you free that man. I fear for Roma." For an instant all his iron self-control deserted him, and he cried, "Oh, Laureolus, Laureolus, how I regret that I chose you to be Emperor! How wrong I was! —Can't you see that Timoleon has to die, for the good of us all? I demand his execution!"

"How strangely you address your Emperor," said Laureolus, in a quiet voice altogether devoid of anger. "It is as if you can't quite bring yourself to believe that I *am* Emperor. Well, Apollinaris, we are indeed your sovereign, and we refuse to accept what you speak of as your 'demand.' Furthermore: your resignation as Consul is accepted. You have overstepped your Consular authority, and there is no longer any room for you in our government as the new period of healing begins. We offer you exile in any place of your choice, so long as it's far from here: Aegyptus, perhaps, or maybe the isle of Cyprus, or Pontus—"

"No."

"Then suicide is your only other option. A fine old Roman way to die."

"Not that either," said Apollinaris. "If you want to be rid of me, Laureolus, have me taken to the plaza of Marcus Anastasius and chop my head off in front of all the people. Explain to them, if you will, why it was necessary to do that to someone who has served the Empire so long and so well. Blame all the recent bloodshed on me, perhaps. Everything, even the executions that Torquatus ordered. You'll surely gain the people's love that way, and I know how dearly you crave that love."

Laureolus's expression was utterly impassive. He clapped his hands and three men of the Guard entered.

"Conduct Count Apollinaris to the Imperial prison," he said, and turned away.

Charax said, "He wouldn't dare to execute you. It would start an entirely new cycle of killings."

"Do you think so?" Apollinaris asked. They had given him the finest cell in the place, one usually reserved for prisoners of high birth, disgraced members of the royal family, younger brothers who had made attempts on the life of the Emperor, people like that. Its walls were hung with heavy purple draperies and its couches were of the finest make.

"I think so, yes. You are the most important man in the realm.

Everyone knows what you achieved in the provinces. Everyone knows, also, that you saved us from Torquatus and that you put Laureolus on the throne. You should have been made Emperor yourself when Demetrius died. If he kills you the whole Senate will speak out against him, and the entire city will be outraged."

"I doubt that very much," said Apollinaris wearily. "Your view of things has rarely been so much in error. But no matter: did you bring the books?"

"Yes," Charax said. He opened the heavy package he was carrying. "Lentulus Aufidius. Sextus Asinius. Suetonius. Ammianus Marcellinus. Julius Capitolinus, Livius, Thucydides, Tacitus. All the great historians."

"Enough reading to last me through the night," said Apollinaris. "Thank you. You can leave me now."

"Sir—"

"You can leave me now," said Apollinaris again. But as Charax walked toward the door he said, "One more thing, though. What about Timoleon?"

"He has gone free, sir."

"I expected nothing else," Apollinaris said.

Once Charax was gone he turned his attention to the books. He would start with Thucydides, he thought—that merciless account of the terrible war between Athens and Sparta, as grim a book as had ever been written—and would make his way, volume by volume, through all of later history. And if Laureolus let him live long enough to have read them all one last time, perhaps then he would begin writing his own here in prison, a memoir that he would try to keep from being too self-serving, even though it would be telling the story of how he had sacrificed his own life in order to preserve the Empire. But he doubted that Laureolus would let him live long enough to do any writing. There would be no public execution, no—Charax had been correct about that. He was too much of a hero in the public's eyes to be sent off so callously to the block, and in any event Laureolus's stated intention was to give the executioners a long respite from their somber task and allow the city to return to something approaching normal.

He reached for the first volume of Thucydides, and sat for a time reading and rereading its opening few sentences.

A knock at his door, then. He had been waiting for it.

"Come in," he said. "I doubt that it's locked."

A tall, gaunt figure entered, a man wearing a hooded black cape that left his face exposed. He had cold close-set eyes, a taut fleshless face, rough skin, thin tight-clamped lips.

"I know you," said Apollinaris calmly, though he had never seen the man in his life.

"Yes, I believe you do," the other said, showing him the knife as he came toward him. "You know me very well. And I think you've been expecting me."

"So I have," said Apollinaris.

It was the first day of the new month, when the Prefect of the Fiscus Imperialis and the Prefect of the Fiscus Publicus traditionally lunched together to discuss matters that pertained to the workings of the two treasuries. Even now, many weeks along in the reign of the new Emperor, the Emperor's private purse, the Fiscus Imperialis, was still under the charge of Quintus Cestius, and the other fund, the Fiscus Publicus, was, as it had been for years, administered by Sulpicius Silanus. They had weathered all the storms. They were men who knew the art of surviving.

"So Count Valerian Apollinaris has perished," Cestius said. "A pity, that. He was a very great man."

"Too great, I think, to be able to keep out of harm's way indefinitely. Such men inevitably are brought down. A pity, I agree. He was a true Roman of the old sort. Men like that are very scarce in these dreadful times."

"But at least peace is restored. The Empire is whole again, thanks be to Count Apollinaris, and to our beloved Emperor Laureolus."

"Yes. But is it secure, though? Have any of the real problems been addressed?" Silanus, that sly little man of hearty appetite and exuberant spirit, cut himself another slab of meat and said, "I offer you a prediction, Cestius. It will all fall apart again within a hundred years."

"You are too optimistic by half, at least," said Quintus Cestius, reaching for the wine, though he rarely drank.

"Yes," said Silanus. "Yes, I am."

A.U.C. 2603: VIA ROMA

A carriage is waiting for me, by prearrangement, when I disembark at the port in Neapolis after the six-day steamer voyage from Britannia. My father has taken care of all such details for me with his usual efficiency. The driver sees me at once— I am instantly recognizable, great strapping golden-haired barbarian that I am, a giant Nordic pillar towering over this busy throng of small swarthy southern people running to and fro—and cries out to me, *"Signore! Signore! Venga qua, signore."*

But I'm immobilized in that luminous October warmth, staring about me in wonder, stunned by the avalanche of unfamiliar sights and smells. My journey from the dank rainy autumnal chill of my native Britannia into this glorious Italian land of endless summer has transported me not merely to another country but, so it seems, to another world. I am overwhelmed by the intense light, the radiant shimmering air, the profusion of unknown tropical-looking trees. By the vast sprawling city stretching before me along the shores of the Bay of Neapolis. By the lush green hills just beyond, brilliantly bespeckled with the white winter villas of the Imperial aristocracy. And then too there is the great dark mountain far off to my right, the mighty volcano, Vesuvius itself, looming above the city like a slumbering god. I imagine that I can make out a faint gray plume of pale smoke curling upward from its summit. Perhaps while I am here the god will awaken and send fiery rivers of red lava down its slopes, as it has done so many times in the immemorial past.

No, that is not to happen. But there will be fire, yes: a fire that utterly consumes the Empire. And I am destined to stand at the very edge of it, on the brink of the conflagration, and be altogether unaware of everything going on about me: poor fool, poor innocent fool from a distant land.

"*Signore! Per favore!*" My driver jostles his way to my side and tugs impatiently at the sleeve of my robe, an astonishing transgression against propriety. In Britannia I surely would strike any coachman who did that; but this is not Britannia, and customs evidently are very different here. He looks up imploringly. I'm twice his size. In comic Britannic he says, "You no speak Romano, *signore?* We must leave this place right away. Is very crowded, all the people, the luggage, the everything, I may not remain at the quay once my passenger has been found. It is the law. *Capisce, signore? Capisce?*"

"*Si, si, capisco,*" I tell him. Of course I speak Roman. I spent three weeks studying it in preparation for this journey, and it gave me no trouble to learn. What is it, after all, except a mongrelized and truncated kind of bastard Latin? And everyone in the civilized world knows Latin. "*Andiamo, si.*"

He smiles and nods. "*Allora. Andiamo!*"

All around us is chaos—newly arrived passengers trying to find transportation to their hotels, families fighting to keep from being separated in the crush, peddlers selling cheap pocket-watches and packets of crudely tinted picture postcards, mangy dogs barking, ragged children with sly eyes moving among us looking for purses to pick. The roaring babble is astonishing. But we are an island of tranquility in the midst of it all, my driver and I. He beckons me into the carriage: a plush seat, leather paneling, glistening brass fittings, but also an inescapable smell of garlic. Two noble auburn horses stand patiently in their traces. A porter comes running up with my luggage and I hear it being thumped into place overhead. And then we are off, gently jouncing down the quay, out into the bustling city, past

the marble waterfront palaces of the customs officials and the myriad other agencies of the Imperial government, past temples of Minerva, Neptune, Apollo, and Jupiter Optimus Maximus, and up the
winding boulevards toward the district of fashionable hotels on the
slopes that lie midway between the sea and the hills. I will be staying
at the Tiberius, on Via Roma, a boulevard which I have been told is
the grand promenade of the upper city, the place to see and be seen.

We traverse streets that must be two thousand years old. I amuse
myself with the thought that Augustus Caesar himself may have rid-
den through these very streets long ago, or Nero, or perhaps Claudius,
the ancient conqueror of my homeland. Once we are away from the
port, the buildings are tall and narrow, grim slender tenements of six
and seven stories, built side by side with no breathing space between
them. Their windows are shuttered against the midday heat, impenetrable, mysterious. Here and there among them are broader,
shorter buildings set in small gardens: huge squat structures, gray
and bulky, done in the fussy baroque style of two hundred years ago.
They are the palatial homes, no doubt, of the mercantile class, the
powerful importers and exporters who maintain the real prosperity
of Neapolis. If my family lived here, I suppose we would live in one
of those.

But we are Britannic, and our fine airy home sits on a great
swath of rolling greensward in the sweet Cornish country, and I am
only a tourist here, coming forth from my remote insignificant
province for my first visit to great Italia, now that the Second War of
Reunification is at last over and travel between the far-flung sectors
of the Empire is possible again.

I stare at everything in utter fascination, peering so intensely that
my eyes begin to ache. The clay pots of dazzling red and orange
flowers fastened to the building walls, the gaudy banners on long
posts above the shops, the marketplaces piled high with unfamiliar
fruits and vegetables in green and purple mounds. Hanging down
along the sides of some of the tenement houses are long blurry
scrolls on which the dour lithographed portrait of the old Emperor
Laureolus is displayed, or of his newly enthroned young grandson
and successor, Maxentius Augustus, with patriotic and adoring inscriptions above and below. This is Loyalist territory: the Neapoli-

tans are said to love the Empire more staunchly than the citizens of Urbs Roma itself.

We have reached the Via Roma. A grand boulevard indeed, grander, I would say, than any in Londin or Parisi: a broad carriageway down the middle bordered with the strange, unnaturally glossy shrubs and trees that thrive in this mild climate, and on both sides of the street the dazzling pink and white marble façades of the great hotels, the fine shops, the apartment buildings of the rich. There are sidewalk cafés everywhere, all of them frantically busy. I hear waves of jolly chatter and bursts of rich laughter rising from them as I pass by, and the sound of clinking glasses. The hotel marquees, arrayed one after the next virtually without a break, cry out the history of the Empire, a roster of great Imperial names: the Hadrianus, the Marcus Aurelius, the Augustus, the Maximilianus, the Lucius Agrippa. And at last the Tiberius, neither the grandest nor the least consequential of the lot, a white-fronted building in the Classical Revival style, well situated in a bright district of elegant shops and restaurants.

The desk clerk speaks flawless Britannic. "Your passport, sir?"

He gives it a haughty sniff. Eyes my golden ringlets and long drooping mustachio, compares them with the closer-cropped image of my passport photo, decides that I am indeed myself, Cymbelin Vetruvius Scapulanus of Londin and Caratacus House in Cornwall, and whistles up a *facchino* to carry my bags upstairs. The suite is splendid, two lofty-ceilinged rooms at the corner of the building, a view of the distant harbor on one side and of the volcano on the other. The porter shows me how to operate my bath, points out my night-light and my cabinet of liqueurs, officiously tidies my bedspread. I tip the boy with a gold solidus—never let it be said that a Scapulanus of Caratacus House is ungenerous—but he pockets it as coolly as if I have tossed him a copper.

When he is gone, I stand a long while at the windows before unpacking, drinking in the sight of the city and the sparkling bay. I have never beheld anything so magnificent: the wide processional avenues, the temples, the amphitheaters, the gleaming palatial towers, the teeming marketplaces. And this is only Neapolis, the second city of Italia! Next to it, our cherished Londin is a mere muddy provincial backwater. What will great Roma be like, if this is Neapolis?

I feel an oddly disconcerting and unfamiliar sensation that I suspect may be an outbreak of humility. I am a rich man's son, I can trace my ancestry more or less legitimately back to kings of ancient Britain, I have had the benefits of a fine education, with high Cantabrigian honors in history and architecture. But what does any of that matter here? I'm in Italia now, the heartland of the imperishable Empire, and I am nothing but a brawny bumptious Celt from one of the outer edges of the civilized world. These people must think I wear leather kilts at home and rub the grease of pigs into my hair. I can see that I may be going to find myself out of my depth in this land. Which will be a new experience for me; but is that not why I have come here to Italia, to Roma Mater—to open myself to new experiences?

The shops of the Via Roma are closed when I go out for an afternoon stroll, and there is no one to be seen anywhere, except in the crowded cafés and restaurants. In the heat of this place, businesses of all sorts shut down at midday and reopen in the cooler hours of early evening. The windows display an amazing array of merchandise from every part of the Empire, Africa, India, Gallia, Hispania, Britannia, even Hither Asia and the mysterious places beyond it, Khitai and Cipangu, where the little strange-eyed people live: clothing of the latest fashions, antique jewelry, fine shoes, household furnishings, costly objects of all sorts. Here is the grand abundance of Imperium, indeed. With the war finally at an end, shipments of luxury goods must converge constantly on Italia from all its resubjugated provinces.

I walk on and on. Via Roma seems endless, extending infinitely ahead of me, onward to the vanishing point of the horizon. But of course it *does* have an end: the street's own name announces its terminal point, Urbs Roma itself, the great capital city. It isn't true, the thing they always say in Italia, that all roads lead to Roma, but this is one that actually does: I need only keep walking northward and this boulevard will bring me eventually to the city of the Seven Hills. There's time for that, though. I must begin my conquest of Italia in easy stages: Neapolis and its picturesque environs first, then a gradual advance northward to meet the formidable challenge of the city of the Caesars.

People are emerging from the cafés now. Some of them turn and stare openly at me, the way I might stare at a giraffe or elephant parading in the streets of Londin. Have they never seen a Briton before? Is yellow hair so alien to them? Perhaps it is my height and the breadth of my shoulders that draws their scrutiny, or my golden earring and the heavy Celtic Revival armlet that I affect. They nudge each other, they whisper, they smile.

I return their smiles graciously as I pass by. *Good afternoon, fellow Roman citizens,* I am tempted to say. But they would probably snicker at my British-accented Latin or my attempts at their colloquial Roman tongue.

There is a message waiting for me at the hotel. My father, bless him, has posted letters of introduction ahead to certain members of the Neapolitan aristocracy whom he has asked to welcome me and ease my entry into Roman society. Before leaving the hotel for my walk I had sent a message announcing my arrival to the people I was meant to meet here, and already there has been a reply. I am invited in the most cordial terms to dine this very evening at the villa of Marcellus Domitianus Frontinus, who according to my father owns half the vineyards between Neapolis and Pompeii and whose brother Cassius was one of the great heroes of the recently concluded war. A carriage will pick me up at the Tiberius at the eighteenth hour.

I am suffused with a strange joy. They are willing to make the visiting barbarian feel welcome on his first night in the mother country. Of course Frontinus ships ten thousand cases of his sweet white wines to my father's warehouses in Londin every year and that is a far from inconsiderable bit of business. Not that business matters will be mentioned this evening. For one thing I know very little of my father's commercial dealings; but also, and this is much more to the point, we are patricians, Frontinus and I, and we must behave that way. He is of the ancient Senatorial class, descended from men who made and unmade Caesars a thousand years ago. And I carry the blood of British kings in my veins, or at least my father says I do and my own name—Cymbelin—proclaims it. Caratacus, Cassevelaunus, Tincommius, Togodumnus, Prasutagus: at one time or another I have heard my father claim descent from each of those grand old Celtic chieftains, and Queen Cartamandua of the Brigantes for good measure.

Well, and Cartamandua expediently signed a treaty with the Roman invaders of her country, and sent her fellow monarch Caratacus to Roma in chains. But all that was a long time ago, and we Britons have been pacified and repacified on many occasions since then, and everyone understands that the power and the glory will reside, now and always, in the great city that lies at the other end of the Via Roma from here. Frontinus will be polite to me, I know: if not for the sake of the heroic though unvictorious warriors who are my putative ancestors, then for the ten thousand cases of wine that he means to ship to Londin next year. I will dine well tonight, I will meet significant people, I will be offered easy entree to the great homes of Neapolis and, when I am ready to go there, the capital as well.

I bathe. I shave. I oil my ringlets, and not with the grease of pigs; and I select my clothing with great care, a silken Byzantine tunic and matching neckerchief, fine leggings of scarlet Aegyptian linen, sandals of the best Syrian workmanship. With, of course, my golden earring and my massive armlet to provide that interestingly barbaric touch for which they will value me more highly.

The carriage is waiting when I emerge from the hotel. A Nubian driver in crimson and turquoise; white Arabian horses; the carriage itself is of ebony inlaid with strips of ivory. Worthy, I would think, of an Emperor. But Frontinus is only a wealthy patrician, a mere southerner at that. What do the Caesars ride in, I wonder, if this is the kind of vehicle a Frontinus sends to pick up visiting young men from the backward provinces?

The road winds up into the hills. A cloud has drifted over the city and the early evening sunlight tumbles through it like golden rain. The surface of the bay is ablaze with light. Mysterious gray islands are visible in the distance.

The villa of Marcellus Domitianus Frontinus is set in a park so big it takes us fifteen minutes to reach the house once we are past the colossal iron gate. It is a light and graceful pavilion, the enormous size of which is carefully masked by the elegance of its design, set on the very edge of a lofty slope. There is a look of deceptive fragility about it, as though it would be sensitive to the slightest movements of the atmosphere. The view from its portico runs from Vesuvius in the east to some jutting cape far off down the other shore of the bay. All around it are marvelous shrubs and trees in bloom, and the fragrance they exhale is the fragrance of unthinkable wealth. I begin to wonder how much those ten thousand cases of wine can matter to this man.

Yet Frontinus himself is earthy and amiable, a stocky balding man with an easy grin and an immediately congenial style.

He is there to greet me as I step down from the carriage. "I am Marcello Domiziano," he tells me, speaking Roman, grinning broadly as he puts out his hand. "Welcome to my house, dear friend Cymbelin!"

Marcello Domiziano. He uses the Roman, not the Latin, form of his name. In the provinces, of course, we pretentiously allow ourselves Latin names, mingling them to some degree with Britannic or Gallic or Teutonic localisms; but here in Italia the only people who have the privilege of going by names in the ancient Latin mode are members of the Senatorial and Imperial families and high military officers, and the rest must employ the modern Roman form. Frontinus rises above his own privilege of rank: I may call him Marcello, the way I would one of his field hands. And he will call me Cymbelin. Very swiftly we are dear friends, or so he wants me to feel, and I have barely arrived.

The gathering is under way already, on a breeze-swept open patio with a terrazzo floor, looking outward toward the city center far below. Fifteen, perhaps twenty people, handsome men, stunning women, everyone laughing and chattering like the people in the sidewalk cafés.

"My daughter, Adriana," Frontinus says. "Her friend Lucilla, visiting from Roma."

They are extraordinarily beautiful. The two of them surround me and I am dazzled. I remember once in Gallia, at a great villa somewhere near Nemausus, I was led by my host into the heart of a mirror maze that he had had built for his amusement, and instantly I felt myself toppling dizzily forward, vanishing between the infinitely reduplicated images, and had to pull myself back with an effort, heart pounding, head spinning.

It is like that now, standing between these two girls. Their beauty dazes me, their perfume intoxicates me. Frontinus has moved away, leaving me unsure of which is the daughter and which is the friend; I look from one to the other, confused.

The girl to my left is full-bodied and robust, with sharp features, pale skin, and flaming red hair arrayed close to her skull in tight coils, an antique style that might have been copied from some ancient wall painting. The other, taller, is dark and slender, almost frail, with heavy rows of blue faience beads about her throat and shadowy rings painted beneath her eyes. For all her flimsiness she is very sleek, soft-skinned, with a glossy Aegyptian look about her. The red-haired one must be Frontinus's daughter, I decide, comparing her sturdy deep-chested frame to his; but no, no, she is the visitor from Roma, for the taller, darker one says, speaking not Roman but Latin, and in a voice smooth as Greek honey, "You do honor to our house, distinguished sir. My father says that you are of royal birth."

I wonder if I am being mocked. But I see the way she is measuring me with her eyes, running over my length and breadth as though I am a statue in some museum's hall of kings. The other one is doing the same.

"I carry a royal name, at any rate," I say. "Cymbelin—you may know him as Cunobelinus, in the history books. Whose son was the warrior king Caratacus, captured and pardoned by the first Emperor Claudius. My father has gone to great pains to have our genealogy traced to their line."

I smile disarmingly; and I see that they take my meaning precisely. I am describing the foolish pretensions of a rich provincial merchant, nothing more.

"How long ago was that, actually?" asks the redhead, Lucilla.

"The genealogical study?"

"The capturing and pardoning of your great ancestor."

"Why—" I hesitate. Haven't I just said that it was in the time of Claudius the First? But she flutters her eyes at me as though she is innocent of any historical information. "About eighteen centuries ago," I tell her. "When the Empire was still new. Claudius the First was the fourth of the Caesars. The fifth, if you count Julius Caesar as an Emperor. Which I think is the proper thing to do."

"How precise you are about such things," Adriana Frontina says, laughing.

"About historical matters, yes. About very little else, I'm afraid."

"Will you be traveling widely in Italia?" asks Lucilla.

"I'll want to see the area around Neapolis, of course. Pompeii and the other old ruins, and a few days on the isle of Capreae. Then up to Roma, certainly, and maybe farther north—Etruria, Venetia, even as far up as Mediolanum. Actually, I want to see it all."

"Perhaps we can tour it together," Lucilla says. Just like that, bluntly, baldly. And now there is no flutter of innocence whatever in her wide-set, intelligent eyes, only a look of unmistakable mischief.

Of course I have heard that the women of Roma are that way. I am startled, all the same, by her forwardness, and for the moment I can find no reply; and then all the others come flocking around me. Marcellus Frontinus bombards me with introductions, reciting name after name, spilling them forth so quickly that it's impossible for me to match name to face.

"Enrico Giunio, the Count of Pausylipon, and Countess Emilia. My son, Druso Tiberio, and his friend Ezio. Quintillo Fabio Puteolano. Vitellio di Portofino; his wife, Claudia; their daughter, Crispina. Traiano Gordiano Tertullo, of Capreae—Marco Ulpio Africano—Sabina Metella Arboria—" A blur of names. There is no end to them. One alone out of all of them registers with real impact on me: "My brother, Cassio," Frontinus says. A slender, olive-skinned man with eyes like bits of polished coal: the great war hero, this is, Cassius Lucius Frontinus! I begin to salute him, but Frontinus rattles out four more introductions before I can. People seem to be materializing out of thin air. To Adriana I whisper, "Has your father invited all of Neapolis here tonight?"

"Only the interesting ones," she says. "It isn't every day that a British king visits us." And giggles.

Swarms of servants—slaves?—move among us, bringing things to eat and drink. I am cautious in the first few rounds, reminding myself that this is only my first day here and that the fatigue of my journey may lead me into embarrassments, but then, to avoid seeming impolite, I select a goblet of wine and a small meat-cake, and hold them without tasting them, occasionally lifting them to my mouth and lowering them again untouched.

The high lords and ladies of Neapolitan society surround me in swirling clusters, peppering me with questions to which they don't really appear to be expecting answers. Some speak in Roman, some in Latin. How long will I be here? Will I spend my entire time in Neapolis? What has aroused my interest in visiting Italia? Is the economy of Britannia currently flourishing? Does everyone speak only Britannic there, or is Latin widely used also? Is there anything in Britannia that a traveler from Italia would find rewarding to see? How does British food compare with Italian food? Do I think that the current Treaty of Unity will hold? Have I been to Pompeii yet? To the Greek temples at Paestum? On and on. It is a bombardment. I make such replies as I can, but the questions overlap my answers in a highly exhausting way. I am grateful for my stout constitution. Even so, after a time I become so weary that I begin to have trouble understanding their quick, idiomatic Roman, and I revert entirely to the older, purer Latin tongue, hoping it will encourage them to do the same. Some do, some don't.

Lucilla and Adriana remain close by my side throughout the ordeal, and I am grateful for that also.

These people think of me as a new toy, I realize. The novelty of the hour, to be examined in fascination for a little while and then discarded.

The wind off the bay has turned chilly with the coming of evening, and somehow, almost imperceptibly, the gathering has moved indoors and upstairs, to a huge room overlooking the atrium that will apparently be our banqueting hall.

"Come," Adriana says. "You must meet Uncle Cassio."

The famous general is far across the room, standing with arms folded, listening with no show of emotion while his brother and another man carry on what seems to be a fierce argument. He wears a tightly cut khaki uniform and his breast is bedecked with medals and ribbons. The other man, I remember after a moment, is the Count of Pausylipon, whom Frontinus had so casually referred to as "Enrico Giunio." He is gaunt, tall—nearly as tall as I am—hawk-faced, animated: his expression seems close to apoplectic. Marcello Domiziano is just as excited, neck straining upward, face pushed close to the other's, arms pinwheeling in emphatic gesticulations. I get the sense that these two have been bitterly snarling and snapping at each other over some great political issue for years.

They are speaking, I gather, of nothing less than the destiny of Roma itself. The Count of Pausylipon appears to be arguing that it is of the highest importance that the Empire should continue to survive as a single political entity—something that I did not think anyone seriously doubted, now that Reunification had been accomplished. "There's a reason why Roma has lasted so long," the Count was saying. "It's not just about power—the power of one city over an entire continent. It's about stability, coherence, the supremacy of a system that values logic, efficiency, superb engineering, planning. The world is the better for our having ruled it so long. We have brought light where only the darkness of barbarism would have existed otherwise."

These did not seem to me like controversial propositions. But I could see by the expression on the florid face of Marcello Domiziano and his obvious impatience to respond that there must be some area of strong disagreement between the two men, not in any way apparent to me. And Adriana, leaning close to me as she leads me across the room, whispers something that amidst all the noise I am unable clearly to make out, but which obscures what Marcello Domiziano has just said to the Count.

Despite all the furor going on at his elbow, it appears almost as though the famous general is asleep on his feet—a knack that must be useful during lulls in long battles—except that every few moments, in response, I suppose, to some provocative remark by one combatant or the other, his eyelids widen and a brilliant, baleful glare is emitted by those remarkable coal-bright eyes. I feel hesitant at joining this peculiar little group. But Adriana steers me over to them.

Frontinus cries, "Yes, yes, Cymbelin! Come meet my brother!" He has noticed my hesitation also. But perhaps he would welcome an interruption of the hostilities.

Which I provide. The dispute, the discussion, whatever it is, evaporates the moment I get there, turning into polite vaporous chitchat. The Count, having calmed himself totally, an impressive display of patrician self-control, offers me a lofty, remote nod of acknowledgment, gives Adriana and Lucilla a pat on the shoulder apiece, and excuses himself to go in search of a fresh drink. Frontinus, still a little red in the face but cheerful as ever, commends me to his brother's attention with an upturned palm. "Our British friend," he says.

"I am honored, your Excellence," I say, making a little bow to Cassius Lucius Frontinus.

"Oh, none of that, now," says Uncle Cassio. "We aren't in the camp." He speaks in Latin. His voice is thin and hard, like the edge of a knife, but I sense that he's trying to be genial.

For a moment I am giddy with awe, simply at finding myself in his presence. I think of this little man—and that is what he is, little, as short as his brother and very much slighter of build—striding untiringly from Dacia to Gallia and back in seven-league boots, putting out the fires of secession everywhere. The indomitable general, the savior of the Empire.

There will be fire of a different sort ablaze in the Empire soon, and I am standing very close to its source. But I have no awareness of that just yet.

Cassius Frontinus surveys me as though measuring me for a uniform. "Tell me, are all you Britons that big?"

"I'm a bit larger than average, actually."

"A good thing. We came very close to invading you, you know, very early in the war. It wouldn't have been any picnic, facing a whole army of men your size."

"Invading Britannia, sir?" Lucilla asks.

"Indeed," he says, giving the girl a quick chilly smile. "A preemptive strike, when we thought Britannia might be toying with joining the rebellion."

I blink at him in surprise and some irritation. This is a sore place for us: why is he rubbing it?

Staunchly I say, "That would never have happened, sir. We are Loyalists, you know, we Britons."

"Yes. Yes, of course you are. But the risk was there, after all. A fifty-fifty chance is the way it seemed to us then. It was a touchy moment. And the High Command thought, let's send a few legions over there, just to keep them in line. Before your time, I suppose."

I'm still holding my goblet of wine, still untasted. Now, nervously, I take a deep draught.

Against all propriety I feel impelled to defend my race. With preposterous stiffness I say, "Let me assure you, general, that I am not as young as you may think, and I can tell you that there was never the slightest possibility that Britannia would have gone over to the rebels. None."

A flicker of—amusement?—annoyance?—in those terrible eyes, now.

"In hindsight, yes, certainly. But it looked quite otherwise to us, for a while, there at the very beginning. Just how old were you when the war broke out, my lad?"

I hate being patronized. I let him see my anger.

"Seventeen, sir. I served in the Twelfth Britannic Legion, under Aelius Titianus Rigisamus. Saw action in Gallia and Lusitania. The Balloon Corps."

"Ah." He isn't expecting that. "Well, then. I've misjudged you."

"My entire nation, I would say. Whatever rumors of British disloyalty you may have heard in that very confused time were nothing but enemy fabrications."

"Ah, indeed," says the general. "Indeed." His tone is benign, but his eyes are brighter and stonier than ever and his jaws barely move as he says the words.

Adriana Frontina, looking horrified at the growing heat of our exchanges, is frantically signaling me with her eyes to get off the subject. Her red-haired friend Lucilla, though, merely seems amused by the little altercation. Marcellus Frontinus has turned aside, probably not coincidentally, and is calling instructions to some servants about getting the banquet under way.

I plunge recklessly onward, nonetheless. "Sir, we Britons are just as Roman as anyone in the Empire. Or do you think we still nurse private national grievances going back to the time of Claudius?"

Cassius Frontinus is silent a moment, studying me with some care.

"Yes," he says, finally. "Yes, I do, as a matter of fact. But that's beside the point. Everybody who got swept up into the Empire once upon a time and never was able to find their way out again has old grievances buried somewhere, no matter how Roman they claim to be now. The Teutons, the Britons, the Hispaniards, the Frogs, everyone. That's why we've had two nasty breakups of the system in less than a century, wouldn't you say? But no, boy, I didn't mean to impugn the loyalty of your people, not in the slightest. This has all been highly unfortunate. A thousand pardons, my friend."

He glances at my goblet, which I have somehow drained without noticing.

"You need another drink, is that not so? And so do I." He snaps his fingers at a passing servitor. "Boy! Boy! More wine, over here!"

I have a certain sense that my conversation with the great war hero Cassius Lucius Frontinus has not been a success, and that this might be a good moment to withdraw. I shoot a helpless glance at Adriana, who understands at once and says, "But Cymbelin has taken enough of your time, Uncle. And look, the praefectus urbi has arrived: we really must introduce our guest to him."

Yes. They really must, before I make a worse botch of things. I bow again and excuse myself, and Adriana takes me by one arm and Lucilla seizes the other, and they sweep me away off to the opposite side of the great hall.

"Was I very horrid?" I ask.

"Uncle likes men who show some spirit," Adriana says. "In the army nobody dares talk back to him at all."

"But to be so rude—he the great man that he is, and I just a visitor from the provinces—"

"He was the one that was rude," says Lucilla hotly. "Calling your people traitors to the Empire! How could he have said any such thing!" And then, in a lower voice, purring directly into my ear: "I'll take you to Pompeii tomorrow. It won't be nearly so boring for you there."

She calls for me at the hotel after breakfast, riding in an extraordinarily grand quadriga, mahogany-trimmed and silk-tasseled and gilded all over, drawn by two magnificent white horses and two gigantic duns. It makes the one that Marcellus Frontinus sent for me the night before seem almost shabby. I had compared that one to the chariot of an Emperor; but no, I was altogether wrong: surely this is closer to the real thing.

"Is this what you traveled down in from Roma?" I ask her.

"Oh, no, I came by train. I borrowed the chariot from Druso Tiberio. He goes in for things of this sort."

At the party I had had only the briefest of encounters with young Frontinus and was highly unimpressed with him: a soft young man, pomaded and perfumed, three or four golden rings on each hand, languid movements and delicate yawns, distinctly a prince. Shamelessly exchanging melting glances all evening long with his handsome friend Ezio, who seemed as stupid as a gladiator and probably once was one.

"What can a quadriga like this cost?" I ask. "Five million sesterces? Ten million?"

"Very likely even more."

"And he simply *lends* it to you for the day?"

"Oh, it's only his second best one, wouldn't you know? Druso's a rich man's son, after all, very spoiled. Marcello doesn't deny him a thing. I think it's terrible, of course."

"Yes," I say. "Dreadful."

If Lucilla picks up the irony in my voice, she gives no sign of it.

"And yet, if he's willing to lend one of his pretty chariots to his sister's friend for a day or two—"

"Why not take it, eh?"

"Why not indeed."

And so off we go down the coast road together, this lovely voluptuous red-haired stranger from Roma and I, riding toward

Pompeii in a quadriga that would have brought a blush to the cheek of a Caesar. Traffic parts for us on the highway as though it *is* the chariot of a Caesar, and the horses streak eastward and then southward with the swiftness of the steeds of Apollo, clipclopping along the wide, beautifully paved road at a startling pace.

Lucilla and I sit chastely far apart, like the well-bred young people that we are, chatting pleasantly but impersonally about the party.

"What was all that about," she says, "the quarrel that you and Adriana's uncle were having last night?"

"It wasn't a quarrel. It was—an unpleasantness."

"Whatever. Something about the Roman army invading Britannia to make sure you people stayed on our side in the war. I know so little about these things. You weren't *really* going to secede, were you?"

We have been speaking Roman, but if we are going to have this discussion I must use a language in which I feel more at home. So I switch to Latin and say, "Actually, I think it was a pretty close thing, though it was cruel of him to say so. Or simply boorish."

"Military men. They have no manners."

"It surprised me all the same. To fling it in my face like that—!"

"So it was true?"

"I was only a boy when it was happening, you understand. But yes, I know there was a substantial anti-Imperial faction in Londin fifteen or twenty years ago."

"Who wanted to restore the Republic, you mean?"

"Who wanted to pull out of the Empire," I say. "And elect a king of our own blood. If such a thing as our own blood can be said still to exist in any significant way among Britons, after eighteen hundred years as Roman citizens."

"I see. So they wanted an independent Britannia."

"They saw a chance for it. This was only about twenty years after the Empire had finished cleaning up the effects of the first collapse, you know. And then suddenly a second civil war seemed likely to begin."

"That was in the East, wasn't it?"

I wonder how much she really knows about these matters. More than she is letting on, I suspect. But I have come down from Cantabrigia with honors in history, after all, and I suppose she is trying to give me a chance to be impressive.

"In Syria and Persia, yes, and the back end of India. Just a little frontier rebellion, not even white people that were stirring up the fuss: ten legions could have put the whole thing down. But the Emperor Laureolus was already old and sick—senile, in fact—and no one in the administration was paying attention to the outer provinces, and the legions weren't sent in until it was too late. So there was a real mess to deal with, all of a sudden. And right in the middle of that, Hispania and Gallia and even silly little Lusitania decided to secede from the Empire again, too. So it was 2563 all over again, a second collapse even more serious than the first one."

"And Britannia was going to pull out also, this time."

"That was what the rabble was urging, at any rate. There were some noisy demonstrations in Londin, and posters went up outside the proconsul's palace telling him to go back to Roma, things like that: '*Britannia for the Britons!*' Throw the Romans out and bring back the old Celtic monarchy, is what people were yelling. Well, of course, we couldn't have that, and we shut them up very quickly indeed, and when the war began and our moment came, we fought as bravely as any Romans anywhere."

" 'We?' " she says.

"The decent people of Britannia. The intelligent people."

"The propertied people, you mean?"

"Well, of course. We understood how much there was to lose— not just for us, for everyone in Britannia—if the Empire should fall. What's our best market? Italia! And if Britannia, Gallia, Hispania, and Lusitania managed to secede, Italia would lose its access to the sea. It would be locked up in the middle of Europa with one set of enemies blocking the land route to the east and the other set closing off the ocean to the west. The heart of the Empire would wither. We Britons would have no one to sell our goods to, unless we started shipping them westward to Nova Roma and trying to peddle them to the redskins. The breakup of the Empire would cause a worldwide depression—famine, civil strife, absolute horror everywhere.

The worst of the suffering would have fallen on the people who were yelling loudest for secession."

She gives me an odd look.

"Your own family claims royal Celtic blood, and you have a fancy Celtic name. So it would seem that your people like to look back nostalgically to the golden days of British freedom before the Roman conquest. But even so you helped to put down the secessionist movement in your province."

Is she mocking me too? I am so little at ease among these Romans.

A trifle woodenly I say, "Not I, personally. I was still only a boy when the anti-Imperial demonstrations were going on. But yes, for all his love of Celtic lore my father has always believed that we had to put the interests of Roman civilization in general ahead of our petty little nationalistic pride. When the war did reach us, Britannia was on the Loyalist side, thanks in good measure to him. And as soon as I was old enough, I joined the legions and did my part for the Empire."

"You love the Emperor, then?"

"I love the Empire. I believe the Empire is a necessity. As for this particular Emperor that we have now—" I hesitate. I should be careful here. "We have had more capable ones, I suppose."

Lucilla laughs. "My father thinks that Maxentius is an utter idiot!"

"Actually, so does mine. Well, but Emperors come and go, and some are better than others. What's important is the survival of the Empire. And for every Nero, there's a Vespasianus, sooner or later. For every Caracalla, there's a Titus Gallius. And for every weak and silly Maxentius—"

"Shh," Lucilla says, pointing to our coachman then to her ears. "We ought to be more cautious. Perhaps we're saying too much that's indiscreet, love. We don't want to do that."

"No. Of course not."

"*Doing* something indiscreet, now—"

"Ah. That's different."

"Very different," she says. And we both laugh.

We are passing virtually under the shadow of great Vesuvius

now. Imperceptibly we have moved closer to each other while talking, and gradually I have come to feel the pressure of her warm thigh
against mine.

Now, as the chariot takes a sharp turn of the road, she is thrown
against me. Ostensibly to steady her, I slip my arm around her shoulders and she nestles her head in the hollow of my neck. My hand
comes to rest on the firm globe of her breast. She lets it remain there.

We reach the ruins of Pompeii in time for a late lunch at a luxurious hostelry just at the edge of the excavation zone. Over a meal of
grilled fish and glittering white wine we make no pretense of hiding
our hunger for one another. I am tempted to suggest that we skip the
archaeology and go straight to our room.

But no, no chance of that, a guide that she has hired is waiting for
us after lunch, an excitable little bald-headed Greek who is bubbling
with eagerness to convey us into the realm of antiquity. So off we go
into the torrid Pompeiian afternoon, full of wine and lust, and he
marches us up one dry stony street and down the next, showing us the
great sights of the city that the volcano engulfed eighteen hundred
years ago in the second month of the reign of the Emperor Titus.

It's terribly fascinating, actually. We modern Romans have the il-
lusion that we still continue to design our cities and houses very
much in the style of the ancients; but in fact the changes, however
gentle they may have been from one century to the next, have been
enormous, and Pompeii—sealed away under volcanic debris eighteen centuries ago and left untouched until its rediscovery just a few
decades ago—seems truly antique. Our bubbly Greek shows us the
homes of the rich men with their sumptuous paintings and statuary, the
baths, the amphitheater, the forum. He takes us into the sweaty little
whorehouse, where we see vivid murals of heavy-thighed prostitutes
energetically pleasuring their clients, and Lucilla giggles into my ear
and lightly tickles the palm of my hand with her fingertip. I'm ready to
conclude the tour right then and there, but of course it can't be done:
there is ever so much more to see, our relentless guide declares.

Outside the Temple of Jupiter Lucilla asks me, all innocence,
"What gods do you people worship in Britannia? The same that
we do?"

"The very same, yes. Jupiter, Juno, Apollo, Mithras, Cybele, all the usual ones, the ones that you have here."

"Not special prehistoric pagan gods of your own?"

"What do you imagine we are? Savages?"

"Of course, darling! Of course! Great lovely golden-haired savages!"

There is a gleam in her eye. She is teasing, but she means what she says, as well. I know she does.

And she too has hit a vulnerable point; for despite all our Roman airs, we Britons are *not* really as much like these people as we would like to think, and we *do* have our own little lingering ancient allegiances. Not I myself, particularly; for such religious needs as I may have, Jupiter and Mercury are quite good enough. But I have friends at home, quite close friends, who sacrifice most sincerely to Branwen and Velaunus, to Rhiannon and Brighida, to Ancasta, to the Matres. And even I have gone—once, at least—to the festival of the Llewnasadh, where they worship Mercury Lugus under his old British name of Llew.

But it is all too foolish, too embarrassing, worshiping those crude old wooden gods in their nests of straw. Not that Apollo and Mercury seem any less absurd to me, or Mithras, or any of the dozens of bizarre Eastern gods that have been going in and out of fashion in Roma for centuries, Baal and Marduk and Jehovah and the rest. They are all equally meaningless to me. And yet there are times when I feel a great vacancy inside of me, as I look up at the stars, wondering how and why they all were made, and not knowing, not having even the first hint.

I don't want to speak of such things with her. These are private matters.

But her playful question about our local gods has wounded me. I am abashed; I am red-cheeked with shame at my own Britishness, which I have sensed almost from the start is one of the things about me, perhaps the most important thing, that makes me interesting to her.

We leave the ruins, finally.

We return to our hotel. We go to our room. Our suite has a terrace overlooking the excavations, a bedroom painted with murals in the Pompeiian style, a marble bath big enough for six. We undress each other with deliberate lack of haste. Lucilla's body is strongly built, broad through the hips and shoulders, full in buttock and breast and thigh: to me an extremely beautiful body, but perhaps she inwardly fears that it lacks elegance. Her skin is marvelous, pale as fine silk, with the lightest dusting of charming pink freckles across her chest and the tops of her shoulders, and—an oddity that I find very diverting—her pubic hair is black as night, the starkest possible contrast to the fiery crimson hair higher up.

She sees the direction of my gaze.

"I don't dye it," she informs me. "It just came that way, I don't know why."

"And this?" I say, placing my finger lightly on the tattoo of a pine tree that runs along the inside of her right thigh. "A birthmark, is it?"

"The priests of Atys put it there, when I was initiated."

"The Phrygian god?"

"I go to his temple, yes. Now and then. In springtime, usually."

So she has indeed played a little game with me.

"Atys! A devotee of Atys of Phrygia! Oh, Lucilla, Lucilla! You had the audacity to tell me that you think Britons are savages because some of us worship pagan gods. While all the time you had the mark of Atys on your own skin, right next to your—your—"

"To my what, love? Go on, say its name."

I say it in Britannic. She repeats it, savoring the word, so strange to her ears, so barbaric.

"Now kiss it," she says.

"Gladly," I tell her, and I drop to my knees and do. Then I sweep her up in my great barbaric arms and carry her to the bath, and lower her gently into it, and lie down beside her myself. We soak for a time; and then we wash each other, laughing; and then, still wet, we spring from the tub and race toward the bed. She is looking for savagery, and I give her savagery, all right, hearty barbarian caresses that leave her gasping in unintelligible bursts of no doubt obscene Roman; and what she gives me in return is the subtle and artful Roman manner of loving, tricks going back to Caesar's time, cunning ripplings of the interior muscles and sly strokes of the fingertips that drive me to the edge of madness; and no sooner have we done with each other than we find ourselves beginning all over again.

"My wild man," she murmurs. "My Celt!"

From Pompeii we proceed down the coast to Surrentum, a beautiful seaside town set amid groves of orange and lemon trees. We tell our driver to wait for us there for a couple of days, and take the ferry across to the romantic isle of Capreae, playground of Emperors. Lucilla has wired ahead to book a room for us at one of the best hotels, a hilltop place called the Punta Tragara that has, she says, a magnificent view of the harbor. She has been to Capreae before. With whom, I wonder, and how many times.

Lucilla and I lie naked on the terrace of our room, reclining on thick sheepskin mats, enjoying the mild autumn evening. The sky and the sea are the same shade of gray-blue. It's hard to tell where the boundary lies between the one and the other. Thickly wooded cliffs rise vertically from the water just across from us. Heavy-winged birds swoop through the dusk. In town, far below, the first lights of evening begin to shimmer.

"I don't even know your name," I say, after a while.

"Of course you do. It's Lucilla."

"You know what I mean. The rest of it."

"Lucilla Junia Scaevola," she says.

"Scaevola? Related to the famous *Consul* Scaevola, by any chance?"

I'm only making idle talk. Scaevola is hardly an uncommon Roman name, of course.

"He's my uncle Gaius," she says. "You'll get to meet him when we go up to Roma. Adriana adores him, and so will you."

Her casual words leave me thunderstruck. Consul Scaevola's niece, lying naked here beside me?

Gods! These girls and their famous uncles! Uncle Gaius, Uncle Cassius. I am in heady company. The whole Roman world knows Gaius Junius Scaevola—chosen again and again as Consul, three

terms, perhaps four, the most recent time just a couple of years before. By all accounts he's the second most powerful man in the
realm, the great strong figure who stands behind the wobbly young
Emperor Maxentius and keeps him propped up. *My uncle Gaius,*
this one says, so very simply and sweetly. I'll have quite a lot to tell
my father when I get back to Cornwall.

Consul Scaevola's niece rears up above me and dangles her
breasts in my face. I kiss their pink patrician tips and she drops
down on top of me like one of those fierce swooping birds descending on its prey.

In the cool of the morning we take a long hike up one of the hills behind town to the Villa Jovis, the Imperial palace that has been there
since the time of Tiberius. He used to have his enemies thrown from
the edge of the cliff there.

Of course we can't get very close to it, since it's still in use, occupied by members of the Imperial family whenever they visit
Capreae. Nobody seems to be in residence right now but the gates
are heavily guarded anyway. We can see it rising grandly from the
summit of its hill, an enormous pile of gleaming masonry surrounded by elaborate fortifications.

"I wonder what it's like in there," I say. "But I'll never know, I
guess."

"I've been inside it," Lucilla tells me.

"You have?"

"They claim that some of the rooms and furnishings go all the
way back to Tiberius's reign. There's an indoor swimming pool with
the most absolutely obscene mosaics all around it, and that's where
he's supposed to have liked to diddle little boys and girls. But I think
it's all mostly a fake put together in medieval times, or even later.
The whole place was sacked, you know, when the Byzantines in-
vaded the Western Empire six hundred years ago. It's pretty certain
that they carried the treasures of the early Emperors off to Constantinopolis with them, wouldn't you think?"

"How did you happen to see it?" I ask. "You were traveling with
your uncle, I suppose."

"With Flavius Rufus, actually."

"Flavius Rufus?"

"Flavius Caesar. Emperor Maxentius's third brother. He loves southern Italia. Comes down here all the time."

"With you?"

"Once in a while. Oh, silly, silly! I was *sixteen.* We were just friends!"

"And how old are you now?"

"Twenty-one," she says. Six years younger than I am, then.

"Very close friends, I suppose."

"Oh, don't be such a fool, Cymbelin!" There is laughter in her eyes. "You'll meet him, too, when we're in Roma."

"A royal prince?"

"Of course! You'll meet *everyone.* The Emperor's brothers, the Emperor's sisters, the Emperor himself, if he's in town. I grew up at court, don't you realize that? In my uncle's household. My father died in the war."

"I'm sorry."

"Commanded the Augustus Legion, in Syria, Aegyptus, Palaestina. Palaestina's where he died. You've heard of the Siege of Aelia Capitolina? That's where he was killed, right outside the Temple of the Great Mother just as the city was falling to us. He was standing near some old ruined stone wall that survives from the temple that was there before the present one, and a sniper got him. Cassius Frontinus delivered the funeral oration himself. And afterward my uncle Gaius adopted me, because my mother was dead, too, had killed herself the year before—that's a long story, a scandal at the court of the old Emperor—"

My head is swimming.

"Anyway, Flavius is like a brother to me. You'll see. We came down here and I stayed the night in the Villa Jovis. Saw all the naughty mosaics in Tiberius's swimming pool, swam in it, even— there was a gigantic feast afterward, wild boar from the mountains here, mountains of strawberries and bananas, and you wouldn't believe how much wine—oh, cheer up, Cymbelin, you didn't think I was a *virgin,* did you?"

"That isn't it. Not at all."

"Then what is it?"

"The thought that you really know the royals. That you're still so young and you've done so many astonishing things. And also that the man I was arguing with the other night was actually Cassius Lucius Frontinus the famous general, and that you're the niece of Gaius Junius Scaevola the Consul, and that you've been the mistress of the Emperor's brother, and—don't you see, Lucilla, how hard all this is for me? How bewildering?"

"My poor confused barbarian!"

"I wish you wouldn't call me that. Even if it's more or less true."

"My gorgeous Celt, then. My beautiful blond-haired Briton. That much is all right to say, isn't it?"

We hire one of the little one-horse carriages that are the only permissible vehicles on Capreae and ride down to the beach to spend the afternoon swimming naked in the warm sea and sunning ourselves on the rocky shore. Though it is late in the day and late also in the year, Lucilla's flawless skin quickly turns rosy, and she's hot and glowing when we return to our room.

Two days, two unforgettable nights, on Capreae. Then back to Surrentum, where our charioteer is dutifully waiting for us at the ferry landing, and up to Neapolis again, an all-day drive. I am reluctant to part from her at my hotel, urging her to spend the night with me there, too, but she insists that she must get back to the villa of Frontinus.

"And I?" I say. "What do I do? I have to dine alone, I have to go to bed alone?"

She brushes her lips lightly across mine and laughs. "Did I say that? Of course you'll come with me to Frontinus's place! Of course!"

"But he hasn't invited me to return."

"What a fool you can be sometimes, Cymbelin. I invite you. I'm Adriana's guest. And you're mine. Go upstairs, pack up the rest of your things, tell the hotel you're checking out. Go on, now!"

And so it is. In Druso Tiberio's absurdly splendid quadriga we ride back up the hill to the villa of Marcellus Domitianus Frontinus, where I am greeted with apparently unfeigned warmth and no trace of surprise by our jolly host and given a magnificent suite of rooms overlooking the bay. Uncle Cassio is gone, and so are the other house guests who were there on the night of the party, and I am more than welcome.

My rooms just happen to adjoin those of Lucilla. That night, after a feast of exhausting excess at which Druso Tiberio and his gladiator playmate Ezio behave in a truly disgusting way while the elder Frontinus studiedly turns his attention elsewhere, I hear a gentle tapping at my door as I am preparing for bed.

"Yes?"

"It's me."

Lucilla. "Gods be thanked! Come in!"

She wears a silken robe so sheer she might as well have been naked. In one hand she carries a little candelabrum, in the other a flask of what appears to be wine. She is still tipsy from dinner, I see. I take the candelabrum from her before she sets herself afire, and then the flask.

"We could invite Adriana in, too," she says coyly.

"Are you crazy?"

"No. Are you?"

"The two of you—?"

"We're best friends. We share everything."

"No," I say. "Not this."

"You *are* provincial, Cymbelin."

"Yes, I am. And one woman at a time is quite enough for me."

She seems disappointed. I realize that she has promised to provide me to Adriana for tonight. Well, this is Imperial Italia, where the old traditions of unabashed debauchery evidently are very much alive. But though I speak of myself as Roman, I'm not as Roman as all that, I suppose. Adriana Frontina is extraordinarily beautiful, yes, but so is Lucilla, and Lucilla is all I want just now, and that is that. Simple provincial tastes. No doubt I'll live to regret my decision; but this night I am unwavering in my mulish simplicity.

Lucilla, disappointed or not, proves passionate enough for two. The night passes in a sleepless haze. We go at each other wildly, feverishly. She teaches me another new trick or two, and claps her hands at her own erotic cleverness. There are no women like this in Britannia: none that are known to me, at any rate.

At dawn we stand together on the balcony of my bedroom, weary with the best of all possible wearinesses, relishing the sweet cool breeze that rises from the bay.

"When do you want to go north?" she asks.

"Whenever you do."

"What about tomorrow?"

"Why not?"

"I warn you, you may be shocked by a few of the things you see going on in Urbs Roma."

"Then I'll be shocked, I suppose."

"You're very easily shocked, aren't you, Cymbelin?"

"Not really. Some of this is new to me, that's all."

Lucilla chuckles. "I'll educate you in our ways, never fear. It'll all get less frightening as you get used to it. You poor darling barbarian."

"You know I asked you not to—"

"You poor darling Celt, I mean," Lucilla says. "Come with me to Roma, love. But remember: when in Roma, it's best to do as the Romans do."

"I'll try," I promise.

Yet another chariot is put at our disposal for the journey: this one Ezio's, which he drove down in alone from Urbs Roma. He's going back north next week with Druso Tiberio, and they'll ride in one of his, but Ezio's chariot has to be returned to the capital somehow, too. So we take it. It's not nearly as grand as the one Lucilla and I had just been using, but it's far more imposing than you would expect someone like Ezio to own. A gift from Druso Tiberio, no doubt.

The whole household turns out to see us off. Marcello Domiziano urges me to think of his villa as his home whenever I am in Neapolis. I invite him to be my family's guest in Britannia. Adriana gives Lucilla a more than friendly hug—I begin to wonder about them—and kisses me lightly on the cheek. But as I turn away from her I see a smoldering look in her eyes that seems compounded out of fury and regret. I suspect I have made an enemy here. But perhaps the damage can be repaired at a later time: it would be pleasant enough work to attempt it.

Our route north is the Via Roma, and we must descend into town to reach it. Since we have no driver, I will be the charioteer, and Lucilla sits beside me on the box. Our horses, a pair of slender, fiery Arabians, are well matched and need little guidance from me. The day is mild, balmy, soft breezes: yet another bright, sunny, summer-like day here in the eighth month of the year. I think of my homeland, how dark and wet it must be by now.

"Does winter ever reach Italia?" I ask. "Or have the Emperors made special arrangements with the gods?"

"Oh, it gets quite cold, quite wet," Lucilla assures me. "You'll see. Not so much down here, but in Roma itself, yes, the winters can be extremely vile. You'll still be here at the time of the Saturnalia, won't you?"

That's still two months away. "I hadn't really given it much thought. I suppose I will."

"Then you'll see how cold it can get. I usually go to someplace like Sicilia or Aegyptus for the winter months, but this year I'm going to stay in Roma." She snuggles cozily against me. "When the rains come we'll keep each other warm. Won't that be nice, Cymbelin?"

"Lovely. On the other hand, I wouldn't mind seeing Aegyptus, you know. We could take the trip together at the end of the year. The Pyramids, the great temples at Menfe—"

"I have to stay in Italia this winter. In or at least near Roma."

"You do? Why is that?"

"A family thing," she says. "It involves my uncle. But I mustn't talk about it."

I take the meaning of her words immediately.

"He's going to be named Consul again, isn't he? *Isn't* he?"

She stiffens and pulls her breath in quickly, and I know that I've hit on the truth.

"I mustn't say," she replies, after a moment.

"That's it, though. It has to be. The new year's Consuls take of-

fice on the first of Januarius, and so of course you'll want to be there
for the ceremony. What will this be, the fourth time for him? The
fifth, maybe."

"Please, Cymbelin."

"Promise me this, at least. We'll stay around in Roma until he's
sworn in, and then we'll go to Aegyptus. The middle of January, all
right? I can see us now, heading up the Nilus from Alexandria in a
barge for two—"

"That's such a long time from now. I can't promise anything so
far in advance." She puts her hand gently on my wrist and lets it
linger there. "But we'll have as much fun as we can, won't we, even
if it's cold and rainy, love?"

I see that there's no point pressing the issue. Maybe her Januarius is already arranged, and her plans don't include me: a trip to
Africa with one of her Imperial friends, perhaps, young Flavius Caesar or some other member of the royal family. Irrational jealousy momentarily curdles my soul; and then I put all thought of January out
of my mind. This is October, and the gloriously beautiful Lucilla Junia Scaevola will share my bed tonight and tomorrow night and so
on and on at least until the Saturnalia, if I wish it, and I certainly do,
and that should be all that matters to me right now.

We are passing the great hotels of the Via Roma. Their resplendent façades shine in the morning sun. And then we begin to climb
up out of town again, into the suburban heights, a string of minor
villas and here and there an isolated hill with some venerable estate
of the Imperial family sprawling around its summit. After a time we
go down the far side of the hills and enter the flat open country beyond, heading through the fertile plains of Campania Felix toward
the capital city in the distant north.

We spend our first night in Capua, where Lucilla wants me to
see the frescoes in the Mithraeum. I attempt to draw on my letter of
credit to pay the hotel bill, but I discover that there will be no charge
for our suite: the magic name of Scaevola has opened the way for us.
The frescoes are very fine, the god slaying a white bull with a serpent
under its feet, and there is a huge amphitheater here, too—the one
where Spartacus spurred the revolt of the gladiators—but Lucilla

tells me, as I gawk in provincial awe, that the one in Roma is far more impressive. Dinner is brought to us in our room, breast of pheasant and some thick, musky wine, and afterward we soak in the bath a long while and then indulge in the nightly scramble of the passions. I can easily endure this sort of life well through the end of the year and some distance beyond.

Then in the morning it is onward, northward and westward along the Via Roma, which now has become the Via Appia, the ancient military highway along which the Romans marched when they came to conquer their neighbors in southern Italia. This is sleepy agricultural country, broken here and there by the dark cyclopean ruins of dead cities that go back to pre-Roman times, and by hilltop towns of more recent date, though themselves a thousand years old or more. I feel the tremendous weight of history here.

Lucilla chatters away the slow drowsy hours of our drive with talk of her innumerable patrician friends in the capital, Claudio and Traiano and Alessandro and Marco Aureliano and Valeriano and a few dozen more, nearly all of them male, but there are a few female names among them, too, Domitilla, Severina, Giulia, Paolina, Tranquillina. High lords and ladies, I suppose. Sprinkled through the gossip are lighthearted references to members of the Imperial family who seem to be well known to her, close companions, in fact—not just the young Emperor, but his four brothers and three sisters, and assorted Imperial cousins and more distant kin.

I see more clearly than I have ever realized before how vast an establishment the family of our Caesars is, how many idle princes and princesses, each one with a great array of palaces, servitors, lovers and hangers-on. Nor is it only a single family, the cluster of royals who sit atop our world. For of course we have had innumerable dynasties occupying the throne during the nineteen centuries of the Empire, most of them long since extinct but many of the past five hundred years still surviving at least in some collateral line, completely unrelated to each other but all of them nevertheless carrying the great name of Caesar and all staking their claim to the public treasury. A dynasty can be overthrown but somehow the great-great-great-grandnephews, or whatever, of someone whose brother was Emperor long ago can still manage, so it seems, to claim pensions from the public purse down through all the succeeding epochs of time.

It's clear from the way she talks that Lucilla has been the mistress of Flavius Caesar and very likely also of his older brother, Camillus Caesar, who holds the title of Prince of Constantinopolis, though he lives in Roma; she speaks highly also of a certain Roman count who bears the grand name of Nero Romulus Claudius Palladius, and there is a special tone in her voice when she tells me of him that I know comes into women's voices when they are speaking of a man with whom they have made love.

Jealousy of men I have never even met surges within me. How can she have done so much already, she who is only twenty-one? I try to control my feelings. This is Roma; there is no morality here as I understand the word; I must strive to do as the Romans do, indeed.

Despite myself I try to ask her about this Nero Romulus Claudius Palladius, but already she has moved along to a sister of the Emperor whom she's sure I'll adore. Severina Floriana is her name. "We went to school together. Next to Adriana, she's my best friend in the world. She's absolutely beautiful—dark, sultry, almost Oriental-looking. You'd think she was an Arab. And you'd be right, because her grandmother on her mother's side came from Syria. A dancing-girl, once upon a time, so the story goes—"

And on and on. I wonder if I am to be offered to Severina Floriana also.

It is the third day of our journey now. As the Via Appia nears the capital we begin to encounter the Imperial tombs, lining the road on both sides. Lucilla seems to know them all and calls them off for me.

"There's the tomb of Flavius Romulus, the big one on the left— and that one is Claudius IX—and Gaius Martius, there—that's Cecilia Metella, she lived in the time of Augustus Caesar—Titus Gallius—Constantinus V—Lucius and Arcadius Agrippa, both of them—Heraclius III—Gaius Paulus—Marcus Anastasius—"

The weight of antiquity presses ever more heavily on me.

"What about the earliest ones?" I ask. "Augustus, Tiberius, Claudius—"

"You'll see the Tomb of Augustus in the city. Tiberius? Nobody seems to remember where he was buried. There are a lot of them in Hadrianus's tomb overlooking the river, maybe ten of them, Antoninus Pius, Marcus Aurelius, a whole crowd of dead Emperors in there. And Julius Caesar himself—there's a great tomb for him right in the middle of the Forum, but the archaeologists say it isn't really his, it was built six hundred years later—oh, look, Cymbelin—do you see, there? The walls of the city right ahead of us! Roma! Roma!"

And so it is, Urbs Roma, the great mother of cities, the capital of the world, the Imperial metropolis: its white marble-sheathed walls, built and rebuilt so many times, rise suddenly before me. Roma! The boy from the far country, humbled by the grandeur of it all, is shaken to the core. A shiver of awe goes through me so convulsively that it is transmitted through the reins to the horses, one of which glances back at me in what I imagine to be contempt and puzzlement.

Roma the city is like a palimpsest, a scroll that has been written on and cleaned and written on again, and again and again: and all the old texts show through amidst the newest one. Two thousand years of history assail the newcomer's bedazzled eye in a single glance. Nothing ever gets torn down here, except occasionally for the sake of building something even more grand on its site. Here and there can still be seen the last quaint occasional remnants of the Roma of the Republic—the First Republic, I suppose I should say now—with the marble Roma of Augustus Caesar right atop them, and then the Romas of all the later Caesars, Hadrianus's Roma and Septimius Severus's Roma and the Roma of Flavius Romulus, who lived and ruled a thousand years after Severus, and the one that the renowned world-spanning Emperor Trajan VII erected upon all the rest in the great years that followed Flavius's reuniting of the Eastern and Western Empires. All these are mixed together in the historic center of the city, and then too in a frightful ring surrounding them rise the massive hideous towers of modern times, the dreary office buildings and apartment houses of the Roma of today.

But even they, ugly as they are, are ugly in an awesomely grand Roman way. Roma is nothing if not grand: it excels at everything, even at ugliness.

Lucilla guides me in, calling off the world-famous sights as we pass them one by one: the Baths of Caracalla, the Circus Maximus, the Temple of the Divine Claudius, the Tower of Aemilius Magnus, even the ponderous and malproportioned Arch of Triumph that the Byzantine Emperor Andronicus erected in the year 1952 to mark the short-lived Greek victory in the Civil War, and which the Romans have allowed to remain as an all too visible reminder of the one great defeat in their history. But just at the opposite end of the avenue from it is the Arch of Flavius Romulus, too, five times the size of the Arch of Andronicus, to signify the final defeat of the Greeks after their two centuries of Imperial dominion.

The traffic is stupefying and chaotic. Chariots everywhere, horse-drawn trams, bicycles, and something that Lucilla says is very new, little steam-driven trains that run freely on wheels instead of tracks. There seem to be no rules: each vehicle goes wherever it pleases, nobody giving any signals, each driver attempting to intimidate those about him with gestures and curses. At first I have trouble with this, not because I am easily intimidated but because we Britons are taught early to be courteous to one another on the highways; but quickly I see that I have no choice but to behave as they do. *When in Roma,* et cetera—the old maxim applies to every aspect of life in the capital.

"Left here. Now right. You see the Colosseum, over there? Bigger than you thought, isn't it? Turn right, turn right! That's the Forum down there, and the Capitol up on that hill. But we want to go the other way, over to the Palatine—it's the hill up there, you see? The one covered with palaces."

Yes. Enormous Imperial dwellings, two score or even more of them, all higgledy-piggledy, cheek by jowl. Whole mountains of marble must have been leveled to build that incomprehensible maze of splendor.

And we are heading right into the midst of it all. The entrance to the Palatine is well patrolled, hordes of Praetorians everywhere, but they all seem to know Lucilla by sight and they wave us on in. She tries to explain to me which palace is whose, but it's all a hopeless jumble, and even she isn't really sure. Underneath what we see, she says, are the original palaces of the early Imperial days, those of Augustus and Tiberius and the Flavians, but of course nearly every Emperor since then has wanted to add his own embellishments and enhancements, and by now the whole hill is a crazyquilt of Imperial magnificence and grandiosity in twenty different styles, including a few very odd Oriental and pseudo-Byzantine structures inserted into the mix in the twenty-fourth century by some of the weirder monarchs of the Decadence. Towers and arcades and pavilions and gazebos and colonnades and domes and basilicas and fountains and peculiar swooping vaults jut out everywhere.

"And the Emperor himself?" I ask her. "Where in all that does he live?"

She waves her hand vaguely toward the middle of the heap. "Oh, he moves around, you know. He never stays in the same place two nights in a row."

"Why is that? Is he the restless type?"

"Not at all. But Actinius Varro makes him do it."

"Who?"

"Varro. The Praetorian Prefect. He worries a lot about assassination plots."

I laugh. "When an Emperor is assassinated, isn't it usually his own Praetorian Prefect who does it?"

"Usually, yes. But the Emperor always thinks that his prefect is the first completely loyal one, right up till the moment the knife goes into his belly. Not that anyone would want to assassinate a foolish fop like our Maxentius," she adds.

"If he's as incompetent as everyone says, wouldn't that be a good reason for removing him, then?"

"What, and make one of his even more useless brothers Emperor in his place? Oh, no, Cymbelin. I know them all, believe me, and Maxentius is the best of the lot. Long life to him, I say."

"Indeed. Long life to Emperor Maxentius," I chime in, and we both enjoy a good laugh.

The particular palace we are heading for is one of the newest on the hill: an ornate, many-winged guest pavilion, much bedizened with eye-dazzling mosaics, brilliant wild splotches of garish yellows and uninhibited scarlets. It had been erected some fifty years before, she tells me, early in the reign of the lunatic Emperor Demetrius, the last Caesar of the Decadence. Lucilla has a little apartment in it, courtesy of her good friend, Prince Flavius Rufus. Apparently a good many non-royal members of the Imperial Roman social set live up here on the Palatine. It's more convenient for everyone that way, traffic being what it is in Roma and the number of parties being so great.

The beginning of my stay in the capital is Neapolis all over again: there is a glittering social function for me to attend on my very first night. The host, says Lucilla, is none other than the famous Count Nero Romulus Claudius Palladius, who is terribly eager to meet me.

"And who is he, exactly?" I ask.

"His grandfather's brother was Count Valerian Apollinaris. You know who he was?"

"Of course." One doesn't need a Cantabrigian education to recognize the name of the architect of the modern Empire, the great five-term Consul of the First War of Reunification. It was Valerian Apollinaris who had dragged the frayed and crumbling Empire out of the sorry era known as the Decadence, put an end to the insurrections in the provinces that had wracked the Empire throughout the troubled twenty-fifth century, restored the authority of the central government, and installed Laureolus Caesar, grandfather of our present Emperor, on the throne. It was Apollinaris who—acting in Laureolus's name, as an unofficial Caesar standing behind the true one—had instituted the Reign of Terror, that time of brutal discipline that had, for better or for worse, brought the Empire back to some semblance of the greatness that it last had known in the time of Flavius Romulus and the seventh Trajan. And then perished in the Terror himself, along with so many others.

I know nothing of this grand-nephew of his, this Nero Romulus Claudius Palladius, except what I've heard of him from Lucilla. But she conveys merely by the way she utters his name, his full name every time, that he has followed his ancestor's path, that he too is a man of great power in the realm.

And indeed it is obvious to me right away, when Lucilla and I arrive at Count Nero Romulus's Palatine Hill palace, that my guess is correct.

The palace itself is relatively modest: a charming little building on the lower slope of the hill, close to the Forum, that I am told dates from the Renaissance and was originally built for one of the mistresses of Trajan VII. Just as Count Nero Romulus has never bothered to hold the Consulate or any of the other high offices of the realm, Count Nero Romulus doesn't need a grand edifice to announce his importance. But the guest list at his party says it all.

The current Consul, Aulus Galerius Bassanius, is there. So are two of the Emperor's brothers, and one of his sisters. And also Lucilla's uncle, the distinguished and celebrated Gaius Junius Scaevola, four times Consul of Roma and by general report the most powerful man in the Empire next to Emperor Maxentius himself—*more* powerful than the Emperor, many believe.

Lucilla introduces me to Scaevola first. "My friend Cymbelin Vetruvius Scapulanus from Britannia," she says, with a grand flourish. "We met at Marcello Domiziano's house in Neapolis, and we've been inseparable ever since. Isn't he splendid, Uncle Gaius?"

What does one say, when one is a mere artless provincial on his first night in the capital and one finds oneself thrust suddenly into the presence of the greatest citizen of the realm?

But I manage not to stammer and blurt and lurch. With reasonable smoothness, in fact, I say, "I could never have imagined, when I set out from Britannia to see the fatherland of the Empire, Consul Scaevola, that I would have the honor to encounter the father of the country himself!"

At which he smiles amiably and says, "I think you rank me too highly, my friend. It's the Emperor who's the father of the country, you know. As it says right here." And pulls a shiny new sestertius piece from his purse and holds it up so I can see the inscriptions around the edge, the cryptic string of abbreviated Imperial titles that all the coinage has carried since time immemorial. "You see?" he says, pointing to the letters on the rim of the coin just above the eyebrows of Caesar Maxentius. "P.P., standing for *'Pater Patriae.'* There it is. Him, not me. Father of the country." Then, with a wink to take the sting out of his rebuke, such as it had been, he says, "But I appreciate flattery as much as the next man, maybe even a little more. So thank you, young man. Lucilla's not being too much trouble for you, is she, now?"

I'm not sure what he means by that. Perhaps nothing.

"Hardly," I say.

I realize that I'm staring. Scaevola is a gaunt, wiry man of middle height as well, perhaps fifty years old, balding, with his remaining thin strands of hair—red hair, like Lucilla's—pulled taut across his scalp. His cheekbones are pronounced, his nose is sharp, his chin is strong; his eyes are a very pale, icy gray-blue, the blue of a milky-hued sapphire. He looks astonishingly like Julius Caesar, the famous portrait that is on the ten-denarius postage stamp: that same expression of utterly unstoppable determination that arises out of infinite resources of inner power.

He asks me a few questions about my travels and about my homeland, listens with apparent interest to my replies, wishes me well, and efficiently sends me on my way.

My knees are trembling. My throat is dry.

Now I must meet my host the Count, and he is no easy pudding either. Nero Romulus Claudius Palladius is every bit as imposing as I had come to expect, a suave, burnished-looking man of about forty, tall for a Roman and strongly built, with a dense, flawlessly trimmed black beard, skin of a rich deep tone, dark penetrating eyes. He radiates an aura of wealth, power, self-assurance, and—even I am capable of detecting it—an almost irresistible sensuality.

"Cymbelin," he says immediately. "A great name, a romantic name, the name of a king. Welcome to my house, Cymbelin of Britannia." His voice is resonant, a perfectly modulated basso, the voice of an actor, of an opera singer. "We hope to see you here often during your stay in Roma."

Lucilla, by my side, is staring at him in the most worshipful way. Which should trigger my jealousy; but I confess I feel such awe for him myself that I can scarcely object that she is under his spell.

He rests his hand lightly on my shoulder. "Come. You must meet some of my friends." And takes me around the room. Introduces me to the incumbent Consul, Galerius Bassanius, who is younger and more frivolously dressed than I would have thought a Consul would be, and to some actors who seem to expect that I would recognize their names, though I don't and have to dissemble a little, and to a gladiator whose name I do recognize—who wouldn't, considering that he is the celebrated Marcus Sempronius Diodorus, Marcus the Lion-Slayer?—and then to a few flashy young ladies, with whom I make the appropriate flirtatious banter even though Lucilla has more beauty in her left elbow alone than any one of them does in her entire body.

We pass now through an atrium where a juggler is performing and onward to a second room, just as crowded as the first, where the general conversation has an oddly high-pitched tone and people are standing about in strangely stilted postures. After a moment I understand why.

There are royals in here. Everyone is on best court behavior.

Two princes of the blood, no less. Lucilla has me meet them both.

The first is Camillus Caesar, the Prince of Constantinopolis, eldest of the Emperor's four brothers. He is plump, lazy-looking, with oily skin and an idle, slouching way of holding himself. If Gaius Junius Scaevola is a Julius Caesar, this man is a Nero. But for all his soft fleshiness I can make out distinct traces of the familiar taut features that mark the royal family: the sharp, fragile, imperious nose, the heroic chin, above all the chilly eyes, blue as Arctic ice, half hidden though they are behind owlish spectacles. It is as if the stern face of old Emperor Laureolus has somehow become embedded in the meaty bulk of this wastrel grandchild of his.

Camillus is too drunk, even this early in the evening, to say very much to me. He gives me a sloppy wave of his chubby hand and loses interest in me immediately.

Onward we go to the next oldest of the royals, Flavius Rufus Caesar. I am braced to dislike him, aware as I am that he has had the privilege of being Lucilla's lover when she was only sixteen, but in truth he is charming, affable, a very seductive man. About twenty-five, I guess. He too has the family face; but he is lean, agile-looking, quick-eyed, probably quick-witted as well. Since from all I have heard his brother Maxentius is a buffoon and a profligate, it strikes me as a pity that the throne had not descended to Flavius Rufus instead of the other one when their old grandfather finally had shuffled off the scene. But the eldest heir succeeds: it is the ancient rule. With Prince Florus dead three years before his father Laureolus, the throne had gone to Florus's oldest son Maxentius, and the world might be very different today had not that happened. Or perhaps I am overestimating the younger prince. Had Lucilla not told me Maxentius was the best of the lot?

Flavius Rufus—who plainly knows that I am Lucilla's current amusement, and who just as plainly isn't bothered by that—urges me to visit him toward the end of the year at the great Imperial villa at Tibur, a day's journey outside Roma, where he will be celebrating the Saturnalia with a few hundred of his intimate friends.

"Oh, and bring the redhead, too," Flavius Rufus says cheerfully. "You won't forget her, now, will you?"

He blows her a kiss, and gives me a friendly slap on the palm of my hand, and returns to the adulation of his entourage. I am pleased and relieved that our meeting went so well.

Lucilla has saved the best of the family for last, though.

The dearest friend of her childhood, her schoolmate, her honorary kinswoman: the Princess Severina Floriana, sister of the Emperor. Before whom I instantly want to throw myself in utter devotion, she is so overpoweringly beautiful.

As Lucilla had said, Severina Floriana is dark, torrid-looking, exotic. There is no trace of the family features about her—her eyes are glossy black, her nose is a wanton snub, her chin is elegantly rounded—and I know at once that she must not be full sister to the Emperor, that she has to be the child of some subsidiary wife of Maxentius's father: royals may have but one wife at a time, like the rest of us, but it is well known that often they exchange one wife for another, and sometimes take the first one back later on, and who is to say them nay? If Severina's mother looked anything like Severina, I can see why the late Prince Florus was tempted to dally with her.

I was glib enough when speaking with Junius Scaevola and Nero Romulus Claudius Palladius, but I am utterly tongue-tied before Severina Floriana. Lucilla and she do all the talking, and I stand to one side, looming awkwardly in silence like an ox that Lucilla has somehow happened to bring to the party. They chatter of Neapolis's social set, of Adriana, of Druso Tiberio, of a host of people whose names mean nothing to me; they speak of me, too, but what they are talking is the rapid-fire Roman of the capital, so full of slang and unfamiliar pronunciations that I can scarcely understand a thing. Now and again Severina Floriana directs her gaze at me—maybe appraisingly, maybe just out of curiosity at Lucilla's newest acquisition; I can't tell which. I try to signal her with my eyes that I would like a chance to get to know her better, but the situation is so complex and I know I am being reckless—how dare I even *think* of a romance with a royal princess, and how rash, besides, inviting the rage of Lucilla Scaevola by making overtures to her own friend right under her nose—!

In any case I get no acknowledgment from Severina of any of my bold glances.

Lucilla marches me away, eventually. We return to the other room. I am numb.

"I can see that you're fascinated with her," Lucilla tells me. "Isn't that so?"

I make some stammering reply.

"Oh, you can fall in love with her if you like," Lucilla says airily. "I won't mind, silly! Everyone falls in love with her, anyway, so why shouldn't you? She's amazingly gorgeous, I know. I'd take her to bed myself, if that sort of thing interested me a little more."

"Lucilla—I—"

"This is *Roma*, Cymbelin! Stop acting like such a simpleton!"

"I'm here with you. You are the woman I'm here with. I'm absolutely crazy about you."

"Of course you are. And now you're going to be obsessed with Severina Floriana for a while. It's not in the least surprising. Not that you made much of a first impression on her, I suspect, standing there and gawking like that without saying a word, although she doesn't always ask that a man have a mind, if he's got a nice enough body. But I think she's interested. You'll get your chance during Saturnalia, I promise you that." And she gives me a look of such joyous wickedness that I feel my brain reeling at the shamelessness of it all.

Roma! Roma! There is no place on Earth like it.

Silently I vow that one day soon I will hold Severina Floriana in my arms. But it is a vow that I was not destined to be able to keep; and now that she is dead I think of her often, with the greatest sadness, recreating her exotic beauty in my mind and imagining myself caressing her the way I might dream of visiting the palace of the Queen of the Moon.

Lucilla gives me a little push toward the middle of the party and I stagger away on my own, wandering from group to group, pretending to a confidence and a sophistication that at this moment is certainly not mine.

There is Nero Romulus in the corner, quietly talking with Gaius Junius Scaevola. The true monarchs of Roma, they are, the men who hold the real Imperial power. But in what way it is divided between them, I can't even begin to guess.

The Consul, Bassanius, smirking and primping between two male actors who wear heavy makeup. What is he trying to do, reenact the ancient days of Nero and Caligula?

The gladiator, Diodorus, fondling three or four girls at once.

A man I haven't noticed before, sixty or even seventy years old, with a face like a hatchet blade and skin the color of fine walnut, holding court near the fountain. His clothing, his jewelry, his bearing, his flashing eyes, all proclaim him to be a man of substance and power. "Who's that?" I ask a passing young man, and get a look of withering scorn. He tells me, in tones that express his wonder at my ignorance, that that is Leontes Atticus, a name that means nothing to me, so that I have to ask a second question, and my informant lets me know, even more contemptuously, that Leontes Atticus is merely the wealthiest man in the Empire. This fierce-eyed parched-looking Greek, I learn, is a shipping magnate who controls more than half the ocean trade with Nova Roma: he takes his fat percentage on most of the rich cargo that comes to us from the savage and strange New World far across the sea.

And so on and on, new guests arriving all the time, a glowing assembly of the great ones of the capital crowding into the room, everyone who is powerful or wealthy or young, or if possible all three at once.

There is fire smoldering in this room tonight. Soon it will burst forth. But who could have known that then? Not I, not I, certainly not I.

Lucilla spends what seems like an hour conversing with Count Nero Romulus, to my great discomfort. There is an easy intimacy about the way they speak to each other that tells me things I'm not eager to know. What I fear is that he is inviting her to spend the night here with him after the party is over. But I am wrong about that. Ultimately Lucilla returns to my side and doesn't leave it for the rest of the evening.

We dine on fragrant delicacies unknown to me. We drink wines of startling hues and strange piquant flavors. There is dancing; there is a theatrical performance by mimes and jugglers and contortionists; some of the younger guests strip unabashedly naked and splash giddily in the palace pool. I see couples stealing away into the garden, and some who sink into embraces in full view.

"Come," Lucilla says finally. "I'm becoming bored with this. Let's go home and amuse each other in privacy, Cymbelin."

It's nearly dawn by the time we reach her apartments. We make love until midday, and sink then into a deep sleep that holds us in its grip far into the hours of the afternoon, and beyond them, so that it is dark when we arise.

So it goes for me, then, week after week, autumn in Roma, the season of pleasure. Lucilla and I go everywhere together: the theater, the opera, the gladiatorial contests. We are greeted with deference at the finest restaurants and shown to the best tables. She takes me on a tour of the monuments of the capital—the Senate House, the famous temples, the ancient Imperial tombs. It is a dizzying time for me, a season beyond my wildest fantasies.

Occasionally I catch a glimpse of Severina Floriana at some restaurant, or encounter her at a party. Lucilla goes out of her way to give us a chance to speak to each other, and on a couple of these occasions Severina and I do have conversations that seem to be leading somewhere: she is curious about my life in Britannia, she wants to know my opinion of Roma, she tells me little gossipy tidbits about people on the other side of the room.

Her dark beauty astounds me. We fair-haired Britons rarely see women of her sort. She is a creature from another world, blue highlights in her jet-black hair, eyes like mysterious pools of night, skin of a rich deep hue utterly unlike that of my people, not simply the olive tone that so many citizens of the eastern Roman world have, but something darker, more opulent, with a satiny sheen and texture. Her voice, too, is enchanting, husky without a trace of hoarseness, a low, soft, fluting sound, musical and magnificently controlled.

She knows I desire her. But she playfully keeps our encounters beyond the zone where any such thing can be communicated, short of simply blurting it out. Somehow I grow confident, though, that we will be lovers sooner or later. Which perhaps would have been the case, had there only been time.

On two occasions I see her brother the Emperor, too.

Once is at the opera, in his box: he is formally attired in the traditional Imperial costume, the purple toga, and he acknowledges the salute of the audience with a negligent wave and a smile. Then, a week or two later, he passes through one of the Palatine Hill parties, in casual modern dress this time, with a simple purple stripe across his vest to indicate his high status.

At close range I am able to understand why people speak so slightingly of him. Though he has the Imperial bearing and the Imperial features, the commanding eyes and the nose and the chin and all that, there is something about the eager, uncertain smile of Caesar Maxentius that negates all his Imperial pretensions. He may call himself Caesar, he may call himself Augustus, and Pater Patriae and Pontifex Maximus and all the rest; but when you look at him, I discover to my surprise and dismay, he simpers and fails to return your gaze in any steady way. He should never have been given the throne. His brother Flavius Rufus would have been ever so much more regal.

Still, I have met the Emperor, such as he is. It is not every Briton who can say that; and the number of those who can will grow ever fewer from now on.

I send a message home by wire, every once in a while. *Having incredibly good time, could stay here forever but probably won't.* I offer no details. One can hardly say in a telegram that one is living in a little palace a stone's throw from the Emperor's official residence, and sleeping with the niece of Gaius Junius Scaevola, and attending parties with people whose names are known throughout the Empire, and hobnobbing with His Imperial Majesty himself once in a while, to boot.

The year is nearing its end, now. The weather has changed, just as Lucilla said it would: the days are darker and of course shorter, the air is cool, rain is frequent. I haven't brought much of a winter wardrobe with me, and Lucilla's younger brother, a handsome fellow named Aquila, takes me to his tailor to get me outfitted for the new season. The latest Roman fashions seem strange, even uncouth, to me: but what do I know of Roman fashion? I take Aquila's praise of my new clothes at face value, and the tailor's and Lucilla's also, and hope they're not all simply having sport with me.

The invitation that Flavius Rufus Caesar extended to Lucilla and me that first night—to spend the Saturnalia at the Imperial villa at Tibur—was, I discover, a genuine one. By the time December arrives I have forgotten all about it; but Lucilla hasn't, and she tells me, one evening, that we are to leave for Praeneste in the morning. That is a place not far from Roma, where in ancient and medieval times an oracle held forth in the Cave of Destiny until Trajan VII put an end to her privileges. We will stay there for a week or so at the estate of a vastly rich Hispanic merchant named Scipio Lucullo, and then go onward to nearby Tibur for the week of the Saturnalia itself.

Scipio Lucullo's country estate, even in these bleak days of early winter, is grand beyond my comprehension. The marble halls, the pools and fountains, the delicate outer pavilions, the animal chambers where lions and zebras and giraffes are kept, the collections of statuary and paintings and objects of art, the baths, everything is on an Imperial scale. But there is no Imperial heritage here. Lucullo's place was built, someone tells me, only five years ago, out of the profits of his gold mines in Nova Roma, ownership of which he attained by scandalous bribery of court officials during the disastrous final days of the reign of old Caesar Laureolus. His own guests, though they don't disdain his immense hospitality, regard his estate as tawdry and vulgar, I discover.

"I'd be happy to live in such tawdriness," I tell Lucilla. "Is that a terribly provincial thing to say?"

But she only laughs. "Wait until you see Tibur," she says.

And indeed I discover the difference between mere showiness and true magnificence when we move along to the famous Imperial villa just as the Saturnalia week is about to begin.

This is, of course, the place that the great Hadrianus built for his country pleasures seventeen centuries ago. In his own time it was, no doubt, a wonder of the world, with its porticos and fountains and reflecting pools, its baths both great and small, its libraries both Greek and Roman, its nymphaeum and triclinium, its temples to all the gods under whose spell Hadrianus fell as he traveled the length and breadth of the Roman world.

But that was seventeen centuries ago; and seventeen centuries of Emperors have added to this place, so that the original villa of Hadrianus, for all its splendor, is only a mere part of the whole, and the totality must surely be the greatest palace in the world, a residence worthy of Jupiter or Apollo. "You can ride all day and not see the whole thing," Lucilla says to me. "They don't keep it all open at once, of course. We'll be staying in the oldest wing, what they still call Hadrianus's Villa. But all around us you'll see the parts that Trajan VII added, and Flavius Romulus, and the Khitai Pavilions that Lucius Agrippa built for the little yellow-skinned concubine that he brought back from Asia Ultima. And if there's time—oh, but there won't be time, will there—?"

"Why not?" I ask.

She evades my glance. It is my first clue to what is to come.

All day long the great ones of Roma arrive at the Imperial villa for Flavius Rufus's Saturnalia festival. By now I don't need to have their names whispered to me. I recognize Atticus the shipping tycoon, and Count Nero Romulus, and Marco Tullio Garofalo, who is the president of the Bank of the Imperium, and Diodorus the gladiator, and the Consul Bassanius, and pudgy, petulant Prince Camillus, and dozens more. Carriages are lined up along the highway, waiting to disgorge their glittering passengers.

One who does not arrive is Gaius Junius Scaevola. It's unthinkable that he hasn't been invited; I conclude therefore that my guess about his being named Consul once more for the coming year is correct, and that he has remained in Roma to prepare for taking office. I ask Lucilla if that's indeed why her uncle isn't here, and she says, simply, "The holiday season is always a busy time for him. He wasn't able to get away."

He *is* going to be Consul once again! I'm sure of it.

But I'm wrong. The day after our arrival I glance at the morning newspaper, and there are the names of the Consuls for the coming year. His Imperial Majesty has been pleased to designate Publius Lucius Gallienus and Gaius Acacius Aufidius as Consuls of the Realm. They will be sworn into office at noon on the first of Januarius, weather permitting, on the steps of the Capitol building.

Not Scaevola, then. It must be important business of some other kind, then, that keeps him from leaving Roma in the closing days of the year.

And who are these Consuls, Gallienus and Aufidius? For both, it will be their first term in that highest of governmental offices next to that of the Emperor.

"Boyhood friends of Maxentius," someone tells me, with a dismissive sniff. "Schoolmates of his."

And someone else says, "Not only don't we have a real Emperor any more, we aren't even going to have Consuls now. Just a bunch of lazy children pretending to run the government."

That seems very close to treasonous, to me—especially considering that this very villa is an Imperial palace, and we are all here as guests of the Emperor's brother. But these patricians, I have been noticing, are extraordinarily free in their criticisms of the royal family, even while accepting their hospitality.

Which is abundant. There is feasting and theatricals every night, and during the day we are free to avail ourselves of the extensive facilities of the villa, the heated pools, the baths, the libraries, the gambling pavilions, the riding paths. I float dreamily through it all as though I have stumbled into a fairy-tale world, which is indeed precisely what it is.

At the party the third night I finally find the courage to make a mild approach to Severina Floriana. Lucilla has said that she would like to spend the next day resting, since some of the biggest events of the week still lie ahead; and so I invite Severina Floriana to go riding with me after breakfast tomorrow. Once the two of us are alone, off in some remote corner of the property, perhaps I will dare to suggest some more intimate kind of encounter. Perhaps. What I am attempting to arrange, after all, is a dalliance with the Emperor's sister. Which is such an extraordinary idea that I can scarcely believe I am engaged in such a thing.

She looks amused and, I think, tempted by the suggestion.

But then she tells me that she won't be here tomorrow. Something has come up, she says, something trifling but nevertheless requiring her immediate attention, and she must return briefly to Urbs Roma in the morning.

"You'll be coming back here, won't you?" I ask anxiously.

"Oh, yes, of course. I'll be gone a day or two at most. I'll be here for the big party the final night, you can be sure of that!" She gives me a quick impish glance, as though to promise me some special delight for that evening, by way of consolation for this refusal now. And reaches out to touch my hand a moment. A spark as though of electricity passes from her to me. It is all that ever will; I have never forgotten it.

Lucilla remains in our suite the next day, leaving me to roam the villa's grounds alone. I lounge in the baths, I swim, I inspect the galleries of paintings and sculpture, I drift into the gambling pavilion and lose a few solidi at cards to a couple of languid lordlings.

I notice an odd thing that day. I see none of the people I had previously met at the parties of the Palatine Hill set in Roma. Count Nero Romulus, Leontes Atticus, Prince Flavius Rufus, Prince Camillus, Bassanius, Diodorus—not one of them seems to be around. The place is full of strangers today.

And without Lucilla by my side as I make my increasingly uneasy way among these unknowns, I feel even more of an outsider here than I really am: since I wear no badge proclaiming me to be the guest of Junius Scaevola's niece, I become in her absence merely a barely civilized outlander who has somehow wangled his way into the villa and is trying with only fair success to pretend to be a well-bred Roman. I imagine that they are laughing at me behind my back, mocking my style of dress, imitating my British accent.

Nor is Lucilla much comfort when I return to our rooms. She is distant, abstracted, moody. She asks me only the most perfunctory questions about how I have spent my day, and then sinks back into lethargy and brooding.

"Are you not feeling well?" I ask her.

"It's nothing serious, Cymbelin."

"Have *I* done something to annoy you?"

"Not at all. It's just a passing thing," she says. "These dark winter days—"

But today hasn't been dark at all. Cool, yes, but the sun has been a thing of glory all day, illuminating the December sky with a bright radiance that makes my British heart ache. Nor is it the bad time of month for her; so I am mystified by Lucilla's gloomy remoteness. I can see that no probing of mine will produce a useful answer, though. I'll just have to wait for her mood to change.

At the party that night she is no more ebullient than before. She floats about like a wraith, indifferently greeting people who seem scarcely more familiar to her than they are to me.

"I wonder where everyone is," I say. "Severina told me she had to go back to Roma to take care of something today. But where's Prince Camillus? Count Nero Romulus? Have they gone back to Roma, too? And Prince Flavius Rufus—he doesn't seem to be at his own party."

Lucilla shrugs. "Oh, they must be here and there, somewhere around. Take me back to the room, will you, Cymbelin? I'm not feeling at all partyish, tonight. There's a good fellow. I'm sorry to be spoiling the fun like this."

"Won't you tell me what's wrong, Lucilla?"

"Nothing. *Nothing.* I just feel—I don't know, a little tired. Low-spirited, maybe. Please. I want to go back to the room."

She undresses and gets into bed. Facing that party full of strangers without her is too daunting for me, and so I get into bed beside her. I realize, after a moment, that she's quietly sobbing.

"Hold me, Cymbelin," she murmurs.

I take her into my arms. Her closeness, her nakedness, arouse me as always, and I tentatively begin to make love to her, but she asks me to stop. So we lie there, trying to fall asleep at this strangely early hour, while distant sounds of laughter and music drift toward us through the frosty night air.

The next day things are worse. She doesn't want to leave our suite at all. But she tells me to go out without her: makes it quite clear, in fact, that she wants to be alone.

What a strange Saturnalia week this is turning into! How little jollity there is, how much unexplained tension!

But explanations will be coming, soon enough.

At midday, after a dispiriting stroll through the grounds, I return to the room to see whether Lucilla has taken a turn for the better.

Lucilla is gone.

There's no trace of her. Her closets are empty. She has packed and vanished, without a word to me, without any sort of warning, leaving no message for me, not the slightest clue. I am on my own in the Imperial villa, among strangers.

Things are happening in the capital this day, immense events, a convulsion of the most colossal kind. Of which we who remain at the Imperial villa will remain ignorant all day, though the world has been utterly transformed while we innocently swim and gamble and stroll about the grounds of this most lavish of all Imperial residences.

It had, in fact, begun to happen a couple of days before, when certain of the guests at the villa separately and individually left Tibur and returned to the capital, even though Saturnalia was still going on and the climactic parties had not yet taken place. One by one they had gone back to Roma, not only Severina Floriana but others as well, all those whose absences I had noticed.

What pretexts were used to lure Prince Flavius Rufus, Prince Camillus, and their sister Princess Severina away from the villa may never be known. The two newly appointed Consuls, I was told, had received messages in the Emperor's hand, summoning them to a meeting at which they would be granted certain high privileges and benefits of their new rank. The outgoing Consul, Bassanius, still was carrying a note ostensibly from the Praetorian Prefect, Actinius Varro, when his body was found, telling him that a conspiracy against the Emperor's life had been detected and that his presence in Roma was urgently required. The note was a forgery. So it went, one lie or another serving to pry the lordlings and princelings of the Empire away from the pleasures of the Saturnalia at Tibur, just for a single day.

Certain other party guests who returned to Roma, that day and the next, hadn't needed to be lured. They understood perfectly well what was about to happen and intended to be present at the scene during the events. That group included Count Nero Romulus; Atticus, the shipowner; the banker Garofalo; the merchant from Hispania, Scipio Lucullo; Diodorus the gladiator; and half a dozen other patricians and men of wealth who were members of the conspiracy. For them the jaunt to Tibur had been a way of inducing a mood of complacency at the capital, for what was there to fear with so many of the most powerful figures of the realm off at the great pleasure dome for a week of delights? But then these key figures took care to return quickly and quietly to Roma when the time to strike had arrived.

On the fatal morning these things occurred, as all the world would shortly learn:

A squadron of Marcus Sempronius Diodorus's gladiators broke into the mansion of Praetorian Prefect Varro and slew him just before sunrise. The Praetorian Guard then was told that the Emperor had discovered that Varro was plotting against him, and had replaced him as prefect with Diodorus. This fiction was readily enough accepted; Varro had never been popular among his own men and the Praetorians are always willing to accept a change in leadership, since that usually means a distribution of bonuses to insure their loyalty to their new commander.

With the Praetorians neutralized, it was an easy matter for a team of gunmen to penetrate the palace where Emperor Maxentius was staying that night—the Vatican, it was, a palace on the far side of the river in the vicinity of the Mauseoleum of Hadrianus—and break into the royal apartments. The Emperor, his wife, and his children fled in wild panic through the hallways, but were caught and put to death just outside the Imperial baths.

Prince Camillus, who had reached the capital in the small hours of the night, had not yet gone to bed when the conspirators reached his palace on the Forum side of the Palatine. Hearing them slaughtering his guards, the poor fat fool fled through a cellar door and ran for his life toward the Temple of Castor and Pollux, where he hoped to find sanctuary; but his pursuers overtook him and cut him down on the steps of the temple.

As for Prince Flavius Rufus, he awakened to the sound of gunfire and reacted instantly, darting behind his palace to a winery that he kept there. His workmen were not yet done crushing the grapes of the autumn harvest. Jumping into a wooden cart, he ordered them to heap great bunches of grapes on top of him and to wheel him out of the city, concealed in that fashion. He actually succeeded in reaching Neapolis safely a couple of days later and proclaimed himself Emperor, but he was captured and killed soon after—with some help, I have heard, from Marcellus Domitianus Frontinus.

Two younger princes of the royal house still survived—Prince Augustus Caesar, who was sixteen and off in Parisi at the university, and Prince Quintus Fabius, a boy of ten, I think, who dwelled at one of the Imperial residences in Roma. Although Prince Augustus did live long enough to proclaim himself Emperor and actually set out across Gallia with the wild intention of marching on Roma, he was seized and shot in the third day of his reign. Those three days, I suppose, put this young and virtually unknown Augustus into history as the last of all the Emperors of Roma.

What happened to young Quintus Fabius, no one knows for sure. He was the only member of the Imperial family whose body never was found. Some say that he was spirited out of Roma on the day of the murders wearing peasant clothes and is still alive in some remote province. But he has never come forth to claim the throne, so if he is still alive to this day, he lives very quietly and secretively, wherever he may be.

All day long the killing went on. The assassination of Emperors was of course nothing new for Roma, but this time the job was done more thoroughly than ever before, an extirpation of root and branch.

Royal blood ran in rivers that day. Not only was the immediate family of the Caesars virtually wiped out, but most of the descendants of older Imperial families were executed, too, I suppose so that they wouldn't attempt to put themselves forward as Emperors now that the line of Laureolus was essentially extinct. A good many former Consuls, certain members of the priestly ranks, and others suspected of excessive loyalty to the old regime, including two or three dozen carefully selected Senators, met their deaths that day as well.

And at nightfall the new leaders of Roma gathered at the Capitol to proclaim the birth of the Second Republic. Gaius Junius Scaevola would hold the newly devised rank of First Consul for Life—that is to say, Emperor, but under another name—and he would govern the vast entity that we could no longer call the Empire through a Council of the Senate, by which he meant his little circle of wealthy and powerful friends, Atticus and Garofalo and Count Nero Romulus and General Cassius Frontinus and half a dozen others of that sort.

Thus, after nineteen hundred years, was the work of the great Augustus Caesar finally undone.

Augustus himself had pretended that Roma was still a Republic, even while gathering all the highest offices into a single bundle and taking possession of that bundle, thus making himself absolute monarch; and that pretense had lasted down through the ages. I am not a king, Augustus had insisted; I am merely the First Citizen of the realm, who humbly strives, under the guidance of the Senate, to serve the needs of the Roman people. And so it went for all those years, though somehow it became possible for many of the First Citizens to name their own sons as their successors, or else to select some kinsman or friend, even while the ostensible power to choose the Emperor was still in the hands of the Senate. But from now on it would be different. No one would be able to claim the supreme power in Roma merely because he was the son or nephew of someone who had held that power. No more crazy Caligulas, no more vile Neros, no more brutish Caracallas, no more absurd Demetriuses, no more weak and foppish Maxentiuses. Our ruler now would truly be a First Citizen—a Consul, as in the ancient days before the first Augustus—and the trappings of the monarchy would at last be abandoned.

All in a single day, a day of blood and fire. While I lounged in Tibur, at the villa of the Emperors, knowing nothing of what was taking place.

On the morning of the day after the revolution, word comes to the villa of what has occurred in Roma. As it happens, I have slept late that day, after having drunk myself into a stupor the night before to comfort myself for the absence of Lucilla; and the villa is virtually deserted by the time I rouse myself and emerge.

That alone is strange and disconcerting. Where has everyone gone? I find a butler, who tells me the news. Roma is in flames, he says, and the Emperor is dead along with all his family.

"*All* his family? His brothers and sisters too?"

"Brothers and sisters too. Everyone."

"The Princess Severina?"

The butler looks at me without sympathy. He is very calm; he might be speaking of the weather, or next week's chariot races. In the autumn warmth he is as chilly as a winter fog.

"The whole lot, is what I hear. Every last one, and good riddance to them. Scaevola's the new Emperor. Things will all be very different now, you can be sure of that."

All this dizzies me. I have to turn away and take seven or eight gasping breaths before I have my equilibrium again. Overnight our world has died and been born anew.

I bathe and dress and eat hurriedly, and arrange somehow for a carriage to take me to Roma. Even in this moment of flux and madness, a purse full of gold will get you what you want. There are no drivers, so I'll have to find my way on my own, but no matter. Insane though it may be to enter the capital on this day of chaos, Roma pulls me like a magnet. Lucilla must be all right, if her uncle has seized the throne; but I have to know the fate of Severina Floriana.

I see flames on the horizon when I am still an hour's ride from the city. Gusts of hot wind from the west bring me the scent of smoke: a fine dust of cinders seems to be falling, or am I imagining it? No. I extend my arm and watch a black coating begin to cover it.

It's supreme folly to go to the capital now.

Should I not turn away, bypass Roma and head for the coast, book passage to Britannia while it's still possible to escape? No. No. I must go there, whatever the risks. If Scaevola is Emperor, Lucilla will protect me. I will continue on to Roma, I decide. And I do.

The place is a madhouse. The sky streams with fire. On the great hills of the mighty, ancient palaces are burning; their charred marble walls topple like falling mountains. The colossal statue of some early Emperor lies strewn in fragments across the road. People run wildly in the streets, screaming, sobbing. Squads of wild-eyed soldiers rush about amongst them, shouting furiously and incoherently as they try to restore order without having any idea of whose orders to obey. I catch sight of a rivulet of crimson in the gutter and think for a terrible moment that it is blood; but no, no, it is only wine running out of a shattered wineshop, and men are falling on their faces to lap it from the cobblestones.

I abandon my chariot—the streets are too crazy to drive in—and set out on foot. The center of the city is compact enough. But where shall I go? I wonder. To the Palatine? No: everything's on fire up there. The Capitol? Scaevola will be there, I reason, and—how preposterous this sounds to me now—he can tell me where Lucilla is, and what has become of Severina Floriana.

Of course I get nowhere near the Capitol. The entire governmental district is sealed off by troops. Edicts are posted in the streets, and I pause to read one, and it is then I discover the full extent of the alteration that this night has worked: that the Empire is no more, the Republic of the ancient days has returned. Scaevola now rules, but has the title not of Emperor but of First Consul.

As I stand gaping and dazed in the street that runs past the Forum, I am nearly run down by a speeding chariot. I yell a curse at its driver; but then, to my great amazement, the chariot stops and a familiar ruddy face peers out at me.

"Cymbelin! Good gods, is that you? Get in, man! You can't stand around out there!"

It's my robust and jolly host from Neapolis, my father's friend, Marcellus Domitianus Frontinus. What bad luck for him, I think, that he's come visiting up here in Roma at a time like this. But I have it all wrong, as usual, and Marcellus Domitianus very quickly spells everything out for me.

He has been in on the plot from the beginning—he and his brother the general, along with Junius Scaevola and Count Nero Romulus, were in fact the ringleaders. It was necessary, they felt, to destroy the Empire in order to save it. The current Emperor was an idle fool, the previous one had been allowed to stay on the throne too long, the whole idea of a quasi-hereditary monarchy had been proved to be a disaster over and over again for centuries, and now was the time to get rid of it once and for all. There was new restlessness in all the provinces and renewed talk of secession. Having just fought and won a Second War of Reunification, General Cassius Frontinus had no desire to launch immediately into a third one, and he had without much difficulty convinced his brother and Scaevola that the Caesars must go. Must in fact be put where they would never have the opportunity of reclaiming the throne.

Ruthless and bloody, yes. But better to scrap the incompetent and profligate royal family, better to toss out the empty, costly pomp of Imperial grandeur, better to bring back, at long last, the Republic. Once again there would be government by merit rather than by reason of birth. Scaevola was respected everywhere; he would know the right things to do to hold things together.

"But to *kill* them—to murder a whole family—!"

"A clean sweep, that's what we needed," Frontinus tells me. "A total break with the past. We can't have hereditary monarchs in this modern age."

"All the princes and princesses are dead too, then?"

"So I hear. One or two may actually have gotten away, but they'll be caught soon enough, you can be sure of that."

"The Princess Severina Floriana?"

"Can't say," Frontinus replies. "Why? Did you know her?"

Color floods to my cheeks. "Not very well, actually. But I couldn't help wondering—"

"Lucilla will be able to tell you what happened to her. She and the princess were very close friends. You can ask her yourself."

"I don't know where Lucilla is. We were at Tibur together this

week, at the Imperial villa, and then—when everything started
happening—"

"Why, you'll be seeing Lucilla five minutes from now! She's at
the palace of Count Nero Romulus—you know who he is, don't
you?—and that's exactly where we're heading."

I point toward the Palatine, shrouded in flames and black gusts
of smoke behind us.

"Up there?"

Frontinus laughs. "Don't be silly. Everything's destroyed on the
Palatine. I mean his palace by the river." We are already past the Forum area. I can see the somber bulk of Hadrianus's Mausoleum
ahead of us, across the river. We halt just on this side of the bridge.
"Here we are," says Frontinus.

I get to see her one last time, then, once we have made our way
through the lunatic frenzy of the streets to the security of Nero
Romulus's well-guarded riverfront palace. I hardly recognize her.
Lucilla wears no makeup and her clothing is stark and simple—
peasant clothing. Her eyes are somber and red-rimmed. Many of
her patrician friends have died this night for the sake of the rebirth
of Roma.

"So now you know," she says to me. "Of course I couldn't tell
you a thing about what was being planned."

It is hard for me to believe that this woman and I were lovers for
months, that I am intimately familiar with every inch of her body.
Her voice is cool and impersonal, and she has neither kissed me nor
smiled at me.

"You knew—all along—what was going to happen?"

"Of course. From the start. At least I got you out of town to a
safe place while it was going on."

"You got Severina to a safe place, too. But you couldn't keep her
there, it seems."

Her eyes flare with rage, but I see the pain there, too.

"I tried to save her. It wasn't possible. They all had to die,
Cymbelin."

"Your own childhood friend. And you didn't even try to warn her."

"We're *Romans,* Cymbelin. It had become necessary to restore the Republic. The royal family had to die."

"Even the women?"

"All of them. Don't you think I asked? Begged? No, said Nero Romulus. She's got to die with them. There's no choice, he said. I went to my uncle. You don't know how I fought with him. But nobody can sway his will, nobody at all. No, he said. There's no way to save her." Lucilla makes a quick harsh motion with her hand. "I don't want to talk about this any more. Go away, Cymbelin. I don't even understand why Marcello brought you here."

"I was wandering around in the street, not knowing where to go to find you."

"Me? Why would you want to find me?"

It's like a blow in the ribs. "Because—because—" I falter and fall still.

"You were a very amusing companion," she says. "But the time for amusements is over."

"Amusements!"

Her face is like stone. "Go, Cymbelin. Get yourself back to Britannia, as soon as you can. The bloodshed isn't finished here. The First Consul doesn't yet know who's loyal and who isn't."

"Another Reign of Terror, then?"

"We hope not. But it won't be pretty, all the same. Still, the First Consul wants the Second Republic to get off to the most peaceful possible—"

"The First Consul," I say, with anger in my voice. "The Second Republic."

"You don't like those words?"

"To kill the Emperor—"

"It's happened before, more times than you can count. This time we've killed the whole system. And will replace it at long last with something cleaner and healthier."

"Maybe so."

"Go, Cymbelin. We are very busy now."

And she turns away and leaves the room, as though I am nothing to her, only an inquisitive and annoying stranger. It is all too clear to me now that she had regarded me all along as a mere casual plaything, an amusing barbarian to keep by her side during the autumn season; and now it is winter and she must devote herself to more serious things.

And so I went. The last Emperor had perished and the Republic had come again, and I had slept amidst the luxurious comforts of the Imperial villa while it all was happening. But it has always been that way, hasn't it? While most of us sleep, an agile few create history in the night.

Now all was made new and strange. The world I had known had been entirely transformed in ways that might not be fully apparent for years—the events of these recent hours would be a matter for historians to examine and debate and assess, long after I had grown old and died—nor would the chaos at the center of the Empire end in a single day, and provincial boys like me were well advised to take themselves back where they belonged.

I no longer had any place here in Roma, anyway. Lucilla was lost to me—she will marry Count Nero Romulus to seal his alliance with her uncle—and whatever dizzying fantasies I might have entertained concerning the Princess Severina Floriana were best forgotten now, or the ache would never leave my soul. All that was done and behind me. The holiday was over. There would be no further tourism for me this year, no ventures into Etruria and Venetia and the other northern regions of Italia. I knew I must leave Roma to the Romans and beat a retreat back to my distant rainy island in the west, having come all too close to the flames that had consumed the Roma of the Emperors, having in fact been somewhat singed by them myself.

Except for the help that Frontinus provided, I suppose I might have had a hard time of it. But he gave me a safe-conduct pass to get me out of the capital, and lent me a chariot and a charioteer; and on the morning of the second day of the Second Republic I found myself on the Via Appia once more, heading south. Ahead of me lay the Via Roma and Neapolis and a ship to take me home.

I looked back only once. Behind me the sky was smudged with black clouds as the fires on the Palatine Hill burned themselves out.

A.U.C. 2650: TALES FROM THE VENIA WOODS

his all happened a long time ago, in the early decades of the Second Republic, when I was a boy growing up in Upper Pannonia. Life was very simple then, at least for us. We lived in a forest village on the right bank of the Danubius—my parents; my grandmother; my sister, Friya; and I. My father, Tyr, for whom I am named, was a blacksmith, my mother, Julia, taught school in our house, and my grandmother was the priestess at the little Temple of Juno Teutonica nearby.

It was a very quiet life. The automobile hadn't yet been invented then—all this was around the year 2650, and we still used horse-drawn carriages or wagons—and we hardly ever left the village. Once a year, on Augustus Day—back then we still celebrated Augustus Day—we would all dress in our finest clothes and my father would get our big iron-bound carriage out of the shed, the one he had built with his own hands, and we'd drive to the great municipium of Venia, a two-hour journey away, to hear the Imperial band playing waltzes in the Plaza of Vespasianus. Afterward there'd be cakes and whipped cream at the big hotel nearby, and tankards of cherry beer for the grown-ups, and then we'd begin the long trip home. Today, of course, the forest is gone and our little village has been swallowed up by the ever-growing municipium, and it's a twenty-minute ride by car to the center of the city from where we used to live. But at that time it was a grand excursion, the event of the year for us.

I know now that Venia is only a minor provincial city, that compared with Londin or Parisi or Urbs Roma itself it's nothing at all. But to me it was the capital of the world. Its splendors stunned me and dazed me. We would climb to the top of the great column of Basileus Andronicus, which the Greeks put up eight hundred years ago to commemorate their victory over Caesar Maximilianus during the Civil War in the days when the Empire was divided, and we'd stare out at the whole city; and my mother, who had grown up in Venia, would point everything out to us, the Senate building, the opera house, the aqueduct, the university, the ten bridges, the Temple of Jupiter Teutonicus, the proconsul's palace, the much greater palace that Trajan VII built for himself during that dizzying period when Venia was essentially the second capital of the Empire, and so forth. For days afterward my dreams would glitter with memories of what I had seen in Venia, and my sister and I would hum waltzes as we whirled along the quiet forest paths.

There was one exciting year when we made the Venia trip twice. That was 2647, when I was ten years old, and I can remember it so exactly because that was the year when the First Consul died—C. Junius Scaevola, I mean, the Founder of the Second Republic. My father was very agitated when the news of his death came. "It'll be touch and go now, touch and go, mark my words," he said over and over. I asked my grandmother what he meant by that, and she said, "Your father's afraid that they'll bring back the Empire, now that the old man's dead." I didn't see what was so upsetting about that—it was all the same to me, Republic or Empire, Consul or Imperator—but to my father it was a big issue, and when the new First Consul came to Venia later that year, touring the entire vast Imperium province by province for the sake of reassuring everyone that the Republic was stable and intact, my father got out the carriage and we went to attend his Triumph and Processional. So I had a second visit to the capital that year.

Half a million people, so they say, turned out in downtown Venia to applaud the new First Consul. This was N. Marcellus Turritus, of course. You probably think of him as the fat, bald old man on the coinage of the late twenty-seventh century that still shows up in pocket change now and then, but the man I saw that day—I had just a glimpse of him, a fraction of a second as the Consular chariot rode past, but the memory still blazes in my mind seventy years later— was lean and virile, with a jutting jaw and fiery eyes and dark, thick curling hair. We threw up our arms in the old Roman salute and at the top of our lungs we shouted out to him, "Hail, Marcellus! Long live the Consul!"

(We shouted it, by the way, not in Latin but in Germanisch. I was very surprised at that. My father explained afterward that it was by the First Consul's own orders. He wanted to show his love for the people by encouraging all the regional languages, even at a public celebration like this one. The Gallians had hailed him in Gallian, the Britannians in Britannic, the Lusitanians in whatever it is they speak there, and as he traveled through the Teutonic provinces he wanted us to yell his praises in Germanisch. I realize that there are some people today, very conservative Republicans, who will tell you that this was a terrible idea, because it has led to the resurgence of all kinds of separatist regional activities in the Imperium. It was the same sort of regionalist fervor, they remind us, that brought about the crumbling of the Empire a hundred years before. To men like my father, though, it was a brilliant political stroke, and he cheered the new First Consul with tremendous Germanische exuberance and vigor. But my father managed to be a staunch regionalist and a staunch Republican at the same time. Bear in mind that over my mother's fierce objections he had insisted on naming his children for ancient Teutonic gods instead of giving them the standard Roman names that everybody else in Pannonia favored then.)

Other than going to Venia once a year, or on this one occasion twice, I never went anywhere. I hunted, I fished, I swam, I helped my father in the smithy, I helped my grandmother in the Temple, I studied reading and writing in my mother's school. Sometimes Friya and I would go wandering in the forest, which in those days was dark and lush and mysterious. And that was how I happened to meet the last of the Caesars.

* * *

There was supposed to be a haunted house deep in the woods. Marcus Aurelius Schwarzchild it was who got me interested in it, the tailor's son, a sly and unlikable boy with a cast in one eye. He said it had been a hunting lodge in the time of the Caesars, and that the bloody ghost of an Emperor who had been killed in a hunting accident could be seen at noontime, the hour of his death, pursuing the ghost of a wolf around and around the building. "I've seen it myself," he said. "The ghost of the Emperor, I mean. He had a laurel wreath on, and everything, and his rifle was polished so it shined like gold."

I didn't believe him. I didn't think he'd had the courage to go anywhere near the haunted house and certainly not that he'd seen the ghost. Marcus Aurelius Schwarzchild was the sort of boy you wouldn't believe if he said it was raining, even if you were getting soaked to the skin right as he was saying it. For one thing, I didn't believe in ghosts, not very much. My father had told me it was foolish to think that the dead still lurked around in the world of the living. For another, I asked my grandmother if there had ever been an Emperor killed in a hunting accident in our forest, and she laughed and said no, not ever: the Imperial Guard would have razed the village to the ground and burned down the woods, if that had ever happened.

But nobody doubted that the house itself, haunted or not, was really there. Everyone in the village knew that. It was said to be in a certain dark part of the woods where the trees were so old that their branches were tightly woven together. Hardly anyone ever went there. The house was just a ruin, they said, and haunted besides, definitely haunted, so it was best to leave it alone.

It occurred to me that the place might just actually have been an Imperial hunting lodge, and that if it had been abandoned hastily after some unhappy incident and never visited since, it might still have some trinkets of the Caesars in it, little statuettes of the gods, or cameos of the royal family, things like that. My grandmother collected small ancient objects of that sort. Her birthday was coming, and I wanted a nice gift for her. My fellow villagers might be timid

about poking around in the haunted house, but why should I be? I
didn't believe in ghosts, after all.

But on second thought I didn't particularly want to go there
alone. This wasn't cowardice so much as sheer common sense,
which even then I possessed in full measure. The woods were full
of exposed roots hidden under fallen leaves; if you tripped on one
and hurt your leg, you would lie there a long time before anyone
who might help you came by. You were also less likely to lose your
way if you had someone else with you who could remember trail
marks. And there was some occasional talk of wolves. I figured the
probability of my meeting one wasn't much better than the likelihood of ghosts, but all the same it seemed like a sensible idea to
have a companion with me in that part of the forest. So I took my
sister along.

I have to confess that I didn't tell her that the house was supposed to be haunted. Friya, who was about nine then, was very
brave for a girl, but I thought she might find the possibility of ghosts
a little discouraging. What I did tell her was that the old house might
still have Imperial treasures in it, and if it did she could have her
pick of any jewelry we found.

Just to be on the safe side we slipped a couple of holy images
into our pockets—Apollo for her, to cast light on us as we went
through the dark woods, and Woden for me, since he was my father's special god. (My grandmother always wanted him to pray to
Jupiter Teutonicus, but he never would, saying that Jupiter Teutonicus was a god that the Romans invented to pacify our ancestors. This
made my grandmother angry, naturally. "But we are Romans," she
would say. "Yes, we are," my father would tell her, "but we're Teutons also, or at least I am, and I don't intend to forget it.")

It was a fine Saturday morning in spring when we set out, Friya
and I, right after breakfast, saying nothing to anybody about where
we were going. The first part of the forest path was a familiar one:
we had traveled it often. We went past Agrippina's Spring, which in
medieval times was thought to have magical powers, and then the
three battered and weatherbeaten statues of the pretty young boy
who was supposed to be the first Emperor Hadrianus's lover two
thousand years ago, and after that we came to Baldur's Tree, which

my father said was sacred, though he died before I was old enough to attend the midnight rituals that he and some of his friends used to hold there. (I think my father's generation was the last one that took the old Teutonic religion seriously.)

Then we got into deeper, darker territory. The paths were nothing more than sketchy trails here. Marcus Aurelius had told me that we were supposed to turn left at a huge old oak tree with unusual glossy leaves. I was still looking for it when Friya said, "We turn here," and there was the shiny-leaved oak. I hadn't mentioned it to her. So perhaps the girls of our village told each other tales about the haunted house too; but I never found out how she knew which way to go.

Onward and onward we went, until even the trails gave out, and we were wandering through sheer wilderness. The trees were ancient here, all right, and their boughs were interlaced high above us so that almost no sunlight reached the forest floor. But we didn't see any houses, haunted or otherwise, or anything else that indicated that human beings had ever been here. We'd been hiking for hours, now. I kept one hand on the idol of Woden in my pocket and I stared hard at every unusual-looking tree or rock we saw, trying to engrave it on my brain for use as a trail marker on the way back.

It seemed pointless to continue, and dangerous besides. I would have turned back long before, if Friya hadn't been with me; but I didn't want to look like a coward in front of her. And she was forging on in a tireless way, inflamed, I guess, by the prospect of finding a fine brooch or necklace for herself in the old house, and showing not the slightest trace of fear or uneasiness. But finally I had had enough.

"If we don't come across anything in the next five minutes—" I said.

"There," said Friya. "Look."

I followed her pointing hand. At first all I saw was more forest. But then I noticed, barely visible behind a curtain of leafy branches, what could have been the sloping wooden roof of a rustic hunting lodge. Yes! Yes, it was! I saw the scalloped gables, I saw the boldly carved roof-posts.

So it was really there, the secret forest lodge, the old haunted

house. In frantic excitement I began to run toward it, Friya chug-
ging valiantly along behind me, struggling to catch up.

And then I saw the ghost.

He was old—ancient—a frail, gaunt figure, white-bearded, his
long white hair a tangle of knots and snarls. His clothing hung in
rags. He was walking slowly toward the house, shuffling, really, a
bent and stooped and trembling figure clutching a huge stack of kin-
dling to his breast. I was practically on top of him before I knew he
was there.

For a long moment we stared at each other, and I can't say which
of us was the more terrified. Then he made a little sighing sound and
let his bundle of firewood fall to the ground, and fell down beside it,
and lay there like one dead.

"Marcus Aurelius was right!" I murmured. "There really is a
ghost here!"

Friya shot me a glance that must have been a mixture of scorn
and derision and real anger besides, for this was the first she had
heard of the ghost story that I had obviously taken pains to conceal
from her. But all she said was, "Ghosts don't fall down and faint, silly.
He's nothing but a scared old man." And went to him unhesitatingly.

Somehow we got him inside the house, though he tottered and
lurched all the way and nearly fell half a dozen times. The place
wasn't quite a ruin, but close: dust everywhere, furniture that looked
as if it'd collapse into splinters if you touched it, draperies hanging
in shreds. Behind all the filth we could see how beautiful it all once
had been, though. There were faded paintings on the walls, some
sculptures, a collection of arms and armor worth a fortune.

He was terrified of us. "Are you from the quaestors?" he kept
asking. Latin was what he spoke. "Are you here to arrest me? I'm
only the caretaker, you know. I'm not any kind of a danger. I'm only
the caretaker." His lips quavered. "Long live the First Consul!" he
cried, in a thin, hoarse, ragged croak of a voice.

"We were just wandering in the woods," I told him. "You don't
have to be afraid of us."

"I'm only the caretaker," he said again and again.

We laid him out on a couch. There was a spring just outside the house, and Friya brought water from it and sponged his cheeks and brow. He looked half starved, so we prowled around for something to feed him, but there was hardly anything: some nuts and berries in a bowl, a few scraps of smoked meat that looked like they were a hundred years old, a piece of fish that was in better shape, but not much. We fixed a meal for him, and he ate slowly, very slowly, as if he were unused to food. Then he closed his eyes without a word. I thought for a moment that he had died, but no, no, he had simply dozed off. We stared at each other, not knowing what to do.

"Let him be," Friya whispered, and we wandered around the house while we waited for him to awaken. Cautiously we touched the sculptures, we blew dust away from the paintings. No doubt of it, there had been Imperial grandeur here. In one of the upstairs cupboards I found some coins, old ones, the kind with the Emperor's head on them that weren't allowed to be used any more. I saw trinkets, too, a couple of necklaces and a jewel-handled dagger. Friya's eyes gleamed at the sight of the necklaces, and mine at the dagger, but we let everything stay where it was. Stealing from a ghost is one thing, stealing from a live old man is another. And we hadn't been raised to be thieves.

When we went back downstairs to see how he was doing, we found him sitting up, looking weak and dazed, but not quite so frightened. Friya offered him some more of the smoked meat, but he smiled and shook his head.

"From the village, are you? How old are you? What are your names?"

"This is Friya," I said. "I'm Tyr. She's nine and I'm twelve."

"Friya. Tyr." He laughed. "Time was when such names wouldn't have been permitted, eh? But times have changed." There was a flash of sudden vitality in his eyes, though only for an instant. He gave us a confidential, intimate smile. "Do you know whose place this was, you two? The Emperor Maxentius, that's who! This was his hunting lodge. Caesar himself! He'd stay here when the stags were running, and hunt his fill, and then he'd go on into Venia, to Trajan's

palace, and there'd be such feasts as you can't imagine, rivers of
wine, and the haunches of venison turning on the spit—ah, what a
time that was, what a time!"

He began to cough and sputter. Friya put her arm around his
thin shoulders.

"You shouldn't talk so much, sir. You don't have the strength."

"You're right. You're right." He patted her hand. His was like a
skeleton's. "How long ago it all was. But here I stay, trying to keep
the place up—in case Caesar ever wanted to hunt here again—in
case—in case—" A look of torment, of sorrow. "There isn't any Caesar, is there? First Consul! Hail! Hail Junius Scaevola!" His voice
cracked as he raised it.

"The Consul Junius is dead, sir," I told him. "Marcellus Turritus
is First Consul now."

"Dead? Scaevola? Is it so?" He shrugged. "I hear so little news.
I'm only the caretaker, you know. I never leave the place. Keeping it
up, in case—in case—"

But of course he wasn't the caretaker. Friya never thought he was: she
had seen, right away, the resemblance between that shriveled old man
and the magnificent figure of Caesar Maxentius in the painting behind him on the wall. You had to ignore the difference in age—the
Emperor couldn't have been much more than thirty when his portrait
was painted—and the fact that the Emperor was in resplendent be-
medalled formal uniform and the old man was wearing rags. But they
had the same long chin, the same sharp, hawklike nose, the same penetrating icy-blue eyes. It was the royal face, all right. I hadn't noticed;
but girls have a quicker eye for such things. The Emperor Maxentius's
youngest brother was who this gaunt old man was, Quintus Fabius
Caesar, the last survivor of the old Imperial house, and, therefore, the
true Emperor himself. Who had been living in hiding ever since the
downfall of the Empire at the end of the Second War of Reunification.

He didn't tell us any of that, though, until our third or fourth
visit. He went on pretending he was nothing but a simple old man
who had happened to be stranded here when the old regime was
overthrown, and was simply trying to do his job, despite the difficul-

ties of age, on the chance that the royal family might some day be re-stored and would want to use its hunting lodge again.

But he began to give us little gifts, and that eventually led to his admitting his true identity.

For Friya he had a delicate necklace made of long slender bluish beads. "It comes from Aegyptus," he said. "It's thousands of years old. You've studied Aegyptus in school, haven't you? You know that it was a great empire long before Roma ever was?" And with his own trembling hands he put it around her neck.

That same day he gave me a leather pouch in which I found four or five triangular arrowheads made of a pink stone that had been carefully chipped sharp around the edges. I looked at them, mysti-fied. "From Nova Roma," he explained. "Where the redskinned people live. The Emperor Maxentius loved Nova Roma, especially the far west, where the bison herds are. He went there almost every year to hunt. Do you see the trophies?" And, indeed, the dark musty room was lined with animal heads, great massive bison with thick curling brown wool, glowering down out of the gallery high above.

We brought him food, sausages and black bread that we brought from home, and fresh fruit, and beer. He didn't care for the beer and asked rather timidly if we could bring him wine in-stead. "I am Roman, you know," he reminded us. Getting wine for him wasn't so easy, since we never used it at home, and a twelve-year-old boy could hardly go around to the wineshop to buy some without starting tongues wagging. In the end I stole some from the Temple while I was helping out my grandmother. It was thick sweet wine, the kind used for offerings, and I don't know how much he liked it. But he was grateful. Apparently an old couple who lived on the far side of the woods had looked after him for some years, bring-ing him food and wine, but in recent weeks they hadn't been around and he had had to forage for himself, with little luck: that was why he was so gaunt. He was afraid they were ill or dead, but when I asked where they lived, so I could find out whether they were all right, he grew uneasy and refused to tell me. I wondered about that. If I had realized then who he was, and that the old couple must have been Empire loyalists, I'd have understood. But I still hadn't figured out the truth.

Friya broke it to me that afternoon, as we were on our way home. "Do you think he's the Emperor's brother, Tyr? Or the Emperor himself?"

"What?"

"He's got to be one or the other. It's the same face."

"I don't know what you're talking about, sister."

"The big portrait on the wall, silly. Of the Emperor. Haven't you noticed that it looks just like him?"

I thought she was out of her mind. But when we went back the following week, I gave the painting a long close look, and looked at him, and then at the painting again, and I thought, yes, yes, it might just be so.

What clinched it were the coins he gave us that day. "I can't pay you in money of the Republic for all you've brought me," he said. "But you can have these. You won't be able to spend them, but they're still valuable to some people, I understand. As relics of history." His voice was bitter. From a worn old velvet pouch he drew out half a dozen coins, some copper, some silver. "These are coins of Maxentius," he said. They were like the ones we had seen while snooping in the upstairs cupboards on our first visit, showing the same face as on the painting, that of a young, vigorous bearded man. "And these are older ones, coins of Emperor Laureolus, who was Caesar when I was a boy."

"Why, he looks just like you!" I blurted.

Indeed he did. Not nearly so gaunt, and his hair and beard were better trimmed; but otherwise the face of the regal old man on those coins might easily have been that of our friend the caretaker. I stared at him, and at the coins in my hand, and again at him. He began to tremble. I looked at the painting on the wall behind us again. "No," he said faintly. "No, no, you're mistaken—I'm nothing like him, nothing at all—" And his shoulders shook and he began to cry. Friya brought him some wine, which steadied him a little. He took the coins from me and looked at them in silence a long while, shaking his head sadly, and finally handed them back. "Can I trust you with a secret?" he asked. And his tale came pouring out of him. The truth. The truth that he had held locked up in his bosom all those long years.

He spoke of a glittering boyhood, almost sixty years earlier, in that wondrous time between the two Wars of Reunification: a magical life, endlessly traveling from palace to palace, from Roma to Venia, from Venia to Constantinopolis, from Constantinopolis to Nishapur. He was the youngest and most pampered of five royal princes; his father had died young, drowned in a foolish swimming exploit, and when his grandfather Laureolus Augustus died the Imperial throne would go to his brother Maxentius. He himself, Quintus Fabius, would be a provincial governor somewhere when he grew up, perhaps in Syria or Persia, but for now there was nothing for him to do but enjoy his gilded existence.

Then death came at last to old Emperor Laureolus, and Maxentius succeeded him; and almost at once there began the four-year horror of the Second War of Reunification, when somber and harsh colonels who despised the lazy old Empire smashed it to pieces, rebuilt it as a Republic, and drove the Caesars from power. We knew the story, of course; but to us it was a tale of the triumph of virtue and honor over corruption and tyranny. To Quintus Fabius, weeping as he told it to us from his own point of view, the fall of the Empire had been not only a harrowing personal tragedy but a terrible disaster for the entire world.

Good little Republicans though we were, our hearts were wrung by the things he told us, the scenes of his family's agony: the young Emperor Maxentius trapped in his own palace, gunned down with his wife and children at the entrance to the Imperial baths. Camillus, the second brother, who had been Prince of Constantinopolis, pursued through the streets of Roma at dawn and slaughtered by revolutionaries on the steps of the Temple of Castor and Pollux. Prince Flavius, the third brother, escaping from the capital in a peasant's wagon, hidden under huge bunches of grapes, and setting up a government-in-exile in Neapolis, only to be taken and executed before he had been Emperor a full week. Which brought the succession down to sixteen-year-old Prince Augustus, who had been at the university in Parisi. Well named, he was: for the first of all the Emperors was an Augustus, and another one two thousand years later was the last, reigning all of three days before the men of the Second Republic found him and put him before the firing squad.

Of the royal princes, only Quintus Fabius remained. But in the confusion he was overlooked. He was hardly more than a boy; and, although technically he was now Caesar, it never occurred to him to claim the throne. Loyalist supporters dressed him in peasant clothes and smuggled him out of Roma while the capital was still in flames, and he set out on what was to become a lifetime of exile.

"There were always places for me to stay," he told us. "In out-of-the-way towns where the Republic had never really taken hold, in backwater provinces, in places you've never heard of. The Republic searched for me for a time, but never very well, and then the story began to circulate that I was dead. The skeleton of some boy found in the ruins of the palace in Roma was said to be mine. After that I could move around more or less freely, though always in poverty, always in secrecy."

"And when did you come here?" I asked.

"Almost twenty years ago. Friends told me that this hunting lodge was here, still more or less intact as it had been at the time of the Revolution, and that no one ever went near it, that I could live here undisturbed. And so I have. And so I will, for however much time is left." He reached for the wine, but his hands were shaking so badly that Friya took it from him and poured him a glass. He drank it in a single gulp. "Ah, children, children, what a world you've lost! What madness it was, to destroy the Empire! What greatness existed then!"

"Our father says things have never been so good for ordinary folk as they are under the Republic," Friya said.

I kicked her ankle. She gave me a sour look.

Quintus Fabius said sadly, "I mean no disrespect, but your father sees only his own village. We were trained to see the entire world in a glance. The Imperium, the whole globe-spanning Empire. Do you think the gods meant to give the Imperium just to anyone at all? Anyone who could grab power and proclaim himself First Consul? Ah, no, no, the Caesars were uniquely chosen to sustain the Pax Romana, the universal peace that has enfolded this whole planet for so long. Under us there was nothing but peace, peace eternal and unshakable, once the Empire had reached its complete form. But with the Caesars now gone, how much longer do you think the peace will last? If one man can take power, so can another, or another. There will be five First Consuls at once, mark my words. Or fifty. And every province will want to be an Empire in itself. Mark my words, children. Mark my words."

I had never heard such treason in my life. Or anything so wrongheaded.

The Pax Romana? *What* Pax Romana? There had never been such a thing, not really. At least never for very long. Old Quintus Fabius would have had us believe that the Empire had brought unbroken and unshakable peace to the entire world, and had kept it that way for twenty centuries. But what about the Civil War, when the Greek half of the Empire fought for fifty years against the Latin half? Or the two Wars of Unification? And hadn't there been minor rebellions constantly, all over the Empire, hardly a century without one, in Persia, in India, in Britannia, in Africa Aethiopica? No, I thought, what he's telling us simply isn't true. The long life of the Empire had been a time of constant brutal oppression, with people's spirits held in check everywhere by military force. The real Pax Romana was something that existed only in modern times, under the Second Republic. So my father had taught me. So I deeply believed.

But Quintus Fabius was an old man, wrapped in dreams of his own wondrous lost childhood. Far be it from me to argue with him about such matters as these. I simply smiled and nodded, and poured more wine for him when his glass was empty. And Friya and I sat there spellbound as he told us, hour after hour, of what it had been like to be a prince of the royal family in the dying days of the Empire, before true grandeur had departed forever from the world.

When we left him that day, he had still more gifts for us. "My brother was a great collector," he said. "He had whole houses stuffed full of treasure. All gone now, all but what you see here, which no one remembered. When I'm gone, who knows what'll become of them? But I want you to have these. Because you've been so kind to me. To remember me by. And to remind you always of what once was, and now is lost."

For Friya there was a small bronze ring, dented and scratched, with a serpent's head on it, that he said had belonged to the Emperor Claudius of the earliest days of the Empire. For me a dagger, not the jewel-handled one I had seen upstairs, but a fine one all the same, with a strange undulating blade, from a savage kingdom on an island in the great Oceanus Pacificus. And for us both, a beautiful little figurine in smooth white alabaster of Pan playing on his pipes, carved by some master craftsman of the ancient days.

The figurine was the perfect birthday gift for grandmother. We gave it to her the next day. We thought she would be pleased, since all of the old gods of Roma are very dear to her; but to our surprise and dismay she seemed startled and upset by it. She stared at it, eyes bright and fierce, as if we had given her a venomous toad.

"Where did you get this thing? Where?"

I looked at Friya, to warn her not to say too much. But as usual she was ahead of me.

"We found it, grandmother. We dug it up."

"You dug it up?"

"In the forest," I put in. "We go there every Saturday, you know, just wandering around. There was this old mound of dirt—we were poking in it, and we saw something gleaming—"

She turned it over and over in her hands. I had never seen her look so troubled. "Swear to me that that's how you found it! Come, now, at the altar of Juno! I want you to swear to me before the Goddess. And then I want you to take me to see this mound of dirt of yours."

Friya gave me a panic-stricken glance.

Hesitantly I said, "We may not be able to find it again, grandmother. I told you, we were just wandering around—we didn't really pay attention to where we were—"

I grew red in the face, and I was stammering, too. It isn't easy to lie convincingly to your own grandmother.

She held the figurine out, its base toward me. "Do you see these marks here? This little crest stamped down here? It's the Imperial crest, Tyr. That's the mark of Caesar. This carving once belonged to the Emperor. Do you expect me to believe that there's Imperial treasure simply lying around in mounds of dirt in the forest? Come, both of you! To the altar, and swear!"

"We only wanted to bring you a pretty birthday gift, grandmother," Friya said softly. "We didn't mean to do any harm."

"Of course not, child. Tell me, now: where'd this thing come from?"

"The haunted house in the woods," she said. And I nodded my confirmation. What could I do? She would have taken us to the altar to swear.

Strictly speaking, Friya and I were traitors to the Republic. We even knew that ourselves, from the moment we realized who the old man really was. The Caesars were proscribed when the Empire fell; everyone within a certain level of blood kinship to the Emperor was condemned to death, so that no one could rise up and claim the throne in years hereafter.

A handful of very minor members of the royal family did indeed manage to escape, so it was said; but giving aid and comfort to them was a serious offense. And this was no mere second cousin or great-grandnephew that we had discovered deep in the forest: this was the Emperor's own brother. He was, in fact, the legitimate Emperor himself, in the eyes of those for whom the Empire had never ended. And it was our responsibility to turn him in to the quaestors. But he was so old, so gentle, so feeble. We didn't see how he could be much of a threat to the Republic. Even if he did believe that the Revolution had been an evil thing, and that only under a divinely chosen Caesar could the world enjoy real peace.

We were children. We didn't understand what risks we were taking, or what perils we were exposing our family to.

Things were tense at our house during the next few days: whispered conferences between our grandmother and our mother, out of our earshot, and then an evening when the two of them spoke with father while Friya and I were confined to our room, and there were sharp words and even some shouting. Afterward there was a long cold silence, followed by more mysterious discussions. Then things returned to normal. My grandmother never put the figurine of Pan in her collection of little artifacts of the old days, nor did she ever speak of it again.

That it had the Imperial crest on it was, we realized, the cause of all the uproar. Even so, we weren't clear about what the problem was. I had thought all along that grandmother was secretly an Empire loyalist herself. A lot of people her age were; and she was, after all, a traditionalist, a priestess of Juno Teutonica, who disliked the revived worship of the old Germanic gods that had sprung up in recent times—"pagan" gods, she called them—and had argued with father about his insistence on naming us as he had. So she should have been pleased to have something that had belonged to the Caesars. But, as I say, we were children then. We didn't take into account the fact that the Republic dealt harshly with anyone who practiced Caesarism. Or that whatever my grandmother's private political beliefs might have been, father was the unquestioned master of our household, and he was a devout Republican.

"I understand you've been poking around that old ruined house in the woods," my father said, a week or so later. "Stay away from it. Do you hear me? Stay away."

And so we would have, because it was plainly an order. We didn't disobey our father's orders.

But then, a few days afterward, I overheard some of the older boys of the village talking about making a foray out to the haunted house. Evidently Marcus Aurelius Schwarzchild had been talking about the ghost with the polished rifle to others beside me, and they wanted the rifle. "It's five of us against one of him," I heard someone say. "We ought to be able to take care of him, ghost or not."

"What if it's a ghost rifle, though?" one of them asked. "A ghost rifle won't be any good to us."

"There's no such thing as a ghost rifle," the first speaker said. "Rifles don't have ghosts. It's a real rifle. And it won't be hard for us to get it away from a ghost."

I repeated all this to Friya.

"What should we do?" I asked her.

"Go out there and warn him. They'll hurt him, Tyr."

"But father said—"

"Even so. The old man's got to go somewhere and hide. Otherwise his blood will be on our heads."

There was no arguing with her. Either I went with her to the house in the woods that moment, or she'd go by herself. That left me with no choice. I prayed to Woden that my father wouldn't find out, or that he'd forgive me if he did; and off we went into the woods, past Agrippina's Spring, past the statues of the pretty boy, past Baldur's Tree, and down the now-familiar path beyond the glossy-leaved oak.

"Something's wrong," Friya said, as we approached the hunting lodge. "I can tell."

Friya always had a strange way of knowing things. I saw the fear in her eyes and felt frightened myself.

We crept forward warily. There was no sign of Quintus Fabius. And when we came to the door of the lodge we saw that it was a little way ajar, and off its hinges, as if it had been forced. Friya put her hand on my arm and we stared at each other. I took a deep breath.

"You wait here," I said, and went in.

It was frightful in there. The place had been ransacked—the furniture smashed, the cupboards overturned, the sculptures in fragments. Someone had slashed every painting to shreds. The collection of arms and armor was gone.

I went from room to room, looking for Quintus Fabius. He wasn't there. But there were bloodstains on the floor of the main hall, still fresh, still sticky.

Friya was waiting on the porch, trembling, fighting back tears.

"We're too late," I told her.

It hadn't been the boys from the village, of course. They couldn't possibly have done such a thorough job. I realized—and surely so did Friya, though we were both too sickened by the realization to discuss it with each other—that grandmother must have told father we had found a cache of Imperial treasure in the old house, and he, good citizen that he was, had told the quaestors. Who had gone out to investigate, come upon Quintus Fabius, and recognized him for a Caesar, just as Friya had. So my eagerness to bring back a pretty gift for grandmother had been the old man's downfall. I suppose he wouldn't have lived much longer in any case, as frail as he was; but the guilt for what I unknowingly brought upon him is something that I've borne ever since.

Some years later, when the forest was mostly gone, the old house accidentally burned down. I was a young man then, and I helped out on the firefighting line. During a lull in the work I said to the captain of the fire brigade, a retired quaestor named Lucentius, "It was an Imperial hunting lodge once, wasn't it?"

"A long time ago, yes."

I studied him cautiously by the light of the flickering blaze. He was an older man, of my father's generation.

Carefully I said, "When I was a boy, there was a story going around that one of the last Emperor's brothers had hidden himself away in it. And that eventually the quaestors caught him and killed him."

He seemed taken off guard by that. He looked surprised and, for a moment, troubled. "So you heard about that, did you?"

"I wondered if there was any truth to it. That he was a Caesar, I mean."

Lucentius glanced away. "He was only an old tramp, is all," he said, in a muffled tone. "An old lying tramp. Maybe he told fantastic stories to some of the gullible kids, but a tramp is all he was, an old filthy lying tramp." He gave me a peculiar look. And then he stamped away to shout at someone who was uncoiling a hose the wrong way.

A filthy old tramp, yes. But not, I think, a liar.

He remains alive in my mind to this day, that poor old relic of the Empire. And now that I am old myself, as old, perhaps, as he was then, I understand something of what he was saying. Not his belief that there necessarily had to be a Caesar in order for there to be peace, for the Caesars were only men themselves, in no way different from the Consuls who have replaced them. But when he argued that the time of the Empire had been basically a time of peace, he may not have been really wrong, even if war had been far from unknown in Imperial days.

For I see now that war can sometimes be a kind of peace also: that the Civil Wars and the Wars of Reunification were the struggles of a sundered Empire trying to reassemble itself so peace might resume. These matters are not so simple. The Second Republic is not as virtuous as my father thought, nor was the old Empire, apparently, quite as corrupt. The only thing that seems true without dispute is that the worldwide hegemony of Roma these past two thousand years under the Empire and then under the Republic, troubled though it has occasionally been, has kept us from even worse turmoil. What if there had been no Roma? What if every region had been free to make war against its neighbors in the hope of creating the sort of Empire that the Romans were able to build? Imagine the madness of it! But the gods gave us the Romans, and the Romans gave us peace: not a perfect peace, but the best peace, perhaps, that an imperfect world could manage. Or so I think now.

In any case the Caesars are dead, and so is everyone else I have written about here, even my little sister, Friya; and here I am, an old man of the Second Republic, thinking back over the past and trying to bring some sense out of it. I still have the strange dagger that Quintus Fabius gave me, the barbaric-looking one with the curious wavy blade, that came from some savage island in the Oceanus Pacificus. Now and then I take it out and look at it. It shines with a kind of antique splendor in the lamplight. My eyes are too dim now to see the tiny Imperial crest that someone engraved on its haft when the merchant captain who brought it back from the South Seas gave it to the Caesar of his time, four or five hundred years ago. Nor can I see the little letters, S P Q R, that are inscribed on the blade. For all I know, they were put there by the frizzy-haired tribesman who fashioned that odd, fierce weapon: for he, too, was a citizen of the Roman Empire. As in a manner of speaking are we all, even now in the days of the Second Republic. As are we all.

A.U.C. 2723: TO THE
PROMISED LAND

They came for me at high noon, the hour of Apollo, when only a crazy man would want to go out into the desert. I was hard at work and in no mood to be kidnapped. But to get them to listen to reason was like trying to get the River Nilus to flow south. They weren't reasonable men. Their eyes had a wild metallic sheen and they held their jaws and mouths clamped in that special constipated way that fanatics like to affect. As they swaggered about in my little cluttered study, poking at the tottering stacks of books and pawing through the manuscript of my nearly finished history of the collapse of the Empire, they were like two immense irresistible forces, as remote and terrifying as gods of old Aegyptus come to life. I felt helpless before them.

The older and taller one called himself Eleazar. To me he was Horus, because of his great hawk nose. He looked like an Aegyptian and he was wearing the white linen robe of an Aegyptian. The other, squat and heavily muscled, with a baboon face worthy of Thoth, told me he was Leonardo di Filippo, which is of course a Roman name, and he had an oily Roman look about him. But I knew he was no more Roman than I am. Nor the other, Aegyptian. Both of them spoke in Hebrew, and with an ease that no outsider could ever attain. These were two Israelites, men of my own obscure tribe. Perhaps di Filippo had been born to a father not of the faith, or perhaps he simply liked to pretend that he was one of the world's masters and not one of God's forgotten people. I will never know.

Eleazar stared at me, at the photograph of me on the jacket of my account of the Wars of the Reunification, and at me again, as though trying to satisfy himself that I really was Nathan ben-Simeon. The picture was fifteen years old. My beard had been black then. He tapped the book and pointed questioningly to me and I nodded. "Good," he said. He told me to pack a suitcase, fast, as though I were going down to Alexandria for a weekend holiday. "Moshe sent us to get you," he said. "Moshe wants you. Moshe needs you. He has important work for you."

"Moshe?"

"The Leader," Eleazar said, in tones that you would ordinarily reserve for Pharaoh, or perhaps the First Consul. "You don't know anything about him yet, but you will. All of Aegyptus will know him soon. The whole world."

"What does your Moshe want with me?"

"You're going to write an account of the Exodus for him," said di Filippo.

"Ancient history isn't my field," I told him.

"We're not talking about ancient history."

"The Exodus was three thousand years ago, and what can you say about it at this late date except that it's a damned shame that it didn't work out?"

Di Filippo looked blank for a moment. Then he said, "We're not talking about that one. The Exodus is now. It's about to happen, the new one, the real one. That other one long ago was a mistake, a false try."

"And this new Moshe of yours wants to do it all over again? Why? Can't he be satisfied with the first fiasco? Do we need another? Where could we possibly go that would be any better than Aegyptus?"

"You'll see. What Moshe is doing will be the biggest news since the burning bush."

"Enough," Eleazar said. "We ought to be hitting the road. Get your things together, Dr. Ben-Simeon."

So they really meant to take me away. I felt fear and disbelief. Was this actually happening? Could I resist them? I would not let it happen. Time for some show of firmness, I thought. The scholar standing on his authority. Surely they wouldn't attempt force. Whatever else they might be, they were Hebrews. They would respect a scholar. Brusque, crisp, fatherly, the *melamed,* the man of learning. I shook my head. "I'm afraid not. It's simply not possible."

Eleazar made a small gesture with one hand. Di Filippo moved ominously close to me and his stocky body seemed to expand in a frightening way. "Come on," he said quietly. "We've got a car waiting right outside. It's a four-hour drive, and Moshe said to get you there before sundown."

My sense of helplessness came sweeping back. "Please. I have work to do, and—"

"Screw your work, professor. Start packing, or we'll take you just as you are."

The street was silent and empty, with that forlorn midday look that makes Menfe seem like an abandoned city when the sun is at its height. I walked between them, a prisoner, trying to remain calm. When I glanced back at the battered old gray façades of the Hebrew Quarter where I had lived all my life, I wondered if I would ever see them again, what would happen to my books, who would preserve my papers. It was like a dream.

A sharp dusty wind was blowing out of the west, reddening the sky so that it seemed that the whole Delta must be aflame, and the noontime heat was enough to kosher a pig. The air smelled of cooking oil, of orange blossoms, of camel dung, of smoke. They had parked on the far side of Amenhotep Plaza just behind the vast ruined statue of Pharaoh, probably in hope of catching the shadows, but at this hour there were no shadows and the car was like an oven. Di Filippo drove, Eleazar sat in back with me. I kept myself completely still, hardly even breathing, as though I could construct a sphere of invulnerability around me by remaining motionless. But when Eleazar offered me a cigarette I snatched it from him with such sudden ferocity that he looked at me in amazement.

We circled the Hippodrome and the Great Basilica where the judges of the Republic hold court, and joined the sparse flow of traffic that was entering the Sacred Way. So our route lay eastward out of the city, across the river and into the desert. I asked no questions. I was frightened, numbed, angry, and—I suppose—to some degree curious. It was a paralyzing combination of emotions. So I sat quietly, praying only that these men and their Leader would be done with me in short order and return me to my home and my studies.

"This filthy city," Eleazar muttered. "This Menfe. How I despise it!"

In fact it had always seemed grand and beautiful to me: a measure of my assimilation, some might say, though inwardly I feel very much the Israelite, not in the least Aegyptian. Even a Hebrew must concede that Menfe is one of the world's great cities. It is the most majestic city this side of Roma, so everyone says, and so I am willing to believe, though I have never been beyond the borders of the province of Aegyptus in my life.

The splendid old temples of the Sacred Way went by on both sides, the Temple of Isis and the Temple of Sarapis and the Temple of Jupiter Ammon and all the rest, fifty or a hundred of them on that great boulevard whose pavements are lined with sphinxes and bulls: Dagon's temple, Mithras's and Cybele's, Baal's, Marduk's, Zoroaster's, a temple for every god and goddess anyone had ever imagined, except, of course, the One True God, whom we few Hebrews prefer to worship in our private way behind the walls of our own Quarter. The gods of all the Earth have washed up here in Menfe like so much Nilus mud. Of course hardly anyone takes them very seriously these days, even the supposed faithful. It would be folly to pretend that this is a religious age. Mithras's shrine still gets some worshipers, and of course that of Jupiter Ammon. People go to those to do business, to see their friends, maybe to ask favors on high. The rest of the temples might as well be museums. No one goes into them except Roman and Nipponese tourists. Yet here they still stand, many of them thousands of years old. Nothing is ever thrown away in the land of Misr.

"Look at them," Eleazar said scornfully, as we passed the huge half-ruined Sarapion. "I hate the sight of them. The foolishness! The waste! And all of them built with our forefathers' sweat."

In fact there was little truth in that. Perhaps in the time of the first Moshe we did indeed labor to build the Great Pyramids for Pharaoh, as it says in Scripture. But there could never have been enough of us to add up to much of a workforce. Even now, after a sojourn along the Nilus that has lasted some four thousand years, there are only about twenty thousand of us. Lost in a sea of ten million Aegyptians, we are, and the Aegyptians themselves are lost in an ocean of Romans and imitation Romans, so we are a minority within a minority, an ethnographic curiosity, a drop in the vast ocean of humanity, an odd and trivial sect, insignificant except to ourselves.

The temple district dropped away behind us and we moved out across the long slim shining arch of the Augustus Caesar Bridge, and into the teeming suburb of Hikuptah on the eastern bank of the river, with its leather and gold bazaars, its myriad coffeehouses, its tangle of medieval alleys. Then Hikuptah dissolved into a wilderness of fig trees and canebrake, and we entered a transitional zone of olive orchards and date palms; and then abruptly we came to the place where the land changes from black to red and nothing grows. At once the awful barrenness and solitude of the place struck me like a tangible force. It was a fearful land, stark and empty, a dead place full of terrible ghosts. The sun was a scourge above us. I thought we would bake; and when the car's engine once or twice began to cough and sputter, I knew from the grim look on Eleazar's face that we would surely perish if we suffered a breakdown. Di Filippo drove in a hunched, intense way, saying nothing, gripping the steering stick with an unbending rigidity that spoke of great uneasiness. Eleazar too was quiet. Neither of them had said much since our departure from Menfe, nor I, but now in that hot harsh land they fell utterly silent, and the three of us neither spoke nor moved, as though the car had become our tomb. We labored onward, slowly, uncertain of engine, with windborne sand whistling all about us out of the west. In the great heat every breath was a struggle. My clothing clung to my skin. The road was fine for a while, broad and straight and well paved, but then it narrowed, and finally it was nothing more than a potholed white ribbon half covered with drifts. They were better at highway maintenance in the days of Imperial Roma. But that was long ago. This is the era of the Consuls, and things go to hell in the hinterlands and no one cares.

"Do you know what route we're taking, doctor?" Eleazar asked, breaking the taut silence at last when we were an hour or so into that bleak and miserable desert.

My throat was dry as strips of leather that have been hanging in the sun a thousand years, and I had trouble getting words out. "I think we're heading east," I said finally.

"East, yes. It happens that we're traveling the same route that the first Moshe took when he tried to lead our people out of bondage. Toward the Bitter Lakes, and the Reed Sea. Where Pharaoh's army caught up with us and ten thousand innocent people drowned."

There was crackling fury in his voice, as though that were something that had happened just the other day, as though he had learned of it not from the Book of Aaron but from this morning's newspaper. And he gave me a fiery glance, as if I had had some complicity in our people's long captivity among the Aegyptians and some responsibility for the ghastly failure of that ancient attempt to escape. I flinched before that fierce gaze of his and looked away.

"Do you care, Dr. Ben-Simeon? That they followed us and drove us into the sea? That half our nation, or more, perished in a single day in horrible fear and panic? That young mothers with babies in their arms were crushed beneath the wheels of Pharaoh's chariots?"

"It was all so long ago," I said lamely.

As the words left my lips I knew how foolish they were. It had not been my intent to minimize the debacle of the Exodus. I had meant only that the great disaster to our people was sealed over by thousands of years of healing, that although crushed and dispirited and horribly reduced in numbers we had somehow gone on from that point, we had survived, we had endured, the survivors of the catastrophe had made new lives for themselves along the Nilus under the rule of Pharaoh and under the Greeks who had conquered Pharaoh and the Romans who had conquered the Greeks. We still survived, did we not, here in the long sleepy decadence of the Imperium, the Pax Romana, when even the everlasting Empire had crumbled and the absurd and pathetic Second Republic ruled the world?

But to Eleazar it was as if I had spat upon the scrolls of the Law. "*It was all so long ago,*" he repeated, savagely mocking me. "And therefore we should forget? Shall we forget the Patriarchs, too? Shall we forget the Covenant? Is Aegyptus the land that the Lord meant us to inhabit? Were we chosen by Him to be set above all the peoples of the Earth, or were we meant to be the slaves of Pharaoh forever?"

"I was trying only to say—"

What I had been trying to say didn't interest him. His eyes were shining, his face was flushed, a vein stood out astonishingly on his broad forehead. "We were meant for greatness. The Lord God gave His blessing to Abraham and said that He would multiply Abraham's seed as the stars of the heaven, and as the sand which is upon the seashore. And the seed of Abraham shall possess the gate of his enemies. And in his seed shall all the nations of the Earth be blessed. Have you ever heard those words before, Dr. Ben-Simeon? And do you think they signified anything, or were they only the boasting of noisy little desert chieftains? No, I tell you we were meant for greatness, we were meant to shake the world: and we have been too long in recovering from the catastrophe at the Red Sea. An hour, two hours later and all of history would have been different. We would have crossed into Sinai and the fertile lands beyond; we would have built our kingdom there as the Covenant decreed; we would have made the world listen to the thunder of our God's voice; and today the entire world would look up to us as it has looked to the Romans these past twenty centuries. But it is not too late, even now. A new Moshe is in the land and he will succeed where the first one failed. And we *will* come forth from Aegyptus, Dr. Ben-Simeon, and we *will* have what is rightfully ours. At last, Dr. Ben-Simeon. At long last."

He sat back, sweating, trembling, ashen, seemingly exhausted by his own eloquence. I didn't attempt to reply. Against such force of conviction there is no victory; and what could I possibly have gained, in any case, by contesting his vision of Israel triumphant? Let him have his faith; let him have his new Moshe; let him have his dream of Israel triumphant. I myself had a different vision, less romantic, more cynical. I could easily imagine, yes, the children of Israel escaping from their bondage under Pharaoh long ago and crossing into Sinai, and going on beyond it into sweet and fertile Palaestina. But what then? Global dominion? What was there in our history, in our character, our national temperament, that would lead us on to that? Preaching Jehovah to the Gentiles? Yes, but would they listen, would they understand? No. No. We would always have been a special people, I suspected, a small and stubborn tribe, clinging to our knowledge of the One God amidst the hordes who needed to believe in many. We might have conquered Palaestina, we might have taken Syria too, even spread out a little further around the perimeter of the Great Sea; but still there would have been the Assyrians to contend with, and the Babylonians, and the Persians, and Alexander's Greeks, and the Romans, especially the stolid dull invincible Romans, whose destiny it was to engulf every corner of the planet and carve it into Roman provinces full of Roman highways and Roman bridges and Roman whorehouses. Instead of living in Aegyptus under the modern Pharaoh, who is the puppet of the First Consul who has replaced the Emperor of Roma, we would be living in Palaestina under the rule of some minor procurator or proconsul or prefect, and we would speak some sort of Greek or Latin to our masters instead of Aegyptian, and everything else would be the same. But I said none of this to Eleazar. He and I were different sorts of men. His soul and his vision were greater and grander than mine. Also his strength was superior and his temper was shorter. I might take issue with his theories of history, and he might hit me in his rage; and which of us then would be the wiser?

The sun slipped away behind us and the wind shifted, hurling sand now against our front windows instead of the rear. I saw the dark shadows of mountains to the south and ahead of us, far across the strait that separates Aegyptus from the Sinai wilderness. It was late afternoon, almost evening. Suddenly there was a village ahead of us, springing up out of nowhere in the nothingness.

It was more a camp, really, than a village. I saw a few dozen lopsided tin huts and some buildings that were even more modest, strung together of reed latticework. Carbide lamps glowed here and there. There were three or four dilapidated trucks and a handful of battered old cars scattered haphazardly about. A well had been driven in the center of things and a crazy network of above-ground conduits ran off in all directions. In back of the central area I saw one building much larger than the others, a big tin-roofed shed or lean-to with other trucks parked in front of it.

I had arrived at the secret headquarters of some underground movement, yet no attempt had been made to disguise or defend it. Situating it in this forlorn zone was defense enough: no one in his right mind would come out here without good reason. The patrols of the Pharaonic police did not extend beyond the cities, and the civic officers of the Republic certainly had no cause to go sniffing around in these remote and distasteful parts. We live in a decadent era, but at least it is a placid and trusting one.

Eleazar, jumping out of the car, beckoned to me, and I hobbled after him. After hours without a break in the close quarters of the car I was creaky and wilted. The reek of gasoline fumes had left me nauseated. My clothes were acrid and stiff from my own dried sweat. The evening coolness had not yet descended on the desert and the air was hot and close. To my nostrils it had a strange vacant quality, the myriad stinks of the city being absent. There was something almost frightening about that. It was like the sort of air the Moon might have, if the Moon had air.

"This place is called Beth Israel," Eleazar said. "It is the capital of our nation."

Not only was I among fanatics; I had fallen in with madmen who suffered the delusion of grandeur. Or does one quality go automatically with the other?

A woman wearing man's clothing came trotting up to us. She was young and very tall, with broad shoulders and a great mass of dark thick hair tumbling to her shoulders and eyes as bright as

Eleazar's. She had Eleazar's hawk's nose, too, but somehow it made her look all the more striking. "My sister, Miriam," he said. "She'll see that you get settled. In the morning I'll show you around and explain your duties to you."

And he walked away, leaving me with her.

She was formidable. I would have carried my bag, but she insisted, and set out at such a brisk pace toward the perimeter of the settlement that I was hard put to keep up with her. A hut all my own was ready for me, somewhat apart from everything else. It had a cot, a desk and typewriter, a washbasin, and a single dangling lamp. There was a cupboard for my things. Miriam unpacked for me, setting my little stock of fresh clothing on the shelves and putting the few books I had brought with me beside the cot. Then she filled the basin with water and told me to get undressed. I stared at her, astounded. "You can't wear what you've got on now," she said. "While you're having a bath I'll take your things to be washed." She might have waited outside, but no. She stood there, arms folded, looking impatient. I shrugged and gave her my shirt, but she wanted everything else, too. This was new to me, her straightforwardness, her absolute indifference to modesty. There have been few women in my life and none since the death of my wife; how could I strip myself before this one, who was young enough to be my daughter? But she insisted. In the end I gave her every stitch—my nakedness did not seem to matter to her at all—and while she was gone I sponged myself clean and hastily put on fresh clothing, so she would not see me naked again. But she was gone a long time. When she returned, she brought with her a tray, my dinner, a bowl of porridge, some stewed lamb, a little flask of pale red wine. Then I was left alone. Night had fallen now, desert night, awesomely black with the stars burning like beacons. When I had eaten I stepped outside my hut and stood in the darkness. It scarcely seemed real to me, that I had been snatched away like this, that I was in this alien place rather than in my familiar cluttered little flat in the Hebrew Quarter of Menfe. But it was peaceful here. Lights glimmered in the distance. I heard laughter, the pleasant sound of a kithara, someone singing an old Hebrew song in a deep, rich voice. Even in my bewildering captivity I felt a strange tranquility descending on me. I knew that I was in the presence of a true community, albeit one dedicated to some bizarre goal beyond my comprehension. If I had dared, I would have gone out among them and made myself known to them; but I was a stranger, and afraid. For a long while I stood in the darkness, listening, wondering. When the night grew cold I went inside. I lay awake until dawn, or so it seemed, gripped by that icy clarity that will not admit sleep; and yet I must have slept at least a little while, for there were fragments of dreams drifting in my mind in the morning, images of horsemen and chariots, of men with spears, of a great black-bearded angry Moshe holding aloft the tablets of the Law.

A small girl shyly brought me breakfast. Afterward Eleazar came to me. In the confusion of yesterday I had not taken note of how overwhelming his physical presence was: he had seemed merely big, but now I realized that he was a giant, taller than I by a span or more, and probably sixty minas heavier. His features were ruddy and a vast tangle of dark thick curls spilled down to his shoulders. He had put aside his Aegyptian robes this morning and was dressed Roman style, an open-throated white shirt, a pair of khaki trousers.

"You know," he said, "we don't have any doubt at all that you're the right man for this job. Moshe and I have discussed your books many times. We agree that no one has a firmer grasp of the logic of history, of the inevitability of the processes that flow from the nature of human beings."

To this I offered no response.

"I know how annoyed you must be at being grabbed like this. But you are essential to us; and we knew you'd never have come of your own free will."

"Essential?"

"Great movements need great chroniclers."

"And the nature of your movement—"

"Come," he said.

He led me through the village. But it was a remarkably uninformative walk. His manner was mechanical and aloof, as if he were following a preprogrammed route, and whenever I asked a direct question he was vague or even evasive. The big tin-roofed building in the center of things was the factory where the work of the Exodus was being carried out, he said, but my request for further explanation went unanswered. He showed me the house of Moshe, a crude shack like all the others. Of Moshe himself, though, I saw nothing. "You will meet him at a later time," Eleazar said. He pointed out another shack that was the synagogue, another that was the library, another that housed the electrical generator. When I asked to visit the library he merely shrugged and kept walking. On the far side of it I saw a second group of crude houses on the lower slope of a fair-sized hill that I had not noticed the night before. "We have a population of five hundred," Eleazar told me. More than I had imagined.

"All Hebrews?" I asked.

"What do you think?"

It surprised me that so many of us could have migrated to this desert settlement without my hearing about it. Of course, I have led a secluded scholarly life, but still, five hundred Israelites is one out of every forty of us. That is a major movement of population, for us. And not one of them someone of my acquaintance, or even a friend of a friend? Apparently not. Well, perhaps most of the settlers of Beth Israel had come from the Hebrew community in Alexandria, which has relatively little contact with those of us who live in Menfe. Certainly I recognized no one as I walked through the village.

From time to time Eleazar made veiled references to the Exodus that was soon to come, but there was no real information in anything he said; it was as if the Exodus were merely some bright toy that he enjoyed cupping in his hands, and I was allowed from time to time to see its gleam but not its form. There was no use in questioning him. He simply walked along, looming high above me, telling me only what he wished to tell. There was an unstated grandiosity to the whole mysterious project that puzzled and irritated me. If they wanted to leave Aegyptus, why not simply leave? The borders weren't guarded. We had ceased to be the slaves of Pharaoh two thousand years ago. Eleazar and his friends could settle in Palaestina or Syria or anyplace else they liked, even Gallia, even Hispania, even Nova Roma far across the ocean, where they could try to convert the redskinned men to Israel. The Republic wouldn't care where a few wild-eyed Hebrews chose to go. So why all this pomp and mystery, why such an air of conspiratorial secrecy? Were these people up to something truly extraordinary? Or, I wondered, were they simply crazy?

That afternoon Miriam brought back my clothes, washed and ironed, and offered to introduce me to some of her friends. We went down into the village, which was quiet. Almost everyone is at work, Miriam explained. But there were a few young men and women on the porch of one of the buildings: this is Deborah, she said, and this is Ruth, and Reuben, and Isaac, and Joseph, and Saul. They greeted me with great respect, even reverence, but almost immediately went back to their animated conversation as if they had forgotten I was there. Joseph, who was dark and sleek and slim, treated Miriam with an ease bordering on intimacy, finishing her sentences for her, once or twice touching her lightly on the arm to underscore some point he was making. I found that unexpectedly disturbing. Was he her husband? Her lover? Why did it matter to me? They were both young enough to be my children. Great God, why did it matter?

Unexpectedly and with amazing swiftness my attitude toward my captors began to change. Certainly I had had a troublesome intro-duction to them—the lofty pomposity of Eleazar, the brutal direct-ness of di Filippo, the ruthless way I had been seized and taken to this place—but as I met others I found them generally charming, graceful, courteous, appealing. Prisoner though I might be, I felt myself quickly being drawn into sympathy with them.

In the first two days I was allowed to discover nothing except that these were busy, determined folk, most of them young and evi-dently all of them intelligent, working with tremendous zeal on some colossal undertaking that they were convinced would shake the world. They were passionate in the way that I imagined the Hebrews of that first and ill-starred Exodus had been: contemptuous of the sterile and alien society within which they were confined, striving to-ward freedom and the light, struggling to bring a new world into be-ing. But how? By what means? I was sure that they would tell me more in their own good time; and I knew also that that time had not yet come. They were watching me, testing me, making certain I could be trusted with their secret.

Whatever it was, that immense surprise which they meant to spring upon the Republic, I hoped there was substance to it, and I wished them well with it. I am old and perhaps timid but far from conservative: change is the way of growth, and the Empire, with which I include the Republic that ostensibly has replaced it, is the enemy of change. For twenty centuries Roma has strangled mankind in its benign grip. The civilization that it has constructed is hollow, the life that most of us lead is a meaningless trek that had neither values nor purpose. By its shrewd acceptance and absorption of the alien gods and alien ways of the peoples it had conquered, the Empire had flattened everything into shapelessness. The grand and useless temples of the Sacred Way, where all gods were equal and equally insignificant, were the best symbol of that. By worshiping everyone indiscriminately, the rulers of the Imperium had turned the sacred into a mere instrument of governance. And ultimately their cynicism had come to pervade everything: the relationship between man and the Divine was destroyed, so that we had nothing left to venerate except the status quo itself, the holy stability of the world government. I had felt for years that the time was long overdue for some great revolution, in which all fixed, fast-frozen relationships, with their train of ancient and venerable prejudices and opinions, would be swept away—a time when all that is solid melts into air, all that is holy is profaned, and man is at last compelled to face with sober senses his real conditions of life. Was that what the Exodus somehow would bring? Profoundly did I hope so. For the Empire was defunct and didn't know it. Like some immense dead beast it lay upon the soul of humanity, smothering it beneath itself: a beast so huge that its limbs hadn't yet heard the news of its own death.

On the third day di Filippo knocked on my door and said, "The Leader will see you now."

The interior of Moshe's dwelling was not very different from mine: a simple cot, one stark lamp, a basin, a cupboard. But he had shelf upon shelf overflowing with books. Moshe himself was smaller than I expected, a short, compact man who nevertheless radiated tremendous, even invincible, force. I hardly needed to be told that he was Eleazar's older brother. He had Eleazar's wild mop of curly hair and his ferocious eyes and his savage beak of a nose; but because he was so much shorter than Eleazar his power was more tightly compressed, and seemed to be in peril of immediate eruption. He seemed poised, controlled, an austere and frightening figure.

But he greeted me warmly and apologized for the rudeness of my capture. Then he indicated a well-worn row of my books on his shelves. "You understand the Republic better than anyone, Dr. Ben-Simeon," he said. "How corrupt and weak it is behind its façade of universal love and brotherhood. How deleterious its influence has been. How feeble its power. The world is waiting now for something completely new: but what will it be? Is that not the question, Dr. Ben-Simeon? *What will it be?*"

It was a pat, obviously preconceived speech, which no doubt he had carefully constructed for the sake of impressing me and enlisting me in his cause, whatever that cause might be. Yet he did impress me with his passion and his conviction. He spoke for some time, rehearsing themes and arguments that were long familiar to me. He saw the Roman Imperium, as I did, as something dead and beyond revival, though still moving with eerie momentum. Call it an Empire, call it a Republic, it was still a world state, and that was an unsustainable concept in the modern era. The revival of local nationalisms that had been thought extinct for thousands of years was impossible to ignore. Roman tolerance for local customs, religions, languages, and rulers had been a shrewd policy for centuries, but it carried with it the seeds of destruction for the Imperium. Too much of the world now had only the barest knowledge of the two official languages of Latin and Greek, and transacted its business in a hodgepodge of other tongues. In the old Imperial heartland itself Latin had been allowed to break down into regional dialects that were in fact separate languages—Gallian, Hispanian, Lusitanian, and all the rest. Even the Romans at Roma no longer spoke true Latin, Moshe pointed out, but rather the simple, melodic, lazy thing called Roman, which might be suitable for singing opera but lacked the precision that was needed for government. As for the religious diversity that the Romans in their easy way had encouraged, it had led not to the perpetuation of faiths but to the erosion of them. Scarcely anyone except the most primitive peoples and a few unimportant encapsulated minorities like us believed anything at all; nearly everyone gave lip service instead to the local version of the official Roman pantheon and any other gods that struck their fancy, but a society that tolerates all gods really has no faith in any. And a society without faith is one without a rudder: without even a course.

These things Moshe saw, as I did, not as signs of vitality and diversity but as confirmation of the imminence of the end. This time there would be no Reunification. When the Empire had fallen, conservative forces had been able to erect the Republic in its place, but that was a trick that could be managed only once. Now a period of flames unmatched in history was surely coming as the sundered segments of the old Imperium warred against one another.

"And this Exodus of yours?" I said finally, when I dared to break his flow. "What is that, and what does it have to do with what we've been talking about?"

"The end is near," Moshe said. "We must not allow ourselves to be destroyed in the chaos that will follow the fall of the Republic, for we are the instruments of God's great plan, and it is essential that we survive. Come: let me show you something."

We stepped outside. Immediately an antiquated and unreliable-looking car pulled up, with the dark slender boy Joseph at the stick. Moshe indicated that I should get in, and we set out on a rough track that skirted the village and entered the open desert just behind the hill that cut the settlement in half. For perhaps ten minutes we drove north through a district of low rocky dunes. Then we circled another steep hill and on its farther side, where the land flattened out into a broad plain, I was astonished to see a weird tubular thing of gleaming silvery metal rising on half a dozen frail spidery legs to a height of some thirty cubits in the midst of a hubbub of machinery, wires, and busy workers.

My first thought was that it was an idol of some sort, a Moloch, a Baal, and I had a sudden vision of the people of Beth Israel coating their bodies in pigs' grease and dancing naked around it to the sound of drums and tambourines. But that was foolishness.

"What is it?" I asked. "A sculpture of some sort?"

Moshe looked disgusted. "Is that what you think? It is a vessel, a holy ark."

I stared at him.

"It is the prototype for our starship," Moshe said, and his voice took on an intensity that cut me like a blade. "Into the heavens is where we will go, in ships like these—toward God, toward His brightness—and there we will settle, in the new Eden that awaits us on another world, until it is time for us to return to Earth."

"The new Eden—on another world—" My voice was faint with disbelief. A ship to sail between the stars, as the Roman skyships travel between continents? Was such a thing possible? Hadn't the Romans themselves, those most able of engineers, discussed the question of space travel years ago and concluded that there was no practical way of achieving it and nothing to gain from it even if there was? Space was inhospitable and unattainable: everyone knew that. I shook my head. "What other world? Where?"

Grandly he ignored my question. "Our finest minds have been at work for five years on what you see here. Now the time to test it has come. First a short journey, only to the Moon and back—and then deeper into the heavens, to the new world that the Lord has pledged to reveal to me, so that the pioneers may plant the settlement. And after that—ship after ship, one shining ark after another, until every Israelite in the land of Aegyptus has crossed over into the promised land—" His eyes were glowing. "Here is our Exodus at last! What do you think, Dr. Ben-Simeon? What do you think?"

I thought it was madness of the most terrifying kind, and Moshe a lunatic who was leading his people—and mine—into cataclysmic disaster. It was a dream, a wild feverish fantasy. I would have preferred it if he had said they were going to worship this thing with incense and cymbals, than that they were going to ride it into the darkness of space. But Moshe stood before me so hot with blazing fervor that to say anything like that to him was unthinkable. He took me by the arm and led me, virtually dragged me, down the slope into the work area. Close up, the starship seemed huge and yet at the same time painfully flimsy. He slapped its flank and I heard a hollow ring. Thick gray cables ran everywhere, and subordinate machines of a nature that I could not even begin to comprehend. Fierce-eyed young men and women raced to and fro, carrying pieces of equipment and shouting instructions to one another as if striving to outdo one another in their dedication to their tasks. Moshe scrambled up a narrow ladder, gesturing for me to follow him. We entered a kind of cabin at the starship's narrow tip; in that cramped and all but airless room I saw screens, dials, more cables, things beyond my understanding. Below the cabin a spiral staircase led to a chamber where the crew could sleep, and below that, said Moshe, were the rockets that would send the ark of the Exodus into the heavens.

"And will it work?" I managed finally to ask.

"There is no doubt of it," Moshe said. "Our finest minds have produced what you see here."

He introduced me to some of them. The oldest appeared to be about twenty-five. Curiously, none of them had Moshe's radiant look of fanatic zeal; they were calm, even business-like, imbued with a deep and quiet confidence. Three or four of them took turns explaining the theory of the vessel to me, its means of propulsion, its scheme of guidance, its method of escaping the pull of the Earth's inner force. My head began to ache. But yet I was swept under by the power of their conviction. They spoke of "combustion," of "acceleration," of "neutralizing the planet-force." They talked of "mass" and "thrust" and "freedom velocity." I barely understood a tenth of what they were saying, or a hundredth; but I formed the image of a giant bursting his bonds and leaping triumphantly from the ground to soar joyously into unknown realms. Why not? Why not? All it took was the right fuel and a controlled explosion, they said. Kick the Earth hard enough and you must go upward with equal force. Yes. Why not? Within minutes I began to think that this insane starship might well be able to rise on a burst of flame and fly off into the darkness of the heavens. By the time Moshe ushered me out of the ship, nearly an hour later, I did not question that at all.

Joseph drove me back to the settlement alone. The last I saw of Moshe he was standing at the hatch of his starship, peering impatiently toward the fierce midday sky.

My task, I already knew, but which Eleazar told me again later that dazzling and bewildering day, was to write a chronicle of all that had been accomplished thus far in this hidden outpost of Israel and all that would be achieved in the apocalyptic days to come. I protested mildly that they would be better off finding some journalist, preferably with a background in science; but no, they didn't want a journalist, Eleazar said, they wanted someone with a deep understanding of the long currents of history. What they wanted from me, I realized, was a work that was not merely journalism and not merely history, but one that had the profundity and eternal power of Scripture. What they wanted from me was the Book of the Exodus, that is, the Book of the Second Moshe.

They gave me a little office in their library building and opened their archive to me. I was shown Moshe's early visionary essays, his letters to intimate friends, his sketches and manifestos insisting on the need for an Exodus far more ambitious than anything his ancient namesake could have imagined. I saw how he had assembled—secretly and with some uneasiness, for he knew that what he was doing was profoundly subversive and would bring the fullest wrath of the Republic down on him if he should be discovered—his cadre of young revolutionary scientists. I read furious memoranda from Eleazar, taking issue with his older brother's fantastic scheme; and then I saw Eleazar gradually converting himself to the cause in letter after letter until he became more of a zealot than Moshe himself. I studied technical papers until my eyes grew bleary, not only those of Moshe and his associates but some by Romans nearly a century old, and even one by a Teuton, arguing for the historical necessity of space exploration and for its technical feasibility. I learned something more of the theory of the starship's design and functioning.

My guide to all these documents was Miriam. We worked side by side, together in one small room. Her youth, her beauty, the dark glint of her eyes, made me tremble. Often I longed to reach toward her, to touch her arm, her shoulder, her cheek. But I was too timid. I feared that she would react with laughter, with anger, with disdain, even with revulsion. Certainly it was an aging man's fear of rejection that inspired such caution. But also I reminded myself that she was the sister of those two fiery prophets, and that the blood that flowed in her veins must be as hot as theirs. What I feared was being scalded by her touch.

The day Moshe chose for the starship's flight was the twenty-third of Tishri, the joyful holiday of Simchat Torah in the year 5730 by our calendar, that is, 2723 of the Roman reckoning. It was a brilliant early autumn day, very dry, the sky cloudless, the sun still in its fullest blaze of heat. For three days preparations had been going on around the clock at the launch site and it had been closed to all but the inner circle of scientists; but now, at dawn, the whole village went out by truck and car and some even on foot to attend the great event.

The cables and support machinery had been cleared away. The starship stood by itself, solitary and somehow vulnerable-looking, in the center of the sandy clearing, a shining upright needle, slender, fragile. The area was roped off; we would watch from a distance, so that the searing flames of the engines would not harm us.

A crew of three men and two women had been selected: Judith, who was one of the rocket scientists, and Leonardo di Filippo, and Miriam's friend Joseph, and a woman named Sarah whom I had never seen before. The fifth, of course, was Moshe. This was his chariot; this was his adventure, his dream; he must surely be the one to ride at the helm as the *Exodus* made its first leap toward the stars.

One by one they emerged from the blockhouse that was the control center for the flight. Moshe was the last. We watched in total silence, not a murmur, barely daring to draw breath. The five of them wore uniforms of white satin, blindingly bright in the morning sun, and curious glass helmets like diver's bowls over their faces. They walked toward the ship, mounted the ladder, turned one by one to look back at us, and went up inside. Moshe hesitated for a moment before entering, as if in prayer, or perhaps simply to savor the fullness of his joy.

Then there was a long wait, interminable, unendurable. It might have been twenty minutes; it might have been an hour. No doubt there was some last-minute checking to do, or perhaps even some technical hitch. Still we maintained our silence. We could have been statues. After a time I saw Eleazar turn worriedly toward Miriam, and they conferred in whispers. Then he trotted across to the blockhouse and went inside. Five minutes went by, ten; then he emerged, smiling, nodding, and returned to Miriam's side. Still nothing happened. We continued to wait.

Suddenly there was a sound like a thundercrack and a noise like the roaring of a thousand great bulls, and black smoke billowed from the ground around the ship, and there were flashes of dazzling red flame. The *Exodus* rose a few feet from the ground. There it hovered as though magically suspended, for what seemed to be forever.

And then it rose, jerkily at first, more smoothly then, and soared on a stunningly swift ascent toward the dazzling blue vault of the sky. I gasped; I grunted as though I had been struck; and I began to cheer. Tears of wonder and excitement flowed freely along my cheeks. All about me, people were cheering also, and weeping, and waving their arms, and the rocket, roaring, rose and rose, so high now that we could scarcely see it against the brilliance of the sky.

We were still cheering when a white flare of unbearable light, like a second sun more brilliant than the first, burst into the air high above us and struck us with overmastering force, making us drop to our knees in pain and terror, crying out, covering our faces with our hands.

When I dared look again, finally, that terrible point of ferocious illumination was gone, and in its place was a ghastly streak of black smoke that smeared halfway across the sky, trickling away in a dying trail somewhere to the north. I could not see the rocket. I could not hear the rocket.

"It's gone!" someone cried.

"Moshe! Moshe!"

"It blew up! I saw it!"

"Moshe!"

"Judith—" said a quieter voice behind me.

I was too stunned to cry out. But all around me there was a steadily rising sound of horror and despair, which began as a low choking wail and mounted until it was a shriek of the greatest intensity coming from hundreds of throats at once. There was fearful panic, universal hysteria. People were running about as if they had gone mad. Some were rolling on the ground, some were beating their hands against the sand. "Moshe!" they were screaming. "Moshe! Moshe! Moshe!"

I turned toward Eleazar. He was white-faced and his eyes seemed wild. Yet even as I looked at him I saw him draw in his breath, raise his hands, step forward to call for attention. Immediately all eyes were on him. He swelled until he appeared to be five cubits high.

"Where's the ship?" someone cried. "Where's Moshe?"

And Eleazar said, in a voice like the trumpet of the Lord, "He was the Son of God, and God has called him home."

Screams. Wails. Hysterical shrieks.

"Dead!" came the cry. "Moshe is dead!"

"He will live forever," Eleazar boomed.

"The Son of God!" came the cry, from three voices, five, a dozen. "The Son of God!"

I was aware of Miriam at my side, warm, pressing close, her arm through mine, her soft breast against my ribs, her lips at my ear. "You must write the book," she whispered, and her voice held a terrible urgency. "*His* book, you must write. So that this day will never be forgotten. So that he will live forever."

"Yes," I heard myself saying. "Yes."

In that moment of frenzy and terror I felt myself sway like a tree of the shore that has been assailed by the flooding of the Nilus; and I was uprooted and swept away. The fireball of the *Exodus* blazed in my soul like a second sun indeed, with a brightness that could never fade. And I knew that I was engulfed, that I was conquered, that I would remain here to write and preach, that I would forge the gospel of the new Moshe in the smithy of my soul and send the word to all the lands. Out of these five today would come rebirth; and to the peoples of the Republic we would bring the message for which they had waited so long in their barrenness and their confusion, and when it came they would throw off the shackles of their masters; and out of the death of the Imperium would come a new order of things. Were there other worlds, and could we dwell upon them? Who could say? But there was a new truth that we could teach, which was the truth of the second Moshe who had given his life so that we might go to the stars, and I would not let that new truth die. I would write, and others of my people would go forth and carry the word that I had written to all the lands, and the lands would be changed.

Perhaps I am wrong that the Republic is doomed. What is more likely true, I suspect, is that this world was meant to be Roma's; so it has been for thousands of years, and evidently it always will be, even unto eternity. Very well. Let them have it. We will not challenge Roma's eternal destiny. We will simply remove ourselves from its grasp. We have a destiny of our own. Some day, who knew how soon, we would build a new ship, and another, and another, and they will carry us from this world of woe. God has sent His Son, and God has called Him home, and one day we will all leave the iron rule of this eternal Roma behind and follow Him on wings of flame, up from the land of bondage into the heavens where He dwells eternally.